Praise for *Out of th*

"One of my favorite cities during on
the Ruins is a historically rich and heart-wrenching glimpse into the
San Francisco earthquake and the resilient faith, love, and spirit
that rises from the ashes—both in the city itself and in the hearts
and souls of a man and woman destined to fall in love."
—**Julie Lessman**, award-winning author of The Daughters of
Boston and Winds of Change series

"*Out of the Ruins*, set in San Francisco in 1905 and 1906, is a
shining example of historical romance. I was right there with the
characters, breathing in the smoke and dust, shaking and falling
with the earthquake. In this her second novel, Karen Barnett is
an up-and-coming author, writing quality historical fiction that is
realistic and grappling with faith issues woven in intrinsically. I'm
pleased to be able to endorse *Out of the Ruins*."
—**Lauraine Snelling**, best-selling author of the Red River of the
North series

"An earthquake, a medical drama, inner turmoil, and a touching romance! Karen Barnett masterfully weaves these together with
heartfelt emotion, believable characters, and impressive research. I
couldn't stop flipping pages. *Out of the Ruins* is a story to savor!"
—**Sarah Sundin**, award-winning author of *On Distant Shores*

"From the optimism of medical breakthroughs to the tragedy
of the great San Francisco earthquake and fire, *Out of the Ruins*
immerses the reader in the hopes and fears of unforgettable turn-of-
the-century characters."
—**Regina Jennings**, author of *Caught in the Middle*

"Karen Barnett's exquisite touch with emotional interplay and
romantic nuance shines in *Out of the Ruins*, thrilling readers with
a powerful story set during San Francisco's most enthralling and
heart-wrenching moment."
—**Michael K. Reynolds**, author of the acclaimed Heirs of Ireland
series

Out of the Ruins

Book 1
The Golden Gate Chronicles

Karen Barnett

Abingdon fiction™
a novel approach to faith

Library of Congress Cataloging-in-Publication Data has been
requested.

Printed in the United States of America

1 2 3 4 5 6 7 8 9 10 / 19 18 17 16 15 14

In Memory of Brandon Aufranc

2000 – 2012

Thank you to the brave scientists, doctors, and nurses who are working to make cancer a thing of the past.

Acknowledgments

Writing a novel feels like a solitary venture at times, but it takes many people to make a story come to life.

Thank you to . . .

My husband, Steve, and our two children. You three are my inspiration.

My first readers: Katie Miller, Morgan Miller, Leiah Greene.

Critique support: Heidi Gaul, Marilyn Rhoads, Patricia Lee, Tamera Bowers, Connie Hamon, and Michelle Ule.

Radiology advice: Amber Nealy.

The history-loving people of San Francisco, especially . . .

Autumn and Anastasia Zimmerman, who escorted me around the city during my research trip and continue to send me books and links. Bless you!

The San Francisco City Guides—a non-profit, primarily volunteer operation that offers educational walking tours of the city (www.sfcityguides.org)

The Donaldina Cameron House (www.cameronhouse.org)

Cheryl King and Old First Presbyterian Church, Sacramento Street

The San Francisco Cable Car Museum (www.cablecarmuseum .org)

The Virtual Museum of the City of San Francisco (www.sfmuseum .org)

The online resources of The Bancroft Library

Mount Hermon Christian Writers Conference, particularly the intermediate mentorship track with Randy Ingermanson (2009), Brandilyn Collins (2010), and Mary DeMuth (2012).

The American Christian Fiction Writers (ACFW), especially the 2012 Genesis Contest coordinators and judges.

Oregon Christian Writers (OCW) for encouragement, teaching, and introducing me to my publisher.

Author Tricia Goyer, who read a snippet of this story back in 2009 and introduced me to my fabulous agent, Rachel Kent. Rachel, thank you for sticking with me through it all. Thank you to the entire Books & Such community.

Ramona Richards, Cat Hoort, and all of the wonderful folks at Abingdon Press for taking a chance on this fledgling author. Thanks to Teri for your keen editing skills.

And to my God—for quiet whispers of support, and for leading me with strains of "Come Thou Fount" every time I doubted my calling. Thanks, Jesus, for being patient with me.

The mountains may shift,
and the hills may be shaken,
but my faithful love won't shift from you,
and my covenant of peace won't be shaken,
says the LORD, the one who pities you.

Isaiah 54:10 CEB

Come Thou Fount of Every Blessing

Come Thou Fount of every blessing
Tune my heart to sing Thy grace;
Streams of mercy, never ceasing,
Call for songs of loudest praise
Teach me some melodious sonnet,
Sung by flaming tongues above.
Praise the mount! I'm fixed upon it,
Mount of Thy redeeming love.

Here I raise my Ebenezer;
Hither by Thy help I'm come;
And I hope, by Thy good pleasure,
Safely to arrive at home.
Jesus sought me when a stranger,
Wandering from the fold of God;
He, to rescue me from danger,
Interposed His precious blood.

O to grace how great a debtor
Daily I'm constrained to be!
Let thy goodness, like a fetter,
Bind my wandering heart to thee.
Prone to wander, Lord, I feel it,
Prone to leave the God I love;
Here's my heart, O take and seal it,
Seal it for thy courts above.

Part 1

1

San Jose, California
August 16, 1905

$\mathcal{T}$he doctor could be wrong." Abby's words cut through the suffocating silence in the bedroom. She placed her fingers on the sun-warmed windowsill, but it did little to thaw the chill gripping her heart.

Cecelia's voice barely stirred the air. "He's not."

Abby glanced down at the novel she'd been reading, her thumb holding a place between the pages. If only she could stick her thumb on this day and prevent life from moving forward. When had time become the enemy?

She rose from the window seat and paced back to the wooden chair pulled close to her sister's bedside. The faded rosebud quilt covered Cecelia's body like a shroud. Abby kept her voice crisp and no-nonsense. "Papa telephoned Cousin Gerald last night. Gerald thinks there might be doctors in San Francisco who could actually do something, despite what Dr. Greene says."

Cecelia opened her eyes, the flash of blue seeming out of place in her otherwise colorless face. Her unbound hair—once like so many strands of golden silk—now covered the white pillowcase, tangled and matted.

Abby fingered her own brown braid. She hadn't even bothered to pin it up this morning. "I'm not giving up, and neither should you."

Cecelia's eyes closed again, dark circles framing their sunken depths. "I'm too tired. If God's calling, I'm ready to go home."

Abby thumped the novel down on the bedside table. "Stop saying that. I'm not going to let you die and leave me here alone."

Her sister shifted under the covers, as if the very weight of the quilt caused her pain. "You're—" she stopped for a breath, "not alone."

The deluge of fear returned, sweeping over Abby like waves across the shore. Who would she be without Cecelia?

She returned to the window, staring at the summer sky strewn with a few lacelike clouds. Back when they were children, Papa always called Cecelia his "sky-girl" because of her blue eyes and her grace. And a sky-girl she remained, even as they aged. Until this illness, Cecelia had moved with charm and style, bringing light to a room simply by entering. Young men flocked to her side, anxious to spend a moment captivated by her beauty and her gift for conversation.

Abby, a year younger—nineteen to Cecelia's twenty—had none of her sister's poise. Instead, she took turns stumbling over her tongue and her feet. And with her brown hair and eyes, and those incessant freckles, the only thing she ever attracted were mosquitoes on a warm summer evening. If Cecelia was the sky, Abby was the earth.

So while Cecelia danced at the parties, Abby strolled in the family orchard, content to talk to the peach trees. There she could speak her mind without worrying about social graces.

But if Cecelia left her . . .

"Abby—" Cecelia broke off with a weak cough.

Abby crossed the room in a heartbeat. "What is it? What do you need?"

Her sister lay silent for a long moment, staring up at her. Finally, after a labored breath she pushed the words out. "Have you prayed?"

"What?" Abby sank down into the high-backed chair where she had spent so many hours. "Cecelia . . ." Her voice faltered.

Cecelia sighed, her eyelids closing. "I thought maybe you would make an exception . . . for me."

Abby's heart sank down into her stomach. Her sister never did play fair.

"Just talk to Him. It's all I ask."

Fidgeting, Abby twisted the hem of her apron. Her sister's ragged breathing snatched at her heart. Abby squeezed the fabric into a ball. "Fine. I will."

The corners of Cecelia's mouth turned upward with a meager hint of a smile. "God will answer." She stirred under the covers once more. "You'll see."

When her sister's breathing finally evened into sleep, Abby reached over and smoothed the quilt. As she gazed at Cecelia's chalk-white face, Abby's throat clenched. The doctor's words chanted in her mind like a group of bullies in a schoolyard.

She tiptoed to the doorway. Catching a quick glimpse in the looking glass, Abby frowned at her unkempt hair and wrinkled dress. Turning away, she continued down the hall, pausing to glance into the nursery where her brother napped. The sight of his flushed cheeks brought a different kind of ache to her heart. No one but four-year-old Davy slept well these days.

She stole down the stairs and out through the kitchen, hearing her parents' hushed voices in the family room. They must be discussing the doctor's announcement, even though he'd left no room for debate.

Pushing open the back door, Abby escaped into the fresh air, untainted by sickness and the decaying scent of fading hope. She trudged through the pasture and up the hillside toward the orchard, dragging the weight of her family's problems with her. By the time she reached the edge of the trees, beyond sight of the house, the heaviness lessened and she picked up her skirts and fled.

As she charged into the orchard, Abby's throat ached with words held captive. *First Dr. Greene discounts Cecelia's symptoms, now he has the audacity to say we should prepare for the worst?*

Abby curled her fingers around the branch of a large cherry tree, placed a foot against the trunk, and hoisted herself upward into its leafy heights. Seeking to lose herself in the greenery, she climbed until her rust-colored skirt wedged between two branches. Holding on with one hand, Abby yanked the fabric loose with the other. Several years had passed since she had climbed one of these trees, and her arms and legs trembled with the effort. *My skirts were shorter back then, and I never cared about soiling them. A grown woman doesn't climb trees.*

Unless her sister is dying.

When a bough bent under her shoes, she halted. Wrapping one arm around the trunk, Abby laid her head against the tree. She slapped the palm of her hand against the bark until her skin stung.

Cecelia's request echoed. *"Just talk to Him. It's all I ask."*

Abby sighed, brushing a loose strand of hair from her face. Maybe prayer came easily to some people, but to her, God seemed too far away and indifferent. She took a deep breath and closed her eyes. "God, save her. I'll do anything—anything you want."

The words sounded foolish, like a child wishing on a star. Abby forced herself to continue. "She believes You love us. If it's true, then it makes sense You should heal her whether or not I ask. You know Mama and Papa couldn't bear to live without her. And Davy—" her breath caught in her throat as she thought about her baby brother.

Straddling a branch, Abby rested her back against the tree's strength and let her legs dangle. "The doctor says there's nothing more he can do." Abby paused, letting the thought soak in. "So, I guess it's up to You to take the cancer away."

Her stomach twisted at the word. Mama didn't like it spoken aloud, as if naming the disease would make the nightmare real.

The doctor had no such reservations. With today's visit, he added an even more formidable word: leukemia. "Some cancers you can cut out, but leukemia is in the blood." He raised his hands in surrender. "You can't fight it."

Abby tightened her fist and pressed it against her thigh. *Maybe you won't fight it, but I will. Somehow.*

She continued her prayer, speaking as much to herself as to any higher power. "I—I don't want to live here without her." She picked at a piece of lace dangling loose from its stitching along the hem of her dress. "I don't want to be alone."

Abby gazed up through the tree limbs. When her eyes blurred, the branches looked like jagged cracks in the sky. Was God even listening? Why should He care about her wishes? She'd never wanted anything beyond her family and the orchard she loved. The peach and cherry trees were better friends than any schoolmate, standing forever faithful in their well-ordered rows. She'd tended them by her father's side since she was old enough to hold the pruning shears. Papa promised someday they would belong to her. What more could she need?

The sound of footsteps crunching through the leaves stole the thought from her mind. She pulled her feet up to the limb and gripped the branch above her head to steady herself.

A man strolled through the orchard, his hands thrust deep into the pockets of his gray twill pants, a dark jacket slung casually over one shoulder.

Abby bit her lip and leaned to the side for a better view. As she shifted her weight, the limb cracked, the sound echoing through the orchard. Abby grabbed the branch above her just as her perch gave way. Swinging awkwardly, she wrapped her ankles around the tree trunk.

"I'm okay," she whispered, under her breath.

"Are you sure about that?" An amused voice floated up.

The man had removed his derby and looked up at her with eyes as brown as Aunt Mae's irresistible chocolate fudge.

From her clumsy vantage point, Abby examined his strong jaw and pleasing smile. *Of course—he's handsome, and I'm hanging from a tree like a monkey.*

"There's a sturdy-looking branch just below you and to the left."

Stretching out a foot, she groped for the limb with her toe. Locating it, Abby tucked her skirts tight around her legs before scurrying down.

The stranger reached up his hand to assist her on the last step to the earth. "I suppose I should apologize for frightening you."

Abby plucked a twig from her apron. "You surprised me." She regretted not taking time to fix her hair before leaving the house. Or put on a hat. What must he think?

A crooked smile crossed the man's face. "Well, then we're even, because no one ever told me girls grew on trees here in California. If I'd known, I might have gone into farming instead of medicine."

He slid his hands back into his pockets. "I certainly didn't expect a beautiful woman to fall out of one."

A wave of heat climbed Abby's neck. "I didn't fall out." She straightened her skirt, annoyed to find this smooth-talking stranger waltzing through her family's orchard. Beautiful, indeed. She narrowed her eyes at him. "Who are you, anyway?"

As he nodded, the light glinted off of his dark hair. "My name is Robert King—Dr. King. I'm Dr. Larkspur's new assistant. Are you Miss Fischer?"

The breath caught in Abby's throat. "Dr. Larkspur—you mean Gerald? He's here?"

"Yes, we drove all night—"

"I'm sorry—I've got to go." Abby grabbed up her skirts and raced back through the meadow toward the house, her braid bouncing against her back. Halfway across the field she realized her rudeness at leaving their guest in the orchard, but she pushed onward. Manners could wait.

Spotting an automobile in front of the house, surprise slowed her steps. Automobiles belonged to rich men. She'd never thought of her mother's cousin in those terms.

With a fresh burst of speed, Abby pounded up the stairs onto the back porch, finishing her prayer in a rush. "God, I'll do anything. I'll be anything. Whatever You want—name it. Just make her better."

As she grasped the doorknob, Abby paused to catch her breath. "And You'd better be listening God, because I'm going to make one last promise. If You dare take her away . . . "

She pulled the door open, casting one last glance toward the stranger in the orchard.

" . . . I'll never speak to You again."

2

$\mathcal{R}$obert took a deep breath, the earthy smell of the country air delighting his senses after so many months in San Francisco. He crossed his arms and leaned against the gnarled trunk of the cherry tree, chuckling as the lady scampered across the field like a rabbit. When Gerald had spoken of his cousin Clara's two daughters, Robert pictured them being much younger. Miss Abby Fischer was clearly an adult, probably only a few years younger than Robert, even though her undisciplined behavior suggested otherwise.

And the shreds of leaves tangled in her hair only made her more intriguing.

He shook himself out of his thoughts. Gerald had probably examined the patient by now. Robert had wanted to give his friend privacy for the exam, but now impatience drew him forward.

Since he'd heard about this case, anticipation burned like a fire in his blood. Cecelia Fischer sounded like the ideal candidate for their research project. And, if they succeeded, not only would they make medical history, but Robert would have his pick of positions and research grants. On impulse, Robert had suggested they drive Gerald's new automobile instead of hiring a horse and buggy for the trip.

His friend's brows had furrowed. "Is it wise? Are the roads good enough?"

"I think it's worth the gamble."

Now Robert pressed his hands against his aching back. Bouncing down the rutted road all night had left him stiff and sore, not to mention the two times he'd repaired flat tires by lantern light.

Gerald showed an amazing lack of sympathy. "Your idea, remember?" A wry smile lit up his features.

Remarkably, they made it in one piece.

Apparently, his mentor was willing to take chances—as long as he had an assistant to deal with the consequences.

Convincing him to take a risky gamble with his cousin's health might be an altogether different matter.

Abby hurried down the hallway, thankful for the thick carpet runner muffling her footsteps. Mingled scents of roses and pipe tobacco perfumed the air. She paused in the shadows outside the half-closed door, pulling off her apron and running a hand over her skirt to remove any evidence of her afternoon activities. *I should go change my clothes and fix my hair before I greet everyone.*

Gerald's voice carried out into the hallway. "It's a difficult case."

Abby held her breath.

Her father had spent years ridding himself of his German accent, but in this moment, he sounded as if he had stumbled back in time. "*Bitte.* . . . There must be something you can do."

"Herman, Clara—you know I care for Cecelia as if she were my own sister, but in cases like this—"

The familiar weight crushed against Abby's chest. As she swung open the door, silence dropped over the room like a velvet theater curtain. Gerald sat beside the fireplace, his somber expression making him appear much older than his twenty-eight years. Her mother sat in the upholstered chair opposite him, while Abby's father leaned on the mantel.

Their sudden silence grated at her heart. Abby folded both arms across her midsection hiding trembling hands under her elbows.

"Don't let me stop you. 'There's nothing we can do.' Isn't that what you were planning to say?"

Mama frowned, her dark green gown casting a sallow hue on her downturned face.

Gerald smoothed his vest. "Abby, as I was telling your parents, Cecelia is in a terrible state."

"It's not exactly news to us."

"Abigail, show some respect." Mama lifted her head, her pale hair tied back in a tight knot, so unlike the soft pompadour she generally wore.

Abby bit her tongue and walked to her mother's side, resting her hand on the back of the chair. "I'm sorry, but Gerald didn't drive all night just to give us bad news. He must have found something."

Gerald studied the floor as if weighing his words.

Abby forced herself to remain still even though the unremitting tick of the mantel clock jarred at her nerves. Every passing second brought Cecelia's fate a step closer.

Her father stepped away from the fireplace and stood over Gerald, his massive height throwing a large shadow over the younger man. "Abigail is right, *ja*? What is it? You have found something we can do?"

Gerald leaned back in his chair, lines creasing his forehead. "Perhaps, but now I've had a chance to examine her . . ." He lifted his hands and dropped them back onto his knees, eyes lowered.

"No. I don't accept that." Abby rushed forward. "I won't let you give up on her like every other doctor we've seen. Just tell us what we have to do."

"You don't understand." Gerald ran a hand through his hair. "We'd have to transport her to a hospital in San Francisco. Even if she survived the journey, the treatment is difficult. If I'd known earlier, maybe we could have attempted it. But she's far too weak." He reached out and touched her father's arm. "This would be torture to you and your family, and in the end it would likely accomplish nothing."

Abby's throat constricted. "Nothing? Are you saying my sister's life is worth nothing?"

A shadow crossed her cousin's face. "Abby—"

"No!" She threw up her hand to stop his words. "You said likely. Then there is a chance. And any chance she will survive is worth attempting."

A strangled sob cut through the air from the direction of her mother's chair.

Abby pressed onward. "Tell us, Gerald—what are your colleagues in San Francisco doing our doctor can't?"

"My assistant and I have been offered a small research project at Lane Hospital—part of the medical college." He stood and paced to the far side of the room, near the door. "But I fear you'd be pinning your hopes on a risky experimental treatment—one Cecelia doesn't have the strength to survive."

Abby moved to follow, ready to grab Gerald's jacket and shake some sense into him.

Her father dropped his large hands onto her shoulders and squeezed. "Answer the question, Gerald. What exactly is this new treatment? Could it save *meine* . . . my daughter?"

Footsteps in the hall drew their attention. Abby held her breath as the young man from the orchard stepped into the room.

His dark eyes gleamed under the parlor's electric lights as he spoke a single word.

"X-rays."

3

The force of Miss Fischer's intense gaze sent a charge rushing through Robert's body, reminding him of the time he had accidentally brushed a fingertip across a live wire while helping his father string electrical line.

She took a step closer to him. "What are X-rays?"

Gerald clamped a hand onto Robert's shoulder. "Herman, Clara—I don't believe you have met my new assistant. Dr. King, may I present my family—" his grip tightened as he spoke. "My cousins, Mr. and Mrs. Herman Fischer and their daughter, Miss Abigail Fischer."

As the man released his hold, Robert fought the urge to rub his shoulder. He nodded to the family. "Please, accept my apology for interrupting your conversation. I shouldn't have spoken out of turn."

Mr. Fischer shook Robert's hand, the farmer's rough skin showing evidence of hard work. "What are these X-rays?"

Gerald cut in. "X-ray treatment is very new. We have no guarantees it would help Cecelia at all. Frankly, I'm not certain it would be a wise choice in your daughter's case."

Robert set his jaw. Caution wasn't going to save any lives. Some treatment must be better than no treatment.

Twisting a handkerchief in her lap, the mother frowned. "Isn't there some type of medicine you can give her here?"

Shaking his head, Gerald ran a hand across his chin. "Nothing beyond what your own physician has already recommended. Arsenic is the standard treatment for leukemia. And morphine for the pain."

The young Miss Fischer stood behind her mother's chair, her lips pressed into a thin line. "But you already said the medicines won't help her."

"They will make it easier," he said.

Scowling at her cousin, Miss Fischer dug fingers into the finely upholstered chair. "Easier for her to die?" She fixed her gaze on Robert. "What about these X-rays?"

The strength of her hope crossed the space between them like ripples in a pond. Explanations hovered on the tip of his tongue, but a brief glance at his mentor's face warned him to remain silent. He set his jaw and kept the words to himself.

The father folded his arms across his broad chest. "We will send Cecelia to San Francisco. If this treatment has even a slim chance of working, we must try." Bushy whiskers did little to obscure the lines of resolution around his mouth.

Rising to stand beside her husband, Mrs. Fischer placed her small hand in his. Shadows hovered around her eyes, but she lifted her chin in a mirror of her husband's strength.

A wave of excitement built in Robert's chest. Gerald's opposition was losing steam as the desperate family drew together.

Gerald pushed a hand against his brow. "Herman . . ."

The young woman stepped out from behind the chair, coming to stand beside her mother and turning her attention back to Robert. "Dr. King, do you believe the treatment could work?"

The yearning in her coffee-colored eyes captivated Robert, blurring his thoughts until his mentor's disapproval scattered to the edges of his consciousness. Whatever this chestnut-haired beauty desired, he wanted to give it to her, no matter the consequences.

"It's her only chance."

Abby forced her lips into a straight line, squashing the smile threatening to spread across her face. *Finally.* Her toe tapped under her long skirt, but she folded her hands around her elbows, locking them to her sides. It wouldn't do to start dancing around the room.

Gerald tugged at his collar, as if the garment were snug about his throat. "We need to move her to San Francisco immediately if there is to be any chance for success. Dr. King and I will take her in the automobile. One of you should come, also."

Papa nodded. "Clara will go. The rest of the family will follow as soon as we are able."

"I'll pack a bag for Cecelia." Abby glanced over at her cousin's assistant, his dark-eyed gaze quickening her pulse as she hurried from the room.

The murmured conversation faded into the background as she climbed the stairs, attempting to shift her focus from the intriguing Dr. King to which items Cecelia might need for a hospital stay in San Francisco.

A man with all the answers drops into my life as I am praying? Maybe God is listening after all.

"Miss Fischer—"

The deep voice broke through the chaos of her thoughts. Abby clutched at the banister and peered down at Dr. King, waiting on the landing. All sensible words fled her mind, perspiration gathering on the back of her neck. Abby retraced her path until she stood facing him.

The young doctor examined her with deep-set eyes. "I hope Dr. Larkspur will forgive me. I'm afraid I overstepped myself back there."

She ran her hand along the stair rail. "I'm glad you did." She lowered her arm, clamping her fingers together to keep them still. "Besides, Gerald would have told us eventually. He never could stand up against Papa."

Dr. King leaned against the post. "Your father strikes me as a formidable man. Have they clashed before?"

The men's voices wafted into the hall, Gerald's mellow tones obscured by the staccato consonants of her father's accent.

"Many times." A smile pulled at her lips. Standing on the bottom step, she stood at perfect eye-level with the doctor. The glimmer of hope he represented—for Cecelia—spread through her, like the dawn's warmth touching frozen ground. Abby lowered her eyes, focusing instead on his hand curled around one of the carved balusters.

"Dr. King . . ." She took a deep breath, trying to slow the hammering in her chest. Cecelia was much better at this. "I want to thank you."

"Thank me? For what?"

Abby risked meeting his eyes. *For being an answer to prayer.* "For allowing us to hope." A tremor raced through her. Why was it so difficult to speak to a man?

"You might not thank me in a few days." His brows pinched together. "Even with the treatment, it's still unlikely she will recover."

Leave it to a doctor to light a spark of optimism, then turn around and pour cold water all over it. She smoothed her hands across the fabric of her skirt. "It will work. I know it will."

"You should be prepared. If your cousin is correct, there is a strong possibility your sister won't survive the trip to the city, much less the treatment."

Abby pushed her chin forward. "My sister is stronger than she looks."

Dr. King waved his hand, dismissing her comment. "You don't know this condition. Leukemia steals every ounce of strength a person has. It consumes from the inside out."

Abby's chest tightened. "I'm quite familiar with this disease. I've watched its evil spread through my sister's body, like a fungus invades the roots of a tree and causes them to rot out from below." She clenched her fists, hiding them behind her back.

Dr. King's mouth snapped shut. He glanced down for a moment before meeting her gaze. "I—I'm sorry. I misspoke." His lips pressed into a thin line. "Again."

Abby nodded. She understood the challenge of controlling one's tongue. She hunted for a new topic of conversation. "Can you explain to me how these X-rays help? No one has mentioned this treatment to us before."

"It's all still very experimental. When X-rays were first discovered, it was immediately obvious how they could be used to identify fractures and dislocations of the bones and joints. A few years ago, a researcher in Chicago discovered one of his cancer patients improved when he irradiated the tumors. Apparently, the radiation not only penetrates the body, it appears to target and kill cancerous cells specifically. Gerald and I have been invited to participate in a study at Lane Hospital, in connection with Cooper Medical College. In fact, we'd already been screening patients before we received the news from your family."

Abby's heart beat faster. "Could it actually cure her?"

Robert shook his head. "We're not certain. But it could help her regain some vitality and provide more time. If she survives long enough for the treatment to work."

"She will." Abby squeezed her fingers into a fist. *She has to.*

Abby hovered in the doorway as Mama explained the situation to Cecelia.

Her sister's eyes widened. "San Francisco? Today?"

"It's for the best, sweetheart." Her mother perched on the edge of the bed and caressed Cecelia's arm.

Cecelia brushed her hand away. "No. I don't want to."

Abby marched in. "Don't be ridiculous. Gerald is going to drive you to the city in his automobile—won't it be exciting?"

"I can't even . . ." her sister paused for breath, "walk down the stairs."

"Dr. King is waiting to help you." Abby wrapped her fingers around the bedpost.

Cecelia's gaze fixed on Abby's face and lingered there. "Dr. King?"

"Gerald's assistant." *His handsome new assistant.* Heat crept up Abby's hairline, but she kept her face firm.

"We must get you ready." Mama gathered an extra quilt from the end of the bed.

Cecelia sighed and looked down at herself. "Not like this."

The tension in Abby's chest eased. Cecelia hadn't thought about her appearance in days. Nothing like having a man nearby to make her take notice.

"Nonsense." Mama took charge. "I've brought you my best dressing gown and we'll wrap you in quilts to keep you from getting chilled. Who will see you?"

Cecelia glanced toward the window, blinking in the strong light. With a sigh, she nodded.

Abby clutched the dressing gown to her chest while Mama helped Cecelia to her feet. Cecelia lifted her arms, wincing as the fabric settled over her bony frame. Her complexion faded to the color of damp fireplace ashes and she swayed against Mama's arm.

Mama touched her hair. "Don't worry, sweetheart. You can rest soon."

"My locket." Cecelia reached a shaking hand toward the nightstand.

Abby scurried over and retrieved the gold necklace. She ran a finger over the design of a flower etched on the front. It contained no portrait. Always the romantic, Cecelia reserved it for a future sweetheart.

Even though Cecelia had worn it faithfully for years, the weight had become an irritation in her weakened state. Abby wrapped the necklace in a handkerchief and tucked it into the pocket of Cecelia's silk gown.

Stepping into the hall, Abby's breath caught in her chest when she spotted Dr. King waiting. "Are you leaving already?"

He gestured to the stairway. "There's no time to waste. If the treatment has any likelihood of working, we should begin immediately. Dr. Larkspur and your father went to prepare the car. Is she ready?"

Abby nodded, holding the door open for him.

He stepped into the bedroom. "Miss Fischer? Can I assist you down the stairs?"

Cecelia's eyes closed and she went limp in her mother's arms.

Dr. King rushed to her side, lifting Cecelia back to the bed.

Her eyes fluttered open. "Wh—what?"

The doctor straightened, his face shadowed. "I think perhaps Dr. Larkspur was correct. Maybe this isn't wise."

Cecelia touched his sleeve. "No, I . . . I'm fine. I just felt a little dizzy." She struggled to sit up. "I'm ready now."

Abby held her breath.

Dr. King nodded and bent down, sliding his arms under Cecelia's shoulders and knees and lifting her like one would a sleeping child, her head falling against his shoulder.

Abby's stomach churned as her gaze drifted across Cecelia's body, taking in her sunken cheeks and birdlike legs barely obscured by Mama's pale pink dressing gown. Her sister's abdomen bulged, in stark contrast—an enlarged spleen, Dr. Greene had explained.

The weight of Gerald's warnings warred with Abby's resolve, the tension in her chest making it difficult to draw a breath. Cecelia might not survive the journey. She gulped back a sudden wash of emotion and leaned against the doorframe for strength.

Dr. King turned toward the door, her sister's body firm in his grip.

"I . . . I . . ." Abby's heart throbbed. *I've changed my mind.* The words refused to leave her mouth.

He glanced toward her, waiting.

Cecelia opened her eyes and lifted her head—a slow, pained motion. "Abby," her voice rasped. "I'll see you . . . there."

Abby nodded, swallowing hard. *Is this really the answer to my prayer?* She stepped aside to let him pass.

Mama followed close behind, clutching several quilts to the bosom of her green dress.

Abby pressed back against the door, the sound of her own breathing loud in her ears.

Yes. I'll see you there.

4

*R*obert wrenched the steering wheel back in line with the road ahead, gritting his teeth as the automobile bucked a second time. After having learned to drive on the cobblestone streets of San Francisco, this road—if one could even call it that—reminded him of a smallpox photo from his textbook of infectious diseases.

Gerald's voice rose from the back seat. "Steady, Robert. Slow down. Let's see if we can't even the ride out a touch."

Gripping the wheel with his gloved hands, Robert nodded. "Sorry. I'll try not to let it—" The words had barely escaped his mouth when the tires bounced over a small crater in the road. Robert gritted his teeth, easing back on the throttle until the vehicle edged along slower than a gimpy mule slogging off to the glue factory. The delays made his skin crawl. Time was running short for their patient, but every jounce and bump produced a cry of pain from the backseat.

He shoved his hat lower over his eyes, the glare of the late afternoon sun cutting through the trees lining the roadway. Two months ago, he'd taken his first drive behind the wheel of Gerald's automobile, giddy with the vehicle's power and speed. He drove straight into a ditch. Horses had the sense not to gallop off the road and generally corrected for their driver's oversight. Motorcars, on the other hand, took finesse. It took a bit of effort, but he mastered the art of precise steering.

Robert cast a quick glance over his shoulder. Gerald's gaze remained locked on his cousin, his fingers gripping her wrist, as if assuring himself of a steady pulse. Cecelia, her pallid face framed by a rose-colored quilt, stared vacantly ahead.

Robert turned his eyes forward, his mouth growing as dry as the dust swirling up from beneath their wheels. He reached for the throttle, his hand closing on the lever.

We need to hurry.

He pulled his arm back. *And yet we can't.*

The engine spluttered, and several loud cracks cut through the evening air. Robert's stomach lurched with the slowing motion of the vehicle. "No, no, no." He leaned forward, fiddling with the controls, but the engine heaved a final hacking cough before hissing into silence.

He smacked the wheel with the heel of his hand. "No! Not now."

"What's the matter?" Mrs. Fischer's voice quavered.

Gerald cleared his throat. "Don't worry, Clara. Robert's become quite the crackerjack mechanic over the past months. I'm sure he'll have us back on the road in no time."

Robert stripped off his jacket and rolled up his sleeves. "Sure." He sighed. "No time."

Abby swung her arms as she chased Davy down the wooded path. "When did you get so fast?" She panted in mock exhaustion, allowing the little boy's legs time to pull far ahead, her laughter mingling with the scolding cries of the birds flitting into the trees. The pair burst out of the woods and into the yard as the sun began to dip low in the western sky, emblazoning the horizon above the peach orchard with wide stripes of crimson and plum-colored light. The cooling air tasted sweet and she breathed deeply, gulping in the fresh evening breeze.

Rushing forward, Abby swept her brother up into her arms, twirling him about in the fading light.

He screamed and kicked in protest. "No, I won! I won!"

"Of course you did, you little racehorse. You're even faster than Cousin Gerald's automobile. Now you better get washed up for bed." She set Davy down on the top step of the porch and followed him inside.

She left the door standing open, the evening birdsong bringing life into the quiet house. "Papa?" She walked down the hall, following the lingering scent of her father's pipe.

He glanced up from the newspaper, his lanky legs crossed at the knees as he reclined in the chair by the fireplace.

She hurried to his side, the news spilling from her mouth before he had a chance to inquire. "Mrs. Franklin says Mama telephoned an hour ago. They made good time—only one breakdown, which she said Dr. King put to rights quickly enough. Cecelia is all settled at the hospital."

He lowered the paper, the lines around his brown eyes deepening. "How is she?"

"She did fine on the journey. Some pain, but it's to be expected." Abby sat in her mother's chair. "Gerald is going to give her morphine, to help her rest."

"When will they begin the treatments?"

"First thing in the morning—if she has a good night." Abby let her mind drift, imagining her sister bathed in the healing lights of a humming machine. "Isn't it extraordinary? A light that can kill cancer—like the sun's rays chasing away the morning dew."

A gleam appeared in her father's eyes. "It's what makes this country great. Folks aren't afraid of embracing progress. This century has already seen many advances."

Abby ran her hands down the arms of the chair. "And progress is what's going to save Cecelia."

"God willing." Her father mumbled the words around the stem of his pipe as he lifted the paper.

"Of course." Abby rose from the chair. *God willing.*

San Francisco, California
Wednesday, August 30, 1905

The street squeezed in, the tall homes looming over Abby's head. She clutched at the edge of the buggy seat with one hand and kept Davy locked tight on her lap with the other.

A trickle of sweat wandered down her father's face, his knuckles whitening on the reins as he urged the horses up the steep hill. A shiny black automobile careened around them, cutting back just in time to avoid colliding with the cable car. The growl of the motor blended with the clatter of hooves against the hard cobblestones.

Abby pulled Davy close, her brother's mouth silenced by the wealth of activity surrounding them. She took a deep breath to clear her head, wrinkling her nose at the mingled scents of exhaust and horse manure.

The elegant homes on O'Farrell Street stood shoulder-to-shoulder with only a sliver of space separating one building from another. Abby leaned forward in her seat, willing the horses to hurry. Her back ached from the vibrations, her ears buzzing with unfamiliar sounds. By the time Papa steered into the alley snaking behind Aunt Mae's house, Maple Manor, Abby's arms trembled with exhaustion. A gangly maple tree seemed to beckon them as it shielded the tiny yard from the patch of sky visible between the houses.

Papa pulled the horses to a stop, set the brake, and jumped down from the buggy.

Abby handed Davy over to her father and clambered to the ground, relieved to feel her shoes against the solid earth. Adjusting her hat, she glanced up at the stately house—tall and narrow—wedged into a row of identical homes. How could people even breathe here?

Mama hurried down the steps to meet them, her bright smile not enough to hide the lines around her mouth.

"How is Cecelia?" Abby flung the question at Mama before her mother could draw her into an embrace.

"She's resting. They've already done two of the X-ray treatments, but we haven't seen any change yet. It's hard to leave her there, but I wanted to help you two settle in."

Abby stretched her cramped muscles. "We could have done it on our own."

Her mother reached for Davy, squeezing his small body against her side. "She was asleep and the nurses seem to take care of everything. I feel rather useless sitting there and watching."

Davy yanked at her collar. "Mama, I saw autos and trains and all sorts of things." His chatter drowned out any remaining conversation.

Abby gathered her carpetbag and the additional one she had brought for Cecelia and followed her mother into the house.

"Where is everyone?" Abby set the luggage at the bottom of the rear stairs.

Mama gripped Davy's hand. "Aunt Mae moved in with Gerald last month. You know he's been trying to talk his mother into doing it for years. She hasn't had the heart to sell Maple Manor, so Gerald says we are welcome to use it during our stay. We'll join them for supper tomorrow."

Davy tugged their mother toward the kitchen as Abby climbed the creaky stairs, bags banging against her shins with each step. The familiar house seemed cold and empty without Aunt Mae's effervescent personality filling its halls. Her influence remained with paintings, vases, and knickknacks from her world travels lining every wall, shelf, and tabletop.

Abby pushed open the door of the narrow back bedroom—the room she and Cecelia shared during visits. Two single beds stood at the far end, a tiny nightstand wedged between. A tall bookshelf leaned against one long wall, shelves sagging under a load of treasures. Across the room stood an ornate teak wardrobe and a washstand topped by a round gold-framed mirror. The dormer window let in a ribbon of late afternoon light.

The scent of dust and mildew clung to the stagnant air. Abby dropped the bags onto the bed and paced to the window. It took several tugs to open the sash, but she was rewarded by a warm afternoon breeze, perfumed by a climbing rosebush in full bloom.

Abby stretched both arms upward and arched her back, her muscles knotted with the awkward combination of exhaustion and nervous energy. The heavy doors of the wardrobe creaked as she pulled them open and began unpacking, shaking the wrinkles out of skirts and shirtwaists.

When she had finished with the first bag, Abby turned and stared for a long moment at the second. She opened the clasp and sighed, Cecelia's pretty clothes mocking her as she drew them out, one by one. Her sister would need more garments when—not if—she improved.

She caressed Cecelia's favorite blouse, a beautiful robin's-egg blue silk embroidered with delicate ivory roses along the neckline. A lump rose into Abby's throat and she sank down onto the mattress, bedsprings squeaking in protest, the garment pressed to her chest. She closed her eyes, trying to imagine her sister strolling down Market Street in the blue blouse and ivory lace skirt, her matching blue parasol tipped over one shoulder. Yet all she could see was Cecelia hanging limp in Dr. King's arms, her limbs as slack as a sleeping kitten.

Abby loosened her grip on the delicate material and returned to the task at hand. She paused once again as she drew out the final article of clothing. What a useless item—a pistachio-green taffeta gown Cecelia had worn last Easter. Abby had added it to the case at the last moment, knowing how much her sister loved the stylish ensemble. Abby exhaled, holding the elegant dress at arm's length. What had she been thinking to bring it? Cecelia came to San Francisco to convalesce, not to attend fancy dinners. Abby smoothed the silky fabric and hung it beside her own dark skirts.

There's nothing wrong with hoping for the best.

Robert, fighting a yawn, drummed his fingers against his leg. The basement room offered little distraction other than stacks of medical equipment, and he'd already been over every inch of each machine—twice.

Gerald continued to dither, as usual, exercising undue caution. He adjusted the equipment for the tenth time, lifting the apparatus another two inches and fiddling with its angle. He rolled up the cuff of his shirt and placed his arm on the wooden stand. "Okay, flip the switch." Gerald motioned with his free hand.

Robert frowned. "You're checking it on yourself? Again?"

Gerald's eyes widened. "Are you suggesting I test it on my cousin?"

"Of course not." Robert ran his fingers along the edge of the control panel. "But I set it to the same levels we used last time."

"Have you seen the burns on Dr. Bryant's fracture patient? I will not let it happen to Cecelia." Gerald repositioned his arm. "I can't reach the switch from here. Will you please do the honors?"

Robert nodded. "Of course." He scooted closer to the controls. "Are you ready?"

His mentor nodded.

Robert switched on the current. The machinery hummed as the Crookes tube began to glow, casting an unearthly blue light across the room. The hair on the back of his neck rose as a grin spread across his face. The invisible X-ray radiation swept through the room like a wind of change replacing ancient superstitions with cutting-edge science.

Gerald met his gaze, his eyes beaming. "It's brilliant, Robert, brilliant! The march of progress." He glanced down at his arm, his lip twitching. "And I think this is enough. My skin is tingling a bit."

Robert cut the electricity, plunging the room into silence. "It didn't burn, did it?" After securing the switch, he hurried to his friend's side.

Wincing, Gerald lifted his hand, rubbing his fingers over the skin. "No, I don't think so. It is a touch pink, though. Maybe we'd better lower the table another half-inch."

Robert nodded and reached for the lever. "We want to attack the cancer, not her skin." He adjusted the machine and shot Gerald a wink. "Of course, I hear, in Chicago, folks are lining up to use X-rays to get rid of wrinkles."

His friend shook his head with a rueful laugh. "I saw it in the newspaper. Wrinkles, dermatitis, acne, psoriasis . . . " He ran his fingers over his arm. "If it's true, I'm going to have lovely arms—and my cousin will be the most beautiful girl in California."

"I don't know about your arms, but I've seen the photograph hanging in your study—the one of our patient and her sister. I believe your cousins already own the title, X-rays or no."

Gerald checked the adjustments. "Let's see if we can keep it that way, shall we?"

Abby's heart pounded as she climbed the imposing granite steps into Lane Hospital and she regretted not waiting for her parents to accompany her. Her heels clicked against the gray and brown marble mosaic floor, the polished mahogany walls closing in on her soul like the boards of a casket.

A sour-faced nurse guided her to the cancer ward, informing Abby that Cecelia would be back in her room shortly. Abby sank into a wooden chair set next to the empty bed, a thin curtain separating the narrow place from eleven more beds in a long row. She covered her nose, trying to block out the mingled smells of medicine and misery as she swallowed the lump rising in her throat.

Her mother and father would be coming later, but Abby couldn't wait. Two weeks had already been too long. She'd slipped out of the house and boarded the cable car as it rattled its way up the hill to the hospital.

"Look who's here!" Dr. King grinned as he propelled Cecelia into the room in a wheeled chair.

Abby jumped to her feet when she spotted the fresh bit of color gracing Cecelia's skin.

"You made it." Cecelia's voice quavered, a weak smile lifting the corners of her lips.

Abby searched her sister's face, hungry for any sign of improvement. She rushed to her side. "Let me help you."

Cecelia raised her hand. "Don't worry, Dr. King and I have done this many times. We've got it set to memory."

Dr. King stepped forward. "I am your humble servant, Miss Fischer." He chuckled as he lifted her from the chair and placed her on the bed as gently as an autumn leaf alighting on the grass.

Abby adjusted the covers. "Cecelia, you look . . ." she paused, suddenly conscious of Dr. King close at her side.

"Ghastly. I know. The nurse brought me a looking glass." Cecelia leaned back against the pillow.

"No. You seem stronger. Your color is much improved." Abby looked to Dr. King. "Does this mean the X-rays are working?"

Dr. King brushed something from the sleeve of his long white coat. "It's too early to say." The light frolicking in his brown eyes belied his cautious words.

Fighting the urge to throw her arms around him, Abby turned her gaze to Cecelia's rosy cheeks. "It is working. It must be." She perched on the edge of the chair and reached for her sister's hand. "Just look at you."

Cecelia smiled. "I do feel a little stronger, I think."

Abby met Dr. King's gaze, the rush of joy swelling her chest until it ached. God may not have galloped in on a white horse to heal Cecelia—but evidently He had sent the doctor who would.

5

Robert rubbed his eyes and leaned back in the chair, the dull ache in his temples blurring his concentration. The electric lamp cast a harsh glare across the desk littered with stacks of papers and books. He stretched his arms upward, not surprised to hear a faint popping in his shoulders.

Robert slid his father's watch from his vest pocket, warming the gold case in his fingers. He held his thumb against the cover for a moment before clicking it open. Two-thirty? He should have gone to bed hours ago.

He glanced back at the open pages. Buried somewhere in these books were the answers he sought. Every time he considered putting them away, his thoughts jumped back to the patient lying in the hospital ward and the family counting on him to bring her back from the brink of death.

A familiar chill swept over Robert. If this failed, it could jeopardize everything he had built with his mentor. Robert had been fortunate to land this position straight out of medical college. Dr. Gerald Larkspur—methodical, meticulous, and precise—had generously involved Robert in every detail of the practice, from examinations to billing. While most of Robert's classmates were still groveling about, hoping for the opportunity to stitch a wound, Robert prospered under the guiding hand of one of the city's finest physicians.

Best of all, Gerald not only served as Robert's mentor, but their association had also deepened into friendship.

Robert sighed. Unfortunately, his friend remained trapped in the nineteenth century.

Skimming through William Allen Pusey's *The Practical Application of the Röntgen Rays*, Robert pressed a pencil against his chin, a day's worth of stubble scraping against the wood. Pusey's evidence clearly stated more radiation was better than less. Did their patient have time for caution? For precision?

Cecelia Fischer needed more.

Abby Fischer's beaming face filled his mind and he closed his eyes to the page. The woman's passion entranced him. Whenever she looked at him with those glowing eyes, Robert felt he could move heaven and earth, if only to please her.

He'd barely recognized her at the hospital today—her hair pinned at the back of her neck, a crisp white blouse, dark skirt, and matching vest—nothing like the uncouth country girl who nearly fell into his arms two weeks ago. And yet, her honesty and zeal remained unchanged.

God, since when did beautiful girls fall from the sky?

He'd never met anyone quite like her. Most San Francisco socialites strutted about in their feathered hats, concealing any sign of intellect or inner passion. They took pride in spouting frivolous conversation like flocks of twittering songbirds.

Abby Fischer spoke few words, but the expressions drifting across her features announced her inner thoughts like a newspaper boy shouting headlines from the street. The fire burning in her gaze as she argued for her sister's care ignited a matching passion in Robert's chest.

He lifted the book, gripping its cover with renewed vigor. He would wring the answers from its fragile pages if it took all night.

Because if it were up to him—Cecelia Fischer would survive.

Abby tossed and turned on the narrow bed, her dreams filled with scattered images of her sister. One moment, she danced at a grand party, the next she fled through flaming streets. Abby opened her eyes, her nightgown damp with perspiration, the musty scent of the room dragging her back to reality. She pushed up from the bed and swung her feet to the floor.

Padding to the window, Abby drew an arm tightly around her middle, pulled back the curtain, and peered out into the night, the gas streetlamps sparkling like low-hanging stars. *I'd rather see real stars.* She lit a candle and set it on the nightstand by the bed, the flickering glow casting comfort into the stark room.

At home, she would have rushed to check on her sister, certain the dreams were a sign of impending doom. Dr. King had assured her the nurses would telephone if there were any problems. Abby cracked the bedroom door ajar to ensure she would hear its ring. Her family had never owned a telephone before, so she wasn't sure how far the sound would carry.

Abby loosed her long braid and retrieved the tortoise-shell brush from the vanity. Sitting on the edge of the bed, she watched the candle flicker. *At least the X-rays are working.* She drew the bristles in long strokes through her hair, the muscles in her neck relaxing with the soothing rhythm.

Her mind wandered back to Dr. Robert King. The image of his warm eyes and smile remained imprinted on her heart. Abby paused mid-stroke and tapped the handle against her chin. Cecelia would laugh if she knew. Her sister had always tried to entice her into conversations about men, but Abby became an expert at changing topics. Besides, no man ever gave Abby a second glance once he spotted Cecelia. Abby had never needed skills in the fine arts of conversation and flirting—an area best left to the master.

Laying the brush on the nightstand, she grasped the candle and walked to the vanity. Surveying her reflection, Abby cocked her head to the side and drew her brown hair over her shoulder. In the dim light, she could almost imagine herself beautiful. Abby lifted her lips into the coy smile she'd seen Cecelia employ with such ease.

A gargoyle grinned back.

Abby covered her mouth in horror. *Better not do that.*

Abby sat back in her chair, resting the novel on her lap and meeting her sister's gaze. Cecelia's face had definitely gained new life—color and sparkle had returned. The luminosity of those familiar eyes brought a lump to Abby's throat.

"Why did you stop reading?" Cecelia's brow wrinkled.

"I can't get over the change in you over the past few days."

Cecelia ran her fingers along the snowy-white sheet covering her legs. She lay propped up with several large pillows, her blond hair brushed and braided, the gold locket gleaming against her chest. "I am having trouble believing it myself."

Abby shook her head. "It's astonishing how an energy field helped more in a few days than all of the medicines Dr. Greene has given you over the past six months."

"Dr. Greene did what he could." Cecelia stifled a yawn with the back of her hand.

"I'm tiring you. I should go." Abby tucked a bookmark into the novel. "Mama and Papa will be coming to see you at noon. You'll want to be rested.

"And here I thought you were waiting to get a glimpse of my handsome doctor." Cecelia smiled, lips parting.

Abby's cheeks warmed. "Don't be ridiculous."

"I'm sick, not blind. And I'm pleased for you. Robert is very nice." Her sister fiddled with the locket, sliding it back and forth on the delicate chain.

A cold prickle washed over Abby's skin. "Robert, is it?"

"Dr. King. He seems too young to call 'Doctor.' He's only twenty-five, you know."

The prickles grew thorns. "He's your doctor, Cecelia. Mama wouldn't approve of you flirting with him."

Cecelia's chin jutted forward. "Calling him by his first name is not flirting. Now who's being ridiculous?" The sudden pout gave way to a smile, like a glimmer of sun after a quick storm. "You do care for him—I can see it in your face." She folded her arms across her chest and raised one eyebrow. "Here I am in the hospital and you're setting your sights on my dashing, young physician."

"Hush," Abby jumped to her feet. "Someone will hear you." She glanced around the hospital ward, but the nearby patients didn't stir. She pointed a finger at her sister. "None of that kind of talk or I'm leaving. Besides, you're the one who told me to pray, and Dr. King was God's answer. For you, not for me."

Cecelia yawned a second time, snuggling deeper into the pillows. "You can leave if you like. Robert's coming in a few minutes. I'm sure he won't mind keeping me company." She closed her eyes, a triumphant smile lighting on her face.

Abby flopped back onto the hard chair. "I'd almost forgotten what you're really like."

Cecelia opened one eye. "What?"

"Incorrigible. Impossible. Insufferable." Abby hadn't bickered with her sister in months. Her heart rose.

"Irreplaceable." Cecelia finally allowed her eyes to close, a small dimple appearing in her cheek.

"That, too." Abby flipped open the novel and stared at the words swimming across the page. She would wait for Dr. King, if for no other reason than to keep an eye on her sister.

Robert nearly collided with two nurses as he paced down the hospital hallway, still thumbing Pusey's *Practical Application*. He apologized, the women's giggles sending heat crawling up his neck as he juggled the heavy tome. Gerald stood at the desk nearby, a telephone receiver in his hand.

Robert excused himself and hurried over to join his partner just as Gerald replaced the receiver on the stand. "Gerald, I wanted to speak with you, if you have a moment."

Gerald ran a hand across the back of his neck, "I just spoke with my cousin Clara. She and Herman will be coming in at noon to meet with me. I'd like for you to be there, also."

"Of course." Robert clasped the book to his chest as he eyed his friend. "You look terrible. Did you spend the night?"

"Mrs. Joyce passed during the wee hours."

Robert's heart dropped. In his fascination with the leukemia case, he'd somewhat lost sight of Gerald's other patients. "I—I'm sorry."

"It's for the best. She's been battling edema from dropsy for years. There was nothing more we could do. I'm glad to see her out of pain." He shook his head. "There are days when it feels like all we do is watch our patients suffer. No matter how much science moves forward, death still wins in the end."

Robert's father's voice echoed through his memory, reciting a favorite Scripture. "O death, where is thy sting? O grave, where is thy victory?" How had he always maintained such hope in the face of stark reality?

Robert reached for Gerald's shoulder. "Your cousin seems to be improving all the time. It must be somewhat of a relief, right?"

Gerald glanced up. "Of course." He eyed the book in Robert's hand. "You look pretty exhausted, yourself. Been burning the midnight oil?"

"I've been reading some of the recent research regarding X-ray technology." Robert hesitated. "I've found some case studies I think you should read. They suggest we should be using higher intensity radiation."

Gerald's eyes narrowed. "We've been over this."

Robert flipped the book open. "But if you'd take a look at the research—"

"Why are you pushing this so hard? Cecelia's responding to the low-level treatments. Why take the risk?"

Robert straightened his shoulders. Stiff competition in medical college had trained him to defend his conclusions with conviction, but facing off against a friend required prudence. "There may be additional risk in the long-term if we continue with this conservative approach. We might be giving the malignancy a chance to spread. I believe we should hit it hard and fast."

"We need to make sure Cecelia can handle strong doses of radiation—build up her vitality first."

Robert pointed to the pages of the book. "Pusey says the patient may not have time to wait."

Gerald sighed, rolling his eyes toward the ceiling. "Give me the book. I'll take a look at it."

"It's all I ask."

6

*A*bby opened her eyes, blinking against the hazy sunshine spilling through the bedroom window. A motor purred outside, catching her attention. The front door rattled and she sat up with a start, book falling to the floor.

Cousin Gerald must have given the family a ride home from church in his automobile. Glancing at the gold-framed clock, she blinked in surprise. Several hours had passed since she had stretched out on the bed to read the dog-eared copy of Kipling's *The Jungle Book* she'd found on the shelf. Abby stretched and slid her feet to the cold floor.

"Abigail?" A quick rap sounded on the bedroom door. Mama peeked in, tiny wrinkles lining her forehead. She crossed the rug in an instant, placing a cool hand on Abby's face. "How are you feeling?"

Abby's stomach turned and she brushed the hand away. "Just a headache. How was church?"

Mama perched on the edge of the bed, unpinning her feather-bedecked hat and resting it on her lap. "The service was beautiful. The choir sang like angels. It's not like church back home, of course, but it was very nice." Her voice faded as her finger traced the pattern in the rosebud quilt Abby had brought from home, the twin to Cecelia's. Mama's eyes darkened.

She looked at Abby from under impossibly long lashes, her lips pressed to a thin line. "Aunt Mae is looking forward to having us for Sunday dinner."

Abby gazed at the floor. She'd rather spend the day at Cecelia's side or here in the quiet house.

"I know you're not feeling your best, but it would make everyone happy to have you there. Aunt Mae was disappointed when you weren't at church. You know how she loves to see you. Gerald even asked if he should come and check on you."

Abby covered her eyes with her hands, "No—please." *This is what comes of feigning sickness rather than going to church.*

"I understand. But I think you will feel better if you join everyone for dinner." A tremor crept into Mama's voice. "It isn't good to be alone at a time like this. We all need to be together now, more than ever."

Abby chewed on her lip. Her mother's request hung in the air. *She needs me.*

"Dr. King will be joining us as well."

Abby's chin jerked up before she could catch herself. She lowered her eyes, but not before spotting her mother's raised brows. An uncomfortable silence filled the room.

Mama stood. "Come, now. Let's not keep everyone waiting."

Abby sighed and rose to her feet.

Her mother smiled in triumph, but the expression faded as she eyed Abby's rumpled brown skirt. Crossing to the wardrobe, she opened the door. She examined the plain shirtwaists and skirts with a frown. "Didn't you bring a dinner dress?"

"I didn't think I would need one."

Mama's hand stopped when she reached Cecelia's Easter gown.

"Mama, no."

"It's the only suitable article of clothing in here. Your sister won't mind." She pulled the garment from the wardrobe and laid it across the bed. "Now, off with your old skirt and I will help you with your laces."

Abby leaned against the bedpost for a moment, staring in dismay at the stylish gown. She remembered Mother and Cecelia choosing the material last year. Ivory lapels framed the pistachio-green gown, Irish lace on the cuffs and high collar softening the fashionable color Cecelia had so adored. The elegant dress deserved to grace the figure of a young woman stepping into the world of high society, not a freckled country girl who felt more at home tending to the orchard.

Taking a deep breath, Abby slipped off her comfortable white shirtwaist and brown skirt and pressed a hand against the front of her corset with a frown. The two sisters had not been cut from the same cloth. Whenever they traded clothes, the results were the same.

If this X-ray treatment fails, we might never share clothes again. Her throat tightened, as if the corset squeezed her neck rather than her middle.

Her mother wrapped Abby's laces between her fingers and pulled, drawing the undergarment in like the coils of a hungry snake. Abby closed her eyes, imagining the constriction as glue holding her together while she spent the afternoon making small talk with relatives.

After her mother fastened the laces, Abby reached for the gown. After fastening the lace collar around her throat, she ran a finger between it and her skin to secure a few decent breaths of air.

Mama frowned as she tugged and adjusted the dress, trying to get it to fit on Abby's sturdier frame. Finally, she stepped back and stared, a series of emotions passing across her gentle face like cloudbursts wandering through a summer sky. Turning away, she lifted a finger to the corner of her eye as if brushing away an errant lash. "It's such a lovely garment."

Abby glanced in the looking glass, a sinking sensation in her stomach. "Yes, lovely." *On Cecelia.*

Her mother cleared her throat. "I'll leave you to finish getting ready. Be quick, please. Gerald and Dr. King are waiting to drive us over."

Abby stared down at the dress as her mother's footsteps receded. After a few moments of silence, she hurried down the hall to her parents' bedchamber. The long looking glass conveyed the unpleasant truth. Even worse than she feared. The lace and ruffles drew attention to the straining bodice, the yellowish-green color of the fabric accentuating the dark circles under her eyes. She rotated, frowning at the huge ivory bow hanging crooked on her backside. Abby tugged at it, but the ludicrous ornament refused to be straightened, its reflection mocking her from the mirror.

I can't wear this. I won't wear this.

She turned and faced her reflection head-on, running her hands down the ivory lapels. *What choice do I have?*

She poured some of Mama's lilac-scented oil in her hand and ran sweet-smelling fingers through her long locks before braiding. Borrowing a few hairpins, she coiled the plaits into a knot at the nape of her neck. Not fancy, but at least her hair looked tidy.

She pinched her freckled cheeks and cast a final scornful glance over her shoulder at the bow on her rump.

Abby paused at the top of the stairs to smooth some of the puckers from her bodice and noticed Robert King examining a painting in the front hall. A crisp white celluloid collar and black tie peeked out above his wine-colored vest and black suit jacket, his dark hair parted in the center.

Abby's breath caught in her throat. She retreated a few steps and stole a glance from around the corner, taking this rare opportunity to inspect the young man from a safe distance. Dr. King tugged at the edges of his suit coat, shifting from foot to foot. *Curious. He radiated self-assurance the last time we met.*

Leaning back against the wall, she took a deep breath. Maybe Dr. King lacked confidence after all. Abby glanced down at the gown before reaching up to smooth her hair. She'd never cared much about her appearance before. *It's just this dress.* She tugged at the snug collar, beads of perspiration forming where the stiff lace scratched against her skin. She took another quick gander down the stairs, hoping Dr. King had gained the nerve to move into the parlor.

No such luck.

Abby backed a few steps into the upstairs hall, considering a retreat to the rear staircase. Clenching her fists, she chided herself. *Why hide now? I'm going to see him all afternoon.*

Cecelia would march straight down those steps and greet the doctor to put their guest at ease. Lifting her head and squaring her shoulders, Abby fanned the tiny spark of her sister's courage into a burgeoning flame. Before stepping around the corner and onto the stairs, she reached one hand behind her back, flattening the enormous bow.

Dr. King glanced upward, his smile affecting an instantaneous transformation from nervous guest to sophisticated gentleman.

Abby's brief flicker of composure fizzled like a match in the face of a stiff breeze. She paused on the middle landing and clutched the banister, steadying herself as she stared down at him.

"Hello, Miss Fischer. I'm glad to see you have recovered enough to join us." His eyes shone, warm and welcoming, putting images of steaming cups of hot chocolate in her mind.

"Dr. King." Abby managed to nod, her back stiffening to maintain formality even as her knees threatened to give way.

"You look . . ." his gaze dropped to the dress before returning to her face, "very nice."

A lump formed in her throat. *He's indulging me.* "Thank you." Keeping the massive bow hidden, she gathered her skirt to descend the last three steps. The edge of her shoe caught on the gown's trailing hem and Abby stumbled, pitching forward in a most unladylike tumble toward the Oriental rug.

Dr. King reached for her arm, preventing her from landing facedown and bow-up.

The brush of his fingers against her arm made her jump. She pulled away, cheeks burning. "Thank you, Dr. King."

A dimple showed in his cheek. "You do know how to make an entrance, Miss Fischer. Are you sure you are feeling well enough to go to dinner?"

She straightened her skirt and backed up to the wall. "Yes. I just took a bad step. Thank you for your assistance."

Dr. King moved closer, a smile playing at the corners of his mouth. "Please, don't speak of it. It's an honor to catch you—again."

Abby battled a sudden urge to dash back up the stairs.

Mama swept into the room with a dramatic swish of her elegant cream-colored skirt adorned with silk roses. Davy squealed atop his father's shoulders as Papa ducked low through the doorway, Cousin Gerald trailing behind.

Gerald tucked his gold watch back into his vest pocket and smiled, his blue eyes twinkling. "Abby, you look lovely. I trust you are fully recovered?"

Abby folded her arm behind her back, wishing she had put on her gloves. If anyone reached for her hand, they would be rewarded with a very damp handshake indeed. "Perhaps I needed some rest."

Gerald nodded. "It has been a difficult few weeks. But I am relieved you will be joining us for dinner. My mother is preparing a feast fit for royalty." He leaned close and winked, lowering his voice to whisper, "If you hadn't shown up, she might have come over here, herself, to retrieve you."

Abby suppressed a shudder.

Gerald offered his arm. "Shall we go and present ourselves for inspection?"

Abby placed one hand behind her back, pushing down the bow. She didn't want to lead this parade. "Why don't you go on ahead? I need to retrieve my hat and gloves."

She lingered in the parlor until the others moved outside. When the door clicked shut, she sighed, her neck muscles relaxing. Abby tied a green ribbon around her casual boater, thankful she controlled at least one item of her ensemble, and jammed a long silver pin through the straw hat, securing it to her bun. Scooping up her handkerchief and lace gloves, Abby hurried back into the hall. A wave of consternation swept over her as she spotted Robert standing by the door.

"I didn't want you to think we'd left without you." Bathed in colored light from the two stained glass windows framing the doorway, Dr. King looked like a footman from the Palace Hotel. He reached for the knob and swung the door wide. "After you."

Abby stepped sideways as she crossed the threshold, careful to keep her posterior hidden from view. "Thank you, Dr. —" A sudden jerk from behind rocked her back on her heels. Her throat tightened as she peered over her shoulder and spotted the dreaded bow hooked over the crystal doorknob. Grabbing the frame, she twisted her shoulders until she faced Dr. King. "I believe I have forgotten my gloves. Would you be so kind as to check if I left them on the hall table?"

He cocked one eyebrow. "Aren't you holding a pair in your hand?"

Abby crumpled them against her chest. "Did I say gloves? I meant my Bible. I wanted to show something to Aunt Mae."

Her breathing slowed as the doctor retreated into the hall. Rising up on her toes, she twisted her hips as if preparing for a waltz turn. The sound of ripping generated a new flutter in her chest. Biting her lip, Abby wound her finger under the ribbon and tugged.

"Allow me." Dr. King's fingers brushed against her own.

Abby closed her eyes, wishing for a crack in the floor to swallow her whole.

Dr. King's breath warmed the back of her neck, under her knotted hair. "I didn't see a Bible on the table."

As the bow slipped free, Abby lunged forward to escape the stifling sensation produced by his close proximity. "I must have been mistaken. No matter." Stopping at the edge of the porch, Abby pressed a cool hand against her cheek. Her family gathered around the automobile waiting on the cobblestone street. She paused, trying to think of a suitable phrase of thanks to offer to the doctor without risking further embarrassment.

Abby turned to speak, but the words froze in her throat at the sight of his amused smile. *Is he laughing?*

All gratitude evaporated from her heart. She hurried down the steps, careful to lift the long skirt clear of her stumbling feet.

Robert ducked his head, a smile threatening to take hold of his face. Abby Fischer was a gem among women. He'd never met someone who could transport him from anxiety to amusement in a few moments.

Every time he laid eyes on her, she looked more beautiful than the last, and yet one could see honesty laid out on her face, especially in those deep, brown eyes. His soul ached to know her better, to discover the spirit blossoming within.

Get a hold of yourself. Robert shuddered. Miss Fischer was his friend's cousin and his patient's sister—two excellent reasons to steer clear.

He followed her down the stairs to the street, his eyes drawn to the cockeyed ribbon bouncing along on her backside.

Robert sucked in a deep breath. *It's going to be a long day.*

7

$\mathcal{T}$he ride in Gerald's automobile stole Abby's breath and sent gooseflesh creeping across her skin. Wedged between Mama and Papa in the rear seat, she closed her eyes rather than watch as they careened past buggies, delivery wagons, and cable cars.

Gerald turned onto Gough Street, traveling two more blocks before stopping in front of his house. He set the brake, the automobile's engine rattling to a blessed stillness.

Abby's hand trembled as she lifted the long green skirt and stepped onto the running board. If she survived the entire day without tripping over the hem, staining the fine silk, or popping a seam, she'd consider it a miracle.

Dr. King appeared at her side, hand outstretched.

She forced a nonchalant expression and placed her gloved hand in his. Distracted by the pressure against her fingers, she stepped to the cobblestone street with little awareness of her feet.

Davy clambered onto the bottom rail of the wrought iron gate, catching a quick ride as it swung out onto the sidewalk. Abby released Dr. King's hand and hurried to peel her brother from the fence.

Mama exited the motorcar clutching Papa's arm, the feathered plumes of her hat waggling like the remnants of a battered rooster after a cockfight. Abby brushed back the green ribbon on her own simple straw boater, thankful she opted not to pack the gown's matching bonnet. A lacy veil and a trickling cascade of white feathers—she would have been a sight, indeed.

Great Aunt Mae swung the door wide. "Welcome, welcome. Come in everyone, get out of the sun." She lifted an age-speckled hand, casting a shadow across her face. "My goodness it's bright."

Abby hung toward the back of the group, preferring a few moments in the sun to the dark house, every tall window shrouded by draperies.

Aunt Mae clasped her son's arm, pulling him through the doorway. "The hospital telephoned a moment ago, Gerald. Cecelia is still sleeping. I told them you would be in *after* supper." Her lips pinched together.

"Thank you, Mother. I'll ring them back." Gerald leaned down and brushed a kiss against her cheek.

Abby stripped off her gloves. Gerald wouldn't mind if she accompanied him to the hospital—assuming she survived the next few hours.

"Abigail, my dear child, come in and let me look at you." Aunt Mae seized Abby's hand, towing her into the shadowy front hall.

Abby dragged her shoes across the expensive Persian rug as the rest of the family filed away through the parlor.

The sunlight pouring in the doorway glinted among the silver strands in Aunt Mae's hair as the elderly woman paraded Abby around the front hall. "What a festive dress. Turn please, and let me look at you."

"It's Cecelia's, actually." Abby sashayed to the side, trying to avoid performing a full roundabout.

Aunt Mae captured Abby's elbow and turned her around. Taking hold of the bow, the older woman clucked her tongue. "My, my, what has happened here? This bow is all askew." The ribbon tugged at Abby's waist as Aunt Mae tinkered with it. "Come into the kitchen. It won't take but a moment to fix that."

Abby trailed in her wake, chiding herself for ever packing Cecelia's gown.

"I hope you are fully recovered because I have been cooking since yesterday and could probably feed all the soldiers at the Presidio."

The deep, rich scent of pot roast and fresh-baked bread set Abby's mouth to salivating as her aunt rummaged through a basket resting on a corner table. She withdrew a gleaming pair of shears. "Aha." She snapped the scissor in the air and waved her fingers in a circle, gesturing for Abby to turn.

Abby's stomach tightened. She reached behind her back, covering the silk bow with her hands. "What are you going to do?"

"I know a thing or two about dresses, dear. I had three girls—and practically raised your mother and her sister."

Abby lowered her hands to her sides and moved in a half-circle. She peeked over her shoulder. "Yes, but . . ."

Her aunt whacked a palm against Abby's back. "Hold still, missy, or I might just cut a hole in your bustle."

Abby swung her gaze forward, willing her spine rod-straight. The last thing the hideous frock needed was a giant hole where she was supposed to sit.

"There." Aunt Mae laughed. "Much better."

Abby froze mid-turn.

The bow dangled from Aunt Mae's fingertips. "You didn't want this ridiculous thing, did you?"

"No, but . . ." Abby explored her back with searching fingers.

"Don't worry, it looks fine. Better, in fact. The silly frill was only attached by a few threads. No one will notice." She pressed the bow into Abby's hands. "Maybe you can put it in your hair or something." Aunt Mae's lips tightened, tiny lines forming around her mouth. "If it were me, I'd bury it in the backyard."

Abby laughed, a bit of tension uncoiling from her shoulders.

Davy ran past and plowed into Aunt Mae. "Cookie!" His joyful shriek cut through the steamy kitchen.

Mama hurried in, fingers reaching for her son's shirt-tail. "Davy! Do not speak to your great-aunt in such a way."

Abby wadded the ribbon in her fist, pushing it behind her back.

Davy paused. "May I have a cookie?" His voice trailed up, expectantly.

Aunt Mae scooped Davy into her arms. "Oh, Clara, please." She huffed, causing the tiny silver curls on her forehead to bounce.

"After a long morning at church, hungry little boys can't be expected to have perfect manners." She touched the tip of his nose with her finger. "You know Great-Auntie always has a cookie ready for you."

He squirmed free.

Aunt Mae reached for the jar, stashed in a sunny corner of the kitchen. "Snickerdoodle or molasses, my sweet?"

Davy scrunched his eyebrows before an impish smile brightened his face. "Both?" He shot a wary glance at his mother. "Both, please?"

Aunt Mae's laugh almost obscured Mama's groan. Aunt Mae patted his shoulder. "Have one now and a different one after dinner."

"Aunt Mae," Mama intercepted Davy's hands as he lunged for the container.

"Now, hush. This is my house—actually, I suppose it's my son's house—but it's my privilege to hand out treats." The small woman tapped the toe of her high-buttoned shoe. "Let him enjoy it or there will be no dessert for you later, my dear!"

Mama heaved a sigh of surrender.

Cousin Gerald's laugh echoed from the next room. "She never fed us sugar before dinner when we were little, Clara. Mama's going soft."

Great Aunt Mae clucked her tongue. "'Behold, what manner of love the Father hath bestowed upon us, that we should be called the sons of God.' And if He can bestow love on His children, so can I. Or at least on the children visiting this house."

The jar cradled in the crook of her elbow, the older woman turned to Abby. "Now, young lady, you were always partial to the molasses ones, right?" She pressed a cookie into Abby's hand.

Abby's throat tightened. Crumbs dropped from her fingers while she crumpled the bow in her other hand. Cecelia lay in a hospital bed while the rest of the family joked and laughed and ate. A sour taste sprang to her mouth.

Aunt Mae took Mama's arm. "I intend to bestow my love on your entire family, my dear. I am pleased you and Herman could join us today. Having you in town has made me very happy indeed—even though it comes under such tragic circumstances. Until I get him married off, Gerald and I rattle around this big house all alone. And my son doesn't seem to be in any hurry to do so."

Mama leaned into the embrace. "It's good to be with family."

Aunt Mae patted her arm. "Yes, child. You know we're always here for you. I'm praying for Cecelia with every breath."

Abby escaped to the pantry. Leaning against the shelves, she closed her eyes for a brief moment. *Get through supper, and you can go to the hospital with Gerald.* Grasping a long white apron hanging from a peg, she tucked the bow and the uneaten cookie into a pocket.

When she stepped back into the kitchen, the two ladies had turned their attentions to dinner. Mama gripped the oven handle with a towel, leaning low to peer inside, the scent of peach pie anointing the warm room. Aunt Mae caught Abby's eye and gestured with a dripping wooden spoon. "Carrots and onions, dear one."

Abby pushed the sharp knife into the onion, the pungent odor tickling her nose. She pushed the vegetables across the block, chopping in a steady rhythm, creating neat piles of carrots and onions. Abby only half-listened as her mother and aunt discussed the building of the glamorous new Fairmont Hotel. Why should she care? She lifted a wrist to brush against her stinging eyes. Her thoughts wandered as Aunt Mae's words hummed in her ear like a bumblebee around a honeysuckle vine.

"The paper claims Caruso will give a marvelous performance in *Carmen*, though I've never been fond of him, myself. The opera society has put together a rather remarkable program this year. San Francisco is certainly making a name for itself when it comes to the arts. *The Call* wrote we are beginning to rival New York and Chicago—trading in the 'wild west' and gold-panning forty-niners for a new image."

Mama sighed and leaned back against the cupboard. "I can't remember the last time I went to the opera. It must have been shortly after Herman and I married." Her voice lowered. "He never wanted to go back."

Aunt Mae pointed her gravy-coated spoon toward her. "Now you are staying in the city, we should make some plans. It would be just the thing to lift your spirits. You can't be at the hospital all of the time. And it would be such a treat for Abby." She fixed her bright eyes on Abby. "Wouldn't it be fun, my dear?"

Abby blinked away the stinging onion tears, swallowing hard, and managing a quick nod. "Yes, of course." *Another reason to wear this dreadful gown.*

As Aunt Mae slid the pie from the oven, the sugary juices bubbling up through the lattice top, Abby closed her eyes, trying to pull her mind away from the operas, crowded cities, and onion fumes. Gripping a large carrot, she shoved the knife downward. A squeaking gasp broke from her mouth even before she realized what she had done. The knife clattered to the floor as Abby lost her grip, dazed by the sight of blood welling from her finger.

Aunt Mae rushed to Abby's side with a clean dishtowel, clasping it around the wound. Mama's face blanched at the sight of the blood sprinkled across the glistening white pile of sliced onions.

Steering Abby into a nearby chair, Aunt Mae tightened her lips into a thin line. "Let me look at it, child." She loosened the towel and examined the injury, her eyebrows drawing together like purse strings. "You still have all your fingers, but the cut looks deep. Clara, go find Gerald. He may want to put in a stitch or two."

Mama's pale skin had taken on a greenish cast. She rushed through the swinging door into the hall.

Aunt Mae twisted the cloth around the wound. "How did you manage not to get any on your dress? How very fortunate!"

Abby glanced down at the gown and sighed.

Mama stepped back into the room with Dr. King on her heels. His gaze darted about the kitchen.

Abby closed her eyes. *The tree, the doorknob . . . now this.*

Her mother's voice trembled. "Gerald and Herman took Davy out for a walk."

"Of course they did." Aunt Mae raised her chin. "It's more likely they went out to smoke their pipes. I told Gerald I wouldn't move in here unless he stopped smoking the disgusting thing in the house." She took a deep breath. "I'm certain Dr. King can take care of this."

Abby's stomach churned.

Dr. King glanced at Abby. "If it isn't too serious, perhaps Miss Fischer would prefer to wait for her cousin."

Holding her breath, Abby darted a gaze toward her aunt. "Yes, I think—"

"Nonsense," Aunt Mae snapped with all the sympathy of a sergeant major, giving the young man a gentle shove. "Gerald told me you were the top of your class. I'm sure you can handle a few simple sutures."

A hissing from the stovetop drew Aunt Mae back toward the food preparations. "Come, Clara, let's give him some space, shall we?" She beckoned to Abby's mother.

Dr. King crouched down on his heels and reached for Abby's hand.

Her palms grew damp. Drawing them close to her chest, Abby cradled the bloodstained towel against the apron bodice. "I don't think it's so bad. It probably doesn't even need stitches."

"Let's take a look. All right?"

Lowering her hand to his outstretched one, Abby averted her eyes. As Dr. King unwound the towel, curiosity overcame her nerves and she bent forward for a glimpse of the wound. Her hand trembled she stared at the gaping, oozing wound on her pointer finger, perhaps a half-inch long. She leaned back against the chair, swallowing a whimper.

Dr. King pressed the towel back into place. "Your aunt is right. It needs to be sutured. I'll get some things from Gerald's study." His brows wrinkled above his deep, brown eyes. "Are you certain you wouldn't rather wait for him?"

Of course, I want to wait for him. She stared down at the doctor's hand cradling hers, his slight olive skin tone in sharp contrast to her own pale fingers. "No, it's fine."

"All right, then." He lifted her arm. "Hold the hand up to slow the bleeding. I'll be right back."

As the kitchen door swung on its hinges, the odors of the cooking food combined with the sweltering heat pressed in on Abby. One last glance at the reddening dishtowel overwhelmed her resolve. She dashed for the back door and stumbled down the stairs into the yard before her stomach heaved.

Abby's mother helped her back inside and into the sitting room. Aunt Mae brought a damp cloth for her forehead and a cup of chamomile tea.

Abby settled down on the rose-colored damask chaise longue, closing her eyes in the quiet. The throbbing in her finger competed with the churning sensations in her gut. As if this day hadn't been embarrassing enough—now she lay like some wounded heroine in a romance novel.

Except this day had been anything but romantic.

Her stomach did another carousel-like twirl at the sound of footsteps entering the room and a chair being drawn close. The doctor's instruments jangled against each other, a grating dissonance in the otherwise tranquil room.

"Miss Fischer?" The doctor spoke in soft tones. "Are you ready?"

"As ready as I will ever be." She swallowed, pushing the acidic taste back down her throat as she opened her eyes.

Dr. King rested her wrist against a cushion he'd set upon a low table.

Abby pressed her other arm against her stomach, pushing away the cold prickles crawling over her skin. *This is nothing compared to what Cecelia endures.*

Dr. King swabbed the wound with iodine-soaked gauze, staining her skin a distasteful shade of orange. Reaching into a leather bag, he withdrew a small silver case, turning away as he opened it.

She leaned forward, craning her neck for a glimpse. Spotting a deadly looking syringe, Abby's breath caught in her throat. "What's that?"

"It's Novocain." He held up the glistening needle and flicked the glass tube several times with a fingernail. "It will numb your skin so you don't feel the sutures."

She frowned. "What about feeling the needle?"

"Trust me, this is better."

Abby held her breath as he positioned it against her finger. The twinge of pain reminded her of a wasp sting.

"Now, we wait." He turned his attention to the medical bag. Selecting several gleaming instruments, he arranged them on a pristine white cloth, touching and straightening each one in turn. With a quick nod, he excused himself from the room.

Abby sat back against the cushion, the silence a soothing balm. She wiggled her fingers in awe as an icy sensation took hold, the ache receding into the cold.

If only someone would invent Novocain for emotions.

Robert stood at the window in Gerald's study, peering down the street for a sign of his friend's return. He wiped damp palms on his trouser legs. *You've done this a hundred times in the hospital. Why is this any different?*

The young woman's teary brown eyes flooded Robert's thoughts and he shoved his trembling hands into his pockets. Perhaps he should ask her to keep her eyes closed. Most patients preferred not to see the suturing process anyway.

Then again, Abby Fischer was no ordinary patient.

The street remained empty. Robert glanced at the grandfather clock, wishing the steady tick would calm his nerves. He took a deep breath and strode down the dim hallway to the sitting room, his shoes sinking into the plush rug.

Miss Fischer's head rested against the crocheted antimacassar draped over the couch's back. Her ivory skin revealed a hint of green, similar to her eye-catching gown.

Robert pulled his gaze away and settled into the chair across from her. "The anesthetic should have worked its magic by now." He cradled her wrist, stroking her fingers. "Can you feel it?"

A pink flush rose on Miss Fischer's freckled cheeks, a stark contrast to her frost-kissed hand. "It's a strange sensation. It's almost as if my hand belonged to someone else."

He released his hold, resisting the urge to warm her skin with his own. Selecting a curved needle from the cloth, he threaded it with catgut. "Even with the Novocain, this is still going to hurt a little. I will need you to hold perfectly still."

Her wide-eyed expression made it difficult to concentrate. *Pretend she's a stranger. Pretend she's a man. Pretend she's your mother, for goodness sakes. Whatever it takes.* He adjusted the needle in the forceps, begging God for steady hands. He hadn't been this tense since Dr. Emil Dawson breathed down his neck during his first surgery. And it had been a splenectomy.

Imagine she's some man off the street. Only with soft skin and perfectly rounded fingernails. Maybe a banker.

Robert pressed the edges of the laceration together and lined up the needle for the initial jab.

At the sharp prick, Miss Fischer gasped and jerked her arm back.

Be gentle, you idiot. He pressed her wrist back against the towel. "Do you want me to ask your aunt or mother to help?"

She shrank in the seat. "No. I can hold still. I promise." Miss Fischer's chin quivered.

He closed his eyes for a moment. "Relax."

"What do you think I'm trying to do?"

He chuckled, easing his grip on her hand. "I was actually talking to myself. But, yes, you relax, too."

Robert pressed the needle into her skin, using the edge of his hand to brace her finger against the table. Drawing the thread taut, he pulled the edges of the wound closed with ease. "Are you doing all right?"

She spoke through clenched teeth. "Yes, fine. Thank you. You may proceed."

Robert bent his head low over his work, making quick work of the few stitches. Tying off the final suture, he snipped the thread close to the skin. "I'm sure your cousin will want to take a look at it when he gets home." He smiled, the tension easing from his shoulders. "Make sure to inform him of my wonderful bedside manner."

Miss Fischer cradled the injured finger against her chest. "Thank you, Dr. King." She gazed at the stitches. "Your sewing is much better than my own. I am fortunate you were here."

"Treating two lovely sisters in one day—I believe I am the fortunate one."

Her shy smile sustained him as he cleaned Gerald's instruments and returned them to the doctor's study. He would need to remember to replace the vial of Novocain with the supply from their downtown office. Pressing a hand against his eyes, he recalled the expression on Miss Fischer's face as he brought out the syringe. A woman of few words, perhaps, but one could get lost in her dark, expressive eyes. The Miss Abby Fischer he'd seen today—frail as a butterfly when he took her hand—stood in sharp contrast to the picture of confidence and strength she presented at her sister's bedside.

A knot formed in his stomach as he remembered his own rush of emotion while touching her hand. *Not very professional.* Robert shook his head.

Gerald cleared his throat as he stood in the doorway, fiddling with his watch fob. "It appears I missed all the excitement."

Robert jerked from his reverie and latched the glass door on the cabinet.

"I took a look at Abby's finger—splendid job. I couldn't have done better."

Robert breathed out, his muscles loosening. "It was only a few sutures. I did plenty in medical school."

Gerald joined him at the cabinet, chuckling. "Yes, but not on my cousin."

"I suppose I'm growing accustomed to treating your family members."

A shadow crossed the other man's face. "Hmm. Let's hope it doesn't become a habit." Gerald dropped down into his desk chair, letting it turn side to side on its swivel post. "Still, Cecelia is making remarkable progress. It's quite astounding."

A surge of pride lifted Robert's spirits as he sat in an armchair nestled in the corner of the office. "Have you thought more about what I said earlier?"

Gerald leaned back, running a hand through his hair. "Yes. And I read the studies you gave me." His face sobered. "It's a good thing I have you to keep me on track." He turned toward the photos lining his desk. "I understand why they say you shouldn't treat a loved one. I'm terrified of making a mistake, of being blamed—of blaming myself—I err on the side of caution. But Pusey's research is clear."

Robert leaned forward. "Then we'll increase the treatments?"

Gerald nodded. "If there's any chance for this to work long-term, we have no choice." His eyes darkened. "But keep an eagle eye on her, Robert. I don't want any burns or such. The machines are to be calibrated every time."

"Of course."

"If we see any negative side effects from the increased radiation, we're going to reevaluate."

Robert stood, energy buzzing in his chest. "I'll document everything. We're going to make history after all."

Gerald gazed out the window. "I'm not in this for history. You're welcome to the glory. I'd simply like to have my cousin back."

Robert's thoughts pulled back to the image of Cecelia Fischer lying in the hospital bed, coupled with Abby Fischer's adoring gaze when she'd recognized her sister's vast improvement. "If I get my way, we're going to have both."

8

    *A*bby settled onto a wrought-iron bench nestled beneath the grape arbor. The late afternoon breeze, scented with lavender, rustled the leaves, the trailing vines whispering words of solace to her soul.

She closed her eyes, desperate to restore her composure after the disastrous dinner conversation. Without Cecelia's lively presence to distract everyone, Abby's lack of conversational grace glared like the summer sun. Spreading her skirt wide across the bench, Abby admired how the color blended with the emerald shades of the garden. Perhaps no one would even see her. Twenty minutes to calm her nerves would be a blessed relief.

As if in response to her thoughts, the back door opened. Abby ducked her head. *Maybe if I hold perfectly still . . .*

Dr. King stood on the top step, his dark hair gleaming in the sun. After glancing around the yard, he ambled down the stairs and made a beeline for her hideaway. "Your great-aunt suggested I come and check on you. You don't look like you need a physician this time, but maybe she thought you could use a friend."

Abby stared down at the green silk covering her legs. "I don't need anything." *Cecelia would invite him to sit.*

Not waiting for the invitation, Dr. King sat beside her.

Abby shifted farther along the bench to give him adequate space. "You don't have to keep me company."

Dr. King leaned forward, resting elbows on his knees. "I have six sisters. Did you know that?"

Abby chewed on her lip. More conversation.

"One older, five younger. You should have seen them cry when I left for school." He stretched out his long legs and leaned back against the bench. "Our house was always full of giggling and chatter. Your family is altogether too quiet for my tastes."

Abby felt his eyes on her. She twiddled her fingers, watching the dapples of sunlight dance across her palms. *This is my cue. Say something.* She licked her lips. "Cecelia is our conversationalist."

"And what about you?"

Her shoulders tensed. "I—I'm not."

"All right, tell me about your family."

What would Cecelia say? How would she act? Abby struggled to pull her thoughts together.

He brushed her elbow with his own. "Better yet, tell me something about you."

The touch of his arm sent a shock through her system. Abby's tongue grew thick and stuck to the roof of her mouth. "It's too difficult. Can't we talk about the weather or something?" A squawking giggle escaped from her mouth, sending a fresh wave of heat up her neck.

He tipped back his head and stared up at the leafy vines. "If you insist. But it's not nearly as interesting."

She darted a glance at his face, her sister's admonishing voice sounding in her head: *Don't sit there like a lump, Abigail. Talk!*

"Cecelia's not just my sister—she's my best friend." *My only friend.* The words rushed out. Her stomach clenched. Not a good beginning.

He leaned forward, a glimmer in his eye. "Why?"

Abby picked at her bandaged finger. "She's easy to talk to. She understands me." Abby glanced up, half-expecting to see mockery in his eyes.

His warm gaze surprised her. "And other people don't?"

"Not really."

"Do you give them a chance?"

She plucked a tendril from the grape vine, straightening the curlicue with her fingers before letting it spring back. "I'm not sure I know what you mean."

Dr. King leaned back and studied her. "If you don't talk to people, give someone an opportunity to get to know you—how can you expect them to understand? You're keeping everyone at arm's length."

"Maybe there's nothing worth talking about."

He smiled. "I highly doubt it. Your eyes alone speak volumes."

Abby ducked her head as a sudden chill raced across her skin.

He leaned closer, placing his hand on her arm, "Abby—"

The back door slammed and Dr. King yanked away as if her arm were a hot stovetop.

Davy galloped across the yard, launching himself into Abby's lap.

Papa followed, tapping a pipe against his palm. "Dr. King, I see you found my wandering daughter."

"Yes, sir." Dr. King sprang from the bench, gesturing for her father to sit.

Papa clamped the pipe between his lips, ignoring the younger man's civility. "When Abby was *ein Kind*—a child—we always had to go searching for her. Eventually she'd traipse in, her skirts wet and muddy from playing in the creek."

Abby cuddled Davy, hiding her face in his skinny neck. *Thanks, Papa.*

"Of course it was never hard to find her sister." Papa's face softened. "You just had to listen. She would sing wherever she went, just like her mama."

A prickle danced across Abby's skin. "'Come Thou Fount of Every Blessing.' It is her favorite. She and Mama sang it together with beautiful harmonies."

Robert tipped his head toward her. "What about you?"

A laugh rose in her belly, not quite reaching her mouth. "Not me."

A cacophony of fire bells out front drew their attention to the street. Davy squealed in delight. "Can I go see?" He thrust away from Abby and bounded toward the sound of pounding hooves.

Papa and Dr. King hurried after him.

Abby jumped up and followed them through the yard and into the narrow slot between Gerald's house and the neighbor's.

Papa grabbed Davy by the seat of his short trousers, swinging the boy up onto his shoulders.

They arrived at the front gate as the fire wagon hurtled past with a rush of wind. The horses leaned into their harnesses, sides heaving and flecked with foam. The burly firemen hung onto the back and sides of the wagon as it careened down the street, a group of laughing boys and barking dogs in pursuit.

Papa clasped Davy's shoes as they drummed against his chest. "San Francisco has the most modern fire department in the world." He turned to Abby. "Progress, Abigail! Many things are changing with this new century—automobiles, flying machines, modern medicines. Nothing is outside of our grasp. Pretty soon, society will have all the answers." Papa placed a hand on the fence, staring out into the street, his voice quieting. "And children won't have to die before their parents."

Abby wove a hand under his elbow and rested her head against Papa's shoulder.

Monday, September 11, 1905

The electric lights emitted a soft buzz, not casting enough illumination to chase the gloom from the windowless laboratory. Robert took a deep breath of the dank air as he adjusted the X-ray machine's settings, hoping to distract his attention from the young woman standing at the table in the center of the large room.

Abby Fischer laid her hand on the wooden box containing the glass plate. Her round eyes shimmered, a rare smile lifting the corners of her mouth. "Like this?"

Robert hoped she couldn't hear the sound of his heart hammering against his ribs. "Let me show you." He stepped closer, intoxicated by the flowery scent emanating from her hair. Lowering his arm, Robert slid his hand down Miss Fischer's wrist, his fingers settling against hers.

The enticing warmth of her skin overwhelmed his senses. He rifled through his memory for a benign image, settling on a diagram of the hand from his medical text. *Scaphoid, lunate, triquetrum, pisiform, trapezium.* He laid her hand flat against the box. *Trapezoid, capitate, hamate . . .* Perspiration glazed his palms. "We'll get a better image if you spread your fingers a little." He pulled away. "Try to hold as still as you can."

She gazed at him, brows lifted and lips parted.

Stepping backward, Robert collided with a rolling metal cart loaded with equipment, sending a cascade of loose items clattering to the tile floor. "Who left this sitting here?" He heaped the objects onto the cart and thrust it into the corner, the action steadying his nerves.

Why had he brought her here? When had he become such a grandstander? He shouldn't be using the equipment for mere entertainment.

Robert reached for the controls, glancing over his shoulder to where Miss Fischer stood facing him, arm in position, her smile practically glowing in its intensity.

"Hold your breath."

She blew out a puff of air with a laugh. "What do you think I've been doing all this time?"

The tension in Robert's chest eased as a chuckle escaped his lips. "Let me know when you're ready."

She glanced down at the table and back to the equipment hovering above. "You're sure this doesn't hurt?"

"Does it hurt to get your picture taken?"

"Depends on the photographer, I suppose." She took a few deep breaths. "All right. I'm ready."

"Don't move until I tell you." He reached for the switch. "Here goes."

The hum of the machinery never failed to make Robert's heart race, but this time it stole the very air from his lungs. Miss Fischer's skin gleamed under the cerulean glow radiating from the Crookes tube. She was simply the most beautiful woman he'd ever seen—in any light.

Robert leaned against the counter. If only it were a real camera, he'd keep the portrait close. With regret, he cut the power to the X-ray machine. "All done."

Miss Fischer pulled her hand from the table and wiggled her fingers. "I didn't feel a thing. When will I see the results?"

Robert reset the machine for the next procedure. "I'll make a print to show you tomorrow, but I can't let you keep it. Hospital property and all." He smiled. *Plus, I have no intention of parting with it.*

September 18, 1905

Abby shifted in the hard hospital chair, gazing at Cecelia as she slept. Two patients chatted in the neighboring beds, the scent of breakfast—oatmeal, toast, and coffee—lingering in the air. The morning sun shining from the far window emphasized Cecelia's new rosy complexion.

The rapid pace of her recovery had taken everyone by surprise. Almost every physician in the hospital had stopped by in recent days to witness the dramatic changes. Abby and her parents alternated being at Cecelia's side for as many hours as visiting rules allowed. Abby vied for the morning shift, to help Cecelia before and after the treatments and to be nearby when the doctors made their rounds.

Gerald frowned as he sauntered into the room, his gaze scanning a handful of papers.

Abby's throat squeezed at her cousin's expression. "What's the matter?"

He glanced up, eyes glazed as if not seeing her. A moment passed before he shook his head. "Nothing. Nothing at all. All good news, in fact." His brows pulled together, a tiny crease forming between them. Gerald glanced back at the papers.

Abby stepped forward and touched her cousin's elbow. "Then why the troubled face?"

His demeanor softened. "I'm having trouble accepting these numbers. Such a radical improvement in a few short weeks. It's a great deal to take in."

She swiped at his arm with her palm. "Don't scare me so."

The seed of joy planted in her chest three weeks ago was rapidly maturing and sprouting fruit. "I prayed for a miracle. And it's what we've received."

He nodded. "I believe in miracles. I suppose I shouldn't be surprised to witness one."

"What miracle?" Cecelia's voice croaked from the bed.

Abby hurried to her side. "I'm sorry. We didn't mean to wake you."

Cecelia cleared her throat. "How can I sleep when you two keep fussing?" She reached for the water glass resting on the tray near the bed. "Where's Robert?"

Gerald's brows lifted. He shook his head. "Robert, eh? I need to keep an eye on my young friend. He's apparently charmed the entire family."

"He is definitely charming." Cecelia took a sip of water and shot a pointed glance at her sister.

Abby gripped the bed railing. "It's his intelligence saving you, not his charm. He's passionate about the science of modern medicine." A flush crept up her neck.

Cecelia returned the glass to the table and relaxed back against the pillows. "I thought you said it was God's miracle."

"Right." Abby bit her lip. "God's doing this. I believe it."

"Do you?" Cecelia's eyes glinted.

Gerald folded the papers and slid them into a coat pocket. "I'll leave you ladies to debate divinity versus science. Dr. King will be here soon to take you down for the next treatment, Cecelia. We've decided to double your radiation again. You'll be spending even more time in the lab, I'm afraid."

Her brow furrowed. "Double it? Why? You increased it last week."

Abby lifted her hands to her chest. "I thought you said the therapy was working?"

"It is. But now the cancer is retreating, we want to make sure it doesn't try to come back." He leaned over the bed and touched Cecelia's chin. "We may actually be able to give you a full life."

Abby couldn't fight the smile spreading across her face. She grasped Gerald's arm. "You're a miracle worker. You and Dr. King."

Cecelia pursed her lips. "Only God makes miracles, Abby."

"But He's using them to do it."

"What are we doing?" Dr. King pushed a wheelchair into the room.

Abby breathed a sigh of relief that the conversation had turned away from the young doctor's charms.

Gerald put an arm around Dr. King's shoulder. "You're working miracles, Robert, and taking Cecelia in for an extra serving of X-ray fun."

Chuckling, Dr. King held his hands in front of him. "Let me warm up my fingers. They need to be ready to hit the button and release the magic."

Abby brightened. "Can I come? I enjoyed seeing the lab last time. I'd love to watch one of Cecelia's treatments. Maybe I can help." She gripped the bedpost to steady herself. The words had sprung from her lips before she'd stopped to consider them. *I need to stop following him like a stray dog.*

Gerald frowned at his assistant. "You took Abby to the lab?"

The younger man's face reddened. "Only a quick tour."

Abby stared at her feet, rather than risk Cecelia's inquisitive glance. No doubt, she'd be interrogated later.

Gerald's brows lifted, his gaze darting between the two ladies. "I see. No wonder my cousins are enjoying your attention so much." He turned toward Abby, face somber. "I suppose there's no harm. Just stay out of the way."

"Of course."

Gerald focused on his assistant, eyes hooded. "Come by the office when you are finished. We need to talk."

Robert helped Cecelia onto the table, adjusting the white sheet—blinding under the glare of the electric lights—around the young woman's emaciated frame. He struggled to concentrate on the patient, rather than the lovely creature hovering at his elbow. The chilled basement air, like a crypt, did little to stem the fine sheen of sweat dampening the back of his shirt.

"What can I do?" Abby's breath tickled his neck.

He set his jaw, sucking in air through gritted teeth. "You can stand back." How would he concentrate with her here?

She jerked away. "I'm sorry."

Cecelia smiled. "Robert's done this a hundred times. He knows what he's doing."

Robert's resolve melted at the sight of Abby's red-tipped ears, her arms wrapped around her slim waist. "Come with me." He motioned her over to the controls.

She followed, lagging behind several steps.

Robert pulled out the stool from the control panel. "Please, sit." He took Abby's elbow, guiding her to the high seat. He pointed at the dials and switches. "Would you like to know how these work?"

Her eyes widened as she tucked the brown skirt under her legs. "Yes, please."

He gestured to the dials on the left. "These control the radiation settings. When we're taking an X-ray image, we keep the levels at a minimum—say a one or two, depending on what part of the body we're examining. We've been elevating your sister's levels progressively and keeping records of her reactions. She's up to an eight-point-five today."

Abby's lips thinned. "Is that safe? Can they go too high?"

He straightened to full height. "It's perfectly safe—as long as we keep an eye on the numbers and don't leave her under the lights too long. I've rigged a timer." He pointed to another dial. "It will shut the machine down if you go beyond the safe limits."

He fiddled with a few of the knobs. He'd adjusted them before bringing the women into the lab, but it never hurt to look efficient. "You have to be careful to keep the coils the right distance from the body or you can end up causing deep tissue burns. Gerald and I test them daily."

"How do you test them?"

He pressed his hands into his pockets. "On ourselves. If we weren't one hundred percent sure of the safety of the equipment, we wouldn't trust it with our patients."

"Very admirable."

"Shall we double-check the settings? I'll read the numbers, you check the dials." He pointed at the row of knobs. "From left to right." He pulled open the notebook and flipped through the pages. "One-point-six, two, eight-point-five, eight-point-six . . ." He rattled off the series of numbers, glancing over Abby's head as she touched each knob with a smooth-tipped fingernail.

A yawn from the direction of the table encouraged him to pick up the pace. Completing the checklists, he took the controls and finished the treatment while Abby observed.

Returning to the cancer wing, Robert stood back as Abby settled her sister back into the hospital bed. She nestled a plump pillow behind Cecelia's shoulders and tucked in the edges of the sheet, like a mother would for a child.

What a wonderful nurse she would make. Such a tender touch. Hairs lifted on Robert's arms. He pulled his gaze back to the medical charts, marking the treatment details in Cecelia's records.

Abby straightened, a line pinching between her brows. "Is she supposed to be this pink?"

Robert stepped to the bedside, a knot forming in his stomach.

Cecelia shifted on the pillows, pressing a hand against her flaming cheek. "Why is it so warm in here?"

Robert grasped her wrist, sliding back the long sleeve of her dressing gown. The tender skin of her inner arm blazed crimson, warm against his fingers. Replacing the sleeve, he lowered her arm against the mattress while his thoughts raced. "Looks like a slight burn. I'll have a nurse come in and give you a cool bath."

Plastering a reassuring smile on his face, Robert excused himself and hurried out to the nurse's station. After giving careful instructions to the duty nurse, he checked his pocket watch and strode toward Gerald's office.

Abby's voice caught his attention. "Dr. King?"

The young woman clutched a novel to her chest as she hastened to catch up. "Will Cecelia be all right? Did I do something wrong with the dials in the laboratory?"

The concern in Abby's eyes tugged at his heart. "No—I mean, yes, she'll be fine, and no, you didn't do anything wrong. I checked the levels myself, twice. It's only a slight erythema." He paused, searching for a better explanation. "The redness is like a mild sunburn. It's nothing to worry about." *Besides, Gerald will worry enough for all of us.*

Abby sighed, the air rushing from between pink lips as she pressed a gloved hand against her heart. "I thought maybe I was to blame. Trouble seems to shadow my footsteps."

"The coil might have malfunctioned. I'll replace it tonight."

The lines smoothed from her face. "Thank you for letting me sit in on the treatment. I am grateful for everything you have done for my sister."

Warmth radiated through him. "Not at all, Miss Fischer. You were an excellent assistant. In fact, I was thinking what a wonderful nurse you would be."

She lowered her eyes, running fingers along the spine of the book. "I'm much better with plants. I can graft a fruit tree and prune branches, but I could never do this sort of work."

"It's not so different, if you think about it. If you'd like, you can help me again tomorrow."

She lifted her chin, eyes shining. "Really? I'd love to."

A rush of electricity raced through his limbs, her smile intoxicating. He glanced back to Cecelia's room. "Are you staying?"

She shook her head. "No, Mama is with her now. Cecelia seems particularly tired after today's treatment. I thought I'd take the cable car home."

Robert glanced to the window—sunshine poured through the glass, the temperature in the hall rising with each passing minute. He could do with some fresh air. *And a few more smiles.*

"May I see you home? Gerald left his automobile here. I could drive you."

Abby's lips parted, eyes growing large. "Well, I don't—"

"I know—let me take you to lunch. There's a man with a lunch cart at Golden Gate Park who makes the best steak sandwiches." His pulse quickened. *A sunny sky, a lovely companion.*

Her face paled, dark eyelashes standing out against her light skin. "I'm not sure."

He stepped closer. "It's the least I can do after your help this morning."

She blinked, glancing down at her feet. "I suppose it would be all right."

A smile spread across his face, the wearying day forgotten. He thrust out his arm, swallowing the moment of elation before he got carried away. "Shall we?"

Abby hesitated a moment before weaving a hand through the crook of his elbow, a tentative smile stealing the tautness from her face.

They were boarding the cable car before Robert remembered Gerald's request. He owed his friend—his boss—an apology. Robert glanced down at Abby's fingers resting on his arm, his chest swelling in response. *The apology can wait.*

9

*A*bby lowered herself to the ground, resting her back against the tree trunk and tipping her head until she could stare up into its leafy heights. The soft breeze lifted the wisps of hair escaping from her bun and sent them fluttering into her face. Brushing them from her eyes, she pulled in a deep breath, the scent of the bay tickling her nose. How long had it been since she'd breathed easily?

Abby pulled off her gloves and ran her hands across the soft grass stems as if she could pull their life into her tired body.

"I've never seen you look more content." Dr. King strode across the open expanse balancing two paper-wrapped bundles an arm's length from his suit jacket. He plopped down next to her. "I wasn't sure what you wanted, so you'll have to trust my judgment."

She smiled. Hadn't she been doing so since the moment they met? Abby unwrapped the sandwich and used a cautious finger to lift the bun. "What is this?"

"Steak with horseradish, pickles, onions, and mustard."

She pressed a hand against her mouth. "You're jesting."

He cocked one brow. "Frank makes the best horseradish, pickle, onion, and mustard steak sandwiches in town."

She lifted the sandwich, wrinkling her nose at the pungent odor. "Let me guess, he makes the only horseradish, pickle—"

"Don't make fun until you've tried it. Have I led you astray before?" He grinned.

She met his eyes. "No. Never."

"Of course, you haven't known me very long."

"Long enough." She drew the sandwich to her lips, took a small bite and chewed carefully, the flavors exploding across her tongue. "I remember Papa saying he loved horseradish, but since Mama couldn't stand the smell, he gave it up when he was courting her."

"The sacrifices we make for love." The doctor smiled. "You have sauce on your chin."

Abby retrieved a handkerchief from her pocket and mopped her face. "It's sort of hard to avoid, Dr. King." She tucked the brown paper wrapper under the sandwich. If she added some condiment stains to her favorite brown skirt, she might be mistaken for a steak sandwich herself.

His forehead wrinkled, brows drawing together. "Abby, I'm not your doctor. Call me Robert—please?"

A gust of wind set the grass blades aquiver. She swallowed, the sauce blazing its way down her throat and tingling through her sinuses.

He removed his derby and clutched it against his chest. "Your cousin Gerald is my best friend. I'd like for us to be friends as well."

Abby glanced down. A ladybug crawled to the top of a tender green stem beside her. "Certainly, if it's what you prefer," she dabbed the handkerchief to her lips, "Robert." Cecelia had been calling him by his first name for weeks already.

The huge smile spreading across his face sent her heart fluttering, like the ladybug as it lifted from the grass stem and winged its way over her head.

"Wonderful." He held up the remains of his sandwich. "What do you think?" A spot of mustard clung to the corner of his mouth.

Abby's lips twitched as she fought a smile. If only she knew him well enough to reach over and remove the stain, but the notion gave her gooseflesh. "Delicious. I must confess, I'm surprised."

He laughed. "I knew you were a horseradish and onion kind of girl from the moment I first laid eyes on you."

Smelly? She flushed. "In the tree, you mean?"

"Exactly. You didn't look like the typical bland, unadventurous style of woman."

Abby licked the last traces of flavor from her lips. Was that supposed to be a compliment? Mama would be horrified.

She cleared her throat and smiled, hoping she didn't have mustard on her teeth. "Definitely not."

$\mathcal{L}$

Robert fidgeted, the weight of Gerald's glare pressing him further into the seat.

"What were you thinking?" His mentor towered above the oaken desk, fingertips whitening as he flattened them against the blotter. "Gallivanting about town with my cousin?"

"We only went to lunch." Robert tugged on the celluloid collar threatening to close about his throat.

Gerald paced the length of the room, raking fingers through his blond hair until he resembled a cornered porcupine. "Didn't they teach you about the importance of professional distance in medical school?"

Robert leaned back, the swivel chair creaking in protest. "What is this about? You're worried about the case? There's no professional distance here—the patient is a member of your family, for goodness sakes."

Gerald halted. "And it's exactly why I have left most of the work in your hands, while I handle the appointments at our downtown office. You need to maintain objectivity, because I cannot."

"What objectivity? You're my friend and my boss. If I botch this, I'm in danger of losing both." Robert lifted *The Practical Application of Röntgen Rays* from the corner table. He tapped the book's cover. "This is where my heart lies. You know it's so."

"It's not *your* heart I'm worried about. Abby is a special young woman. I won't have her trifled with."

Robert dropped the book onto the desk, the muscles in his neck knotting. "What do you take me for? We've worked together for over a year—have I given you reason not to trust me?"

Gerald's scowl withered. "No, but—"

"I understand your fear, but I'm not trying to seduce Abby. Yes, she's a beautiful and intriguing young woman, but I only want to be her friend." Robert stared out the window, his pulse quickening. *God, let it be the truth.*

Gerald exhaled, as noisy as a fireplace bellows. "Robert, you thrive on respect and admiration. Abby is vulnerable right now and you've ridden to the rescue. If she elevates you on a hero's pedestal, you're going to have a nasty fall back to reality."

"You make me sound like some idol to be worshiped." Robert frowned. "I don't believe you know your cousin as well as you think. She's no fool."

"I'm aware of that." Gerald ran his hand back through his hair, smoothing it. "She's a very determined young woman. Cecelia wouldn't be here otherwise." He shook his head. "And if she's already set her sights on you, I'm afraid it may take an act of God to change her mind."

Warmth flashed through Robert's chest before dissolving and leaving a hollow ache in its place. He scrubbed a hand across his face. *What have I become?*

Abby clenched the brass railing, bracing herself as the cable car rolled to a stop. Bunching her skirt in one hand, she managed to hop to the street without twisting an ankle or falling on her face.

Rather than catching the connecting line to take her down to O'Farrell, Abby set out on foot. Sweat dampened the silk chemise hiding under her corset. Stopping for a breath, she unbuttoned her jacket to let the bay-freshened air cool her body. If it weren't for the cacophony of vehicles and voices, she could almost imagine herself climbing the hill behind the orchard, escaping into the shady grove of trees for a quiet moment. *Soon enough. Cecelia's improving every day.*

Abby whacked her reticule against her hip to get herself moving. Maple Manor lay just beyond and Mama needed her help with Davy. It was impossible to leave her brother—the one-man demolition team—alone for more than a few moments in the borrowed house. Her stomach fluttered. Why had she traipsed off to the park with Robert and not even considered coming to collect Davy?

Robert. His name tickled the edges of her mind, but Abby shook it away. She didn't have time to lose herself in romance.

Maybe when Cecelia is well. The tingle running up her back took her by surprise. Never before had a man waltzed his way into her head and heart. But then, she'd never met someone like Robert. Like a vine, thoughts of him coiled through Abby's every waking moment.

She pushed through the gate at Maple Manor, closed it behind her, and leaned upon the wooden slats. And he'd never met someone like her. Or so he said.

Maybe Cecelia was correct—perhaps meeting Robert was part of God's plan for her. One prayer and God dumped a miracle right into Abby's lap. And a man at her feet.

Abby hurried up the walk toward the house, vowing to pray a little more often.

10

$\mathcal{R}$obert picked up Cecelia's hand and slid his fingers to her wrist, noting the heat radiating from her flushed skin. Her pulse raced under his thumb. "Did the nurse put cool compresses against these burns?"

Cecelia grimaced. "Yes."

He checked her other arm, examining clear to her shoulder, his stomach tightening. *Gerald will be furious.* "You received a bit too much radiation this morning, I'm afraid. How do you feel?"

She pulled the dressing gown sleeve over her reddened skin. "It will be fine."

He lowered his voice and stooped close to the bed. "You need to be honest with me. I can't help if you're hiding things."

She turned her gaze to the window, lips firm.

Robert lifted her chart and stared at the numbers. He'd been vigilant, even with Abby underfoot, stealing his attention. Cecelia should not have reacted to the low level of radiation unless the machinery had malfunctioned. He rifled through the papers, observing the patient from the corner of his eye.

She clenched the edge of the blanket and released it, repeating the action every few seconds. "Don't tell Abby." Cecelia's voice crackled in her throat.

The dread in his stomach hardened to stone. "What can't I tell her?"

She fixed him with her gaze. "It's not working. The X-rays. They were for a while, but they're not anymore."

He sat in the chair beside the bed, resting his hands on the mattress. "What makes you think so?"

She bit her lip. "I can feel it. And it's not just today." She glanced down at her hand, lifting it from the covers. "It's not the burn." She let it drop to the mattress and winced. "I feel like I'm swimming in an undertow. It's pulling me further from the shore every day. For a time I felt stronger and I could push against the current, but I can't anymore."

Robert leaned back against the chair, her words like a punch to the gut. "We'll run some more tests. Check your blood. Maybe you're a touch anemic."

"If you must." She sniffed, a faint smile brushing her lips, a light appearing in her eyes. "Enough of that. Tell me about lunch."

"Hunger is a good sign."

"Not *my* lunch, you simpleton. Tell me about your lunch with Abby."

A prickly heat crawled over his skin. "I just had this discussion with Gerald. Like I told your cousin, it was a friendly lunch, nothing more."

Cecelia's smile faded to a pout. "I'm not Gerald. And you're interested in her, I can tell. Your face lights up whenever she's here."

Robert pushed up to his feet, the chair sliding on the tile floor. "Hmm. You must be feverish, delirious." A smile dragged at the corners of his lips.

She reached for his hand, her forehead pinching at the sudden motion. "She cares for you—I've never seen her like this. Don't be embarrassed, please. I don't have time to waste on pretense." Cecelia squeezed his fingers.

For a woman suffering with chronic leukemia, Cecelia's grip crushed like a vise. He matched her intense gaze and lowered his voice to a whisper. "I cannot become entangled with the sister of a patient, no matter my personal feelings."

She released her grasp and her eyes darkened. "I won't always be your patient, Robert. And when I'm gone, I don't want you to let her get away." She touched his sleeve with a gentle brush of her thin fingers. "Promise me."

The piercing blue of her eyes tore into him, burning the words into his heart. How could anyone refuse her—dying or no? He swallowed, letting the internal battle rage. If there were no barriers to his pursuing a relationship with Abby—would he? His heart jumped in response, answering the question before his head could interfere.

But if Cecelia were gone, it would be due to his failure. Would Abby even want him?

No.

His throat closed. As long as Cecelia lived, she would stand in their way. And if—when—she passed. . . . He turned his head away, disliking the bubbling concoction brewing in his stomach. The truth of Gerald's words rang in his ears. Abby didn't care for him— she idolized him for what she thought he could accomplish. Robert swallowed, trying to push past the lump swelling in his throat.

He picked up Cecelia's chart from the edge of the bed. "We'll shorten tomorrow's treatment to give your skin time to heal. No matter what you think you're feeling, everything else points to the fact the X-rays are doing their job. The coil malfunctioned—gave you too big a dose. I'll fix it, so it won't happen again. But don't you start giving up on me."

She leaned back against the pillows, new shadows circling her eyes. "I'm not giving up on *you*, Robert King."

Robert retreated to the safety of the X-ray laboratory. Perhaps if he buried himself in electrical wires and Crookes tubes, he could forget the chaos reigning in his heart.

Gerald pulled the casing apart, running a hand down the wires. "I don't understand what happened. I checked it myself."

"And I double-checked it." Robert brushed a loose hair from his forehead.

Gerald's neck corded as he tugged the wiring loose. "What's this?"

Stepping to his friend's shoulder, Robert peered down into the box. Black soot smeared across Gerald's fingertips. "Burnt wires?"

A crease formed between Gerald's brows. "Did you see anything during the treatment? A flash? Smell anything burning? Popping?"

"Nothing out of the ordinary." Robert fingered the scorched remains. "There should be an emergency cutoff when something like this happens."

Gerald dropped the lid, the metal crashing against the floor like a cymbal and exposing the delicate entrails of the machine. He pulled a wire cutter from the table and shoved it into Robert's hand. "Yes, there should be. And until there is—my cousin comes nowhere near this machine."

"She's due for another treatment in the morning."

Shoulders hunched, his mentor headed for the door. "Then you'd better get to work." As his footsteps faded, silence fell across the room.

Robert gazed down at the mess of wires, head suddenly aching. Clenching the cutters, he banged the tool against the metal casing. He had gone to medical school to fix people, not wires. He rolled his head back against his shoulders, staring at the ceiling. *God, help me.*

Abby sat on the porch stairs, watching Davy play in the tiny patch of a backyard, gathering rocks from the flower beds and lining them up on the stone wall like a platoon of soldiers.

A leather-bound journal lay in her lap, the empty page mocking her. She'd never had trouble writing her feelings before. She lifted the pen and placed it against the page, editing her thoughts before the ink began to flow.

> Cecelia is looking so much better, I can scarce
> believe it. Gerald and Robert keep increasing the
> X-ray treatments. I hope this amazing technology
> will send her cancer fleeing back to the pits of hell
> where it belongs.

She tapped the end of the pen against her lips. She probably shouldn't have written the last part.

> Robert took me to lunch yesterday . . .

Her hand stopped, the ink blotting against the page. How much should she say?

Davy kneeled in the flower bed, excavating the soil with his fingers. Had Robert played like that as a boy? She pushed the thought away, pressing the cap over the pen and closing the journal. *I'm turning into a lovesick fool.*

"Abby?" her brother called, his high-pitched voice grating on her nerves.

She stood, shielding her eyes with a hand. "What is it?"

"Can you help me find more rocks?" He stood, the pockets of his short pants bulging with stony treasure.

She joined him, the soft earth squishing beneath her hard-soled shoes. Back home she might have pulled them off, along with her stockings, to relish the joy of the soil between her toes—but the city pressing in around her made Abby self-conscious.

Crouching down by an azalea, Abby ran her hands over the dirt, picking some small stones from the soil and piling them on a nearby brick. "How many more do you need?"

"Just more. I want to make an army."

Abby laughed. "We all want more don't we? We're never happy with what we have."

He looked at her, his blue eyes round, mouth puckered.

"Never mind." She gazed around the meticulously groomed garden patch. Not the best hunting ground. "Come on." She reached out dirt-covered fingers. "There's plenty of time before bed. Let's walk down to the vacant lot on the corner. I'm sure there's plenty more there."

He crowed, dancing a jig with chubby legs, pants sagging under the weight.

She helped Davy unload his pockets, leaving the stones in a pile on the brick walk.

Mama pushed open the back gate, her eyes downcast and cheeks flushed.

Abby's chest tightened. "What's happened? Why have you returned early?"

Mama closed the gate and leaned against it. "Cecelia was so tired, I decided to let her sleep." She removed her hat, the feathers bouncing with the motion like birds on a twig. "She didn't seem herself." A shadow crossed her face. "Dr. King said the new level of treatment might be tiring her. He's going to run some tests overnight."

Abby took Davy's hand in her own. "I'm certain, whatever it is— Robert will sort it out."

"I'm sure you're right." Mama adjusted the hatband, stroking the glossy black plumes. "He's such a bright young man. We're blessed to have him and Gerald helping us."

Abby followed Davy through the gate. *Blessed.* Her soul launched, like a maple seed twirling away onto the breeze.

Robert strode down the endless corridor, crimping his fingers against his shoulder to ease the tension taking up permanent residence. After another six hours of leaning over the wearisome machine—rewiring, testing, and rewiring again—his muscles craved movement. He pushed open the heavy hospital door, the fresh air blasting away his lethargy and sending a jolt of energy through his system, nearly as effective as the mud-black coffee they brewed in the hospital kitchen. The glaring morning sun caught him off guard and Robert lifted a hand against its glory. He pushed his hat forward, ducking his head from the glare.

A brisk walk might revive him enough for morning rounds. Robert hastened down the granite steps, aiming for Lafayette Square, a self-prescribed touch of grass and flowers the ideal remedy to desperation caused by overexposure to wires, radiation, and sickness.

Robert paused at the corner, waiting as a milk wagon trundled past on Laguna Street, the swaybacked horse barely lifting its head as it dragged the heavy load. *Poor beast. He'll soon be relegated to the glue factory and replaced by an engine.*

A steamer maneuvered around the slower vehicle, the engine chugging and hissing as if laughing at the decrepit animal. Robert hurried across the street and into the square, relishing the contrast as his shoes sank into the spongy lawn.

He made two spirited rounds about the hilltop property, breathing deeply, before settling onto a stone bench. A granite angel knelt in the center of a small rose garden, head bowed into clasped hands. Robert gazed down the hill to the bay as the mingled scents of greenery and exhaust brewed the unmistakable fragrance of the city. He leaned forward, balancing his elbows against his knees and letting his head droop.

The weariness of the morning sent a wave of longing through him. Back in Sacramento, Mother would be dishing out bowls of steaming oatmeal, dotted with butter and brown sugar, his sisters rushing about in their never-ending preparations of dresses, ribbons, stockings. When he'd lived at home, he couldn't wait to escape the crushing insignificance of the morning routine.

What he wouldn't give now for five minutes surrounded by its tender familiarity.

He shook himself, chasing away the thought. Four years of medical school and two years of practice—a tad late for homesickness.

Leaning back against the bench, an overgrown shrub bumped his hat, shoving the derby forward over his eyes. Swiveling, he grasped the twig and prepared to snap it off, but as the velvety leaves tickled his fingers, his thoughts turned to Abby, beautiful in a gown of the same yellowish-green. Surrounded by the grapevines and roses of Gerald's backyard, she'd looked like a fairy hiding in the shadows, preparing her palette of spring colors.

Robert sprang to his feet, thrusting his arms into the sleeves of his jacket. There was no point dwelling on wishes that could never come to pass. Abby Fischer would forever be off-limits. He needed to convince his heart of it. His dreams revolved around science, research, and medicine. He couldn't afford the distraction of fanciful ideas.

A dull ache grew in his throat.

Robert strolled to the edge of the square, jamming his hands into his pockets as he waited for three more wagons to lumber past. As he crossed the road, his left shoe sank into a pile of horse manure. Robert grimaced and scraped it against the cobbles.

At least motorcars don't defecate in the street.

✍

Abby spotted Robert as she hopped down from the cable car, her heart quickening at the sight of his broad shoulders.

Robert shuffled across the intersection, his gait stiff as if he favored one foot.

She hurried after him. "Robert, wait!" A flush spread across her cheeks. Ladies didn't call out in public. It wouldn't do to look too eager. Abby checked her pace and straightened her posture.

As he turned, a smile broke across her face. Her feet skipped forward, despite her best intentions. "I'm glad to see you!" She slowed at the sight of his somber expression, chiding herself for her exuberance. *Stop acting like a child.*

"Abby—I was just thinking about you." His brows scrunched downward and his eyes closed for a brief moment. "I mean, I was thinking of our lunch . . ." He scraped his shoe along the curb. "I was just over at the Square, and . . ." He blew out a breath between his lips and shook his head.

His expression reminded her of Davy when he'd been caught eating jam with his fingers. She glanced at the spreading green lawns, a large white mansion perched at the apex of the hill. "It must have a lovely view."

He chuckled, the lines on his face slackening. "It's no Golden Gate, I'll admit. But when you've been trapped in the basement all night, it's like a corner of Eden."

"You've been here all night?" No wonder he looked so rumpled. Her stomach squeezed. "Is there a problem with Cecelia?"

He glanced toward the hospital. "I assume it's where you are heading?"

She nodded.

"May I escort you?" He offered his arm.

Her gloved hand trembled as she placed it in the crook of his elbow. "You didn't answer my question."

He patted her fingers, sending the quiver streaking up to her shoulder. "Your cousin asked me to make some adjustments to the X-ray machine. It took a little longer than expected."

She managed a full breath—Cecelia hadn't taken a turn for the worse. "I enjoyed our lunch." Abby ventured, determined to attempt some of her sister's boldness.

Darkness passed across his face, like a cloud covering the sun.

Abby's stomach sank. *Why did I say that?*

He cleared his throat, picking up the pace toward the hospital. "Yes, yes. So did I, of course."

Abby swept her gaze forward, blinking several times to clear the sudden stinging sensation in her eyes. *I am a fool. He doesn't feel the same way. I imagined the whole thing.* She bit the inside of her cheek, loosening her grip on his arm. "But it really shouldn't happen again. I need to focus on my sister's health."

"Quite right. I thought the same myself."

Her heart sank lower, her emotions circling like water draining from a basin.

Robert reached a hand into his pocket and withdrew a watch. "But you shouldn't spend every moment by her bedside."

"You're a fine one to speak—didn't you just mention you stayed here all night?" Raw, her words tumbled past her tongue before she could evaluate them.

"It's why I went for a walk. It's always a good idea to step out for fresh air."

A delivery truck rattled past, kicking up swirls of choking dust in its wake. "I'm not sure there is fresh air anywhere in this city. Outside of Golden Gate Park, anyway."

He frowned. "There are some nice areas around the hospital for walking. You just have to know which direction to travel. There are some unpleasant neighborhoods I wouldn't recommend."

Abby shrugged. "I can take care of myself."

Pausing at the corner, Robert froze her with a long look. "Nonsense. I won't have you out walking in dangerous areas."

She placed a hand on her hip. "You were the one suggesting I walk."

"Not unattended."

Shaking her head, Abby clamped her lips shut. No use wasting time conversing with this man who acted like a suitor one moment, a protective brother the next.

"Let me know when you want to walk. I'll escort you. I should get out more often than I do." A strained expression crossed his face. "In fact, I'd be honored to show you around."

Abby paused, turning her back to the hospital entrance and searching Robert's face. *He changes tracks faster than a streetcar. Is this how it works with all men? I don't know how Cecelia stands it.*

Someone collided with her from behind, sending Abby careening forward into Robert's chest. She grabbed his arms to steady herself as a flush of heat climbed her neck.

Robert placed his hands on her shoulders, but his gaze fixed on someone behind her.

Abby pivoted on her heel, spotting a young Chinese woman sprawled on the stone steps. The woman's chest heaved as tears dotted her cheeks, her white blouse and matching loose trousers flecked with blood. Abby reached out to help the woman to her feet, sticky blood on her hands. "Are you hurt?"

"No, no." The woman panted, swinging her head to the side, a long skinny braid flipping over one shoulder. She pointed down the street with a trembling hand. "Miss Cameron need help. But the nurse, she said no Chinese allowed."

Robert took Abby's elbow and guided her back a step. "I'm sorry, but the Chinese are supposed to go to the Dispensary in Chinatown, or to City and County Hospital on Potrero."

The woman grabbed his sleeve. "Need help now. Yoke Hay ran in front of the cable car. She's bleeding." She lifted her bloodstained hand as evidence. "Miss Cameron is coming." She gestured down the street to where a tall, elegant woman hurried toward them, a young child cradled in her arms.

Robert pried his sleeve from the young woman's fingers. "Two blocks that way," he pointed. "California Street. The cable line will take you all the way to Chinatown."

"Robert," Abby gasped. "How could you?"

He turned, lines furrowing his brow. "I'm sorry, but it's hospital policy."

Gripping the injured child to her chest, the older woman's cheeks shone pink from running. "Kum Yong, did you find help?"

The Chinese woman frowned at Robert and Abby, glancing back at the closed hospital doors. "No one will help, Lo Mo. No Chinese allowed."

Abby stared at the sobbing child. The little girl, younger than Davy, howled as she pressed a hand to the side of her head, blood streaming down her tiny arm. "Robert, you can't leave them out on the street."

The second woman straightened, hoisting the girl higher in her arms. "This is ridiculous." Her feathered hat bobbed in indignation, her Scottish brogue tickling Abby's ears. "Out of my way, I'll have a word with the hospital administrator."

Robert sighed. "I'm a physician. Can I be of service?"

Her expression softened. "You are? Will you help my daughter?"

He stepped close to peer at the child, but the girl buried her face in the lady's shoulder, the sage-green jacket now stained with blood.

"Yoke Hay, hold still and let the doctor examine you." The woman frowned.

Robert glanced up at the imposing brick building. "Come with me. We'll sneak in the side entrance. I think we can get all the way to my office without anyone seeing us."

A blaze of heat surged through Abby's throat. "They shouldn't have to sneak anywhere. This is outrageous."

"It's the only way." Robert guided them around the building and into a dim delivery entrance.

The young woman fell in step beside Abby. "Thank you," she whispered.

Abby studied her round face. She'd seen very few Chinese in her small community, though she'd read many newspaper stories about them. "My name is Abby."

The dark eyes brightened. "I am Kum Yong." She nodded to the woman cradling the crying child. "That is Miss Donaldina Cameron. She runs the Mission house."

Abby gripped the handrail of the steep stairway leading to Robert and Gerald's second floor office. "And the little one?" She hesitated.

"Yoke Hay. She's only five. I should have been holding her hand. It's my fault. She dropped her paper and it blew into the street. She went after it before I could catch her."

Robert checked the second-floor hallway before guiding the women out of the stairwell. "We'd best hurry before we attract attention." Robert gestured to his office door, motioning for Miss Cameron to enter.

The women piled into his office and he shut the door behind them. Rolling up his sleeves, he reached into a cabinet and withdrew a handful of bandages.

The young girl cringed, clinging to Miss Cameron's arms in silence, her eyes massive above her wet cheeks. Kum Yong crouched in front of the pair, a smile lifting the corners of her mouth. She chattered to the girl in Chinese, the foreign words dropping from her tongue like notes of music. The girl turned to Kum Yong, bobbing her head in response.

Miss Cameron pulled her close, murmuring a few more Chinese words into her ear as she braced Yoke Hay's small head against her chest.

Abby pondered the odd group. *An unmarried woman with a Chinese daughter?*

Robert leaned down and examined the girl's wound. He ran his fingers across her head and gazed into her dark eyes. "It doesn't look serious. Just a superficial abrasion."

"Thank You, Lord." Miss Cameron sighed, holding Yoke Hay still while Robert worked. "It could have been much worse."

"So much blood." Kum Yong grimaced.

Robert lifted the girl's bobbed black hair away from the cut as he cleaned the area and bandaged the wound. "Head injuries often bleed profusely."

Abby filled a washbasin and helped Kum Yong rinse the blood from her hands.

A rapping on the door caught Abby's attention and everyone froze. The door swung open and a redheaded nurse stared into the room, mouth agape. "Dr. King? What is going on here?"

Abby stepped in front of Kum Yong as Miss Cameron turned her body to shield Yoke Hay from view.

Robert cleared his throat, rolling down his shirtsleeves and attaching his cuffs. "Can I help you, Nurse Maguire?"

The woman frowned, the white cap pulling forward on her curls as her brow scrunched. "Your patient, Miss Fischer, wants to speak with you. I told her I would check to see if you were in." She craned her neck, twisting to see behind Abby.

"I'm finishing up, here." Robert lifted his coat from the back of the chair. "Abby, why don't you go with Nurse Maguire? Tell Cecelia I'll be along directly." He shot Abby a meaningful glance.

Abby straightened. "Yes, of course." She stepped in front of the wide-eyed nurse, blocking the doorway. "Please, lead the way."

The nurse stepped back from the door and sauntered down the hall. "He's not supposed to be treating patients in his office. It is why we have examination rooms. Every patient needs to be checked in."

Abby smiled. "I'll make sure to remind him."

The white-aproned nurse deposited her at Cecelia's door with a sniff, flouncing away down the hall to the main desk.

The odd situation vanished from Abby's thoughts the moment she spotted Cecelia sitting upright in the bed, lowering her feet over the sides. "What are you doing?"

"Going to the chapel to pray."

A wash of conflicting emotions swept over Abby. "Let me get the nurse. We'll get the wheelchair and take you down there."

"I want to walk."

Abby's throat clenched. "Why not pray here? What's the sudden urge to go to the chapel?"

Cecelia's eyes filled with tears. "I need to get out of this room. Can't you understand?"

Reaching out a hand to grasp her sister's arm, Abby nodded. "Of course. If you feel up to it."

"I'm going."

Abby reached for her sister's dressing gown. "I'll get Robert. He can help."

Cecelia pushed her arms through the sleeves of her gown and tied the ribbon around her neck, her complexion fading as she sat perched on the edge of the bed.

"Don't move," Abby ordered.

Her sister shot her a withering look, but remained seated.

Robert leaned on the desk, deep in conversation with the beautiful red-haired nurse.

Abby rushed to his side, ignoring the pointed glare from Nurse Maguire. "Dr. King, we need you."

His head jerked up and he followed Abby back to the ward, arriving in time to see Cecelia tottering to her feet, clutching at the bedrail for support.

"What do you think you're doing?" Robert grasped her arm, steadying her on her feet.

"Prayer. Chapel." The words wheezed from her chest.

"No. Absolutely not." He lowered her to the edge of the bed.

She stared up at him with round blue eyes, lines forming on her glistening brow. "My choice." Cecelia pulled the gown tight around her waist.

Robert frowned. "It's too far. I'll get the chair."

Cecelia pushed up to her feet a second time, beckoning to Abby with a hand. "I'm walking."

Gripping Cecelia's arm, Abby blanched at the sensation of her fingers pressing against her sister's bones through the thin sleeves of her dressing gown.

Robert's face darkened, but he crossed to her opposite side and slid his arm around Cecelia's back. "Take it slow and easy. Short steps."

Abby placed her other arm behind Cecelia for additional support. The brush of Robert's sleeve against her own sent an uncomfortable prickle across her skin.

Cecelia slid a foot forward, a sheen gracing the contour of her brow, her golden braid dangling over one shoulder. Breaths came in short puffs through her parted lips as she dug her fingers into Abby's arm.

The odd-looking group hobbled down the hall about a hundred yards, pausing every five feet, before Robert shook his head and leaned Cecelia back toward his body. Sweeping her up in his arms, he ignored her protests. "I'll take you wherever you want to go. But at this rate, you'll be too weary to pray when you get there."

Abby stepped aside, her relief like a fresh breeze from the bay. She watched as Cecelia laid her head against Robert's shoulder, placing her hand against his chest. Abby couldn't resist touching Robert's elbow in appreciation.

He winked at her over Cecelia's head. "Next stop, prayer chapel."

Robert balanced her featherweight body against his shoulder as Abby pushed open the door to the dimly lit room. He sidled up the center aisle and lowered Cecelia into the front pew. Crouching on his heels, Robert took Cecelia's hands. "Do you want me to stay with you?"

Cecelia's chin trembled. "Are you a praying man, Robert?"

He glanced behind her to where Abby stood fidgeting in the aisle, her gaze darting to the door. Returning his attention to his patient, he nodded. "Sometimes—not as much as I should, perhaps—but I do. Don't go telling everyone. I'm supposed to be a man of science."

A smile blossomed on Cecelia's face. She reached out and touched his shoulder, like a queen bestowing knighthood. "Glad to hear it." Her breathing had eased upon arrival as if the chapel provided much-needed energy. "Abby doesn't pray very much, I'm afraid." She rolled her eyes back toward her sister. "But, when she does, God listens." She smiled at Robert, dropping her hand to her lap. "After all, He sent us you, didn't He?"

Robert glanced between the two sisters, a hot flush climbing his neck. "Yes, well . . ."

Abby sat beside her sister. "I don't know why you had to come all the way to the chapel. You've never been concerned about the locations of your prayers before."

Cecelia sighed. "It's not the location. It's the bed."

Robert pushed to his feet. "Maybe I should step out and let you two talk."

"Take Abby with you."

"What?" Abby's eyes rounded.

Cecelia turned to her sister. "Abby, I need to have a little chat with God. Just us."

Abby stood, hands on hips. "Just so you're praying to get better." She marched down the aisle to the exit.

Robert watched her leave, an ache growing in his chest. "You owe it to her to keep fighting, you know."

Cecelia's gaze drew back to the cross hanging over the altar. "My future is safe in the Lord's hands. It's my sister and my family who need our prayers. I'd appreciate it if you prayed for them."

A tremor cut through him. "I will. But my focus is finding a cure."

The light trickling through the stained glass dotted her hair with color. "Oh, Robert." She sighed, the corners of her mouth turning downward. "I pray someday God will show you your true purpose."

11

*R*obert eased the automobile under the shade of the maple tree in the Fischer's backyard, cutting the power to the engine and relaxing as the sputtering motor lapsed into silence. Dapples of sunlight drifted through the red and orange leaves, casting a golden glow over the afternoon. The sound of childish laughter rang out as Davy Fischer scampered down the wooden stairs and out into the sunshine.

Abby stood in the doorway, a graceful hand cupped over her brow as she watched the boy play. After a moment, she closed the door and settled down on the top step, a book clasped in her hands.

Robert took a deep breath, the peaceful scene chasing away his anxious thoughts. Reaching over the seat, he retrieved a basket from the floorboard. Gerald's mother had entreated him to deliver the supplies and one did not dare refuse Mrs. Larkspur—not if you hoped for a sliver of peach pie at dinner.

He lifted the basket, the aroma of fried chicken wafting through the woven strips of rattan. Inhaling the heavenly fragrance, Robert's stomach gurgled in response. He hooked the wooden handles over his arm and walked down the path from the alley into the yard, raising his hand in greeting.

Davy paused in midstride, changed directions, and raced toward him at top speed.

Robert laughed, setting the food behind him before hoisting the boy into the air.

Closing her book, Abby stood, eyes bright with smiles. "Dr. King—we weren't expecting you."

Robert boosted Davy to his back. "First names, now—you promised." He steadied the boy with one hand and reached down for the basket. "Besides, I come bearing gifts."

Abby peeked under the lid with a grin. "Aunt Mae?"

"Certainly not me. I can cook, but it never smells like this. Usually a little more like charcoal."

"Mama will be pleased. She's been resting this morning and we haven't gotten anything ready for the noon meal yet."

"Chicken?" Davy dug his chin into Robert's neck, bouncing on his back.

"Sure smells like it." Robert raised Davy higher so he could see into the depths of the hamper.

"Aunt Mae always makes fried chicken on Saturdays." Abby replaced the red-checked cloth and closed the lid. "You'll join us, won't you Robert? You don't need to get back right away?"

He grinned. "I thought you'd never ask. Do you think you could share with me, Davy?"

The boy shimmied down his back, landing on the stone walk with a thud. He grasped Robert's hand and tugged him toward the door. "So long's you don't eat too much."

Robert lifted the basket from Abby's arm. "I promise." His eyes met hers, a smile dancing between them.

Prickles danced up and down Abby's spine as she escorted the doctor into the house, heading directly into the small kitchen. "Papa left for home yesterday. He can only leave the orchard in the hands of neighbors for so long. After a while he gets all twitchy, like the trees are calling him." *Papa's gone, Mama's upstairs—what will we talk about?*

Robert placed the hamper on the table. "I imagine you might feel the same."

She pictured her strong, reliable trees in their perfect lines—so unlike people and their peculiarities. "I do miss them." Abby opened the lid, the heady scent engulfing her with its promise of greasy goodness. She closed her fingers around a silver fork, transferring the juicy morsels to a platter. "But, I couldn't leave Cecelia." She wiped her fingers on a clean rag, careful to keep her eyes focused on her work, lest her face betray other reasons keeping her here.

"I'm glad you chose to stay. I appreciate your help in the laboratory." He hooked his thumbs in the pockets of his jacket. "If you do much more, we'll have to put you on the payroll. You're practically a trained technician."

Abby bobbled the tray, nearly sending the chicken diving for the floor.

Robert stepped to her side. "Here, allow me."

She released the heavy platter into his hands with a grateful nod. The basket boasted other goodies—fresh German potato salad, canned peaches, a lemon cake and—of course—molasses cookies. Thankfully, Davy had disappeared upstairs and wasn't yanking on her apron demanding a taste. She bundled the items into serving dishes and set the table, ignoring Robert's gaze. If she thought too much about it, she was sure to drop something.

Footsteps hammering down the back staircase made her start. Davy burst into the kitchen, eyes round. "I can't wake Mama!"

"You shouldn't be . . ." The expression on her brother's face swept the words from her mind. "What do you mean?" Without waiting for his answer, Abby dropped the bowl of potato salad on the table and hurried up the steps. She wiped her hands on her apron before touching the cool metal doorknob.

"Mama?" Abby crept into the shadowed room and bent over the huddled shape on the bed, her mother's shoulder and hip forming rounded lumps under the quilt. Mama's eyes remained closed.

"Are you awake?" Abby brushed the backs of her fingers against her mother's cheek. Heat.

Mama opened her eyes and blinked slowly, her eyes glassy and feverish. "Barely. I don't feel myself, though."

Abby sank down on the edge of the bed. "How long have you been feeling poorly?"

Clearing her throat, Mama winced. "Last night. My throat feels like I've been swallowing glass."

"You're burning up. Dr. King is downstairs—I'll have him come take a look at you."

Her brows lowered into points over her nose. "No, don't bother him. It's just a sore throat."

Abby forced a smile and patted her mother's shoulder. "What fun is having doctors in the family if you can't pull in a favor once in a while?"

Pushing higher on the pillow, Mama's face pinched. "Gerald is family. Dr. King shouldn't feel responsible for us."

"After the number of hours he has spent with Cecelia, I'm sure he'd disagree."

✐❤

Robert ran his fingers along Mrs. Fischer's neck, the swollen lymph nodes obvious to the touch. He nodded to Abby. "You should try to get the fever down, if you can. Keep her cool as much as possible." He stood, stepping out of her way.

Abby took his spot on the edge of the bed, mouth in a pinched frown. "Is it serious?"

"Probably just a mild infection. But it would be best if she remained in bed for a few days. There's been some influenza about town lately. You'll want to be careful." He watched as Abby dipped the cloth in the basin and wrung it out.

Mrs. Fischer shifted under the covers. "What about Cecelia?"

"I'll take care of her." Abby spread the cloth on her mother's forehead.

Robert leaned against the dresser. "It might be best if you kept your distance as well, Abby. Wait a day or two before visiting. Make sure you're not coming down with it, too."

She sprang from the bed. "I feel perfectly fine."

"Just as a precaution. Cecelia couldn't withstand an infection in her condition." He took a step backward as the force of Abby's glare pressed against him. "She will be well looked after, I promise. And I'll make sure Gerald stops by tomorrow to see how you are all getting on."

She set the basin on the floor and gave her mother's arm a pat. "We'll let you get some rest, Mama. I'll be back in a while to check on you."

Robert edged back toward the door as Abby rose and stormed in his direction. He followed her out into the hall, pulling the door shut behind him.

"You're being ridiculous," she sputtered, making her way down the stairs to the kitchen. "I don't have an infection and I can't leave Cecelia alone in the hospital for days on end just to prove it."

"You'd rather march in there and get her sick?"

The lunch remained as they'd left it. Abby flopped down into a chair and took a sip from a glass of water. "Of course not." She scowled down at the food.

Robert sat beside her, her pouting lips tugging at his heart. "She'll get plenty of attention. I'll come by and keep her company whenever I get a free minute."

Abby leaned back against the chair with a groan. "It's maddening."

"I know." Robert studied the waiting meal. The aromas of the food had mellowed with cooling, but still tempted his stomach. He gestured to a crumb-speckled gap on the tablecloth. "Am I mistaken, or is a dish missing?"

Glancing around the bright kitchen, Abby frowned. "Davy? Where are you?"

The chair opposite Robert edged backward, the legs squeaking as they slid across the tile floor. A small face appeared over the top edge of the table, round cheeks dotted with brown spots. "Here I am." The fragrance of molasses drifted through the air.

Robert chuckled, glancing at Abby. "I thought you were the only one in your family with freckles."

Abby stood, glowering. "I am."

Davy swiped a hand across his face, brushing away the evidence.

A gray tabby cat wound through a white picket fence, stopping to roll in the sunshine at Robert's feet. Robert's neck ached as Davy, perched on his shoulders, leaned forward to watch, his weight pressing against Robert's head.

Abby crouched down to stroke the purring feline, her fingers riffling through the striped fur on its belly. It pawed at the edge of her navy blue skirt, as if drawing her close enough to scratch its ears. Abby features softened. "Aren't you sweet?"

Robert's heart lightened, as if the words were for him. Suggesting a walk had been the ideal diversion to take Abby's thoughts off of her mother's illness. They hadn't traveled far, but already the fresh air had brought new life to her step. As soon as she rose, he guided her down a side street filled with elegant homes fronted by lush gardens.

Abby had already pointed out a dozen varieties of trees and flowers, her lilting voice putting names to flowering vines Robert had long appreciated, but never bothered to identify. Her enthusiasm brought a smile to his lips and gave him the energy to walk on, even as Davy's heels kept kicking him in the chest.

"You know every flower, don't you?" He watched her touch a blooming honeysuckle adorning a garden gate.

She laughed, the sound matching the birdsong in the trees. "Not all of them. But they're sort of like old friends. This city is all brick and automobiles, horses and noise." She sighed, with a gentle shake of her head. "I don't belong here." Abby ran her hand along the fence, reaching out to touch a blossom dangling from a trailing rose bush. "But when I see these familiar faces, it's like a bit of home has followed me."

Robert admired how the rosy blush on her cheeks matched the flower in her hand. Before he could stop himself, his hand lifted to touch her face.

Her eyes rounded and she turned her cheek ever-so-slightly into his hand.

His breath caught in his chest. *What am I doing?* "I'm sorry. You had a little—a little bug or something, there." He caught Davy's boot in his hand before it could clunk down against his chest for the sixteenth time.

Abby blinked, brushing a hand across her cheek. "A bug?" Her face flushed. "Did you get it?" Her head tilted to the right, her skin catching the warm glow of the afternoon sun.

Temptation swelled in his gut, his fingers itching to caress her cheekbone, just under those amazing brown eyes. He swallowed, keeping his hands safely locked on the boy's ankles. "Yes. It's gone."

She nodded, a faint smile touching her lips. "Thank you, Dr. King. You're a good friend."

As Abby took a last sniff of the trailing blooms, Robert turned away, focusing his eyes on the brown cobbles at his feet.

"I should walk you home. Gerald will be wondering what's happened to me." Even with his eyes averted, Abby's beauty played havoc with his resolve. He took a deep breath to clear his head, but the fragrance of the roses wrenched his thoughts back to the woman by his side.

Friends.

Thursday, September 28, 1905

Robert leaned against the tall wooden desk, the long corridor silent except for the quiet footfalls of the night nurse on her dawn rounds. He struggled to focus his weary eyes in the dim light, but the numbers continued swimming about the paper. A lump formed in his throat. "These can't be right." He pushed a hand against his forehead, trying to will away the exhaustion threatening to consume him.

The past four days had been a flurry of activity. Though he had promised to spend every free moment at Cecelia's bedside, he'd still managed to sneak away to spend time with Abby as she nursed her mother at home. And together with rounds, research, patients, and tinkering with the equipment—it left little time for sleep.

Late last night, while bent over the dismantled X-ray machine, he'd finally admitted he'd been lying. Both to himself and to Gerald. Touching Abby's face the other day had confirmed his worst fear. A spark of electricity had coursed through his hand and his heart—as if a static charge had been building inside him for weeks. The touch freed the charge and shocked him into awareness.

Unless he'd completely misdiagnosed the situation, she was fond of him as well. She smiled more often at him nowadays, her eyes sparking with bottled-up electricity. Every time they spoke, she shared a little more of her soul, like a bud uncurling into full bloom.

The question now was, should he tell his best friend?

The image faded as Robert glared at the paper, willing the figures to change before his eyes. He dug his fingers against his neck muscles, tense from leaning over the X-ray machine, rewiring, testing, and rewiring again.

And now, looking at the test results—it might be all for naught.

A young orderly hurried past, flashing him a bright smile. Robert crushed the paper in his fist and turned to the duty nurse waiting at the desk. "Run them again."

Her lips thinned to a scratch, wrinkles forming around her mouth. "I ran them twice, Dr. King."

Steam boiled up from the furnace in his stomach. "I don't care if you did it ten times. Run them again." He flattened the paper against the desk and stormed toward the office. He hadn't worked all night to learn Cecelia wouldn't be fit for treatment today.

And from the look of those numbers—maybe not ever.

12

Saturday, September 30, 1905

The fog-drenched air hardly stirred and yet the withered oak leaves shivered under Abby's touch. She glanced toward the tree's roots, imprisoned under a geometric pattern of cobblestones. "You poor thing. I know how you feel."

Abby gave the tree a final pat before she strode up the hospital steps. She retrieved a handkerchief, prepared to cover her nose against the familiar odor of ammonia. If she hurried, she would have time to visit Cecelia before her morning treatment.

Six days without seeing her sister had seemed like an eternity, even with Robert coming to call each day. As much as Abby detested San Francisco, she'd begun to dread the day when her family would leave. Thoughts of Robert consumed her mind—the zeal in his eyes when he spoke about his work, the way he carried Davy high upon his shoulders, the touch of his hand on her cheek. She shook herself. *Stop being such a fool.* Every ounce of common sense had dissolved the day she met this man. She hadn't come to San Francisco in search of romance.

But it was a dizzying, delightful feeling.

She'd never had many friends beyond Cecelia—much less romantic interests. Romance involved talking. And yet, sharing with Robert had grown easier with time. He never laughed at her choice of words or belittled her for having strong opinions. He was strong and reliable, like one of her trees. Would this relationship also bear fruit? The idea tickled her insides.

Abby stifled a yawn as she crossed the gleaming tile floor. She'd stayed up late reading the final chapters of a novel she had purchased from a bookstore on Market Street, the story of a stolen dog returning to its wolf roots in the wilds of Alaska and the Yukon. After she'd finally closed her eyes, she dreamt of running free through a forested wilderness.

A group of nurses stood clustered around the door to the ward like a flock of pigeons. *Something is wrong.* Abby's pace slowed, the hall stretching endlessly before her.

Gerald exited the room, sending the nurses fluttering back to their duties. He walked toward her, eyes fixed on the clipboard in his hand. When he glanced up and saw Abby, he paused—his brows drawing low, matching the downward turn of his mouth.

"What's going on? What's the matter?" Abby's breath vanished from her lungs, a strangled vacuum growing in her chest.

Gerald placed a hand on Abby's shoulder, steering her in the direction of his office. "Cecelia has taken a turn for the worse. She's running a fever and her white blood cell count is rising."

She pulled him to a stop. "What does it mean?"

Gerald exhaled. "It means the cancer is fighting back."

"And the X-rays?"

"We're making adjustments." He shook his head. "Maybe you can lift her spirits. I think you might be the medicine she needs right now. Robert and I will compare notes and decide how to address this new development."

Abby nodded and hurried down the hall to her sister's room, nearly colliding with Robert as he walked out, the door swinging shut behind him.

He grasped an elbow to steady her, his face a grim reflection of Gerald's. "Abby, it's good to see you." The lines around his eyes lessened as he smiled in greeting. "Let's see if you can work your sisterly magic on our patient."

"I'll do my best." She glanced past him, imagining her sister on the other side of the door.

"And maybe we can take another walk this afternoon? I'd like to speak with you in private."

The tension in her chest eased, her arm tingling in his grip. "I'd enjoy an outing."

After a gentle squeeze to her arm, he hurried down the hall.

Abby pushed through the door, the air in the ward smelling stale and lifeless. The pallor of her sister's skin triggered an ache within Abby's stomach. She dug for courage. "Good morning. How are you feeling?"

Cecelia closed her eyes and rolled to her side. "Why must everyone ask me that?"

Abby placed her hands on her hips. "Six days since I last saw you and this is how you greet me?" She walked around the bed and pulled up a chair. "Are you hurting?"

Cecelia's lip trembled for a moment before she pressed them tight together. "I'm tired. I don't want to read today."

"It's too bad because I was going to let you choose between continuing the sappy *Sweetheart, Will You Be True* or digging into this incredible book I found titled *Call of the Wild*." Abby leaned forward, tucking the blanket around Cecelia's shoulder. "True love or wild dogs—as if I had to guess which one you'd prefer."

Without opening her eyes, Cecelia shifted under the covers and grimaced. "Neither."

Abby leaned back against the chair. She'd only missed six days. What had happened?

Even as Cecelia cleared her throat, her voice rasped. "How's Mama?"

"Much better, though her throat is still bothering her. She wishes she could come."

"Better if she doesn't."

Abby slid to the edge of her chair and laid her palms on the bed. "I'm sorry you're feeling so poorly. But Robert and Gerald will sort it out. They'll just dial up the X-rays a little more."

Cecelia buried her head deeper into the pillow. "They've tried. It's not helping like it did before." She opened her eyes, pinning her sister with a steady stare. "It isn't going to work, Abby."

Abby sucked in a quick breath. The whites of her sister's eyes were veiled in a yellowish cast. Abby's mind reeled, searching for something to steady her flailing emotions. "But Robert—"

"Stop it!" Her sister squeezed her eyes shut, pressing the lids together with such force tiny wrinkles formed all around them. "Stop expecting Robert to fix everything."

"I don't . . ." Abby paused, unsure of her answer. *Do I?*

Cecelia yanked the blanket higher on her shoulder. "Do you know what I dream about?"

Abby closed her mouth, glancing down at the weave of the blanket, certain she wouldn't like her sister's answer.

Cecelia's gaze landed somewhere on the wall behind Abby. "I dream about running."

A laugh bubbled from Abby's stomach, but she managed to swallow it. "Running? Really?" Cecelia hadn't run since they were little girls, skipping through the meadow holding hands. Even then, Abby had yanked her along. As they grew, Cecelia strolled, parasol in hand, knees unblemished.

Abby had knees like an old carthorse—rough and scarred.

Cecelia picked at the threadbare edge of her quilt. "I'm running through the meadow at home. It's covered in wildflowers. You would know their names." She coughed, managing two quick barks and a wheeze, the back of her hand covering her mouth. "My hair is down and the wind is whipping it across my back." A tiny smile hovered around her lips as she lowered her hand to the pillow. "I run and run without ever growing winded."

"What are you running from?" Abby leaned forward.

Cecelia's gaze fixed on Abby, as if just noticing her presence. "I'm not running away—I'm just running and it feels marvelous." She sighed. "Like I'm running into Jesus' arms." A tiny smile formed at the corners of her mouth, the lines smoothing from her face.

Abby sat back in the chair. "You can't start thinking like that again." *Not when we've come so far.*

"Whether I live a week, a year, or fifty years—it's up to God, Abby. Not you, and not Robert."

Abby crossed her arms, the room growing stifling. "Why would God bring Robert to us if not to help with your healing?"

Cecelia rolled to her back. "As it says in Isaiah, 'For my thoughts are not your thoughts, neither are your ways my ways,' saith the Lord. 'For as the heavens are higher than the earth, so are my ways higher than your ways, and my thoughts than your thoughts.'"

"Meaning what?"

"It means we don't always understand God's plans for us. But they are always better than what we have planned for Him to do."

Abby set her jaw. So far, she and God had stuck to their little agreement, and she didn't intend to let Him weasel out now.

✐❧

The icy stone chilled Robert's fingers as he ran his hand along the carved scrollwork of the bench, striving to keep his eyes off his beautiful companion.

Abby gazed upward, droplets of fog clinging to her hair. The muted light brushed across her freckled cheeks and illuminated the flecks hiding within her eyes, like gold dust beneath the dark current of a stream.

Robert reached into his pocket, digging for his watch—anything to keep his hands busy. Taking a walk over to the square had sounded like a good diversion. Now he had second thoughts.

"What will you do?" She lowered her chin and met his gaze. "More X-rays?"

He leaned back against the bench. Would there ever be a day when they could simply talk about the weather, the park, the novel she carried in her bag? "Gerald and I have been discussing returning to a more traditional treatment."

Her brows creased. "Like what?"

"Arsenic."

Abby's slender fingers rumpled the fabric of her skirt. "Dr. Greene already tried. It didn't do anything."

"Yes, but a combination of arsenic and X-ray radiation might work in her favor. At least for a time."

"A time." She dropped her chin, her hat tipping sideways at the sudden motion.

He took a deep breath and reached for her hand. "Abby, she's already lived longer than we anticipated."

She stared down at his fingers for a long moment, face unreadable. Glancing up into his eyes, she crinkled her mouth into a weak smile. "If anyone can save Cecelia, you can. Please, don't give up now." A sudden breath of wind sent a green hat ribbon fluttering into her face.

Robert lifted his free hand and brushed it away. "You were wearing this hat the day you came to Gerald's house for supper. The day I stitched your finger."

A pink hue rose among the freckles as Abby smiled, ducking her head.

He ran a thumb along her knuckles and then lifted her hand so he could see the tiny white scar, a visible reminder of his work.

She didn't pull away. "A fine bit of sewing. You can hardly see it now."

Robert slid closer along the smooth marble seat, hungry for a whiff of her lilac-scented hair. "I was nervous. I kept hoping Gerald would return and take charge."

Abby's head jerked back, eyes wide. "You?"

"We'd only just met." He leaned back to capture a glimpse of her eyes under the brim of her hat. "And I know it's unprofessional of me to say, but I—I was overcome by your beauty."

The color drained from her face. "You're making sport of me."

"I most certainly am not."

Her gaze softened. "Don't flatter me. I couldn't bear it."

"The fact you are unaware of your own beauty is all the more compelling." Robert squeezed Abby's hand, a light breeze ruffling the wisps of hair about her face.

She reached up and smoothed his lapel before running a hand down his arm, gaze flickering between his shoulder and face, her lips parted.

Robert's pulse stepped up. He swallowed, unprepared for the onslaught of feelings triggered by her touch. "Abby . . ." He leaned forward, his breath catching in his chest. "I am fond of you. Too fond, I'm afraid."

Abby didn't answer, her brown eyes gleaming. She matched his gaze without wavering.

"I—I shouldn't—" Robert pulled her closer and brushed his lips against hers, the taste of her tender lips rushing over him like a summer storm.

Abby's quick breath grazed his cheek, her fingertips pressing into his inner arm.

What am I doing? Robert retreated a few inches, but desire brought him to a standstill, his thoughts muddying.

She lifted her head, her cheekbone caressing the side of his face and sending his self-control into disarray.

Robert lifted a hand, sliding fingers up her throat to where her pulse fluttered like butterfly wings against his skin. *Patient's sister. Gerald's cousin.* He lowered his chin until his nose brushed her hair, a stray strand tickling his cheek. He touched his lips to the silky skin just below her ear, wrestling against the urge to bury his face in the curve of her neck and never emerge.

Her arm, caught between the bench and his side, traveled upward behind his shoulder, her wandering fingers sending a current sweeping down his spine.

You told Gerald you wouldn't pursue this. Robert drew back, his gaze trailing past Abby's entrancing eyes until it lingered on her moist lips. *I kissed her.* He caught himself before he leaned forward to claim another.

Abby trembled in his grasp.

Even with his throat closing, Robert managed to wrench in a breath. There was too much to lose—his job, Gerald's trust, the research . . .

His hands shook. Robert yanked them away, pushed up from the bench, and turned his back. He scrubbed a palm across his face, as if to brush away the sensation of her touch. *What have I done?*

Abby stood behind him, the rustle of her skirt drawing him back.

Robert turned, his heart aching as he observed the woman standing before him.

Her eyes glistened, mouth pinched like a suture drawn too tight. "Is something . . ." her voice faltered. "Did I . . ."

He set his jaw. "It's my fault. I don't know what I was thinking."

She took a step back, blinking like she'd been thrust into a bright light.

Robert grasped her arm, unable to catch her hand as she withdrew. "I'm so sorry—it's just—"

Abby wrenched her arm free, her chin trembling. "No, I'm the one who's sorry." She shook her head, hat ribbons fluttering as she turned and hurried away.

A sharp pain drove into Robert's chest. He flopped down onto the bench, the afternoon sun burning through the fog like a glaring eye from heaven.

✍❦

Abby fled back to the hospital, locking her gaze on the intricate pattern of red brick cobblestones underfoot rather than risking a backward glance toward the man responsible for the flush on her cheeks. The corset boning crushed against her ribs as she attempted to draw a steady breath. *He didn't know what he was thinking?*

Sweetness rolled across her tongue at the memory of the tender kiss, the feather-soft touch of his lips against hers, the sensation of her muscles unknotting, and the desire to dissolve into his touch. She shivered. A seed had been planted, and now, under these perfect conditions, it had swelled and burst through its seed coat, tiny roots fanning out through her system, drawing life back into itself.

His hollow-eyed pain cut through, stilling the fluttering in her chest. *He regretted kissing me.* Abby curled her fingers into her palm. What had she done wrong?

Cecelia would know. Abby's throat tightened. How could she bring herself to tell her sister about this incident?

And I kissed him back. Abby pressed her knuckles against her cheekbones, heat blazing between her fingers. Her lips still tingled from the kiss. *What was I thinking?*

13

*R*obert's words lodged in Abby's heart like a splinter. She pressed a hand against her chest as she rushed back to Cecelia's room.

Mama and Gerald hovered near the bedside, the air buzzing with the sounds of their hushed voices. Cecelia lay flat, eyes closed and mouth agape, as if in sleep she struggled for breath. Gerald clamped fingers around her wrist, drawing it upward a few inches. Cecelia's sleeve slid back, exposing her long, white arm.

The recollection of the kiss shattered, Abby raced to her mother's side. "What happened?"

A grim expression covered Gerald's face, his light-colored hair rumpled as if he had repeatedly passed his fingers through the strands. "Cecelia's fever has risen to a dangerous level." He took a deep breath and turned to Abby's mother. "We'll try to bring it down with some ice, but I think her final hours are coming more quickly than we anticipated, Clara. Have you gotten word to Herman?"

Mama nodded, her face gray, shoulders curved. "But he won't arrive until tomorrow morning at the earliest."

"What?" Abby's heartbeat pounded in her ears. *I just spoke with her.*

Gerald lowered Cecelia's hand to the bed. "Her pulse is erratic. She may not have much longer."

Abby stumbled backward with a gasp, bumping against the door-frame. "No . . ."

He glanced up at her. "Have you seen Dr. King?"

Her mouth opened, heat returning to her cheeks. "I left him a moment ago, in Lafayette Square."

"Go and get him. No, wait—" Gerald cast another glance at Cecelia. "Stay with your mother and sister. I'll send one of the nurses." He scooped up the clipboard and hurried from the room.

Abby touched the blue silk of her mother's draping sleeve.

Mama sank down in the chair beside the bed, eyes dull. "Oh, God—why now?"

Spidery purple veins marred Cecelia's closed eyelids, her face flushed and cheeks sunken. Her cracked lips parted, faint wheezing breaths rasping in her chest.

A raven-haired nurse arrived with a bucket of ice. Wrapping the blocks in cloths, she wedged the packs under Cecelia's arms and around her torso, covering Cecelia with a thin sheet.

Abby wove her fingers through her sister's, the warmth in Cecelia's skin burning into her own.

Gerald returned minutes later, Robert at his heels, his face somber.

Other than a brief glance in his direction, Abby kept her gaze downward, pushing away all thought of their recent encounter. Her sister lay dying, and what had Abby done? Distracted her doctor from Cecelia's bedside when she needed him most.

Distracted? She'd kissed him. Abby's mouth went dry, her throat as parched as sun-baked mud. She moistened her lips, fighting an urge to wipe them on her sleeve.

Mama stood at the opposite side of the bed, her dark blue eyes glistening with unshed tears. "There must be something else you can do, Gerald. She was responding so well. What happened?"

Gerald stood a step behind Mama, his own eyes rimmed with red. "The radiation put the leukemia into a temporary remission. But the blood tests are showing her organs can't handle the treatment. Her liver and kidneys are shutting down. Clara—" he took her arm, turning her to face him. "Her heart is weakening. She won't withstand the infection."

Abby swallowed. "This is it, then? No more X-rays?"

Robert's face darkened. "At this point, the radiation therapy is causing more harm than good."

The declaration resounded in Abby's chest like a voice echoing through a cavern. Her throat clenched until she could barely force out words. "You can't give up now. You can't." She sank to the edge of the bed, directing her gaze toward Robert. "Don't give up on us."

His cheeks puffed with a long exhale, his eyes round and dark. "There's nothing more—"

"Don't!" Abby jumped to her feet, jabbing the air in front of him with a finger. "Don't say those words. Not to me. Not ever."

Gerald's fingers grazed her arm. "Abby."

Abby flung her elbow, knocking away her cousin's touch. "Take her back to the laboratory. One more treatment. See her through this infection and she'll get stronger again."

Mama's choking voice cut through the room. "Abigail, stop—" A sob stole her remaining words. She bent down, covering Cecelia with caresses. "Cecelia, honey, open your eyes."

Abby bounded toward Robert. "We didn't bring her all this way to have her die in some cold hospital room. Fix this." Her body shuddered as she drew gasping breaths. "Do something. Give her one more chance. She deserves it—I deserve it." She grasped his arms and squeezed.

Robert reached for her shoulders, as if to draw her into an embrace. "Abby, I can't. It's no good."

She pushed against him, his words piercing her soul. "Not can't—won't. You won't do it." A deep pain collected in the back of her throat. She broke away, throwing herself down on the bed beside her mother and sister. Eyes dry, a sob heaved up from her core. Abby clenched her teeth to stop the sound.

Gerald, his hand on Abby's mother's back, gestured with his head. "Robert, take her out, please."

"No!" Abby clutched at the bedcovers.

Robert took her arm and lifted, using his other hand to pry open her grip. "Abby, let's get some air."

She locked her knees as he set her on her feet. "No, please. I don't want to go. Gerald, please."

Robert half-carried, half-dragged, Abby from the room, propelling her forward until the doors of the cancer ward swung closed behind them.

"You can't do this!" Abby flung her body against his in a mad attempt to get past. "It's my sister. I need to be in there. She needs me."

"Exactly." Robert locked his arms around her waist, pressing her back against the wall, his thick brows rumpled. "Cecelia needs her sister. She doesn't need you to be another doctor. She doesn't need to be part of some experimental research program. And she doesn't need a frightened woman ordering people about."

As he touched her cheek, the twisted knot in her stomach loosened. Her hand, gripping the loose fabric of his laboratory coat, sensed the rising and falling of his chest. The steady, even rhythm eased the buzzing in her head.

"She needs to know you will be all right." His voice faltered, but his earnest gaze did not. "She is going to die, regardless. Don't waste this moment moaning in the hall, when you should be saying good-bye."

A tear dripped from Abby's chin. She hadn't even realized she was crying.

The door swung open and Gerald leaned out, his face dark. He eyed Abby for a long moment before speaking. "Cecelia's awake."

A tremor coursed through Abby's arms, her hand still buried in the front of Robert's coat. "I can't let her go."

Robert looked down at her, his gaze fervent. He squeezed her shoulders. "You can."

Robert leaned into the wall, pressing the back of his head against the cool plaster as Abby followed Gerald through the swinging door. He blew out the breath he had been holding for the last several moments. His stomach roiled.

The look on Abby's face had left his heart in shreds no surgery could repair. Robert pressed a palm against his chest, the warmth of Abby's hand lingering on the smooth fabric.

I fell in love with my patient's sister and now the patient is dying. Robert lowered his face to his hands, digging fingers into his hair. Cecelia's case had been hopeless from the start. The goal of the experiment was to determine the effectiveness of X-rays for cancer treatment. It had never been about saving one woman's life.

His head throbbed in rhythm with the taunting voice chanting inside his mind. *Fool. Idiot. Charlatan.* He'd known Abby Fischer was vulnerable. The woman grasped at hope like a lifeline. And he'd offered plenty, like a salesman selling snake oil in the town square.

He paced the hall, palms sweating. Abby had captured his heart, and now the rope of her expectations tangled around his ankles, threatening to drag him down into the abyss.

He'd presented her with hope. She'd responded with love. Who would bear the burden of guilt?

Abby stole back into the room, listening to her mother's soft voice as she whispered to Cecelia.

"My sweet, sweet girl. You rest now."

Cecelia's blue eyes stared out from puffy lids, her unfocused gaze traveling from Mama to Abby.

Abby sank down, perching on the edge of the bed across from her mother. She reached for Cecelia's hand. "How . . ." she searched for words to matter to her sister. "How do you feel?"

Cecelia's eyes closed. "Not so bad." Her voice rattled. "Weary."

Abby grasped at her sister's words. "Maybe it's not as severe as they say. Perhaps if you rested awhile . . ."

Cecelia parted her lips, a long breath crackling in her chest. She opened her eyes. "Can we go home now?"

The hole inside Abby's heart broke open. Tears dampened her cheeks. "Of course." She nodded, swallowing past the lump growing in her throat. "Let's go home."

Mama reached over and took one of Cecelia's hands.

Cecelia lifted the corners of her mouth in a faint smile. "Good." She sighed. "I'll see you there."

Abby listened to her sister's ragged breaths gurgling as they grew more sporadic. After a time, the room fell silent except for Mama's quiet sobs.

Gerald stood behind her mother, his hands resting on her shoulders. "It's over, Clara. She's gone."

Abby pushed to her feet and hurried out to the hall.

Robert, standing at the nurses' station, turned and met her gaze, dark shadows collecting around his eyes.

She brushed past, rushing down the hall. For a heartbeat, she considered hiding in the prayer chapel, but veered away and proceeded to the end of the corridor where a smudged window looked out on a tiny courtyard.

Flattening her palms against the windowpane, Abby tipped her chin upward, gazing toward the sky, flaws in the thick glass creating ripples in the clouds. "We had an agreement, remember?" She narrowed her eyes, glaring at the heavens. "I said if You took her away, I'd never speak to You again." She swallowed the bile rising in her throat. "You didn't honor your end of the bargain." Lowering her chin, Abby rested her forehead against the cool glass. "I'm bound and determined to keep mine."

14

Abby clambered up the steep wooden stairs, ducking her head as she entered the murky attic of Maple Manor. Dust swirled in the dim shadows as she wove through the cluttered space, the noise of the city fading into the distance. She pulled herself into a ball between an old trunk and a stack of forgotten paintings, laying her head on a pile of moth-eaten quilts.

Chest aching, she drew her arms around her middle and squeezed. *Home.* Abby forced her lids to close over gritty eyes and conjured up an image of the orchard, the overladen limbs bending low, the fragrance of overripe fruit clinging to the breeze. The stream gurgled through the pasture, birds singing as they winged their way about the orchard and meadows. Abby moaned, burying her face in the soft quilts, the sour taste of longing clinging to her tongue.

"I'll see you there."

But Cecelia wouldn't come home. She would never run with abandon across the wildflower-strewn meadow, arms outstretched in greeting.

Abby pushed upright, sitting cross-legged on the floor. She unbuttoned her shoes, yanked them off, and threw them toward the doorway. Folding her knees up to her chest, Abby rocked in place, stifling the whimper growing in her throat. She didn't want to be here. She didn't really want to be home. She didn't want to be anywhere.

God let her die. Gerald did nothing. Robert . . .

The words faded, the image of Robert's face rising in her thoughts, the sensation of his lips against hers, the touch of his hand on her skin. Her stomach rolled.

Too late for that. Too late for anything.

✐

Papers lined every inch of Robert's desk—X-ray reports, blood tests, charts, notes, and records. He leaned forward in his chair and let his face fall against his hands. The gaping chasm in his stomach grew. No amount of paperwork would bring Cecelia back. Or Abby.

He reached for the pen. And no amount of procrastination would make it all go away.

"For the sake of the next patient." His professor's voice resounded in his head. *"Always be thinking about your next case."*

Robert clenched his fingers into a white-knuckled fist around the writing implement. In one swift motion, he sent the papers cascading to the floor, a cry bursting from his raw throat.

How could he consider experimenting further when he had already sacrificed one patient on the altar of personal glory?

15

Sunday, October 1, 1905

Colma? Where is that?" Abby pulled out a chair and sat across from her father, the rich scent of roasting ham flavoring the overheated kitchen air.

He gazed at her through world-weary eyes, running a hand over his unshaven chin. "South of the city."

Gerald wandered the edges of the room, avoiding the large central table. "No one has been interred in the city limits for years. The rail line provides funeral service to the Colma cemeteries."

Abby adjusted a hairpin scraping against her scalp. "Why can't we take her home to San Jose?"

No one spoke. Silence hovered in the room.

Gerald paced to the back door. "I think I'll go join Davy." The curtains fluttered as the door closed behind him.

Papa frowned at the table, tracing the grain of the wood with a dirt-crusted fingernail.

Abby slid forward on her chair. "What's going on? Why aren't we taking Cecelia home?"

Pushing to his feet, Papa walked the length of the kitchen and stopped in the entrance to the dining room. "I'm selling the farm, Abby. We'll be staying in San Francisco."

The room revolved slowly, as if being sucked into a whirlpool. "What?" Abby's voice faded to a whisper. "What do you mean?"

Her father rubbed a hand across his neck. "We're drowning in debt. I'd already mortgaged the house and the orchard. Now with medical bills, there's no money to pay."

A buzzing settled in Abby's ears. She gave her head a quick shake. "You never said anything about this before."

He leaned against the doorframe. "No. Your mother and I didn't want to worry you." His accent thickened. He took a deep breath and exhaled, the air escaping in pulsating spurts. "Even with Gerald donating his services, we must pay the hospital."

For the first time, Abby noticed the puffy bags sprawling under his red-rimmed eyes, his shoulders limp as if his arms hung by nothing but a few frayed threads. The sight gnawed at her heart. "I thought we had a record harvest last year."

Papa rubbed a thumb across bushy eyebrow. "*Ja.* But it was not enough—and too late. Prices were down. Way down."

Abby swallowed, pushing down the sob threatening to escape her throat. "We can't sell the farm. I promised Cecelia we would take her home." She dug her fingernails against the wood of the table. "It was her last request." *And those trees are mine. I played under them, worked them since I was a child. How can someone else own them?*

"We have no choice."

Abby remained seated as Papa left to check on her mother. An eerie stillness descended, as if the air had come alive and pressed down upon her, gluing her to the chair. The odor of the cooking meat turned her stomach. Outside, the sounds of automobile engines, horse hooves, and voices melded together. Life continued.

Abby pressed knuckles against her mouth to smother the whimpering moan building in her chest.

Robert leaned against the gate, staring in at the small patch of yard behind Maple Manor, stomach churning. Did he belong here? Would anyone welcome him?

Wisps of smoke sprouted from Gerald's pipe as he rested against the massive maple tree. The pungent odor drifted on the breeze. His friend only smoked when upset—often, lately.

Taking a deep breath and praying for strength, Robert unlatched the gate and waved to Davy busy maneuvering a toy train down the garden path. Gerald glanced up, not bothering to lower the pipe or call a greeting.

Robert ambled over to his friend's side. "How is everyone?"

Smoke seeped from Gerald's mouth as he exhaled, tipping his head back to gaze at the upper-story windows. "I don't think it's sunk in yet. Not really." A pinched line appeared between his brows. "Clara's taken to her bed. I brought some laudanum, but she seems dreadfully calm already. Maybe later." He touched his vest pocket as if checking the medicine's location.

A small bird flitted from the tree, alighting on the edge of the rooftop. Robert followed the bird's movement, watching until it disappeared back into the foliage. "What about Abby?"

Gerald gestured to the steps with a hand. "In the kitchen. Her father is breaking the news about their farm. I decided now was a good time to be scarce."

"The farm?"

He met Robert's eye. "Herman is selling."

A hole seemed to open in Robert's stomach. Abby's orchard? "Too many memories in the old place?"

His friend huffed. "Too many bills, I believe."

"What will they do?"

"I'm not certain. Herman mentioned looking for factory work." Gerald frowned. "But it seems harsh for such a man. He's always been forward thinking and hard-working. I can't imagine him wasting away in a factory."

How much of this is my fault? If I hadn't raised their hopes, would they be in this predicament? Robert pulled off his hat and pressed it against his chest. "Can't we help?"

Gerald clamped the pipe stem between his teeth and took a long puff. "I'm working on some ideas. I've intercepted several of the bills and paid them myself. But the farm has been struggling and Herman still owes their local doctor in addition to the hospital. I told him the family is welcome to this home as long as they need it."

Robert lowered his head, pushing a hand against his temple. "Is there anything I can do?"

"Why should you?" Gerald eyed him, brows raised. "It's not your family. You can't get consumed with the financial problems of every patient or you won't last long in this business."

A veil of blue smoke floated between them. "They're your family and you're my friend."

"There's more. Am I right?"

A weight settled in Robert's chest as he tried not to think about the stolen moment in the park. "I'm not sure what you mean. I'm just concerned for them."

Gerald leaned back against the gnarled trunk of the old tree. "Concerned for them? Or for Abby?"

The accusation hit Robert like a blow to the chest. "She's my friend, too. Isn't it right for me to be concerned?"

Gerald crossed his arms. "You can quit lying to yourself, Robert. And quit lying to me. I've known you too long not to see the signs."

Robert lowered his gaze, staring at the round brim of his hat, clasped in his fist. "I—I don't know what I feel."

"Oh, yes, you do." Gerald tapped the pipe against his palm. He chuckled and slowly shook his head. "Don't say I didn't warn you." The rueful smile faded. "But, I've got one thing to say to you, Robert."

Robert met his friend's gaze. "Yes?"

"Your timing is wretched."

A sigh rose from deep in Robert's chest. "Don't I know it?"

16

Thursday, October 5, 1905

*A*bby wandered through Gerald's house with a cheese-laden platter, surrounded by an assembly of well-meaning strangers. *Who are all these people?*

She returned to the kitchen where two elderly aunts helped Aunt Mae scoop food from steaming casseroles onto serving trays, the room filled with pungent odors of over-cooked fare. Abby dropped the platter into the only open spot on the table and picked up a fresh one filled with stuffed mushrooms. She popped one of the warm morsels into her mouth and chewed, the earthy flavor doing little to ground her in the moment. Her mind insisted on straying home to her orchard, abandoning her body to familial duties.

At least serving kept her hands busy and prevented anyone from cornering her with condolences and platitudes.

Pasting a nonchalant expression on her face, Abby skirted through the crowd of relatives and friends—most of whom she'd never met. Or if she had, she hadn't bothered to remember. She left those details to Cecelia.

A red-haired woman with an expansive coiffure caught her elbow, jarring the tray and sending mushrooms rolling about the plate. "Excuse me, dear. But I just wanted to tell you how devastated I was to learn about your precious sister. Our Ladies Circle has been praying for the sweet girl for weeks. I know how hopeful you all must have been for Dr. Larkspur and Dr. King to work some sort of miracle." She clicked her tongue. "God has another flower for his garden, I suppose. Shame she had to be so young. I saw her portrait—a lovely girl." Her gaze skittered across Abby's frame. "Yes, very tragic."

Abby extricated her arm. "Thank you." The words of gratitude caught in her dry throat. She wandered to the sitting room, where more people gathered, huddled in groups of three or four with just enough room for her to maneuver between them without stepping on anyone's skirt hems. Abby kept her gaze down, not wishing to see the black silk dresses and dark suits. Instead she focused on the men's shoes, the gloss and polish making the footwear shine against the patterned rug.

An elbow collided with her arm scattering the mushrooms around the platter for a second time and sending several diving off the edge. Abby lifted her eyes in time to see Robert's hand reach out to steady the tray. She jerked back, her sudden movement flinging the remaining appetizers airborne.

Stifled gasps and shrieks filled the room as mushrooms rained down on mourner's laps and onto the rug.

Abby's face burned as she clutched the tray to her chest and fled the room. Elbowing her way through the hall, she burst into the kitchen and thrust the tray into another woman's hands. She pushed through the door to the backyard, only to find the garden equally occupied. A stifled sob rose up in her clenched throat.

Robert appeared at her arm. "Come with me." He grasped her hand and ducked to the right, steering Abby into the dark gap between the houses. Dead leaves crunched underfoot as they scurried into the shady passage.

Ragged breaths squeaked in Abby's chest and she pressed her hand against her throat to stop the plaintive sound.

Robert placed a hand on her back. "Deep breaths, slowly now."

She shook, her chest heaving. "You—you startled me."

"I know, I'm sorry."

Calm down. Abby drew a long breath and concentrated on exhaling slowly. As she did so, the trembling eased. She glanced up at Robert's face, the sight bringing a fresh surge of pain. "Why are you here?"

He took a step back, about all he could manage in the confined space between the houses. "I was invited."

She glanced down at the decaying leaves. Nothing could grow in this dark space, not even weeds. "Of course. How silly of me."

He blew a long breath out between his lips. "Abby, I don't know what to say." His eyes held an unspoken invitation.

Abby stepped forward, his magnetic draw tugging at her body. How simple it would be to lay her head on his chest, allow his strong arms to support her. She turned her shoulders away, brushing a hand across the crumbs on her apron. "My sister is dead. There's nothing left to say."

His brows drew low. He reached a hand toward her.

Abby backed, angling toward the yard. "I don't think this is appropriate, Dr. King."

Robert yanked his fingers away like a schoolboy who'd had his knuckles rapped. "I—I'm sorry."

"Sorry for what, exactly?" Abby's throat ached. "Sorry you reached for my hand? Sorry you kissed me?" She choked as the words spewed forth. "Or sorry you didn't save my sister?"

His jaw clenched, cheek twitching. "I'm sorry . . ." his voice dropped to a whisper, "for all of it. I'm sorry I hurt you."

Eyes stinging, Abby grabbed a handful of her gown, twining the glossy fabric around her fingers—the almond-green forever obscured by black dye. "Yes, well, I'm sorry I ever met you." She hurried back into the crowded house, where she could hide in the crowd of well-wishers, cascading tears a welcomed and expected behavior as the sister of the deceased.

Robert's stomach twisted as Abby dashed back to the gathering, the black gown whispering around her ankles. He remained in the quiet crevice between the houses, away from the prying eyes and whispered words. His heart had drawn him to the funeral even as his stomach churned with shame. Everyone knew the part he'd played. People smiled and nodded, but few spoke to him. What would they say? "Oh, yes, *you're* the one . . ."

He rested against the house, his head falling back against the boards. A long-legged spider scuttled across the wall opposite, dragging a silken thread behind. Robert closed his eyes, trying not to think of the threads he had used to pull Gerald into this debacle.

"Leukemia? Really?" Robert's own voice echoed in his mind. *"She could be a candidate for our study. Have you examined her?"* How the blood had pulsed through his veins, shivers of excitement crossing his skin. The opportunity for research, for glory, all within his grasp.

Robert sank down along the wall, crouching on his heels and leaning against the house for strength. Had he really brought them here, to this moment? Abby's accusing eyes left a scorched hole in his heart. He lowered his face into his hands, burying himself in the grief.

In the dark bedroom, Abby slipped off the dress, letting it puddle in a black pool on the floor, the sight of her white petticoat a welcome relief. Reaching down, she lifted the gown and clutched it to her face. The faint aroma of perspiration and grief had replaced the fragrance of Cecelia's perfume among the threads. She shook out the fabric and opened the wardrobe, prepared to hide the dress until tomorrow.

The cabinet seemed more spacious than normal. Abby thumbed through the remaining garments, a cry rising in her chest. She flung the gown into the wardrobe and rushed from the room.

"Mama?" She hurried down the hall and knocked on the door to her mother's bedchamber before flinging it open. "Where are Cecelia's things?"

Mama sat in the wooden rocker, her blond hair hanging over her shoulders like a golden curtain, glimmering in the lamplight. A gilt hairbrush rested on her lap. She didn't bother to turn her gaze, just rocked slowly, staring at a portrait of sunflowers over the bedstead.

Dressed only in her undergarments, Abby knelt at her mother's feet like a small child.

Mama sighed and glanced down, eyes filling. Reaching out a hand, she touched Abby's head. "When will you start taking care of your hair, Abigail? You should be brushing until it shines. Every single night. Turn around."

Unsettled by the glazed look in her mother's eyes, Abby adjusted her position, the wood floor biting against her knees, and leaned back against her mother's legs. The familiar admonishment had been a standard in her home for years, but now she couldn't remember the last time her mother had uttered the words.

The strokes of the brush yanked against her hair, the bristles grinding against her scalp. "Mama, where are Cecelia's dresses?"

The rhythm of the brushing faltered before continuing. "Aunt Mae took your sister's things to the attic." The words barely stirred the air. "She thought it better for us not to be faced with them."

A burning sensation gripped Abby's chest. She reached out and grabbed her mother's wrist, halting the brush mid-stroke. "What if I want to see them?"

Mama sat back in the chair, lowering the brush to her lap. "It's past time for bed, Abigail. You can finish brushing in your room."

Abby rose up on her knees. Placing her hands on Mama's, she blinked back tears. She gazed at her with new eyes—taking note of lines and shadows she'd never noticed before, as if losing Cecelia had aged her overnight. "Good night, Mama."

Abby struggled to her feet, her long white underskirt twisting around her ankles. She yanked it out of the way of her feet. If she were to fall, she wasn't sure she'd ever wish to rise. Pacing back toward her room, she paused at the steps leading up to the attic. Bits and pieces of their life—locked behind closed doors. If only she could lock her feelings away so easily.

17

Thursday, October 19, 1905

*A*bby gripped her brother's hand as they strolled through Golden Gate Park. Davy tugged against Abby's arm every step of the way, her elbow aching like a rusty hinge. The morning air, thick with fog, dampened the wisps of hair escaping from her half-hearted attempt at style. Leaving the pebbled walkway behind, she set out across the grass, Davy's feet doing double-time while hers dragged. The green of the park mocked her homesickness. She didn't want manicured lawns and man-made ponds—the imperfect attempts of city-dwellers to enrich and embrace the natural world. If she couldn't have her peach trees, she wouldn't have any.

"Hurry up, Abby." Davy squeezed her fingers. "Uncle Gerald's meeting us at the lake."

Sighing, she quickened the pace. "It's Cousin Gerald, Davy. He's not your uncle."

"He says he bought me a new boat."

"Yes." Abby bit her tongue rather than spew any harsh words. Davy had spoken of little else all morning, his relentless voice drowning all other thoughts until she consented to escort him to the park. She took a deep breath, wiggling her shoulders to release the tension building in her neck. Two weeks had passed since Cecelia's funeral and life had settled into a predictable pattern of meals and sleep.

Gerald strolled by the stream, a wooden sailboat clutched under one arm.

Davy yanked his hand free and raced forward to meet him.

Her breathing eased, seeing her cousin without his good-looking shadow. Every time she laid eyes on Robert, a new thorn pressed into her heart.

"Hello, little man." Gerald's face brightened as Davy scampered up and grabbed onto his trouser legs.

Abby slowed her pace as Gerald walked her brother down to the creek's bank and set the small vessel afloat. She settled on a bench, wrapping her hands around her knees.

Not content to let the mild current power the craft, Davy pulled off his socks and shoes and waded in to push it along. Gerald climbed the rise and sat beside Abby, his long legs stretched out before him.

They sat for a long time without speaking, watching Davy splash in the chilly water.

Abby breathed slowly, conscious of the air filling her lungs and departing. Ever since witnessing Cecelia's final labored breaths, the process seemed a little less assured.

"Is there word from your father?" Gerald's voice broke into her thoughts.

"He says a few factories are hiring, but he wants to finish preparing the farm for sale." The words tasted like sawdust.

"My mother and I are delighted your family is staying in the city. I know it's little comfort to you, however."

Abby swallowed the snide remarks on her tongue. "It's very kind of you to let us stay on at Maple Manor. It's probably best for Mama. She's always missed city life."

Davy stumbled, plopping onto his seat in the shallow water. He struggled to his feet, short pants dripping.

Gerald chuckled. He turned to her, his blue eyes crinkling around the corners. "I realize you're not content to live in San Francisco, Cousin, but you must admit there are some benefits. Plays, operas, ballets, libraries, museums—endless opportunities. We'll introduce you to some of the finer aspects of city life." He cleared his throat. "After some time has passed, of course."

"There's not enough time in the world for me to feel like doing anything of the sort." Abby adjusted her hat, resetting the pin through her loose bun.

Gerald patted her arm. "In time. I understand you and Robert grew close while caring for Cecelia. Perhaps he would enjoy seeing the sights with us."

Acid burned in Abby's throat. "No, thank you."

Gerald's brow furrowed. "You can't blame him for what happened, Abby. He worked harder than anyone to save her."

Tears burned in her eyes, but she blinked them away. She couldn't tell her cousin she had almost missed saying good-bye to Cecelia because she was too busy kissing Robert in the park. She shrugged off the remembrance, but not before her lips tingled in defiance.

"There comes a point when the suffering becomes too dear and there is no hope in sight—"

"Stop." Abby pushed up to her feet, brushing a blade of grass from her skirt. "I have no desire to relive it."

Gerald stood. "What about Robert? How long will you punish him?"

"Punish him?" Her throat squeezed. "Who is being punished here? He received everything he wished—his precious little experiment. What about me? I lost my sister and my home. I lost everything." She took two stumbling steps backward. "I never want to hear Robert King's name again."

Abby marched to the edge of the stream. Davy had fallen forward, every stitch of his clothing now drenched. "Davy Fischer, get out of that muddy water!"

Davy glanced up, a pout dragging down his lower lip. "My boat!"

Locking hands on her hips, she shot him a glare. "You're supposed to be sailing the boat, not bathing."

Gerald stepped to the bank. "Come on, little man. Enough for today."

Her brother splashed through the water, droplets flying, as he pursued the toy bobbing against a small footbridge.

Abby walked out on the rough wooden surface, her footfalls ringing hollow. Bending down, she stretched her arm toward the craft, lingering just out of reach. She lowered herself to her knees and leaned forward.

"No—I'll get it!" Davy thrashed through the water, spraying her before crashing down on one knee and bursting out in howls.

Abby groaned. She stretched, her fingers closing on the top of the boat's sail, but the bow remained firmly wedged under the bridge. Twisting her arm, she tugged at the mast. The sail popped loose from the toy, tilting her off-balance. Arms flailing, Abby pitched forward, the muddy water closing over her head and rushing into her nose and mouth. She pushed up to her hands and knees in the muck, spluttering.

Cries silenced, Davy stood frozen, jaw hanging. Gerald rushed forward and grabbed her arm, helping her back onto the footbridge. "Are you all right?"

Abby shivered on the wooden deck, water running down in rivulets, her sodden shirtwaist and skirts sticking to her body. She shoved the boat under her arm and reached a hand up to straighten her hat, mud dribbling from the brim. "I'm perfect, Gerald. Just perfect."

Robert glanced out the tall windows of Gerald's third-story downtown office, the glorious view of Market Street obscured by the fog. Seven-year-old Janie Stevens sat on the high table, thin legs kicking a steady rhythm as they dangled in the air. Her mother hovered nearby, shiny red hair tucked under an enormous feathered hat.

Lifting the electric lamp, Robert shone it into the child's eyes and watched each pupil contract in turn. He placed the light on the table and ran careful fingers across her skull from back to front. He lightened his touch when he reached the goose egg on her forehead, hidden by a fringe of brown curls.

Robert perched on a stool and rolled his shoulders to loosen the aching muscles. "It looks like you survived another spill, Janie. But I think you ought to avoid riding your brother's bicycle without his permission."

The girl lifted her chin, wearing her bruises and scrapes like badges of honor. "He said he'd take me for a ride and didn't."

Mrs. Stevens crossed her arms atop her pregnant belly and tapped her foot. "Now Lucas doesn't have a bicycle for his delivery job, and you nearly broke your skull. When are you going to learn to act like a lady?"

Janie giggled, touching the swollen lump on her forehead. "Never, I hope."

Robert smiled as the irritated mother whisked her child from the office, his thoughts wandering back to Abby. Even dangling from a tree branch, the same glint of independence had shown in her eyes.

He stretched his back, grunting as the vertebrae popped. He hadn't slept well in weeks. His mind—his dreams—wouldn't allow it.

Robert scratched a few notes on Janie's chart before returning it to the oak cabinet in the back office. He peeked out into the empty waiting room, stomach rumbling. He hadn't even had time for lunch.

The door swung open, Gerald stepping in from the outer hall. "Is the coast clear?" His blond hair fell forward, unusually ruffled.

Robert let him pass before hurrying to lock the door. "Yes, no thanks to you. Where have you been all day?"

Gerald's shoes squished across the hard floor. "Doing a little sailing." He hung his hat on the coat tree, settled down in the desk chair, and stripped off his shoes and socks.

Gathering some paperwork from the desk, Robert scowled. "I'm taking care of your patients so you can go boating?"

"Isn't that why I have an assistant? So I can wrangle a day off once in a while?" Gerald draped his dripping socks across the top of the radiator. "I took my cousin Davy to the park. We had a little accident with his toy boat." He raised his eyebrows. "You think this is bad, you should see Abby."

Robert froze at the mention of her name. *If only.*

Gerald flopped into the chair and propped his bare feet on the desk, a smirk crossing his face. "She was spitting like an alley cat after someone tossed a bucket of water on it."

Robert sorted the papers and returned them to the cabinet, careful not to respond. If he opened his mouth, he knew his voice would betray his feelings—emotions he had vowed to forget.

His friend leaned back, hands behind his head, his gaze piercing. "She's grieving, Robert."

Robert reopened the drawer, shuffling through more papers even though he could no longer see the words and figures.

Gerald sat forward. "She's going to need your friendship, if nothing else."

Robert slammed the drawer shut. "What do you want me to do? She won't even see me." A potted plant atop the cabinet wobbled.

"Don't let her drive you off. Abby needs to know you still care, no matter what."

Running a hand through his hair, Robert shook his head. "She doesn't want me around. She'll never forgive me. Frankly, I'm not sure I deserve to be forgiven."

Gerald sprang from the chair and paced across the room, his feet slapping against the tile floor. "What are you talking about? You cannot take blame here. You don't deserve it and you have no right to it. Cecelia lived months longer than expected because of your research. The experiment was a success, Robert."

Robert's stomach twisted. "A success?"

Lines formed on Gerald's forehead. "She was my cousin. I hated to watch her die. But we did what we could, and what we learned will help other patients."

"How can I even think of other patients? Every time I see you or Abby, my heart breaks all over again."

Gerald paused. A tentative smile tugged at the corners of his lips. "Why do you think I stayed out of the office all day?"

Robert leaned against the cabinet, arms folded across his chest. "Because you're lazy and you'd rather watch your assistant do the work?"

His friend shot him a withering glance. "Because you needed to get back up on the horse before you forget how to ride. Tomorrow, you go back to the lab. I've got two more patients waiting for your X-ray expertise."

Robert's knees weakened and he slumped into the chair. "What?" His voice trembled. "No."

"The hospital board has heard about our work. They've granted us $4,000 to continue the research and patients are already lining up." Reaching for his still-damp shoes, Gerald pulled them on over his bare feet.

Robert sat forward. "Four thousand?"

"This is what you wanted. Remember? Are you going to shut down the research because you lost one patient? How about the others who are in need of this technology?"

"It wasn't just one patient. It was Cecelia. I pressed you into taking the case, and—"

"And you were right. The X-rays bought her some additional time." Gerald rubbed a hand across his chin. He lifted the socks from the radiator and rolled them into a ball. "I ache for my cousin and her family, but we still have work to do. It would dishonor Cecelia's memory to give up now." He tucked the socks into his coat pocket before heading for the door. Pausing on the threshold, he glanced back at Robert. "So, tomorrow, I'll handle the office appointments. You will meet with the patients at the hospital. And thank the board for their generosity."

Robert rested both elbows on the desk pad, letting his head fall forward into his hands.

Abby leaned against the bay window frame and gazed at the evening sky only half-listening as Great Aunt Mae spouted words of comfort. Gerald's home had an enviable view of the sunset, nearby homes and chimneys silhouetted against the brilliant pink and purple, as if the sky pulled on its finest nightclothes.

Teacups rattled as Aunt Mae gathered the remnants of their dessert. "I'm sure the Lord understands our grief, but I imagine He wants—"

"I really don't care what He wants." Abby sighed.

Aunt Mae lowered herself into a gold mohair chair, her mouth agape. "Abigail!"

Abby bit her lip. She shouldn't have spoken the callous words to her religious-minded aunt, but her heart refused to be silenced. "He took my sister. And my home."

Aunt Mae rose from her chair, padded up behind, and laid a hand on the small of Abby's back. "God has a plan for you, dear. And right now, it includes San Francisco. We don't always understand the Lord's will for us, but His plan is always perfect."

Burning coals lodged in Abby's chest. Hadn't Cecelia said something along those lines on the day she died? Her death had ripped a hole in the fabric of their family—of their lives. No divine plan could stitch it together again. Abby turned from the window, her eyes scrutinizing the fine room with its wine-colored damask paper, a bouquet of dried roses tucked into a blue-green Bristol vase, a patterned rug cushioning their steps. The space had been designed to protect the inhabitants from the pressures of the outside world. And yet, its shelter was but a façade. Abby balled her fists, the tips of her nails digging into the tender flesh of her palms—growing softer every day she spent away from her trees. "Do you really believe He willed this?"

The amber light cast a rosy glow upon Aunt Mae's face, softening the lines hiding around her mouth. "What I know is I couldn't survive my grief without the Lord's strength."

Abby pulled away and sank into a nearby chair. "If this is God's plan, I don't want anything to do with it."

A strained silence fell over the room. Aunt Mae remained at the window, as if searching the clouds for words of comfort. "Give it time, child. You're hurting now—we all are. But give God time to show you His will. He can bring good from bad, blessings from curses. If anyone understands, it's me."

Letting her head fall back against the cushion, Abby gazed at the older woman's stooped shoulders, her age-speckled hand braced against the back of a tall chair. The words made no sense, bouncing off of Abby's raw heart, but she didn't ask her aunt to explain. The last thing she wanted was more talk of God's will. "I should return home. I can help put Davy to bed."

Aunt Mae nodded, the glow fading as the sun lowered in the sky. "I have a book I want you to read. But I'm not going to give it to you just yet. After a little time has passed, perhaps."

Abby retrieved her hat and shawl. The evening air had taken on a chill as of late and she couldn't wait to wrap the knitted garment around her shoulders and close herself up against the world. If Aunt Mae's book was about God, Abby certainly was in no hurry to read it.

18

*R*obert spread his fingers and pressed his hand to the table, using a broom handle to reach the X-ray control panel. He'd been spoiled by Abby's capable assistance in the lab. He needed a better system for controlling the device while testing the radiation strength. But it would entail another long night of wiring. "I should have been an electrician."

A woman's voice floated in the open doorway. "Doctor or electrician, they're both in high demand these days."

Robert jerked his gaze upward, half-expecting to see Abby traipsing through the door.

Nurse Maguire cocked her head, a clipboard balanced on one hip, her white cap floating on a sea of red curls. "Would you like some help, Dr. King?"

Lowering the wooden handle, Robert stepped away from the table. Of course, Abby wasn't there. *Why would she be?* "I could use another pair of hands—well, one hand, actually. Don't you usually work on the fourth floor?"

Nurse Maguire strode inside and took the broom from his fingers, her blinding-white apron cinched tight around a wasp-thin waist. "I'm filling in for Nurse Edgar."

Robert cleared his throat and refocused his eyes on the row of controls. If she tripped, she might snap in half. She was clearly a change from Nurse Edgar whose waist more closely resembled a bumblebee. Or a rhinoceros.

Frowning at the counter cluttered with glass plates and boxes of coils, the nurse clucked her tongue. "I'm surprised she hasn't done some straightening up in here."

"I think Nurse Edgar feared she might stumble over Mr. Hyde or Frankenstein's monster." Robert opened the metal casing on the device and checked the wiring.

"You don't seem much like Dr. Jekyll or Dr. Frankenstein." The woman picked up a burned-out tube and peered through the smoky glass. "Though, after what we've heard about the experiments you've been conducting, it does make one wonder. I'd be happy to help you tidy up a bit." She cocked her head, perusing him with catlike green eyes. "The board thinks you can walk on water, or so I hear." She laid the tube on a rolling cart and turned to face Robert.

Robert stared at the dials, not wanting to think about the board. As soon as he'd stepped into the hospital this morning, one of the trustees cornered him in the hall, requesting a meeting. Robert ran his thumb across the row of switches powering the coils.

"They're saying you're the next Pierre Curie." Her pale brows lifted and she smiled, revealing a dimple in one pink cheek. "But you don't have a Marie, so the comparison only goes so far." She cleared her throat. "I'd be honored to assist you in your research, Doctor."

Robert stomach tightened. "You do know I lost my last patient, right?"

The young woman's smile vanished. "And the fact you care so deeply shows what a wonderful doctor you are." Her fingers brushed his elbow as she leaned in. "Now, what can I do?"

Robert gestured to the table, eager to create some space between his nose and her musky cologne. "Place your forearm on the table and hold very still."

The nurse rolled back her sleeve and laid a milky white arm against the smooth surface. "Like so?"

Averting his eyes, he nodded. "It will do, yes, and because X-rays can penetrate clothing, you won't need to do so next time."

"The newspaper said they can see through a woman's clothing, read her thoughts, and expose her darkest desires—but I don't believe such rubbish." Her lip curled in a saucy grin.

Robert gritted his teeth. "You need to hold still." *And close your mouth.*

As the day wore on Nurse Maguire returned to other duties, much to Robert's relief. He spent the afternoon assessing his new patients, each brimming over with unrealistic hopes. The first, a sixty-two-year-old banker presenting with a carcinoma on the back of his neck. The second, a mother of four whose thyroid sported a grape-sized tumor. When the final patient walked in, clinging to her mother's hand, it took all of Robert's self-discipline not to flee the laboratory. The five-year-old girl suffered from leukemia—not so different from Cecelia Fischer, just much younger.

All three cases were hopeless. Robert's heart ached as he cleaned and organized the equipment for the next round of treatments. He remembered practicing surgeries on cadavers back in medical school. The three patients he'd seen today were little more than living cadavers, donating their bodies to science, enticed with the hope of a healing touch.

His father would say true healing came from God, and doctors were only His instruments. He'd often spent precious time praying with his dying patients, whispering words into their ears even when they were beyond hearing. How had he managed to walk the line between science and religion with such grace? His father's quiet faith never seemed at odds with his profession.

Medical school had hammered Robert's belief system into submission in a few short years. To mention God before one's instructors or classmates brought instant mockery and humiliation. He learned to put God in his back pocket, or better yet—leave Him at church where He belonged.

Robert glared at the dark glass tubes holding a false promise of life for dying patients. His father might have been right. Perhaps someday doctors would achieve the cure for cancer, but it was a long way off. Too many variables. How could they track the dosages? Test the effectiveness? Quantify the results?

He dropped the burned-out tube in the trash bin, the sound of crunching glass matching his mood. If he had his way, he'd cast this research into the bin with the rest. Unfortunately, the hospital board had other ideas.

Science had failed him. Each patient reminded him of the Fischer girls. One he had tried to save. The other he tried not to love.

And with both, he'd failed.

19

The winter crawled past with the San Francisco fogs rolling in and out like a suffocating wet blanket over Abby's soul. The dark days dragged, brightened only by Abby's weekly visits with Aunt Mae. The woman had a knack for teasing a smile from Abby, and she always had a task waiting.

This early spring day, they had spent the afternoon weeding and pruning in the lush garden behind Gerald's house. Abby uncovered the shoots of some bearded irises, overgrown and tangled, languishing in the tiny spot. Aunt Mae used a sharp knife to divide the roots, bagging up several for Abby to take back to Maple Manor—or home, as Mama had begun referring to it.

Weary after her long walk back up the hill, Abby plopped down in the one bright spot not obscured by the massive maple tree. Pushing her gardening trowel into the soft ground, she watched as the dirt crumbled, the dark particles of earth rearranging as they fell. A rich, musky scent rose from the broken soil, filled with the promise of new life.

She blinked back tears, torn apart by the very things she loved. Abby drove the spade deeper, pushing past the rich topsoil into the lighter-colored layer beneath. Reaching down into the hole, she fingered the cold mud, its slick texture clinging to her skin. The image of Cecelia buried in this damp clay chilled her heart. How could God have let this happen?

Shaking her hands, Abby flung the muck back into the hole and continued her work. After loosening the topsoil, she reached for the iris rhizomes and situated them in their new home. It wasn't the right time of year to be transplanting iris, but they might find a way to survive. Leaning down, she spoke to the stubby, green shoots. "Do you feel as out-of-place here as I do?" She tamped the dirt down with her palms.

She felt as dead as those rhizomes appeared, and even so, they were sending up greenery. Abby ran her fingers over the ground, smoothing the surface around the stalks. Would they bloom in this new place? She glanced up at the overhanging limbs of the maple, heavy with buds. Would there be enough light to help them grow?

Sitting back on her knees, she brushed back a loose lock of hair with a dirt-crusted hand. Back home, the fruit trees should be preparing to burst forth into flowers. Early spring always brought joy. The peach trees adorned themselves in gowns of tender pink blossoms and seemed to dance with delight every time the wind caught the limbs, sometimes sending petals flying like snowflakes.

Abby closed her eyes, imagining her orchard, arrayed in its finest. In her daydream, she strolled between the trees, stopping to touch one and then another, relishing the heavy drapery of blooms dripping from the tender branch tips.

Hearing steps behind her, Abby struggled to her feet, mud clinging to her fingers.

Robert leaned against the fence, his arms draped across the boards, his face thinner than she remembered. "I thought I might find you here. Gerald's mother said you could use some help with the garden." His warm eyes beseeched her, like a dog begging to come in from the cold.

Leave it to Aunt Mae. Abby took a step back, her shoe squishing into the soil she'd just turned. She swiped a hand across her damp cheek, the scent of dirt heavy on her skin. *I just smeared mud on my face, didn't I?* "I've finished the planting, thank you."

Robert wrapped his fingers around one of the pickets, his brown derby emphasizing the dark shadows under his eyes. "Ah, good. I don't suppose I'd have been much of an assistant anyway."

Abby dug for a handkerchief, but found none. "Like me in the X-ray lab." She paused, the words sending a tremor through her insides. "Excuse me—" her voice faltered. "I must go."

His pinched brow and shining eyes gouged at her heart. Abby ground the sole of her shoe into the topsoil, brushed muddy hands across her apron, and hurried to the house.

I can't. I just can't.

Part 2

20

Wednesday, April 18, 1906
4:25 a.m.

An alarm bell cracked Robert's dream into a million shards of lost images. He jerked upright, flinging blankets to the side. *Fire wagon?* He launched to his feet, landing with a thump on the rag rug beside the bed.

He swayed for a moment as his senses recovered enough for him to locate the sound in the darkness. With a groan, Robert swiped the clock from the nightstand and silenced the ear-splitting bell. Hands shaking, Robert sank onto the mattress, blood pulsing in time to the rhythm of his heart.

A faint glow from the streetlamp outside filtered through the window of his third-story bedroom. Robert tipped the clock face toward the light and squinted. Four-twenty-five? He pinched the bridge of his nose before rubbing clumsy fingers across his eyelids. Returning the timepiece to the stand, Robert fell back in the blankets, stretching his legs down until his toes brushed the end of the wooden bedstead. He rolled onto his stomach, reaching an arm to each side and stretching his fingers around the edges of the narrow mattress, like a starfish clinging to a tide-swept rock.

With a groan, he lifted his head, blinking his eyes to clear his vision. Early rounds. Who invented such a ludicrous idea?

"Abby?"

Wrapped in the fog of sleep, Abby snuggled deeper under the covers, ignoring the soft tick of the clock and the shuffling footsteps.

"Abby?" The high-pitched voice cut through her bleary mind.

Abby clenched her eyes shut and pulled the covers over her head. "Too early," she mumbled into the blankets. "Too early." Gentle breathing tickled her ear. She pulled the covers down to her chin. Moonlight gleamed through the tall bedroom windows and shimmered in her brother's eyes.

He leaned close. "Are you awake?"

Abby turned and pressed her face into the bedding, the feather pillow absorbing her frustrated groan. "Yes." She took a deep breath, sucking air through the down. "What do you want?"

He shook the edge of the bed. "Can I sleep here with you?"

"Shh, yes. Come on." She reached down and grabbed his wrist, hauling him up into the warm bed.

He bounced on the mattress, the frame squeaking in protest.

"Hush, Davy. Don't wake Mama. Be quiet."

"Mama's singing." His voice chirruped like a morning songbird in the quiet room as he cuddled into Abby's side.

"Mama doesn't want to sing to you now. She's sleeping." She grasped his icy fingers and tried to rub some warmth into them. "Davy, why are you hands sticky? What have you been into?"

His sweet breath flooded her face. "Nothing." Red smears decorated the corners of his mouth.

"Have you been eating jam?"

Davy stuck his gummy fingers in his mouth.

"Oh, sure, now you're quiet," Abby sighed. "Mama won't be pleased. We're down to just a few jars."

Abby fought the urge to roll over and go back to sleep, but she couldn't leave a sticky mess in the bed. And for Davy's sake, it'd be better if she hid the evidence in the kitchen before morning. She pushed back the warm blankets. "Don't touch anything, Davy." She leveled a finger at his sticky face. "Sit still."

Abby slipped her arms into the sleeves of her wrapper, pulling it over her nightdress. Walking on tiptoes to keep the soles of her feet off the cold floor, Abby crossed to the washstand and dampened a washcloth.

Davy's eyelids drooped by the time she returned to the bed.

"Oh, no you don't. If I'm awake—you're awake." She scrubbed his face with the clammy rag as he batted at her wrists. "It's what you get for waking me in the middle of the night with a sticky face." She seized the flailing hands and wiped them clean, too.

Davy twisted his body and pushed his face into the pillow.

"I sure hope I got it all and you're not using my pillow as a napkin." She tugged the covers and flung them over his head. "I'll be back in a minute. I want to make sure you didn't leave the kitchen in a mess."

Moonlight peeked through the kitchen window as Abby stole down the steep back stairs, skipping the creaky third step. The kitchen looked untouched. No cabinets stood open, no sticky spoons littered the table or the floor. At least her brother had been discreet about his nighttime snacking.

Abby wandered through the kitchen and into the dining room. The front parlor door stood ajar. Abby tiptoed to the door and peeked inside. The glass jar lay on its side under a small corner table, its lid reflecting the moonlight. A gentle creak broke the stillness. Abby froze, her breath catching in her chest.

Mama sat in Grandma Etta's rocking chair, pulled close to the large bay windows facing the street. Eyes squeezed shut, the moonlight glistened off of her damp cheeks. The family Bible lay open on her lap, her mouth moving, lips forming quiet words.

The familiar hymn floated across the room. "Come thou fount of every blessing, tune my heart to sing Thy grace. Streams of mercy, never ceasing, call for songs of loudest praise."

Abby's heart ached as the tender notes transported her back to Cecelia's last days. Wrapping arms around her middle, she shivered in the dark hall.

Mama's voice quavered on the last note and she drew a long, tremulous breath, eyes still closed. "Father, we need those streams of mercy right now. You haven't stopped sending them, have you? I don't feel like praising You, and yet, it is what Your Word asks. Help me."

Hot tears welled up in Abby's eyes as she backed from the room. Cecelia's song. No one—not even Mama—should sing Cecelia's song. She held her breath all the way back up the stairs.

Flashes of white danced before her eyes—the nurses' gowns, the hospital walls, the bed linens, Robert's lab coat. She pushed away his image before her mind could travel to unwanted memories.

"Streams of mercy" hinted at misty-cool blues and living greens, like her farm home. There was no place for it here.

Davy lay curled on the bed, eyes closed, and his tiny eyelashes dark and unmoving against his fair skin.

A stone settled into Abby's stomach and she fell to her knees on the hard floor beside the bed, staring at her baby brother. *God could take him, too. God could take everything my heart loves.* Papa had left for the farm this morning—signing the final papers selling their home, her orchard, to strangers.

She laid her cheek on the cool mattress, arms spread across the bedding. The image of her father slaving from dawn till dusk inside a dim factory sent shivers across her skin. It didn't seem right.

Trembling, Abby pushed up to her feet and slid under the covers, the wrap still hugging her shoulders. She slipped an arm under Davy and scooted close, stealing a portion of his warmth. Abby's eyes stung with tears and she slammed them shut, burying her face against the pillow.

21

5:12 a.m.

*A*bby opened her eyes, Davy's fine hair tickling her cheek and the first hints of morning light drifting in the bedroom window. Davy lay like a fallen log on her left arm, leaving her fingers tingling.

An eerie howl twisted through the morning air. The neighbor's dog? Abby lifted her head. The shadows seemed to be holding their breath, as if someone stood nearby. Slipping her arm free, Abby sat upright, a shiver spreading through her body. Her teeth chattered in the early morning chill.

She flexed her hand and shook it, willing the blood back into her fingers. The bed rattled and she froze so as not to rouse her brother. She had hoped for a few moments of silence before Davy awoke, disturbing the peace with his endless chatter.

A wagon rumbled by outside and a second dog added his baying to the first, rising in pitch until it became an unearthly wail sending prickles racing across Abby's skin. The tremor continued. She straightened, her heart rate quickening as she grabbed at the iron bed frame, its vibrations tickling through her fingers.

Earthquake.

❦

Robert walked the quiet wards, coffee cup in hand. The white walls gleamed under the harsh lights. He needed to prepare the X-ray laboratory for the day, but first he wanted to check on Mrs. McCurty. After yesterday's fever, he wasn't eager to take her down for treatment unless she'd shown some improvement overnight.

Taking a gulp of the dark brew, he nodded to the duty nurse before stepping into the cancer ward. Eight beds crowded the small room, each one occupied by a sleeping patient. Robert glanced over at the bed where Cecelia Fischer had slept during her stay, now filled by a portly woman with several gold rings on her pudgy fingers. Her mouth hung open in sleep, gasping snores cutting through the morning stillness.

He walked to the far end where Mrs. McCurty lay curled on her side on the narrow bed closest to the window. Her brown hair tucked into a lace sleeping cap, she looked much younger than her forty-five years. Her lids fluttered open as Robert approached and a faint smile played at the corners of her lips. "There you are, Doctor. The pretty red-headed nurse said you'd be by early and here you are."

Robert set down his cup and reached for her chart. "How are you feeling this morning?"

"Much better. A little stronger every day, just like you promised."

I made no promise. He placed the back of his hand against her forehead. "I think the fever's broken. It's a good sign. We might get you down for some X-ray treatment today after all."

She sighed. "The good Lord's smiling down on me."

Clearing his throat, Robert glanced at the woman's charts. Her faith was admirable, considering what she'd been through so far. And perhaps misplaced, from the look of her tests. He thumbed through the papers.

A faint buzzing caught Robert's attention. Searching for the source of the sound, his gaze settled on his coffee cup, vibrating on the bedside table.

Mrs. McCurty pushed up onto her elbows. "What is happening?"

The floor pulsed under Robert's feet and he clutched the head-board with one hand. His chest tightened. "Only a little tremor . . . usually lasts just a few seconds."

She glanced up at him, her green eyes widening.

Abby's stomach knotted. There had been several small quakes in her lifetime, and each time her heart raced. She let go of the bed frame, digging her hands into the covers and pulling them up to her chin as if they afforded some type of protection.

The bed shook and quivered, shifting across the wooden floor. Abby braced herself as the tremors multiplied, the low table scut-tling away from the bed like a spider running from a rolled-up news-paper. A row of decorative glass bottles on the bookshelf provided music for their own strange dance, shivering and glancing off one another in an awkward rhythm.

With a sudden jerk, the bookcase teetered and the bottles crashed to the floor, books raining from the middle shelves. The rattling grew to a roar, like the sound of a locomotive puffing into the sta-tion. A deep groan cut through the air, as if the house complained about the movement.

Davy whimpered, his eyes fluttering open.

Abby grabbed him with both hands, hugging him tight to her chest, unable to tear her gaze from the alien spectacle.

The wardrobe waltzed sideways. The massive piece of furniture tipped, hanging mid-air long enough for Abby to scramble up onto the pillows, tugging Davy along. It crushed the footboard, tumbling Abby to the floor, her brother landing on her chest with a screech. The doors sprang open, spewing clothing onto the ruined bed.

Scooting backward on her rear, Abby pressed her back against the bedroom door, shoving Davy between her knees and covering his head with her arms. *Deliver us from evil . . .* Words from the ancient prayer jumped, unbidden, into her mind.

The shaking slowed. Abby's heart thumped as she lifted her head, surveying the scene in her room. She relaxed her grip on Davy, placing a hand on the floor to push herself up.

A second jerk knocked her off balance, her brother's shrill scream cutting through the air. She yanked him close, burying his face in her chest. Abby braced herself against the floor on elbows and knees, keeping him covered with her body and watching in terror as the furniture in the room began to rearrange.

A massive crack crawled up the wall, chunks of plaster tearing loose. Like a chick pushing through its cracked shell, a cluster of bricks ripped through the ceiling and clattered down onto the floor and across the bed.

White plaster dust mingled with black soot in a choking cloud filling the room. Abby coughed and gasped, pressing her brother against the floor. This house was going to be their grave.

Robert bent his knees to absorb the shock as the vibrations accelerated into rhythmic pulsing. He gripped Mrs. McCurty's reaching hand, hoping his touch could assuage her fear. Screams and cries rose from the nearby beds as the room shook and rattled, the noise deepening to a guttural roar.

Plaster fell from the ceiling, grazing Robert on the shoulder. He spun on his heel, watching the room dissolve into chaos. The healthier patients clambered from their beds, cowering on the floor and crawling under tables. The infirm covered their heads with arms.

Robert turned back to the woman shrinking in the bed. Scooping her up in his arms, he pulled her to the floor, covering her with his chest and shoulders. Cracks appeared, like some invisible child drawing jagged lines on the wall. The window glass rippled in its frame before the surface shattered, sending splinters dancing across the shuddering floor.

In panic, Robert wove his hands under Mrs. McCurty's arms and pulled her backward, further into the room as the floor surged beneath them. A vicious jolt knocked him off-balance and he landed hard on his backside, the terrified woman falling against him, pinning his legs.

Her screams tore at his ears and he followed her gaze to where the outside wall undulated with the rhythm of the shaking. Robert yanked his leg free, a jab of pain burning through his knee. He scrambled backward, the motion unsettling his stomach. He reached for his patient's arm just as the outer wall gave way and broke up before his eyes. Clouds of dust rose from the opening, the floor now angling downward toward the gap.

Lunging forward, Robert snatched at her arm, as a cracking sound over his head drew his eyes. He lifted a hand to block the falling tiles, the crushing weight smashing him to the floor, pain bursting through his head.

❧

The movement slowed and an eerie silence descended, broken only by Abby's ragged breaths and her brother's muffled whimpers. One last book, teetering on the edge of a shelf, thudded to the floor like an exclamation point on the morning's activity.

"Mama?" Davy hiccupped the word in between whimpering cries.

"Abby? Davy?" Mama's voice wafted down the hall.

Abby pushed up to her knees, trembling. She heaved in a couple of gulping sobs, but the motion seemed far away, as if it belonged to someone else.

The door pushed against her hip. "Abby? Are you all right?"

Scooting out of the way, Abby grabbed the knob and yanked. It opened about two inches and stuck against the frame. Mama's face appeared in the crack. "Abby?"

Stumbling to her feet, Abby pulled frantically at the knob.

Mama shoved from the other side, bursting into the room.

"Mama!" Davy scrambled up from the floor and into Mama's legs, knocking her back into the hall.

"David! Abigail!" Mama swept Davy up in her arms, a black smudge on her cheek. She reached a trembling hand, pulling Abby into the embrace.

Abby's strength crumbled as she leaned against her mother's side, the terror of the past few moments settling deep into her bones. She gazed at the bed, a thick coating of plaster and bricks lying where she and her brother had been sleeping. The knots in her stomach matched the mess in her room.

Mama settled Davy on her hip and squeezed Abby's arm. "Are you hurt? There's a nasty scratch on your cheek."

"No, Mama." Abby's voice cracked.

Mama pulled Davy close, tucking his head under her chin as she swayed back and forth, rocking him like a baby. "Goodness." A breathy laugh rumbled up from her chest. "I'm still shaking!" She held out her trembling hand.

Her laugh scratched like sandpaper on Abby's raw nerves.

As the dust-filled air curled around them, Mama patted Davy's back and sighed. "Thank you Lord, for Your mercy."

"What?" The word exploded from Abby's mouth before she could catch it. "What?"

Mama pushed back a lock of blond hair fallen across her face. "We've been shaken, Abby, but we are all safe."

Davy murmured into her shoulder, "Thanky God."

Mama squeezed him. "Yes. Well said, Davy."

Thank Him? Abby surveyed the broken mess of her room. *You can't be serious.*

22

*T*he pain searing through Robert's head drew him to reluctant wakefulness. *Where am I?* He opened his eyes, grit falling from his lashes, his arm hidden under a mess of splintered wood and chunks of plaster. Groaning, Robert shifted his weight and wrenched the limb free, debris clattering to the floor. His chest ached, but breathing didn't seem overly difficult. *No broken ribs, then.*

He touched the back of his throbbing head, his fingers smearing through warm, sticky blood. *Not a dangerous amount. On the outside, anyway.* He brushed away the thought of a possible intracranial hemorrhage—not much he could do until he figured out what had happened. Robert braced an arm under his body and pushed upward, the room spinning slowly. He shook his head once, ears buzzing like a mass of hornets.

Robert wiped a hand across his eyes, gazing around the room. Bricks, wood, plaster and medical equipment lay in haphazard piles around him, illuminated by the weak sunlight filtering in—*shouldn't there be a wall there?* He swallowed, fighting the nausea building in his stomach. The memory of the shaking trickled back into his mind, shivers coursing through his limbs. Chilled morning air poured in through the gap at the end of the ward. Another few feet and he would have been on the ground, three stories down.

Twisting his head to glance behind him, a stab of pain gripped his neck. He lowered his hand to touch the vertebrae. *Thank God, they're still there.* An unseemly laugh rose from the depths of his chest. *I definitely need to get my head checked.*

The beds and tables lay scattered about in the room, but the patients seemed out of danger, though some were moaning or crying out in fear. He must have received the worst here by the window. Now, why was he there?

Mrs. McCurty.

Robert's throat clenched, the taste of blood and dust mingling with sour acid surging up from his stomach. Thrusting upward to his knees, he dug his arms into the rubble. "Mrs. McCurty?" His voice crackled as if he'd swallowed fragments of brick. He pressed the heel of his hand against his forehead, but continued raking through the jumble of debris.

Voices cried out behind him, preventing him from hearing any sounds from the pile. Robert flung bits of brick and wood out of the way, sharp edges digging into his skin. He located Mrs. McCurty's legs and worked upwards, pushing aside the rubbish covering his patient. Bruised and scraped, she stirred. He pressed two fingers under the angle of her jaw. Her carotid pulse seemed steady, and Robert sat back on his heels.

But, what of the remainder of the hospital? The city?

His breath caught in his chest. *What of Abby?*

5:28 a.m.

Abby's teeth chattered as she dug through the pile of clothes in front of the fallen wardrobe, no longer trusting the floor beneath her feet. She pulled off her nightgown, holding it uncertainly with the tips of her fingers before dropping it onto the pile. She shivered in corset and drawers and poked about for clean stockings. Everything was covered with plaster dust and soot. She located a pair and gave them a few fierce shakes, sending fragments flying. With no place to sit, Abby balanced on one foot and wiped the filth from her bare sole before stuffing grimy toes in the stocking.

Hurry, hurry, hurry.

She didn't bother tightening the corset laces. Not even Mama would notice on a day like this. Abby shimmied into a petticoat, skirt, shirtwaist, and apron, the clothes gritty against her skin. She jammed her feet into her shoes, fastening the buttons in record speed.

Grabbing her brush, Abby dashed into the hall, bumping against the splintered doorframe in her haste. *The locket.* Changing directions, she scampered back into the room. She crawled across the ruined bed, knocking off bricks and chunks of plaster. The nightstand stood wedged in the corner, resting on three legs, balanced against the walls. Abby settled it into place before pulling open the small drawer. Heart pounding in her ears, Abby's fingers scrabbled around the empty drawer. With a cry, she yanked it from the slot. Cecelia's locket popped free and flew through the air, landing in a pile of chalky white plaster.

Abby stooped to retrieve the necklace. Blowing softly to remove the dust from its delicate gold design, she opened the face. Running a finger over the tiny, coiled braid, the golden strands of hair tugged and clung to her heart like ivy on a tree trunk. Abby closed the cover and pulled the chain over her head, tucking it inside her lace collar. She rested her fingers on the lump nestled against the base of her throat. The early morning sun filtered through the window, sending beams of light through the haze. A fevered trembling sank deep into her bones as the eerie silence contradicted the disarray in the room.

Knees wobbling, Abby stumbled down the steep rear stairs and burst out the back door. She stopped in the yard and turned to face the house, her heart thudding. From where she stood, the house appeared little changed. Except for the missing chimney and a few broken windows, the outside of the house looked no different than the day they had arrived.

Hurrying around to the front, Abby stared into the street. Neighbors wandered about like lost children, several wearing little more than dressing gowns. In the distance, a woman cried, her hysterics sending a chill through Abby's body. Mama's words about mercy took root—other families may not have been as fortunate. Had the earthquake been this severe back home? Could Papa be hurt? What about Aunt Mae and Gerald? Robert?

She returned to the back porch as Mama came out, gripping Davy's hand, both of them clean and dressed. Mama might have been ready to go to the market, except for her long braid and the tall stack of cooking pots balanced in the crook of her arm.

"I think we may need to cook outside for awhile, since the chimney is down. Things are bad enough, I don't intend to set Aunt Mae's house ablaze." She released Davy's hand and he bounced out into the yard. She glanced at the neighboring homes. "I hope everyone else is well." A shadow crossed her face.

Abby swallowed. "Papa?"

"I tried the telephone, but it doesn't seem to be working." She took a deep breath, blinking back tears. "We need to pray for him. I'm sure he's just as worried about us, Abby."

Mama put the cooking pots down near the brick garden path. "Perhaps Gerald and Robert can come by later and move the stove outside."

The mention of Robert's name sent a shiver through Abby. Where was he now?

"I'm going to gather some supplies. Will you stay here and watch your brother, please?" Mama climbed the steps to the back door.

Davy snatched his tin bucket of rocks, dumping the contents on the path and sorting them into piles.

Abby laid a hand on the maple's trunk, the tree's deep roots providing an anchor should the ground begin to shake. The earth seemed much less solid and dependable than yesterday. Abby beat a steady rhythm against her leg with the wooden brush still clutched in her fingers, centering her attention on Davy rather than her runaway imagination.

Mama bustled in and out of the house like a squirrel preparing for the winter, adding to the growing pile of items. She paused, her gaze skirting about the yard. "A few more things, I think." She hurried back up the steps and into the doorway.

Davy clambered onto the rocking chair, resting on the path. "What's Mama doing?"

Abby moistened her lips. "We're going to stay outside a while, until we know the house is safe. She's bringing out items we might need."

"We're going to camp? Like the pioneers?" He bounced in the seat, setting the chair into motion.

"Yes, like pioneers. Or gold prospectors."

A rumble and a distant scream alerted Abby before the dreaded motion began. She crouched down, grabbing at the ground as if to hold it still with her hands.

Davy latched onto the chair with both fists, riding it like a boat in stormy seas.

She lurched toward her brother, his wide blue eyes drawing her like a magnet. The earth shivered only for a few brief moments before settling again. Abby pushed out the breath she'd been holding. Even though she was certain he could hear her pounding heart, she tried to calm her voice. "All done now."

"Mama?"

"Wait here. I'll check on her." She hurried to the back door. "Mama? Mama? Are you all right?"

The house remained silent.

Davy peered through the rungs of the chair.

Abby swallowed the lump growing in her throat. "Davy, why don't you find some more stones? See if you can fill the pail. We can pretend we're making soup." Waiting until he turned back to the garden, Abby rushed inside.

"Mama? Answer me!" Her throat grew dry as she searched. "Where are you?"

Mama sat perched halfway up the grand front staircase, holding an empty kerosene lamp and staring off into the distance.

Abby sighed, the knots easing from her stomach. But the vacant look in her mother's eyes gave her pause. "Are you all right?"

Her mother sat like a rock, her knuckles white against the oil lamp.

"Everything's fine, Mama, the shaking's stopped. It's okay, now." Abby climbed the stairs.

"Abby, where is your father?"

Crouched beside her mother, Abby grasped the rail for balance. She swallowed, but couldn't disguise the quaver in her voice. "He's back at the farm. Remember?"

Mama nodded, looking away. "Oh, yes, right."

"Come on. Let's get outside where it's safe."

Her mother stretched a trembling hand upward, like a seedling reaching for the sunlight. As Abby helped her to her feet, Mama released her grip on the lamp. The glass rolled down a few steps and shattered, the acrid scent of kerosene rising into the air.

Abby tugged at her mother's arm and guided her down the stairs, crunching across the broken glass and fallen plaster, and walking out the back door. She directed Mama to the rocking chair.

Davy pattered over, grabbed fistfuls of his mother's skirt, and pulled himself into her lap. Mama patted his back, her eyes staring off into the distance.

Abby gazed at the items cluttering the backyard. What now? She retrieved the hairbrush and dragged the bristles through her tangled hair. Braiding it tightly, she coiled it into a bun at the back of her neck with some hairpins from her apron pocket.

Mama rocked in the chair, her long blond braid spilling over her shoulder, glinting in the glow of the early-morning sun. Davy leaned against her chest.

Gathering the kitchen things, Abby prepared a meager breakfast. She found three plates and filled them with bits of bread, hard-boiled eggs, and cheese. She pulled a box up next to Mama's chair and balanced a plate on it, setting her own and Davy's on the grass.

"Come on, Davy. We'll have a breakfast picnic."

He dashed over and flopped down next to the food. "Do we say grace?" Davy glanced up at Mama from under the brim of his straw hat.

Abby's skin crawled at the blank stare in her mother's eyes. She didn't even acknowledge Davy's question.

"Grace, Mama? Grace?" He pushed up to his knees and leaned against her chair.

"Just eat, Davy!" Abby hissed.

Davy's face pinched, but he gobbled every bit of food from his plate before returning to his rock pile near the maple tree.

Abby tucked the food into a crate and organized their supplies.

Mama shifted in her seat. "Abby, have you tried the telephone?"

"You already did. It wasn't working." Abby's stomach tightened.

"We really should check on Aunt Mae." Mama continued rocking, her eyes glazed and unfocused. "Why don't you pack up some food and walk down the hill and check on her?"

"All right. Will you and Davy be fine without me?" Abby set down the box she held and reached for her hat. The hair rose on her arms at the idea of walking the streets by herself so soon after the quake, but it appealed more than sitting here staring at the house and worrying. Besides, Gerald could have news of the rest of the city. He and Robert might be busy if there were many injuries. Her heart squeezed. *There's nothing wrong with being concerned for Robert's welfare.* Wrapping up some of the breakfast food, she tucked it into the cloth bag.

"Take Davy with you," Mama added as Abby turned to leave.

Davy crouched on his heels near the fence, stripping the leaves off the branch of a boxwood hedge.

Abby sighed and called to him.

His little straw hat shifted as he shook his head. "No. I want to stay."

Abby hurried out the gate and latched it behind her. "He doesn't want to come. I'll be back soon."

Mama didn't reply, the chair creaking as she rocked.

Abby hurried down the alley before Mama could insist Davy accompany her. She certainly didn't want to haul him all the way to Aunt Mae's and back.

23

6:30 a.m.

*A*bby slung the bag over her shoulder as she hurried down the alley toward O'Farrell Street, freedom lightening her steps. The steady breeze tugged at her hat and she lifted her face to the morning sky, gazing around at the nearby houses, pleased to see how little damage had occurred to the sturdy wooden structures. The tall, narrow homes lining the street towered over her like a company of soldiers awaiting orders

People brushed past, their faces tense. A small dog raced along a fence, yelping at Abby through the boards.

To the east, a wisp of yellow smoke rose into the morning air. She remembered watching the fire wagons with Papa and Davy and it brought a wave of longing for her father's presence. If only he hadn't chosen this week to make the final preparations on the farm. She adjusted the heavy bag on her shoulders as the ground rumbled slightly under her feet once more. *This isn't over.*

She waited on two passing wagons before crossing the street. A large crack meandered up the roadway, cobblestones lying at odd angles, like an ocean wave frozen in stones. Picking up the edge of . her skirt, Abby stepped over the crack. A loose cobble shifted under her shoe and she pitched forward, falling hard on hands and knees. Staggering to her feet, she wiped the tiny bits of gravel and a sliver of broken glass from her palms before examining her torn dress and shredded stocking.

Rubbing both palms against her skirt, Abby glanced back to the east. A towering plume of smoke rose from the skyline, billowing upward, moving and changing in the early morning light.

Abby hurried up the street to the west, battling against a sudden desire to run back to her mother and hide behind her skirt like she did when she was a little girl. She brushed the thought away and pressed on toward Gerald's house.

6:35 a.m.

Robert perched on the corner of his desk while Gerald leaned uncomfortably close, shining a bright lamp in his eyes. His friend reeked of sweat and dirt, his vest hanging unbuttoned over a stained, white shirt.

"Pupils match and react to the light. You might have a mild concussion, but I don't think it's serious. Normally, I'd tell you to go to bed and rest a couple of days." Gerald straightened, looking about the ward with a scowl. "But somehow I doubt you're going to listen."

"I'm not sure if I have a bed to go back to. I haven't been home yet." Robert pressed the cold cloth against the back of his head.

"I drove by your apartment building. It appeared to be standing, and it's more than I can say for some areas of town." Gerald pulled back Robert's celluloid collar, peering at his neck. "You look like a porcupine—splinters all down your neck and shoulder. Take off your shirt."

Robert lowered the compress, the throbbing in his head unchanged by the pressure. "What of your family?" He shrugged off his suspenders, unbuttoned his shirt, and yanked it off, grunting with the effort.

"Mother is fine—a bit shaken up, of course."

Twisting the fabric between his fingers, Robert hesitated. "And your cousins?"

Gerald placed his hand on the top of Robert's head, motioning him to tip it forward. He dabbed at the wound with a piece of gauze, and reached for a pair of forceps. "Herman is out of town—signing the final papers on the farm. I haven't heard from Clara yet. The telephone lines are down all over town. I'll try and get out there next."

"You'll be needed here." Robert sucked in his breath as Gerald probed at the wound, picking out bits of debris.

Gerald dropped the bloodstained cloth into a basin. "As will you, if you're fit. You don't require sutures. It's just a bad scrape and a goose egg. How does your head feel? Do you want morphine?" He extracted a splinter from Robert's skin.

Robert bent his neck to the left and right in an attempt to loosen the muscles. "I think I can make do with some aspirin powder and a clean shirt."

"Hold still, would you?" Gerald dropped a fragment of wood into the garbage. "Once things are stable here, we should run down to the office and collect all the paperwork and equipment we can salvage."

Robert paused. "Why would we do that?"

Gerald dropped the forceps on the table and swabbed alcohol across Robert's neck and shoulder. "A fire is burning in the financial district. Broken gas lines, I imagine. I'd hate to lose all the patient records."

Pushing to his feet, Robert swayed for a moment before staggering across the room, his shirt clutched in his hand. Memories of the crumbling wall made his chest tighten as he approached the window, but curling brown smoke chased the image from his mind. "Earthquake, and now a fire? How much more can we endure?"

7:30 a.m.

The elegant three-story home stood undamaged, its unbroken windows greeting Abby like an old friend. Great Aunt Mae swung the door wide and beckoned her inside. "Mercy, child! Look at your face! Are you hurt? What about your mother and brother? Did the house stand? I have been so frightened for you all!"

Abby touched the scratch on her cheek, hesitating in the front hall. "No, I'm fine. We're all fine."

Great Aunt Mae swooped around like a small, fluttering insect, her grasping hands pulling Abby into the parlor. The elderly woman's words spilled over, filling the quiet room. "I'm relieved. This house did so well, I think it's safe to be inside, don't you?" She took Abby's hat, disappearing back into the entry hall.

Abby turned, examining the fine room with a careful eye. With the exception of a few paintings sitting on the floor and some missing vases, one wouldn't even know the house had been disturbed.

Aunt Mae returned, skirts swishing. "Sit, child, sit!" She waved a hand at a chair as she lowered herself onto the settee. "Tell me how things are at home."

Giving her soiled skirt a quick shake, Abby perched on the edge of the expensive mohair chair, tucking her dust-coated shoes as far back as she dared. "Everyone is in good health, Aunt. Some things were knocked over, but—oh, the chimney is down and there are some broken windowpanes." Her words tumbled out in a disorganized mess.

"I am so relieved you are all safe." Aunt Mae leaned back against her chair. "I thought of you poor things alone there during this disaster and I just knew I wouldn't rest until I had word. I tried to get Gerald to go to you at once, but he's been busy here at the house and then he ran off to the hospital. He said young Robert was there doing rounds. He wanted to collect him and get down to their office ahead of the fires."

Robert . . . fires . . . Abby twisted the words together.

"Can you believe my son went up on the roof right after the quake?" Aunt Mae lifted an age-speckled hand to her throat. "I thought I would die of fright. As if the shaking hadn't already unnerved me, Gerald has to go and climb the roof? He said he wanted to get the loose chimney bricks down before we got another shake. I suppose it makes sense, but—mercy! I was terrified the shaking would return while he was still up there. I spent the whole time on my knees—"

As her aunt chattered, Abby fidgeted, distracted by an itch growing under the edge of her corset. Shifting on the edge of the chair, she bit her tongue, waiting for her aunt to take a breath. When the pause arrived, she blurted out, "Mama sent food."

Aunt Mae's face broke into a wide smile. "Clara's always been the sweetest girl. Let's take it into the kitchen. I don't dare light the stove, but I think it is fine to eat in there. I have been so busy sweeping up broken bits, I hadn't even thought about food yet."

Abby stood, brushing a hand across the chair to remove any dust, and followed Aunt Mae. "Does Gerald think the fires will reach his office?"

"It's hard to say. The smoke down there looks bad. And there are so many wooden buildings—just waiting to burn, really. He's more worried about losing his patients' records than his equipment. He has all of his former partner's records—and the man practiced in San Francisco for more than thirty years—plus his own, so it's a load of paper. I imagine he and Robert will be very busy over the next few days. I hate to think how many injuries there could be." The lines deepened around her eyes.

Aunt Mae set the package of food on the table. "Let's clean up your cut, first." She motioned Abby to one of the high-backed kitchen chairs. "It's unfortunate Robert isn't here. He did such a nice job patching you up last time." Aunt Mae pulled another chair close, so they were knee-to-knee. She pressed the cool compress against the scratch, taking Abby's chin in her hand as she worked.

Abby examined her aunt's soft gray eyes, the gentleness of her touch bringing the first moment of ease in the day. Abby let her chin rest in the older woman's grip.

"We're very fortunate, Abigail." Her eyes, usually so quick to laugh, darkened. "I keep thinking about it."

Like a deer caught in a hunter's sights, Abby met her gaze, but set her jaw. *I will not talk to her about this. Not today.*

"It could have been so much worse. God has shown us great love. We've been shaken, but we still stand firm."

Resentment bubbled in Abby's stomach like a teapot. *He can keep His love, if this is what comes of it.* She busied her mind with other thoughts: Mama's pumpkin pie, wading in the stream, walking bare-foot in the grass—anything but Aunt Mae's voice. This was no time to argue.

"God has spared us much heartache today."

Abby's self-control snapped like a twig under Aunt Mae's foot. "How kind of Him. What about these past months? Why couldn't He have spared us their heartache?" Tears stung her eyes. Rather than pulling away from Aunt Mae's grip, she forced her neck stiff as an iron rod.

Aunt Mae dropped the cloth and placed her palm on Abby's hair, framing her face between two trembling hands. "We can't always understand God's ways, child. But your family has endured enough grief for a while. I am thankful we've been passed over this time."

Abby squeezed her eyelids shut to block out Aunt Mae's soul-piercing gaze, hot tears sneaking past their locked gates.

Releasing Abby's chin, Aunt Mae nodded. "We read in the Scriptures, 'God is our refuge and strength, an ever-present help in trouble. Therefore we will not fear, though the earth give way and the mountains fall into the heart of the sea, though its waters roar and foam and the mountains quake with their surging.'" She dropped her hands to her sides. "The Psalms always say it best."

Abby's chest ached. She fought to swallow, burying her words deep within. "I should get back home."

Aunt Mae's brows pinched together, adding years to her already worn face. Thoughts seemed to dance behind those gray eyes, as if eager to be spoken—perhaps even more Bible verses. Instead, she remained silent and patted Abby's knee before lifting a crooked fin-gertip in the air. "Wait just one moment, I have something for you."

She rose with a creak of the chair, pushing one hand against her lower back while she gripped the edge of the table for support.

A cold tendril clutched at Abby's heart as she watched her aunt totter on unsteady feet out of the kitchen. The woman could seem so full of energy at one moment, and so old and feeble the next. Abby sighed, melting into the seat, letting her head fall back. The ceiling in the kitchen resembled a broken eggshell. Her eyes traced the jagged lines as footsteps moved back and forth upstairs.

Rising, she walked to the front hall, retrieving her hat and pinning it in place, frowning at her reflection in the hall glass.

Aunt Mae hobbled down the stairs, gripping the rail with one hand and a small leather-bound book pressed to her bosom with the other. "I know how much you love books, Abigail. I think you should read this. I've been meaning to give it to you for some time now."

Abby wrapped her fingers around the soft, worn cover. She nodded her thanks to Aunt Mae and tucked it into her skirt pocket as she turned to the front door, the view out the small pane windows beckoning her.

"Dear, I know you are in a hurry to get back to your mother . . . " Aunt Mae paused as if carefully considering her words.

Abby kept her grip on the cool metal knob, muscles tensing at the expectation in her aunt's voice.

"I hate to ask this of you," Aunt Mae fiddled with the lace on her sleeve. "I know you need to get home."

Abby's heart dropped. Her aunt never lacked for words. "What is it?"

Sliding a hand under her Abby's arm, Aunt Mae pulled her away from the door. "When I was upstairs I discovered Gerald had forgotten the suture kit from his doctor's bag. He must have removed them last night for cleaning. I think in his rush to leave, he forgot to put them back in. Do you think it would be too much trouble for you to take it to him?"

Abby imagined the long walk downtown to Gerald's office and then back to Maple Manor. *At least it will get me out of here.* "Of course I will."

Relief pooled in her aunt's eyes. "I know he will be so grateful." She thrust the package into Abby's hands. "He should be at the office. If for some reason he's not there, you might check at the hospital."

"I'll find him." Abby stepped out onto the front porch, adjusting her hat and glancing up at the expanding plumes of smoke.

Great Aunt Mae placed a hand on her shoulder. "I'm sorry if I upset you before, dear. I am praying for you." She squeezed, her fingers pressing against Abby's collarbone. "Your heart is wounded, but if you let Him, He will heal it."

Abby tried to draw away, but Aunt Mae held her fast.

"One more verse and then I will hold my tongue. He wants to give you 'beauty for ashes, the oil of joy for mourning, the garment of praise for the spirit of heaviness.' It's from Isaiah."

Abby stepped free. "Good-bye, Aunt Mae."

"May God go with you, child." Aunt Mae stepped up on her toes and threw her arms around Abby's shoulders, planting a kiss on her cheek.

A flood of unwanted emotion surged upward from Abby's stomach. For the briefest moment, she considered melting onto her aunt's shoulder in a puddle of tears. How easy it would be. Instead, she stepped out of Aunt Mae's clinging arms, hurrying down the stairs.

As she walked, the warmth of her aunt's embrace lingered on her skin, like being cuddled in a soft quilt. Her words echoed in Abby's mind: "May God go with you."

24

7:45 a.m.

*R*obert pinched the bridge of his nose with his fingers, trying to ease the pressure behind his eyes. No time to waste, too many patients.

A breath of air tickled the back of his neck from the line of broken windows in the long hall—like a child proudly showing off a row of missing teeth. He lifted his arm to block a sneeze, the scent of smoke and dust tickling his sinuses.

"Am I gonna be all right, Doc?" The old man resembled a granite statue, his gray beard blending with the thick coating of dust clinging to his skin. He clutched an arm to his chest. "I'm a bricklayer. I need both my arms, or I won't be able to work."

Robert grasped the limb, the bones of the forearm shifting under his fingers, the man's face wrinkling like tissue paper at the movement. He longed for an X-ray of the fracture, but the laboratory lay buried under rubble, the machinery a complete loss. "I'll set the bone and splint it for now, Mr. Roderick. Try not to move it more than you must. You should come back in a few days and let us take another look."

The man's bushy white brows pulled low over his rheumy eyes. "I got to get my daughter and grandchildren out of the city, Doc. We live south of the Slot, you know. It's going up in flames."

Robert shook his head. The cable-line running down Market Street, known as the Slot, served as an unofficial divider between the working classes in the south and the businessmen to the north. It seemed unlikely, however, the fires would remain bound by these man-made divisions. He gestured to a couple of nurses who stood nearby and they moved into position to help Mr. Roderick brace himself.

Robert manipulated the ends of the bone back into position and maneuvered a splint in place. The man groaned and winced during the procedure, but managed to remain still until Robert finished.

Robert placed a hand on the man's shoulder. "Wherever you end up after today, have someone take a look at your arm. And be careful with it—no lifting, no motion at all." Robert sighed. Any further advice would be wasted. No motion? Unlikely.

Gerald waited at the door. "That's the last patient for now, Robert. Dr. McKinley has arrived and Dr. Carson will be by later. We need to get downtown and see what we can salvage from the office before all of Market Street is gone."

Robert tied the cloth sling, careful that it supported the splinted arm and patted the older man on his good shoulder before joining his friend. "Have you heard how far the fire has spread?"

Gerald shook his head. "No one seems to know. Evidently there are some problems with the water mains."

As he followed Gerald through the front doors, Robert paused, staring at the roiling clouds billowing upward into the sky. The weight growing all morning in Robert's chest sank into his stomach. What lay before him was no simple fire. It was an inferno.

Abby paused at the corner, nibbling her lip as she pondered the options. Run up the hill and tell Mama she'd agreed to a second errand, or risk a quick dash down to Gerald's office? The towers of smoke curled upward like a giant fist punching at the gates of heaven. If she didn't hurry, she might miss Gerald all together. At the base of the steep hill, the downtown spread out before her. Beyond the ferry building, morning sunlight sparkled on the bay, the haze eating away at the view. Abby's gaze climbed the columns of smoke as they bulged and churned in the sky.

Abby lifted the edge of her skirt and jogged down the hill, gravity hurrying her feet and Aunt Mae's book bouncing against her thigh. A trio of women nodded to her, the feathers on their hats bobbing as they walked.

With each street she passed, the damage multiplied, the city transforming before her eyes. Broken glass crunched beneath her shoes as she stepped over piles of debris—blocks of cement, bricks, twisted pieces of wood. She reached out a trembling hand to touch the corner of a fallen building. Only two walls remained, standing jagged against the sky. Across the road, a second structure stood open to the world, its entire front wall missing, like an oversized dollhouse. A sudden weakness clutched at Abby's legs, as she struggled to accept the reality before her eyes.

"Cecelia," Abby touched the locket nestled under her shirt, "Be glad you didn't see this."

The crowds thickened. People walked westward, away from the smoke, arms spilling over with belongings. Anything with wheels had been pressed into service: carts, baby buggies, and toy wagons. Men and women dragged trunks and cases, the heavy items bumping over the debris-strewn ground.

A red-faced woman pushed a pram, loaded down with belongings, three bundle-toting children trailing in her wake, the youngest clinging to her skirt. Tears streamed down the face of the little child, a heavy shawl tied around her neck over what appeared to be multiple layers of clothing. "Carry me! Carry me!"

In the distance, the top floors of a building burned like a torch, flames licking out of its upper windows and dancing up into the sky like demons, twirling and jumping with sinister glee. A disheveled man pointed a shaking finger at the flames. "God's wrath! God is pouring His wrath out on His people! He punishes this evil generation with fire and death!" Face twisted, spittle hanging at the corner of his mouth, the man's gray hair waved in the breeze as he clutched a floppy hat to his heaving chest.

Few stopped to watch and listen, most people giving the wild-looking man a wide berth.

"Turn and repent! He shakes out His house and possessions! He will drive you from the land!" The man lifted his hands and eyes toward the smoky sky. "In a moment shall they die, and the people shall be troubled at midnight, and pass away: and the mighty shall be taken away without hand."

"Shut up, you old fool!" A gentleman in a long black coat shook a newspaper at the man. "We got enough trouble. We don't need your preaching."

Abby hurried away in the direction of the flames. She had no desire to hear more about God's destruction. Ruin was obvious on all sides. She pushed through the crowd like a fish swimming against the current. Abby pressed both arms to her stomach, gripping elbows with rigid fingers. *Just a few more blocks.*

25

*A*bby tugged open the heavy oak door, the dust-filled building a quiet respite from the chaos of the street. Chunks of plaster and cement littered the wooden stairway. Lifting the hem of her skirt, Abby picked her way through the mess.

Lacelike cracks decorated the windowpane in Gerald's office door. Abby turned the doorknob and crunched across the glass-strewn rug. "Cousin Gerald?" Her voice trembled. She cleared her throat and straightened her shoulders. "Gerald?"

The reception room lay in shambles. Broken glass from the window covered the green settee while smashed vases and artwork littered the floor. Pushing open the door to the inner office, Abby peered inside. Medical instruments lay scattered like a child's playthings.

Gerald entered from a back room, his arms filled with papers, his eyes wide. "Abigail, what are you doing here? Are you all right? Does your family need help?" Gerald plopped the armload onto a table before striding to her side.

Robert, equally burdened, hovered in the doorway.

Abby pulled her gaze from Robert's face, attempting to focus on her cousin. "What? Oh, no—I'm fine. Everyone is well."

Gerald placed his hand on her forearm, his lowered brows creating wrinkles on his forehead. "Then why are you here? You should be at home."

Brushing both hands across her skirt, Abby stared as Robert stepped farther into the room, his unkempt appearance chasing every thought from her mind. Never had she seen him in such a state—his brown hair tousled, vest unbuttoned, shirt stained. *Blood?*

Gerald's pressure on her arm drew her attention back. "Um, I . . . I . . . " Abby struggled to formulate an answer to a question she'd already forgotten.

A glint appeared in Robert's eye. "You didn't come downtown for a stroll."

"Of course not." Abby reached for the bag, turning her gaze back to Gerald. "Great Aunt Mae was concerned you had forgotten some of your instruments. She was afraid you might need them." Abby drew out the carefully wrapped tools.

Gerald's face darkened. "Mother shouldn't have sent you down here. It's not a safe day for a girl to be walking the streets alone." He turned toward Robert. "How would you feel about seeing my cousin home?"

Abby clenched her fingers. "I'm not a child. I don't need an escort." *And certainly not him.*

A smile lit Robert's dirt-smudged face. "It would be an honor."

"Good." Gerald nodded. "I'll meet you at the hospital when you are finished. I think our task here is about complete, anyway."

Abby tugged at the edge of her shirtwaist. "Go back to work, both of you. I will be fine." How could she manage intelligent conversation with Robert for the entire walk home? The moment he'd entered the room, she'd forgotten the purpose of her trip.

"I don't want to spend the rest of the day worrying about whether or not you arrived." Gerald folded his arms across his chest.

Footsteps pounded on the rickety staircase, the steps groaning under the pressure. "Dr. Larkspur?" A raspy voice echoed up the stairwell.

Gerald pushed past Abby as he stepped into the corridor. "Yes?"

A man appeared at the top of the stairs, his face red and dripping with sweat. "Doc, we got a building down, and they're pulling folks out now. You need to patch them up so we can get moved before the fire comes."

"Let me get my bag, and I'll follow you." Gerald ducked into the office, reappearing a moment later with a large black case.

Robert hesitated. "Gerald—should I . . . " He gestured toward Abby.

The red-faced man mopped his brow. "We need all the hands we can get. The fire is bearing down fast."

Abby stepped forward. "Go, both of you. I can return to Maple Manor on my own." A quiver shot through her stomach. "Unless you'd rather I stayed to help?"

Gerald shook his head. "I want you out of harm's way."

Robert buttoned his vest. "I can get Abby home and be back in a heartbeat."

Abby braced her hands against her hips. "I can take care of myself. Those people cannot."

Her cousin closed his eyes, pressing a hand to his forehead. After a slow exhale, he frowned, pointing a finger at her. "Be careful. This is a dangerous situation. I want you to hurry straight back to Maple Manor and stay put. I'll come and check on you and your mother as soon as I can get away."

"I'll be careful, I promise."

Gerald gestured toward the office as he started down the stairs. "Robert, lock those files in the safe and then come join me."

Robert stood at Abby's side, gazing at her for a long moment without speaking. "Are you certain, Abby? I really don't mind seeing you home." He touched her sleeve.

Abby's knees wobbled as butterfly wings tickled her stomach. *Be strong.* She glanced away from his earnest eyes. "I'm sure."

Robert's stomach tightened as he stood at the office window, watching Abby disappear into the mass of people walking the cobblestone streets. He gripped the packet of instruments she'd carried through the city, as if the pressure of his hand could somehow protect her on the journey home. His gaze traveled over the nearby buildings, lifting to where three separate pillars of smoke rose into the skyline, one so close he could see flames dancing out of the windows of a building. *Lord, keep her safe.*

After locking the safe, he hurried after Gerald. Running a hand through his thick hair, Robert replaced his derby. From the expression on Abby's face, he must look a fright. Robert quickened his step, his heart pounding at the idea of what types of injuries they might encounter.

For years he'd dreamed of doing scientific research, fighting to unlock the secrets of disease. Today he'd set broken bones, sutured cuts, and debrided wounds—dirty work, but oddly enjoyable. Robert grimaced, rubbing a hand across the back of his head. Not enjoyable, exactly—just a bit gratifying to see instant results.

Robert rushed over to where Gerald crouched next to a patient. The unconscious fireman lay sprawled on the sidewalk, ankle and foot pinned beneath a massive granite block.

A second fireman, thumb hooked in his suspenders, hovered at Gerald's shoulder. "We've got to get him out of here, Doc. Do what you gotta do."

Gerald sliced through the trouser leg, revealing the bloody remains of the man's lower limb. He sighed. "Completely crushed. There'd be no saving it, anyhow." His gaze met Robert's. "You'll assist me?"

Robert swallowed the bile creeping up his throat, and dug into the open bag for the bottle of ether. Perhaps instant results weren't so gratifying.

26

*A*bby dug her hands deep into the pockets of her skirt as she hurried up the street, away from the rolling clouds of smoke billowing on the skyline. As she pushed her tired legs up the steep hill, she risked a glance over her shoulder. The fires were moving quickly, consuming buildings that moments before had stood untouched. Her stomach churned at the thought of Gerald and Robert working while the danger raced toward them.

Pray for them. Abby could almost hear Cecelia's voice whispering in her ear.

Abby blew out a slow exhale, letting the air buzz through her lips. *A lot of good it did you.*

She strode to the corner and crossed the street, but a wall of smoke filled the space between the buildings. Stumbling back, she turned south to skirt around the worst parts. The distant roar pounded in her temples. An old man with a handful of newspapers clutched to his chest collided with her, sending Abby stumbling into a crooked lamppost.

With only a scornful glance, the man staggered off into the throng.

Brushing off her sleeve, Abby stepped over a pile of terra cotta tiles and blocks of brick and cement. The crowd thinned as she continued south, looking for an easier route home.

As she turned the corner onto Market Street, a blast of heat stung her cheeks. Less than a block away another fire burned, licking through the windows of a church. Abby stopped, entranced by the terrible beauty of the twisting, incandescent flames as they capered about the ruins of the structure.

An explosion tore through the air, echoing down the street like a bouncing rubber ball. Abby's ears buzzed. She backed up against a building as bystanders ran in every direction, like ants from a kicked-over hill.

Eyes stinging from the smoke, Abby dug her fingernails against the brick wall. *This is insanity. The whole city could burn.* She released her grip, edging away from the conflagration, but refusing to turn her back for fear the fire would pursue her like a monster from a nightmare.

A second explosion ripped through a nearby building, slamming her back into the brick storefront. Abby's head cracked against the wall, fireworks dancing in her eyes and a rushing roar filling her ears. Turning her head, tiny pieces of grit and dirt pelted her arms and clothes. Abby coughed, stumbling and sinking down to one knee. Leaning over, she clutched at the earth as her stomach rolled.

As the dust settled, Abby wiped a sleeve across her mouth and pushed to her feet. "Cecelia," she whispered, "What am I doing here?"

10:15 a.m.

Robert pulled the catgut thread through one last suture and dabbed the area with iodine. Everything about today's work gripped at his conscience. His instructors had always emphasized the importance of working in a clean environment, washing hands, sterilizing tools. Dried blood coated his fingers, his shirt covered in filth. How many of these patients would survive today, only to succumb to sepsis in the days to come?

"Doc, you finished? We've got to get a move on." A thin fireman with a beard hovered at his shoulder, his breath adding to the myriad of foul odors hanging in the air and setting Robert's head throbbing.

"Yes, I'm finished." Robert leaned over the prone form on the ground, lifting the patient's eyelids one by one. This man might not even get the opportunity to fret over the loss of his leg. All signs pointed to brain injury.

Robert helped the fireman load the injured man onto a canvas stretcher. "Where are you taking him? I'd like to check on him later."

Weary eyes looked out from the dirt-streaked face. "I'd heard a temporary hospital had been set up at the Mechanic's Pavilion, across from City Hall. But I think the fires have already reached there, so I thought I'd head up toward Golden Gate Park."

"Golden Gate? It's miles from here. You'll never make it on foot."

"Hopefully I'll be able to find a cart to give us a lift." Gesturing to another man, the fireman crouched to lift his end. "No time to argue. We've got to put some distance between us and those flames."

A roar in the background made Robert turn. Fire ripped through the upper stories of a nearby building, smoke rolling up into the sky. A lump crawled into his throat as the inferno increased in ferocity with each passing minute.

Gerald gripped his arm, the flames casting an orange glow on his face. "Come on. We've done all we can—time to get out."

Robert dropped to his knees, gathering the equipment with shaking hands. Without bothering to clean anything, he thrust the tools into the medical bag and snapped the lid, his fingers barely able to secure the leather strap.

Gerald shouted and gestured, his words lost to the roar of the wind. He loped off down the street, toward the hill.

Robert tucked the bag under his arm and chased after his friend, the scorching heat tickling the back of his neck.

27

*A*bby grabbed up her skirt and sprinted through the smoke-filled street, breath rasping in her chest. Ashes floated from the sky like snowflakes, but she didn't take the time to brush them from her hair and dress. *Stupid, stupid girl. Gerald was correct, you should have gone straight home.*

She charged up the hill toward Maple Manor, pushing through the crowd gathered at the corner. *Why are people lingering here?*

"Hey, Miss! Stop! You can't go that way." A voice trailed after her, followed by pounding footsteps. "Wait!" A hand clamped onto Abby's arm, her body jerking back at the sudden interruption. A tall policeman glared down, his grip fierce and his face smeared with a combination of sweat and soot.

"This area is off-limits." He released his hold. "You need to head to safety."

Abby rubbed her arm where his fingers had pinched against the muscle. The policeman's resemblance to her father gave her pause. A lump rose in her throat as she thought about Papa alone at the farm, possibly injured. "I'm trying to go home, sir." She glanced up the hill. "My mother and brother are waiting for me."

"You can't go that way. They are getting ready to dynamite this whole area to clear a firebreak. They want to stop this blaze before it takes everything."

"Dynamite?" Abby swallowed, her throat like sandpaper. "How will explosives help anything?"

"They have to do something. There's no water to be had." He shoved his hat back along his head, exposing a stretch of pink skin between the soot line and the brim. "This whole area has been evacuated."

"I have to get back," Abby crossed her arms, gripping onto her elbows. "They're waiting for me."

"Head for Union Square. They've probably gone there."

Abby's thoughts raced. *Mama leave without her?* It seemed unlikely.

The policeman frowned as if reading her thoughts. "Your family would want you safe, Miss. Go to Union Square. There are people there who can help."

Gazing into his smoke-reddened eyes, she nodded. "Yes, sir. Thank you." *Thank you, but no.*

Falling in with the crowd walking toward the square, Abby glanced over her shoulder, watching as the policeman stopped to converse with a soldier on horseback.

Abby crossed the street and edged around the corner of an alley. Darting down the street and into another side alley, she raced up the hill. After the hubbub of the crowd and the roar of the fires, the silence descending on O'Farrell Street pressed against Abby's chest. Even with the roadblocks, a few people still skulked about, presumably retrieving belongings.

The house appeared unchanged. Abby thundered up the wooden stairs and pushed on the door. The knob turned freely, but the wood stuck in the frame. Abby threw a shoulder against it and burst into the front hall.

"Mama?" Abby's chest tightened until it became hard to draw a breath. She stole to the bottom of the stair, the silence disconcerting. "Mama?" Her voice shook, rising in pitch until it ended with a whimper.

Abby searched the house, her heart growing heavier with each step. As she opened the back door, a piece of Mama's best yellow stationery fluttered like a waving hand. Mama's handwriting was scrawled, as if her fingers had trembled while she wrote.

> Dearest Abigail,
>
> I am praying fervently you are safe and will find this message. I was so scared when the soldiers came and told us to leave. They said Aunt Mae's neighborhood will be evacuated also. I suppose you must be with Gerald and Aunt Mae. I am going to Union Square. Meet me there. I am waiting and praying for you. Do not delay. Come at once.
>
> All my love,
> Mama

Abby clutched the note to her chest, an ache building in her heart. Another small shock rumbled the earth, like a toddler trembling with fear. As if in response, a child's cry cut through the air, the voice so similar to Davy's it brought tears to Abby's eyes. At least she knew he was safe with Mama.

The shaking ceased and she tucked the note into her pocket with Aunt Mae's book. *I will find them. And after this, nothing else will separate us.*

2:00 p.m.

Smoke rolled like fog through the streets, tickling Robert's throat as he plodded behind Gerald. After fleeing the fire zone, they'd stopped three more times to treat the wounded. Sweat dripped down his back. "Where did you leave your automobile?"

Gerald shifted the medical bag to his left arm and dug into his vest pocket, pulling out a watch. "At the hospital." He held the timepiece at arm's length, staring at the numbers. "It's getting late. Have you eaten?"

When had he last eaten? "No."

"Let's head to my house, then. Mother's probably going crazy with worry. She can work through some of it by feeding us." He glanced at Robert, his gaze traveling up and down his frame. "How are you holding up?"

"I'm trying not to dwell on it."

His friend chuckled, but his brows pulled into a frown. "Stay with us tonight. After the blow to the head you took this morning, I'd feel better keeping an eye on you."

"I won't argue." Robert ran a hand over the knot on his scalp. "Are you going to check on the Fischers?"

Gerald nodded. "Once we reach the hospital, we'll drive over there first. Maybe we can collect them. I wouldn't mind having my entire family under one roof tonight." He clapped a hand onto Robert's shoulder and squeezed. "Good work today, by the way."

A smile pulled at Robert's lips—for perhaps the first time all day. Whether it was from Gerald's words or the prospect of seeing Abby again, he wasn't certain. His pace slowed, leg muscles cramping as they pressed up the steep hill. All he really wanted was to see her safe—and then to close his eyes for a few moments. The rest of the world's problems would have to wait until tomorrow.

28

2:15 p.m.

Abby's feet dragged as if she had bricks attached to the bottom of her shoes. Every street seemed blocked. People walked westward now, like the tide shifting. Spotting a soldier helping a gray-haired woman into a heavily laden wagon, Abby rushed toward him. "I'm trying to get to Union Square. Can you help me?"

"The road's closed off between here and there. They're sending everyone to Golden Gate Park and the Presidio."

Abby crossed her arms. "My mother and brother went to Union Square for refuge." The dryness squeezed at her throat until her voice crackled.

The man focused on the cart, refusing to meet her eyes. "Sorry, Miss. Just keep heading west. Find someplace safe to wait out this mess. You can find your family after the danger has passed." As he handed another elderly woman up onto the wagon, he spoke to Abby over his shoulder, "Just be glad you got strong legs. A lot of folks are having trouble today."

Abby swallowed, fighting down the sob wanting to climb her throat. Leaning against a storefront, she closed her eyes for a heartbeat, imagining the joy of a long cool drink of water and falling into bed. Weary of the crushing crowds and the uncertainty, the peaceful darkness of Maple Manor's attic sounded like a haven. If she were there right now, she'd bury herself in Cecelia's quilt and hide.

Golden Gate Park was miles away.

Opening her eyes, Abby pushed off the brick wall and joined the stream of people plodding westward. Her stomach rumbled. She'd only eaten a few bites of breakfast, not aware it would be her only meal of the day.

A hysterical wailing from across the street caught her attention. An old woman, a blanket wrapped around her frail shoulders, huddled near the ruins of a fallen building.

So much grief. So much loss.

Abby stumbled over a pile of rubble, turning her ankle, hot tears stinging her eyes. She sank down onto abandoned trunk pushed up against the side of a building and rested her back against the brick wall. A few moments' rest might help her regain her strength. Abby dug into her pocket after Mama's note, her hand brushing against the book. Pulling it out, she stared at the aged leather, worn smooth by use. The pages crackled as she leafed through, flowery script covering each yellowed sheet from edge to edge. Abby flipped back to the beginning.

Mae Robinson, 1853.

A journal? Several sheets broke loose, fluttering to the ground. With a cry, she slid off the trunk and collected them before the wind could carry them off. Checking the dates at the top of each, Abby matched the loose pages to their locations in the journal before leaning back against the wall to read.

April 19, 1853

It's hopeless, Doc Meyers says. Mama's cough worsened last night and now she's coughing blood into her handkerchief. She tried to hide it, but I saw the wadded piece of linen under her pillow when I changed the bedding. I asked her about it, and she said I was too young to worry. She doesn't seem to realize I'm ten years old and not a baby anymore. Plus, everyone says how smart I am. I know consumption when I see it.

It's not right. She shouldn't have to be in so much pain. I planned to pray for her for a whole hour last night, but I fell asleep on the floor beside my bed. Not sure if God heard me or not.

April 20, 1853

God must not have heard. I'll try again tonight.

Abby kneaded her ankle with firm fingers as she read, the diary braced on her lap.

April 24, 1853

Mama's getting worse. Her skin is a queer gray color and it's hanging loose on her like an old woman. She's got more shadows on her face than I've got under my bed. But I'm still praying. Preacher came by this morning. He didn't talk to me, but told Papa he's praying for a miracle. If the preacher is praying, God must be listening, right?

April 27, 1853

Dear God, I hope you don't mind me writing my prayers. I keep falling asleep when I'm praying and I can't get all the words out. Save my Mama. Make her better. I'll do anything. Just don't take her away. Papa is real sad these days. He didn't mean what he said this morning. He's just worried and doesn't like me asking so many questions. I won't bother him anymore, if You'll just help. Please, God. Please.

Abby's heart cringed at the familiar words of someone crying out to an uncaring God. A lump formed in her throat. She wedged the loose sheets into the journal and slammed the cover shut.

2:30 p.m.

The soldier scowled in the roadway, rifle at the ready, more like a guard at a prison camp than a sentry over a peaceful neighborhood. "This whole area has been evacuated. You've got no business here."

Gerald leaned out of the automobile and waved his medical identification. "I understand. We'll take responsibility for our own safety."

The man didn't blink, his mouth an unwavering line. "I have my orders."

They'd already been stopped three times, each time their status earning them reluctant nods. This statuesque soldier, however, refused to budge. Robert pushed down the heat rising in his gut, consumed by the urge to throw the throttle into high gear and drive around the blockade, but the man's grip on his rifle made him think twice.

Gerald blew out a long breath. "Maybe Clara and Abby went ahead to my house."

"I hope so." Robert braced his arm across the seat back as he looked behind, shifting the automobile into reverse and turning back toward his friend's home. The car lurched as the tires lumbered over loose cobbles during the slow journey.

When they finally drove into the side alley, Mrs. Larkspur rushed out onto the porch. "Thank the Lord, you're safe. I've been so worried." The woman pushed fingers through the tight silver curls above her brow.

Robert climbed out of the car, his joints aching like an old man's, and followed his friend to the house.

Mrs. Larkspur grasped her son's hand, drawing him up the final few steps and into her arms.

Gerald leaned down to return his mother's embrace. "Mother, are Clara and her family here?"

She pulled back. "No. Abby came by this morning, but I haven't seen them since. I keep trying the telephone, but I can't seem to get the foolish thing to work. Maybe you could take a look at it."

Robert halted midway up the stairs, grabbing the railing for support. *Where were they?*

Gerald's shoulders slumped. "Wires are down all over the city. I'm afraid the telephones won't be working for some time."

The older woman settled a hand on one hip. "Well. We get so accustomed to these conveniences and then what happens? We're lost without them." She clucked her tongue. "Just look at you boys. Come in, come in."

Gerald turned to face Robert, lines forming on his face. "We'll get some dinner and then I'll head out and look for them. You need to get some rest."

Robert climbed the steps until he reached eye-level with his friend. "I'm coming with you. An extra set of eyes might be necessary."

29

3:00 p.m.

*We*ary of the scenery and the people about her, Abby focused on her dusty shoes, counting the city blocks as they passed under her feet. Most people walked in silence, the mood darkening by the hour. A cacophony of strange-sounding voices caught Abby's attention and she glanced up, noticing a large group of Chinese—young girls and a few women—the musical tones of their words cutting through the general hush on the cobbled road.

Their long white shirts and loose-fitting white trousers flapped as they walked. Many carried bulky sheet-wrapped bundles clasped in their arms or tied to their backs. A few of the young women toted babies. Two older matrons walked beside the line, like shepherdesses guarding the flock.

Abby fell in behind, transfixed by the unique cadence of their voices.

The girls chattered, staring about the street like sightseers touring the ruins of ancient Rome. One started singing and within a few paces, the whole group joined, smiles spreading across their faces. An elegant woman walking in front of the group turned her head, her gaze traveling over each girl as she joined in the song.

Abby's breath caught at the sight of the familiar figure—the missionary she'd met at the hospital. Abby pressed a hand to her chest. Was the young woman here, too? Kum Yong? She quickened her steps, the melody drawing her in. The tune crept around the edges of her memory. She began to hum and within a few bars she stopped, her fingers traveling up to touch her locket. Cecelia's song.

After finishing a verse in Chinese, they switched into English.

Jesus sought me when a stranger,
Wandering from the fold of God;
He, to rescue me from danger,
Interposed His precious blood.

The song tugged at Abby's heart. She hastened her steps, following as close as she dared, searching the group for the familiar face. The song returned to Chinese, the melody unchanged.

A lump rose in her throat. *Cecelia.* The song wafted through the air, as if her sister called from beyond the grave. Abby shook her head, chasing away the image. Their voices were nothing like Cecelia's, and yet her sister's presence seemed almost palpable, buoyed along by the music.

A young woman at the rear of the line paused, leaning down to examine the twisted rails. The bundle slipped from her back and landed with a thump on the cobblestones. Ducking her head, she grasped the package with both hands, her dark hair glistening in the late afternoon sunshine. Hoisting it to her back, she staggered under the weight.

Sudden boldness gripping her heart, Abby hurried forward. "Let me help you."

A timid smile brightened the woman's smooth face. "I remember you. Hospital—yes?"

"Yes, right. I'm Abby." Abby helped her balance the awkward load, holding it steady while the young woman tied the corners of the sheet around her sides.

White-edged scars twined about the Chinese woman's forearms from elbows to wrists. She tucked her hands up into her sleeves, offering another shy smile and bobbing her head. "Thank you, Abby. Again."

Abby stepped back, stomach fluttering. "How is the little girl?"

The woman grinned. "Yoke Hay is much improved."

One of the older women stopped and frowned back at them. "Is everything all right, Kum Yong?"

"Yes, Mrs. Ling." Kum Yong's hair bounced as she nodded. "This is Abby—she's the one who helped Yoke Hay at the hospital the day she ran in the street."

"My friend Dr. King helped her. I didn't really do anything." The memory of Robert's gentle manner with the tiny girl flooded through Abby's heart.

Kum Yong beamed. "No one else would help until you stepped in."

Abby smiled, fascinated by the way the familiar words were altered by the exotic accent.

The matron clucked her tongue as she looked at the bulging sheet. She touched the makeshift pack. "What are you carrying that is so heavy?"

Kum Yong stared at her feet, clad in simple black slipperlike shoes. "I am carrying Ma-Yi's box of letters."

Mrs. Ling's face darkened. "Lo Mo said to leave those. Only necessities."

The young woman tucked her chin against her chest. "Lo Mo told Ma-Yi to leave them. She did not say I could not carry them. Lo Mo also says 'Carry each other's burdens, and in this way you will fulfill the law of Christ.'" The Chinese girl's chin lifted as she recited the verse, eyes shining.

The older woman huffed. "I'm not sure this is what Lo Mo intended." She pressed her lips into a line. "I suppose one cannot argue with the words of the apostle Paul. And what you wish to carry is your problem. But make sure to keep up."

"Yes, ma'am." Kum Yong bobbed her head.

"Thank you, Miss Abby," Mrs. Ling bent forward in a slight bow, "for your kindness to little Yoke Hay and also for helping this foolish girl with her heavy, unnecessary burden." Mrs. Ling's thin eyebrows pinched. "Are you alone? Where is your family?"

Abby lowered her eyes, the woman's stern, but motherly, gaze sending an ache to her chest. "We've gotten separated. I can't find them."

Mrs. Ling clucked her tongue a second time, shaking her head. "We are taking the Mission girls west to Old First Presbyterian Church. You come with us." She patted Abby's arm. "Miss Cameron would agree."

Unease rippled through Abby. Why should these women help her? She craned her neck for a better glimpse of the graceful missionary at the front of the line.

Mrs. Ling swung her arm, gesturing to the group of girls. "These girls are from the Chinese Mission home, most rescued from slavery in Chinatown. We are going to the Presbyterian church on Van Ness until the fires are over, and then—God willing—we will go home to the Mission."

The hair on Abby's neckline prickled at the word *slavery*, remembering the scars on Kum Yong's arms.

A bright smile lit Kum Yong's face. "You will join us, Abby, won't you? We could help you, like you helped us."

"Jesus helps all, Kum Yong, not just foolish women carting around love letters," Mrs. Ling flicked her fingers against Kum Yong's shoulder.

One of the little girls stumbled, falling forward onto one knee with a cry. Mrs. Ling rushed forward to help her. "Don't tire Abby with all your chatter, Kum Yong," she called back.

Abby and Kum Yong caught up to the group, walking in silence for a few minutes, exchanging shy glances. Questions bubbled in Abby's mind. "Love letters?" The words finally escaped from her lips.

Kum Yong lifted her fingers to her mouth with a giggle. "Ma-Yi has been writing letters with a Chinese man from Minnesota who wishes a bride. They are to be married on Thursday at the Mission house." She shrugged her shoulders. "Now? The fire might eat up the Mission along with Chinatown. But Lo Mo—Miss Cameron—says, it only matters we are safe. The Mission is just a building." She shook her head. "But Ma-Yi is worried her fiancé will not be able to find her if we leave." She pointed at a tall, thin girl near the front of the line, wads of sheets and clothing gripped under one arm. Abby recognized Yoke Hay clutching her free hand.

"Lo Mo told her to trust God. She says today we will all learn to trust Him better."

Abby sighed. "It seems to me today makes it even harder to trust God."

Kum Yong frowned. "Maybe. But, God has kept us safe, so far. And I can't forget how God rescued me from slavery."

Abby's stomach quivered. "In China?"

Kum Yong shifted her load. "No, here in Chinatown."

"But, it's against the law," Abby sputtered, and fell silent, her face burning. As if laws fixed every problem. "How did you become a slave?"

Kum Yong's eyebrows drew together. "I was very young when I lived in China, but I remember a man spoke to my father about taking girls to America. He told my father my sister and I would be daughters for rich Chinese merchants. We would help the wives with their little babies. Everyone in China calls America 'Gold Mountain.' He said we would have plenty of food and fine clothes. We would marry well.

"He gave my father money for my sister and me. Father thought it better to send us to America than for our brothers to die from hunger."

Abby's mouth dropped open, but she snapped it shut. Walking in the shadow of the mansions along Sacramento Avenue, it was difficult to imagine the desperation leading a father to sell his daughters. "So the man lied?"

"Yes. When we got to America, they took my sister away and handed me over to strangers. I learned quickly I was no daughter." Kum Yong drew her hands up into her sleeves, her eyes darkening.

"After many months there, Lo Mo arrived with policemen. They showed the master papers and asked about a slave girl. He said, 'No, no slave girl. Just my loving daughter.'" Kum Yong's lips pulled back from her teeth as she spoke.

"I was terrified. I thought this white stranger was coming to take me to the brothel or a jail."

In spite of the warm late-afternoon sun, an uncomfortable chill swept over Abby, raising gooseflesh on her arms.

Kum Yong shifted her pack again. "Lo Mo told me, 'Jesus can save you from this life. Jesus is a kind master. He will give you rest, not beatings.'"

"How long have you been at the Mission?" Abby steered the conversation away from religion.

"Eight years, now. At first I was like them." Kum Yong gestured to the younger girls, "Going to school at the Mission, learning English. Now, I'm eighteen, I work in the kitchen and help Lo Mo with rescues and in court." She straightened her shoulders. "Lo Mo rescues more girls all the time, most from the brothels. Those girls have a very hard time. I am very thankful Jesus saved me before I ended up there."

Abby shook her head. "Don't you wonder why Jesus didn't save you from all of it? Why would he let you be a slave at all? Why would he allow your family to starve in the first place?"

"I used to ask. But now, I think . . ." Her lips pursed. "If Jesus hadn't let me come to America and be a slave, I might not have known him at all."

A prickle raced across Abby's arms. This girl spoke of God in the same manner as Cecelia. Like a friend. A shiver crawled up her spine. *Why have I never experienced this?*

"Someday . . ." Kum Yong bit her lip. "Someday, I want to go back to China and find my father. I will tell him how much God loves him, too."

Abby's throat tightened. "Aren't you angry with him?" She pushed knuckles against her side. "Fathers are supposed to protect their daughters."

The Chinese woman clasped one arm behind her, pushing the load higher on her back, looking up at the sky as she walked. "I used to be angry. But, I think he meant well. He thought he was doing a good thing." She twisted a lock of hair. "Do you know the story of Joseph? His brothers sold him into slavery, like me. But God used his trouble and raised Joseph up into a position of power in Egypt so he could save his family. God sometimes makes good out of the bad." She set her chin. "I would like to go home someday and save my family—like Joseph."

Abby glanced down at her dusty skirt. "I thought God would help my sister. I asked him to. But she died anyway. He can't make good out of that." She gestured to the city. "And I certainly can't see any good coming out of all this mess."

Kum Yong's eyes widened. She touched Abby's sleeve. "I am sorry about your sister. I miss my sister, too."

Abby blinked back tears, turning her face away.

Kum Yong stepped closer and looped an arm through Abby's as they walked, plodding up the steep hill together.

4:15 p.m.

Robert stared at the giant oak. He balled his hand into a fist, burying it in the pocket of his trousers. A few months ago, he'd sat under the tree with a beautiful woman and gotten her to smile. Today, crowds of refugees surrounded it, milling about like lost sheep.

He jammed a hand through his hair, wincing as his fingers encountered the goose egg at the base of his skull. How could he locate Abby in this throng? He didn't even know if she was here.

Gerald walked down the path toward him. "Any luck?"

Robert shook his head, grinding his foot against the ground. Desperation hung over the park like the smoke clinging to the air. "They could be anywhere."

Sighing, Gerald gestured toward the car. "Let's go. We've looked everywhere. Hopefully they'll make their way back to my house. With your injury, you should be resting. You've done far too much today already."

Robert gave one last glance through the park, praying he'd spot Abby amongst the faces. "I don't like it."

"Nor do I, but what choice do we have? We'll pray God keeps them safe." Gerald ran a hand over his chin.

Robert cocked a brow. "I didn't take you for a praying man."

One corner of Gerald's mouth lifted into a smirk. "Yes, well, if you live with my mother long enough, she rubs off on you, I suppose."

Robert fell in beside his friend, maneuvering through the camp-sites on their way back to the road. "Mrs. Larkspur is quite outspoken about her faith."

Pushing back his hat, Gerald's smile deepened. "The good Lord seems to listen to her, too. She was always praying for me as a kid—mostly so I'd get caught whenever I did something wrong. I always did, too." He rubbed the back of his neck.

"I can't picture you as a troublemaker." Robert chuckled.

"I held my own. But my father was pretty quick with the belt, so between his discipline and my mother's prayers—I didn't stand much of a chance. I learned to walk the straight and narrow."

Robert reached for the automobile door. "In my house, it was my dad who was always praying and quoting Scripture."

His friend slid behind the wheel. "He was a doctor, too, right?"

Robert scanned the crowd one last time before climbing in. "I suppose I found it somewhat confusing. He prayed for his patients' health, yet it looked to me as if his own hands did the healing." Robert shrugged. "When I went away to medical school, I placed my faith on the shelf in favor of science."

"And how has it worked for you?"

Robert braced a foot against the front rail as Gerald eased the auto onto the road. "Fine, until recently." He coughed, the smoky air tickling at his lungs.

The car bumped along the road, weaving past horse-drawn carts sagging under the weight of people's belongings. "Because of Cecelia?"

Robert nodded, the memory bringing a lump to his throat.

Gerald pulled in behind a milk van, grimacing at the slow traf-fic. "She's better off now. You know that. We're the ones who are hurting."

"So, who has the answers? God or science?" Robert rapped his fingers against his knee.

Gerald pulled back on the throttle, the engine idling as they waited for an opportunity to cross the intersection. "Perhaps science is one of God's tools. Here's how I see it . . ." He turned to face Robert. "How does one learn to understand God?"

Robert frowned. "You study Scripture, go to church—listen to the teaching."

Gerald eased the car forward. "And those things are great. But think of God as an artist. If you believe God created the world, His fingerprints must be everywhere, all around us. You learn about an artist by studying his art. The human body is the most complex masterpiece ever created. We've only begun to scratch the surface with our scientific knowledge. To claim we've somehow mastered science is like a baby trying to recite the complete works of Shakespeare."

Gerald tipped his hat back. "I just don't see how science and faith are so different. What is science, but a study of the Maker?"

Robert pondered his friend's words in silence until they stopped in front of the house. "So, why doesn't He give us the answers? Let us heal people?"

"Now there's the big question." Gerald stepped out, closing the door with a bang. "Maybe because He knows we'd take credit."

30

4:40 p.m.

*A*bby tipped her head back, her gaze climbing the tall wooden church steeple, a bold finger pointing at the heavens. Miss Cameron gestured for the group to wait as she entered the building. Mrs. Ling and the other older woman, like a pair of sheepdogs, herded the girls into a tight group.

Abby leaned close to Kum Yong. "Are they afraid someone is going to wander off?"

Kum Yong's inky black brows lifted. "Wander off? Where would we go? No, they are keeping watch for highbinders—men who would try to take us back to slavery."

Miss Cameron, hat in hand, appeared in the doorway and beckoned to the girls. Her silvery hair glinted in the late afternoon light, a sharp contrast to her youthful complexion.

Abby hesitated, trailing after the group as they filed into the sanctuary. The heavy doors closed, locking out the fearful smoky street. She stared up at the huge windows, the colored glass filtering the afternoon light and adding a sense of calm to the cavernous space.

The chatter quieted as the girls piled belongings against the wall and took seats on the wooden pews, rubbing tired necks and looking about with large eyes.

Abby hovered by the entrance, heart fluttering. As much as she wanted to hide in this beautiful place, she knew she didn't belong.

Kum Yong seized Abby's hand and tugged her to Miss Cameron's side. "Lo Mo, do you remember Abby from Lane Hospital?"

Abby glanced down at the floor before meeting Miss Cameron's eyes. The missionary took Abby's hand and squeezed it. "Yes, of course. Welcome, Abby. Mrs. Ling and I were just speaking of you a moment ago. I am glad she invited you to join us. No one should be alone today."

"Thank you, ma'am. I appreciate your kindness."

Abby followed Kum Yong to a bench, collapsing in near exhaustion.

Miss Cameron and the minister spoke in hushed tones, while the Chinese girls chattered to each other in their foreign tongue.

Abby pushed her back against the seat, her tired muscles relaxing. She unfastened her shoe buttons and wrapped firm fingers around her throbbing ankle. Leaning forward, she draped her arms over the pew in front of her and allowed her head to drop down onto her wrists. Wisps of hair fell alongside her face, screening her from the others' eyes.

Even in the moment of quiet, Abby's mind fluttered from one image to another: the crushed buildings, the plumes of smoke, people dragging their belongings, Kum Yong's scars, Mama's glazed eyes, giant cracks in the road, Robert's hand on her arm, Davy's sticky face. Digging into her skirt pocket, she drew out the journal. Perhaps its words could chase away these thoughts. She let the book fall open.

April 23, 1853

Mama seems better today. Maybe it's the sun shining in her window. She says she loves the feel of the light on her face. I wish Papa would take her outside, but he's worried the air would make her worse. I gathered flowers and put them by her bed. She smiled real big. Papa even smiled a bit, too. I'm going to double my prayers tonight and maybe Mama will be even better tomorrow.

April 25, 1853

I didn't write yesterday because it was such a bad day. The sun shone, but Mama said the light hurt. She's coughing more. At one point she couldn't breathe, the coughs came so fast. Her face went blue and her lips stained with blood. I ran from the room, I was so scared. I'm writing this in the yard, under the lilac bushes. They're Mama's favorites, but Papa said no more flowers. He thinks it makes her coughing worse. I'd pull up every flower in the yard if it would make her better.

April 30, 1853

We buried her today down by the lilac tree. Mama loved those lilacs.

Abby closed the book, leaving a finger to hold the place. Twisting a handful of skirt, she took a deep breath, waiting for the pain in her heart to ease. She forced her eyes back to the page.

May 1

I woke up early this morning and ran to Mama's room. I'd forgotten during the night. Can you believe it? It's like she died all over again.

My class memorized the 23rd Psalm for the Sunday school lesson. All the other girls lined up to recite.

Teacher just patted my shoulder as she went past. All the girls whispered behind my back.

I felt sick when I heard the part about "walking through the valley of the shadow of death . . . " Preacher said those words at Mama's funeral. I never wanted to hear those verses again and then in Sunday school I had to hear it eight times.

Abby closed the journal and returned it to her pocket. The minister had read the Psalm at Cecelia's funeral, too. The words floated through her mind like a smoky haze. The valley of the shadow of death was an apt description for San Francisco today.

The windows rattled as another blast of dynamite shook the city.

Several of the girls began to sing. Abby closed her eyes and listened, absently kicking the pew in front of her. The melody pricked her heart until the air felt like a weight crushing against her shoulders. Abby lurched to her feet.

Kum Yong looked up. "What's wrong?"

"I can't stay. I must find my family." Abby stumbled down the row toward the aisle, her chest tightening until she struggled for breath.

Her new friend followed, clutching at her arm. "Stay the night with us. Tomorrow you can find your family. It is not safe to be out at night with the city on fire."

Abby's feet and legs trembled with exhaustion. Mama wouldn't want her out after dark, especially with things in such a muddle, but she must be crazy with worry by now. Abby pushed her hands into her hair. "I don't know how to fix this."

Mrs. Ling appeared at her side. "Yes, Miss Abby, stay. You should not be wandering streets by yourself." The woman placed her small hand on Abby's shoulder. "Sit, child. You look like you are sleeping on your feet already. Your mother would not want you to be in danger."

As if to confirm her words, the windows rattled. A hush descended on the group. Yoke Hay whimpered, tears sliding down her face. Kum Yong scooped up the child, cradling her against her long white blouse and crooning in the girl's ear. Other girls joined in the song, the frightening sounds giving way to the warmth of their voices.

Abby sank back into the pew. Kum Yong sat down, the girl cuddled against her shoulder. "You wouldn't find them in the dark anyway. You will find them tomorrow."

Tears blurred Abby's eyes. One night. That's all it would be.

31

*R*obert tossed off the bedspread and flung himself upright as a rumble tore through the house. He jumped to his feet, stumbling as the ground rose up to meet him, his balance thrown into disarray by the throbbing in his skull. His chest and shoulder hit the floor like a pile of bricks and he lay still, gasping for breath.

The gentle tremor eased, but not before his mind rushed through visions from the previous morning—falling beams, patients screaming, chaos. He dug his fingers into the rag rug, legs trembling, a miniature quake spreading outward from his chest.

Robert rose to his hands and knees, fighting the urge to retch. The dull pain above his eyes retreated into the background as his breathing slowed.

Mrs. Larkspur's tremulous voice carried down the hall. "Gerald?"

Footsteps passed in front of his door, proceeding down the hall. "Everything is all right, Mother. Just a small one. Nothing to worry about."

The footsteps returned, pausing briefly outside his room before continuing. A door closed.

Robert expelled a long breath, feeling his heart rate slow. He pressed both hands against his face, banishing the memories.

As soon as he chased one worry away, another rushed in to fill the void. Where were Abby and Davy and their mother? Were they sleeping in the open somewhere? He pushed to his feet and wandered to the window. Pulling back the loose drapery, he gazed out into the night. The horizon glowed, the inferno still raging in the distance.

Robert clutched the windowsill. She could be anywhere. And here he stood in a safe house, surrounded by people who cared about him. His skin crawled, a sickly sensation starting at his feet and traveling upward across his body.

How can I wait for morning? He yanked his folded trousers from the chair. Who cares if it is the middle of the night?

Pulling on his clothes, he mapped out the city in his mind. Maple Manor was north from Nob Hill. The fires approached from the east and south. Since the family didn't come to the Larkspur house, the officials leading the evacuation must have sent them someplace. Union Square? No, the fires must have long since burned through the area.

They could be anywhere, but his thoughts kept returning to Golden Gate Park, the place of their first picnic.

Robert retrieved his shoes and pushed his feet into them. He gripped the doorknob, slowing his movements to preserve the silence. His footsteps echoed in the quiet hall, so he yanked the shoes back off and walked in his stocking feet. A fresh wave of pain rolled through his head, the dark stairs swimming before his eyes. Robert grasped the railing for support, the bottom stair creaking under his weight.

"Going somewhere?" Gerald's voice broke the stillness of the front room.

Robert paused, squinting against the darkness.

His friend stood in the parlor, his face washed in the orange glow from the bay window, a cup in his hand.

"Can't sleep. I thought I might go out and take another look for—for the Fischers."

Gerald snorted, turning back to the view and taking a sip of the drink. "For Abby, you mean."

"Yes."

"At least you're being honest. It's a step in the right direction. Maybe the thump on your head did you some good after all." Gerald gestured out the window. "It's an unbelievable sight. I just can't get my head to believe what my eyes are seeing—what they've already seen today."

Robert joined him. "I know what you mean."

"So much change in the course of one day. Who'd have thought it possible?"

The night sky crackled with the sound of distant dynamite. Robert pulled his braces up over his shoulders. "And how much more is changing with every passing moment?"

Gerald lowered the cup and met Robert's eyes. "But one thing hasn't changed."

Turning from the window, Robert tipped his head, waiting for his friend to elucidate. "What is it?"

"You. You're rushing off like a knight into battle."

Robert yanked the watch fob, drawing the timepiece from his pocket. "Isn't it what we're supposed to do?"

"You know you won't find her in the dark. It's a fool's errand. You're taking action simply to make yourself feel better, and it won't help Abby one bit. At times like this, we have to trust God to handle things."

Robert opened the watch and tried to read it by the flickering light. "Doesn't God help those who help themselves?" The hour hand had just passed the two.

"The world says so. Scripture says God helps the helpless and when we put our trust in Him, He straightens our paths."

Robert clicked the watch shut and returned it to his trouser pocket. "You're full of wisdom tonight. So, we just let them wander in the dark and the smoke and hope God is watching over them while we sleep?"

Gerald turned, the glow casting an odd mixture of light and shadow across his face. "We don't hope, Robert. We pray, and we trust." He patted Robert's arm before heading for the stairway.

Silence fell across the room like a woolen blanket. Weariness crept over Robert and he leaned forward, letting his weight rest against the window frame. "You're out there somewhere, and I can't do a thing about it." He took a deep breath. Was Gerald right?

"God, show me what to do." His breath fogged the glass as he whispered the words. "I don't want to wait and trust, I want to take action." He allowed the prayer to roll around in his mind. "If I *must* wait . . ." He stepped back so the view would clear. "Then I pray You are with Abby tonight."

He touched the glass. Was the fire growing closer?

Hold her . . . and protect her, Lord. Since I cannot.

2:15 a.m.

Abby stretched out on the pews, the hard wood a welcome cradle to her aching legs. Lying on her stomach, she pushed up on her forearms to look at Kum Yong. The woman's smooth hair gleamed in the dim light as she lay with knees bent, her head resting on her arm, eyes closed. Warmth crept across Abby's skin as she gazed at her new friend.

Cecelia had been an expert at gathering friends. People naturally flocked to her.

Abby had known Kum Yong only for a few hours and she already felt closer to her than any school chum. Why?

Kum Yong opened her eyes and pushed up on her elbows, mirroring Abby's posture. She giggled. "We look like two sea lions on the shore." Kum rested her chin in her hands. "I'm glad you are staying with us, Abby."

The warmth spread through Abby. "I appreciate your kindness. Your friendship."

In the dim light, Kum Yong's teeth shone bright as a broad smile crossed her face. "I am glad to make a new friend."

Abby lowered her head onto her arms and closed her eyes. Exhausted though she was, her mind buzzed with activity. She turned over to her back and stared up into the darkness, thinking about Mama and Davy sleeping in the open. Time dragged, each tick of the clock drawing her a step closer to sunrise and morning.

The windows rattled as a distant blast shook the building. Abby tensed. Each detonation seemed closer than the last. Were they really safe here?

She forced her eyes closed, willing her body to relax. If she could just grab a few minutes of sleep, the morning would soon arrive. Her thoughts drifted back home, imagining she walked through the orchard with Cecelia at her side. Her sister's words rose and fell like notes of music, her face adorned with sunshine-filled smiles. Abby grabbed her sister's hand and the two ran toward home, feet flying over the dusty earth.

Another rocking blast dragged Abby back to the darkened church, the building vibrating like a tolling bell. The blackness of the room closed in, wrenching her gut. Abby rolled to her stomach and buried her face in her arm. Hot tears stung her eyes.

Kum Yong sat upright. She eased down to the narrow space between the pews, placing a cool hand on Abby's shoulder. "Abby?"

Choking back the tears, Abby cleared her throat. "I'm sorry. Did I wake you?"

A soft laugh tickled the darkness. "Who can sleep with all the bangs?" Her hand traveled down Abby's arm until it reached her hand. "Come with me."

Abby pushed up to a sitting position. "Where?"

With a gentle tug, Kum Yong guided her down the center aisle, slinking like a mouse through the shadows. The young woman pushed through a swinging door at the back of the room.

Abby followed her into an equally dim room beyond. A round, stained glass window on the back wall shone like a beacon in the darkness. Kum Yong's face reflected the faint light. They settled on a cushioned bench, sitting shoulder to shoulder.

Kum Yong broke the silence. "Why are you crying? Are you scared? Do you miss your family? Your sister?" She reached over, capturing Abby's hand.

Abby released the breath she hadn't realized she was holding. "Yes—well, no." She shrugged. "It's just all too much. Everything has gone so wrong." She pressed fingers against the bridge of her nose. "Yes, I miss my sister. All the time. Not a moment goes by I don't think of her."

Kum Yong's shoulder pressed up against hers. "Tell me about her."

The lump growing in Abby's throat made it difficult to speak. She coughed into her sleeve, squeezing her eyes shut. After another press from her friend's hand, she took a deep breath, the memories flooding her mind. "She was like sunshine. Everyone was special to her. She never said a bad word about anyone." Abby paused, considering her words. "Well, she teased sometimes, to make people laugh. Never to hurt. Her optimism used to irritate me. I'd be fretting about something and she'd find some way of turning it around. She had a way of making things look better." A tear slipped onto her cheek and Abby lifted a hand to brush it away.

"And now?"

The words jabbed Abby's heart. More tears broke free, wandering down to her jaw line. Her voice cracked. "There is no one to turn it to something good." Abby held her breath, trapping a sob in her throat.

Kum Yong wove her arm behind Abby's back. "You miss her."

A painful hiccup made Abby jerk. "I'm angry with her."

Her friend cocked her head. "Why?"

A rushing current flowed through Abby's arms and legs. "She didn't keep fighting. Because she went away and left me here by myself."

Kum Yong nodded and leaned close, rubbing tiny circles on Abby's back. For a long time the room sat silent except for distant rumbles and the occasional sniff.

At length, Kum Yong lowered her head. "Jesus, please help my friend, Abby."

Abby stiffened.

Kum Yong kept a firm grasp on her hand. "You know her pain, Lord. You understand her anger. Please show her she does not walk this earth alone."

Silent tears dripped down Abby's face, landing on their clasped hands.

"Amen," Kum Yong whispered.

Abby pulled her hand free and pressed both her palms against her eyes.

Kum Yong squeezed her shoulder. "You're not alone."

32

2:35 a.m.

*R*obert plodded up the stairs, his heart heavy. Pray and trust. Pray and wait. Pray and sleep? Somehow, he couldn't imagine it working, but he might as well make the attempt.

He sprawled on the bed, the room dark except for the faint glow from the window—the distant fires felt like they burned within his head as well. Robert pressed his face into the pillow, trying to bury the ache. He rolled to his side, shadows crawling across the wall as his eyelids drooped.

The shadows followed him into sleep.

In his dreams, Robert staggered down countless streets, scanning faceless crowds and calling Abby's name until his voice gave way. His heart pounded as he crawled over rubble and searched through burned-out structures. *I know she's out here somewhere.*

An electrical wire coiled like a hissing snake, arcing and spitting sparks into the night. Robert reeled backward, stumbling into a dark alley. He pressed his back against a wall, fingers splayed out across the rough bricks. The roar of the fire chased every thought from his mind and he ran in blind panic, the blaze licking at his heels.

A single thought cut through the din like a scalpel.

She's at the church.

3:00 a.m.

In the dark recesses of the church, Abby dug for her handkerchief. "I wonder what time it is." She pressed the small square against her eyes, the fabric reeking of smoke, dirt, and sweat. She lifted her arm, burying her nose in her sleeve. The foul odor clung to her clothes and body.

Kum Yong stood by the door, staring into the dark sanctuary.

"What is it?" Abby rose.

"What is Lo Mo doing?" Kum Yong's soft voice stirred the air. In her soft shoes, she walked in perfect silence, stepping around sleeping forms until she reached the front.

Clutching her high-button shoes, Abby crept after her, careful to place her feet in the same places, lest she step on someone's fingers.

Light spilled from a small lamp, creating an inviting half-circle on the wood floor near the altar. Miss Cameron pushed her arms into the sleeves of a long coat. Mrs. Ling fastened a cloak about her rounded shoulders.

Kum Yong's eyes widened as she rushed to the women's sides. "Where are you going, Lo Mo?"

Miss Cameron pinned a feathered hat over her silver hair with an air of confidence belying the lines etched on her forehead. "Don't worry, girls. I just need to get a few things from the Mission house before the fire reaches it."

Kum Yong grasped the edge of Miss Cameron's sleeve. "Take me with you. I want to help."

Mrs. Ling frowned at her outburst. "Kum Yong, foolish girl! Go back to sleep."

"It's all right, Mrs. Ling." Miss Cameron smiled and patted Kum Yong's hand. "I would feel better if you stayed here and helped watch the smaller children."

Kum Yong straightened to her full height. "Ma-Yi and Yoke Soo can look after the little girls. I can help you carry the things back."

Miss Cameron and Mrs. Ling exchanged looks. The missionary pulled on a pair of gloves. "We could use the assistance, I imagine."

Abby stepped out of the doorway. "Then, I will come, too." Her knees trembled.

Miss Cameron's brows arched high above her gray-brown eyes.

"If I can't help my family—at least let me help yours."

Kum Yong grasped Abby's arm. "Please, Lo Mo."

After a long sigh, Miss Cameron nodded. "Very well. You can both join us. But stay close and follow my instructions exactly."

A new energy coursed through Abby, her skin tingling.

Miss Cameron reached a hand out to Mrs. Ling and another to Abby. "I think this is a good time to pray."

Mrs. Ling stepped in next to Kum Yong, closing the circle.

The women's heads bowed. Abby studied their faces as they prayed. Such an unlikely group—the stoop-shouldered Chinese woman, the silvery-haired Christian missionary, and Abby's new big-hearted friend. Faith seemed to wind through their lives like the grapevines trailing up the trellis at Aunt Mae's. A bittersweet longing whispered in the stillness of Abby's heart. She closed her eyes, floating on the words, until Miss Cameron finished the prayer.

Miss Cameron squeezed Abby's hand, her gaze traveling in a circle. "Let's go."

Abby followed the women into the night. The streets were empty now except for a few stragglers still wandering in the dark and others sprawled out, sleeping atop their belongings.

Lifting her gaze, Abby watched as the glowing clouds floated into the night sky, the hairs on her arms rising. Were they really going to march into the firestorm? Suddenly she wanted nothing more than to dash back into the silent church and hide beneath one of the pews.

Mrs. Ling placed hands over her cheeks. "It's come so close. I pray we are not too late."

The fire's glow reflecting in her eyes, Miss Cameron did not glance at the flames, but started up the hill, her skirt flapping as she walked.

Abby hurried to catch up, the two Chinese women on her heels. "What is it you need to save?" *What could be so important?*

Miss Cameron's eyes never strayed from the path. "I'm sure Kum Yong has told you what we do at the Mission. Every time we rescue a girl from slavery, I petition for legal, custodial rights. We maintain paperwork for every girl. With City Hall in ruins and the police busy with the disaster, I would hate to see someone take advantage of the crisis and steal a girl from my care."

Forced to take multiple steps to match the woman's determined stride, Abby lifted the hem of her skirt to keep it out of the way of her rushing feet. Mrs. Ling and Kum Yong jogged along in their wake.

Miss Cameron reached a gloved hand to straighten her hat, adjusting the pin holding it firmly to her hair. She lowered her chin, eyes darkening. "When we left this morning, my only thought was to get my daughters to safety. Now, I need to make sure they remain safe."

Kum Yong caught up, breathing heavily, her eyes glittering in the dim light. "What happens if we can't save the papers?"

"Then we have no proof you girls belong with me. In the time it would take to get the paperwork replaced, the Tongs could make our lives difficult." Miss Cameron shook her head, face grim. "I will not let our work go up in smoke. God would not bring us so far, only to let us fail."

Kum Yong laid a hand on Abby's arm. "Lo Mo," she paused, taking a deep breath. "Abby asked why God allowed me to be a slave. Why didn't He prevent it? And why didn't He save Abby's sister from dying? Why does He let bad things happen?"

Abby's face flushed. This seemed like a bad time to be questioning Miss Cameron.

The woman slackened her pace, as if the question gave her reason to pause. "I imagine many people are asking those types of questions tonight. I don't believe God makes bad things happen, Kum

Yong. He is with us every moment of our lives—through the good and the bad. The Bible says when Jesus' friend Lazarus died, Jesus wept with Lazarus's sisters. It says His heart was 'greatly moved.' He feels our pain, He shares it."

The words pulled at Abby. She swallowed, her mouth dry. "He could have stopped it. If Lazarus was His friend, why didn't He intervene?"

Miss Cameron's chuckle dispelled some of the gloom of the night. "That's exactly what the sisters said. 'Lord, if only you had been here, our brother would not have died!' But Jesus had a plan to show everyone God's glory and His power. He brought Lazarus back from the dead."

The smoke stung Abby's eyes. "Because Lazarus was His friend. He's not going to do the same for my sister."

"I think Jesus wanted people to understand He holds power over death."

"If He has power over death, why didn't He keep my sister alive?"

Miss Cameron waited a long moment before speaking. "Abby, may I ask you a question before I answer that?"

Darkness covered Abby's nod. "Of course."

"Did your sister believe in Jesus? Did she trust Him?"

"Wholeheartedly. During her last few weeks, it's practically all she would speak of." The memory stung.

Miss Cameron turned her head, gazing at Abby with a smile. "Then your sister is not dead in the grave, she is safe in His arms. She is rejoicing in His presence this very moment. She is not wandering frightened through a burning city. She is at peace in a way we cannot fully comprehend."

Abby's breath rattled in her chest as she struggled to the top of the steep hill. She imagined Cecelia laughing and smiling with Jesus, running through the fields of heaven. It is what Cecelia had believed—but was it true? Or just wishful thinking?

Apparently unfazed by the climb, Miss Cameron continued. "God is here as well. He is walking with us now, supporting us with His strong hands. God feels your sadness, Abby. He mourns with you. Not for your sister's death, but for your loss. If you let Him, He will see you through this."

As the woman finished speaking, Abby slowed her steps, falling back to walk with Kum Yong. After passing the top of the hill, they looked down the steep incline toward the glowing inferno below. A hot smoky wind blasted up to meet them. An explosion shook the ground, echoing through the nearby buildings.

Abby and Kum Yong hurried to keep up with Miss Cameron and Mrs. Ling as they trotted down Sacramento Street, the air growing more sweltering with every step.

"The Mission." Mrs. Ling breathed the word like a sigh of relief. The five-story brick building stood silhouetted, like a dark fortress, against the glowing sky. Miss Cameron and Mrs. Ling hastened the last few steps as Kum Yong trailed behind.

Abby paused, straining to read the letters etched in the stone-work above the front door: "Occidental Board of Foreign Missions."

"Good old '920.'" Miss Cameron clapped her palms together like a schoolteacher calling a class to order. "God must have held it together with his bare hands. So many other brick buildings crumbled in the quake."

A policeman hovered near the door and greeted the missionary like a long-lost friend. "Miss Cameron, you must be quick. The firemen are laying dynamite just down the block. They will be here shortly."

Her eyes darkened, her brows pinching together. "They're going to dynamite our Mission house?"

"They are planning on taking out the whole block. They want to stop this thing before it reaches the mansions on Nob Hill. So, you must make haste, Miss. I'll keep watch here."

Face stony, Miss Cameron caught up her skirts and raced up the stairs. Abby and the two women followed. By the flickering glow from the window, Miss Cameron dug through a desk drawer, tossing packets of papers onto the blotter.

Kum Yong appeared in the doorway with a handful of pillowcases.

With trembling hands, Abby scooped papers from the desk, helping the women stuff the cases full.

The policeman's voice rang out from below, "Make haste, Miss Cameron! They are bringing the dynamite!"

Abby rushed to the window. A group of firemen clustered around the front steps. "I think we'd better leave now. Do you have what you need?"

Miss Cameron rose to her feet, papers clutched to her chest. "Yes, I believe so." She stood in silence, her gaze traveling about the room. "This building was a gift from God. May we never forget His loving-kindness."

The firemen waited at the front door, axes balanced on their slumping shoulders.

After thanking the policeman, Miss Cameron turned to the firemen. "Thank you, gentlemen, for your hard work today. We will be praying for your safety."

One of them shook her hand, his face grim. "Thank you, Missus. I am truly sorry about your building."

She placed her other hand on top of his grimy one. "I am thankful my daughters are safe. God has been gracious to us." She stared down the hill toward the glowing flames. "What is the news of Chinatown?"

He glanced at his boots. "It's gone, ma'am."

Her shoulders sagged.

As they stepped outside, Kum Yong crouched down and retrieved something from the ground, slipping it into her pocket as another explosion rocked the ground.

Abby gripped the edge of the building to steady herself.

Miss Cameron gave one last lingering look at the building before leading the group back into the night.

33

6:00 a.m.

$\mathcal{D}$awn light, tainted rusty-orange by smoke, spilled in through the open window. Robert blinked and glanced about the unfamiliar room, disoriented by his troubling dreams. *Where am I?*

Jerking upright with sudden realization, Robert's head spun sending his stomach roiling. He gripped the edges of the mattress as his center of balance tipped, threatening to dump him onto the floor. Robert lowered himself to the pillow with a groan, grinding his knuckles against his temples. After closing his eyes for a brief moment, he pushed himself to his elbows and waited for his equilibrium to settle.

With a deep breath, he pushed himself vertical, swinging his legs over the edge of the bed.

A tap rang out from the door. "Robert, you awake?" Gerald's muffled voice spoke through the room.

Robert grunted and cleared his throat. "Yes."

The door swung open and Gerald crossed the threshold, jamming his arms into his coat sleeves. "Get some sleep after all? How are you feeling?"

Dropping his head forward into his hands, Robert groaned a second time. "Like I fell under a cable car and then performed surgery all night."

Gerald laughed. "Probably not too far off from reality, my friend." He crossed the room and dropped down on the end of the bed, setting the mattress bouncing.

"Quit rocking the boat." Robert didn't lift his head.

"Why don't you stay here. Get some rest and let your head heal. My mother would be more than happy to spend the day fussing over you."

Robert raked his fingers through his hair. "No. I'm coming. As soon as the room stops spinning."

With a chuckle, Gerald rose and headed for the door. "When you're ready, Mother's laid out a spread of food. You ought to stay over more often—I haven't seen a breakfast like this in years. And it's quite a feat, considering she had to cook outside. You look like you could use some black coffee."

The idea of food sent Robert's stomach into a new series of gyrations. He leaned forward, stretching his back as he felt around the floor for his shoes. His head clamored to return to the pillow, but he bunched his muscles and pushed up to his feet, stumbling over to the window. Colossal columns of smoke billowed from the city, jacketing the morning sky with haze.

He pressed his hand to the window, his nausea replaced by cold fingers of dread. Not only had the fires not abated, they had spread, consuming the city block by block during the night. Where would it end?

Was Gerald's home safe? Would any of San Francisco be spared from the gluttonous flames?

He snatched his tie and jacket from the chair. Too much time had wasted already.

6:30 a.m.

"Abby." A hand gripped her shoulder. Abby opened her eyes, gritty with sleep, her knees clenched into her stomach. The flames and the heat of her dreams fled, replaced by Kum Yong's face. "Abby, wake up." She clutched Abby's shoulder, giving it a second shake. "You were dreaming."

Abby sat up and rubbed her eyes.

Kum Yong plopped down. "Nightmare?"

"Yes. Too much talk about fires, I think." Abby swallowed, the burning sensation in her throat subsiding.

Sunlight poured in the high windows of the church. The dark night and the fiery dream faded and Abby stretched arms toward the ceiling, pulling the kinks from her frame. Dirt and sweat caked both skin and clothes. Her toe, tipped with an angry red blister, peeped out from a large hole in her stocking. She flexed her swollen ankle, drawing a circle in the air with her toes. Ignoring the discomfort, Abby pulled on her shoes, and fastened the buttons.

Kum Yong joined the other Chinese girls as they spoke in hushed tones and gathered their things. One of the babies fussed.

Abby closed her eyes for a moment and the images of the night before flooded back. Wiggling her cold fingers, she hooked them under her arms to warm.

Kum Yong finished gathering her things and settled onto the bench beside Abby. "Reverend Guthrie says the fire is traveling this way and it's not safe to stay here any longer. Lo Mo has decided we'll walk around the fires and make our way to the waterfront. We will take a ferry across the bay." She placed her hand on Abby's arm. "Will you come with us?"

"No, I have to find my family. My Mama must be worried."

Kum Yong nodded. "I'll pray for you and your family." She reached into her pocket and drew out a small red chunk of brick, rubbing it between her fingers.

Abby leaned over to look. "What is that?"

"It's a piece of the Mission house. Last week, Lo Mo taught us about the prophet, Samuel. When the Israelites' enemies were attacking, Samuel prayed. God sent thunder and frightened the armies away. So the people wouldn't forget how God had helped them, Samuel set up a stone—Lo Mo called it an 'Ebenezer.' She said it meant 'stone of help.' Samuel said, 'Thus far has the Lord helped us.' "

Kum Yong rolled the small stone between her fingers. "Last night, when I realized the Mission would be destroyed, I decided to save a piece of it. I don't want to forget what God did for me there." She closed her fingers over the chunk of brick and pressed it to her heart. "This is my Ebenezer."

"Like the hymn?" Abby slid closer to her friend. "My sister always sang, 'Here I raise my Ebenezer, hither by Thy help I've come . . .' "

Kum Yong's eyes brightened. "It's my favorite—'Come Thou Fount of Every Blessing.' We sing it all the time."

An ache took hold of Abby's heart. "It was my sister's favorite, too." Her voice faltered.

Kum Yong looked up, her dark eyes burning with intensity. "I'll use the stone to remember you as well."

The words tugged at Abby. "Thank you." She studied the young woman's face. *Is this what real friendship is? Will we ever see each other again?* Abby touched Kum Yong's hand. "Can we still be friends when this is all over?"

Kum Yong's face lit up like a street full of electric lights. "Abby, I promise—I will be your friend forever." She opened her arms.

Abby's heart pounded, as if it had grown too large for her ribs. She fell into Kum's arms, wrapping her arms around the woman's lithe back. Meeting Kum Yong had been like gaining a sister; a small gift to chase away the crushing loneliness of the past few months. Brought together by an earthquake and fire—what could possibly tear them apart?

34

7:30 a.m.

The sea of humanity spread out before him like whitecaps on the bay. Everywhere he looked, Robert spotted Abby—or at least someone who resembled her. He pushed through the crowd, stepping around piles of belongings. Robert turned a slow circle, staring out into the crowd, hoping to see a familiar brown-haired beauty.

Gerald pushed through and joined him, his gaze swiveling from one side to the other. "No sign." He pushed the derby to the back of his head with a sigh. "I'm going to wander down to the east side, why don't you take the west? We'll meet back at the automobile in an hour."

"And what if we haven't found them?"

"I need to check in at the hospital. The fires are moving dangerously close to the area—not to mention my own neighborhood. If they don't get them under control by this evening, I'm not sure what's going to happen."

Robert stepped over a pile of books. "What will these people do? Where will they get food and water?"

"The army is already moving in to offer assistance. And the Red Cross. The real fear is going to be disease. This type of setting is ripe for a typhoid outbreak."

A swarm of boys dashed past, hurdling over obstacles in their play.

Robert took a deep breath. "If you don't see me at the car, go on without me. I'll meet you at the hospital later."

His friend pulled a watch from his pocket and gave Robert a quick slap on the shoulder before picking his way east through the park.

Robert eased through the crowd, heading for the lower reaches of the property where army tents sprouted like toadstools. He was thankful to see someone taking control of the melee. Who knows how long these people would remain itinerant. How many had already lost homes? How many more would follow?

"Help! Oh, please, help!" A woman's shriek sent a shockwave through the camp. A ripple of inquisitive murmurs rose like a frightened flock of starlings.

Pressing between jam-packed bodies, Robert hurried toward the sound, heart quickening.

A young woman crouched over an elderly man, his peppery hair flopping to the side. The woman looked up, her face beseeching the crowd, hat ribbons hanging limp across her shoulders. "Please, help. I can't stop the bleeding!" She pressed a wad of cloth against a jagged wound in the man's leg, red stains spreading up the man's torn trousers.

The man clutched at his leg, a grimace scouring his face. "I'll be all right, Mary Ann. Don't make such a fuss."

Robert lowered himself to his knees, pressing against the woman's hand. "Keep a steady pressure. Don't lift the bandage to check."

He beckoned to a sallow-faced woman hovering nearby. "Can you find some clean linen? We're going to need more bandages. And water."

She gasped and nodded, hurrying off.

"Thank you." Tears streaked the young woman's face, her voice shaking. "He's my father. Are you a doctor?" She wiped her face against her sleeve.

Robert sat back on his heels. "Yes, I'm Dr. King. What happened?" He reached for his bag.

"I'm Mary Ann Marshall. My father was injured in the quake. We got the bleeding stopped last time, but just now . . ." A sob choked off her remaining words as blood dampened the rags under her fingers.

The older man scowled. "I tripped is all. But it's bleeding again."

Robert handed her another cloth. "It must have reopened the wound. Once we get the bleeding stopped, I'll take a look. It might need some stitches."

The gray-haired woman returned with armful of fabric. "I got an old sheet I could cut up. It's worn, but clean. Will it do?"

Robert nodded. "Perfect. Thank you." The bleeding slowed, and Robert risked a quick peek at the laceration, wincing at the extent of the damage. "You should have seen to this before now."

"Yeah, well. No time until now." The girl's father grunted.

After removing the old bandages, Robert wiped the area clean, thankful he'd brought his small medical kit along. He threaded the needle and made quick work of the sutures, the patient managing to lie motionless despite the discomfort.

A pleased ripple coursed through his stomach as he examined the fine, even stitches. How long had he taken to do Abby's? He leaned back, letting his shoulders relax as he returned the curved needle and forceps to their folds in the leather bag. His physician father would be proud. He'd regaled Robert with stories of war-time surgery, but the past two days had been Robert's first experience practicing medicine outside the cozy confines of the hospital and office.

"Now, be sure you keep it clean and dry." He turned his gaze from father to daughter. "Conditions here are less than optimal, but you want to prevent infection."

The man grunted, sitting forward and eyeing the puckered skin under the row of knots. "How long do they have to stay in?"

Robert wiped his hands on a rag, frowning at the bloodstains sullying the shirt he'd borrowed from Gerald. "At least ten days. If you see any signs of infection, see a doctor. Don't delay."

The daughter smiled, pushing back golden hair from her face. "We will. Thank you. I am so thankful God sent you here to us."

Pushing to his feet, Robert scooped up his bag. "Yes, well, I'm glad, too. Good luck."

He brushed stray blades of grass from his knees and settled his hat onto his head, grimacing as it pressed against the lump on the back of his skull. He glanced up at the sun, already climbing high into the sky. He'd missed his meeting time with Gerald. *And I'm no closer to finding Abby and her family.*

9:15 a.m.

Abby limped into Golden Gate Park on sore, tired feet. The grounds swarmed with people, like bees on fields of clover. Dull-eyed men and women sat on trunks and blankets while children raced around in circles, darting between heaps of possessions.

Abby moved among the throng, searching for a familiar face. Thousands of voices speaking quietly to each other created a humming vibration in the early morning air.

A young girl in a too-small dress plowed into Abby's legs, tears cleaning paths down her dirty cheeks. She looked up with haunted eyes, curly brown hair tangled and matted. The child stepped back in fear before turning and disappearing into the multitude.

Abby stood frozen in place, overwhelmed with longing for her own mother. Taking a deep breath, she pushed on, her hope fading with each unfamiliar face. She crossed the park from one corner to the other, stepping around trunks, boxes, and blankets.

The whole city must be hunkered down here. She stretched up on her toes, trying to see over the heads of people gathered nearby. After several moments, she rocked back onto her heels and pressed hands against her hollow chest. *Too many people. Too close.* She wandered to the edge of the park and found an empty spot near the road. Sinking to the ground, Abby dropped her head onto her knees, allowing the tears to flow. A gentle breeze lifted wisps of loose hair. "What now?" She murmured the words into her arm.

Her stomach growled at the smell of food cooking. It took all of her composure not to sniff the air like a hungry dog. Miss Cameron had invited her to share the meager breakfast, but Abby had declined. The missionary had done too much already.

Abby pulled Great Aunt Mae's journal from her pocket, flipping through the pages. A subtle change in the handwriting caught her eye. The words grew larger and more slanted, as if written in a hurry.

June 5, 1856

I'm moving! Can you believe it? My Aunt Joyce and Uncle Harold wired the foundling home in St. Louis and invited me to live with them in Cincinnati. I've never even met these people. My uncle is a teacher and the headmistress says they are good Christian folk. If my Aunt and Uncle are good Christians, maybe they can explain why God did what He did.

"Abby?"

A man's voice caught Abby's attention and her head jerked upward, the sudden motion causing the crowd to swim before her eyes. "Papa?" The word croaked from her parched throat. She glanced around the sea of bodies, heart fluttering in her chest as she held her breath. *No, Papa is home in San Jose.*

"Abby?" The voice grew louder.

She snapped the journal closed, jumping to her feet. Her heart raced, thumping against her ribs.

A familiar figure strode up the hill away from her. The man's coat was draped over one shoulder, his shirt and vest stained, a round black hat perched at an awkward angle on his head.

"Robert?" A gasp of recognition tore through Abby. She pushed past three women standing in a tight huddle.

Robert turned, his brown eyes widening and a grin crossing his unshaven face. He stretched out both arms.

Abby flew into them, latching on as if Robert were a life preserver in a storm-tossed sea.

He crushed her in a bear hug, the momentum lifting her off her feet. "I can't believe I finally found you!"

She pressed her face against his shirt, breathing in his warm scent. "What are you doing here?" The pitch of her voice had risen by at least an octave, sounding foreign to her own ears.

"Gerald and I have been searching for you and your family. We were concerned when we found Maple Manor abandoned." He pulled off his derby and wiped his brow with the back of his hand. His tie hung loose and the collar of his shirt stood askew.

Abby maintained her grip on Robert's waist, gazing up at him. Despite his unwashed state, he'd never looked more handsome.

He reached out a hand and brushed her cheek, his eyes unreadable.

A rush of heat climbed her neck. She let go and stepped back. *I must look a fright.* She pushed the loose strands from her face and tucked them behind her ears.

"I think your cousin has already left for the hospital. I'll walk you back to his house. Where are your mother and brother?"

"I—I don't know" Abby hesitated. "By the time I made it home, they'd already left. I haven't been able to find them."

Robert's brows squeezed together. He gripped her arm, the warmth of his fingers evident through her sleeve. "You been wandering since you saw us downtown?"

Abby nodded. "I had no idea they'd evacuate the area."

Robert groaned. "I knew I should have walked you home. I've had a hard time thinking of anything else since you left." He closed his eyes for a moment. "Oh, and your mother? She must be frantic."

A sick feeling gripped Abby's stomach. "Yes, I am sure she is. And I feel the same about her and Davy."

His gaze searched the crowd. "Well, I'm not leaving you again. We'll find them."

Sudden warmth rushed through Abby. She brushed back her hair a second time, tucking it under her hat. Two days ago she would have bristled at his attention, but after an exhausting day followed by a sleepless night, she wanted nothing more than to fall into his strong arms. *Not because of him. It's just good not to be alone.* "You said you were going to Gerald's house? Maybe my mother went there, too."

"She wasn't there this morning, but maybe she is by now. It's a good place to start, anyway." He turned his gaze toward her, the deep brown of his eyes a temporary refuge.

Abby's heart fluttered and she forced herself to look away from his face. *How quickly the feelings return.* The bloodstains on his shirt drew her eye. She reached out a hand, but caught herself before touching him. "Are you hurt?"

He glanced down. "It's not my blood." He brushed at the stains. "I was helping someone." His red-rimmed eyes, framed by dark circles, suggested the hours he'd probably spent treating the wounded.

This time she didn't resist. Abby stepped forward and gripped his arm, laying her head against his shoulder. "I can't tell you how glad I am to see you." She shouldn't give him the wrong idea, and yet, she couldn't bear to draw away.

His hand wrapped around her back, his chin settling against the top of her straw boater, causing the loose locks to tumble free of their hiding place. After a deep breath, he spoke. "Shall we go?"

Abby pushed the unwanted feelings into her stomach and stepped free of his arm. She trailed after Robert as he picked his way through the muddle of scattered belongings and wove through the crowd. She dared not take her eyes from his back, fighting the urge to grasp the back of his vest like a baby elephant clinging to its mother's tail. Anything to keep from being left behind in this circus.

35

9:45 a.m.

*R*obert yearned to take Abby's hand as they reached a more open area of the park, but forced his into his trouser pocket. He cast a sideways glance at her, noticing how she continually tucked a lock of hair under her flowered hat. It reminded him of the time he'd seen her dangling from the tree limb, hair flying every direction.

The moment she'd flung herself into his arms, he felt two inches taller. And yet, the look of discomfort on her face when she'd drawn away suggested her actions were motivated by fear and exhaustion rather than any change of heart. Lying to himself would serve no purpose.

He fastened his vest over the worst of the dried bloodstains and pulled on his coat. Certainly she wouldn't care to be seen with him looking like a vagabond. He tucked his medical bag under one arm and held the other out to her. "May I?"

She paused her steps, her brown eyes rounding. "Yes, of course." Her arm felt stiff like a tree branch as it looped around his own. She chewed on her bottom lip, lines forming around her eyes.

He paused, Abby's hand on his arm, and stared out at the assembly gathered on the open lawns of Golden Gate. Families huddled together, speaking in hushed tones. Folks sorted through their belongings, bemoaning what had been left behind.

"I can't believe I didn't bring towels," a nearby woman dug through a case. "How will we get by without towels?" Two small boys in short pants pushed and shoved each other behind her back.

Robert turned his head to keep from laughing and caught the twinkle in Abby's eye. The boys didn't much seem to care about their mother's towel anxiety.

A nearby moan drew his attention. Robert slowed his steps, spotting a woman curled on her side on a quilt, a tortured-looking man hovering over her. *Not again. Not now.*

Abby's hand tugged at his arm. She looked back at him, her brows pinching in question. "Robert?" She turned, eyes widening as the woman's moans rose in pitch like an animal-like howl. "Do you think she needs help?"

A wild-eyed man bent over the woman's prone form. "Lillian? What do I do?" He leaned down, his lips pulled back from his teeth and deep grooves lined his forehead. The woman moaned and rolled to her back, exposing a large pregnant belly.

Lifting a hand to shade his eyes, Robert watched the scene from a distance. What an awful place and time to have a baby. Three young children squatted close by, two girls and a boy. The younger two were crying and the older sister, who looked only to be about ten, wrapped her arms around them.

"Are you going to help her?"

Abby's words spurred him into motion. Robert strode to the campsite, taking in more information with every step. The mother had obviously been laboring for some time judging by the sweat dampening her bodice and face.

Everyone's eyes fixed on him as he kneeled at the woman's side. "My name is Dr. King. May I be of assistance?"

The red-faced man exhaled loudly, his shoulders slumping. "Oh, thank you, Lord!" He seized Robert's hand and shook it. "I'm James Davis. My wife here has been fighting the pains for hours now. I talked to the army doctor, but he's too busy over at the med tent."

Robert set his jaw. *No help from the army, then.* "Is she full-term?"

The man shook his head. "Not quite. Lillian should still have a few weeks to go, but with all this—" He raised a shaking hand and gestured toward the surrounding chaos. "And losing our home." His head fell forward, his chin jutting forward. "It's been too much. You know, Doc?"

"I understand."

Lillian lay still, panting, beads of sweat meandering across her brow. Her glazed eyes focused on her husband's face as he spoke, then she turned to stare into Robert's. "You look so young." Her voice barely rose above a whisper. "Not much more'n a boy yourself."

Abby hovered just outside the camp, a haunted look on her face.

Robert crouched at the woman's side. "I'm older than I look, Mrs. Davis. We'll get you through this." He glanced to where the three children huddled together. "Are those your children?"

She rolled her head to the side. "Yes. They shouldn't see me like this."

Mr. Davis sprang to his feet and began herding the children to the next campsite.

"So, you've had three healthy births. This isn't your first."

Her face pinched, eyes closing as she clutched her belly. "Right." She squeezed out the word.

Robert glanced up at Abby. "Will you assist me? I need to examine her."

Abby's mouth opened, like a fish gasping for air. "I know nothing about childbirth."

Mrs. Davis twisted to her side, her dress stretched tight across a huge belly, her face contorting as she drew her knees upward into a tight knot.

Robert rolled up his sleeves. "You were always a good helper in the lab. I need an extra set of eyes and hands. Don't worry, I will tell you what to do."

Abby kneeled on the ground, face white.

Robert smiled, hoping he appeared confident and in control. "I thought you were a farm girl. I figured you would have had lots of experience."

Abby shot him a withering look, settling both hands into her lap. "We raised peaches."

Abby kneeled at the woman's head, her heart fluttering. What did she know about childbirth?

"I'll be right back. I need to find some supplies." Robert pushed up to his feet. "Just keep her calm."

Abby stared at the laboring mother. A baby—in this madness? She pushed a trembling hand against her own stomach. "Hello, Mrs. Davis. My name is Abby."

"Call me Lillian." The mother panted.

"My friend, Dr. King, is going to help you. Is there anything I can do to make you more comfortable?"

"It's too early. Baby . . . isn't due yet." Tears rolled down her flushed cheeks. "I'm thirsty . . ." Lillian groaned, turning away.

The three children had escaped from their father's attention and hovered nearby. They had the same dark hair and green eyes as their mother. Their round faces pulled at Abby's heart. *They must be so frightened.* She reached a hand out to the oldest. "What are your names?"

They stared in silence, tears sparkling on their freckled cheeks.

Another girl, maybe thirteen or fourteen years old, arrived from the next campsite. "I think the girls are Katie and Nora. Isn't that right?" A lilting Irish accent colored her speech.

One girl nodded while the other chewed on a fingernail. The taller of the two pointed at the boy. "He's Norman," she whispered.

The teen girl crouched down. "My name is Harriet. Can I help somehow?"

Abby breathed out, relief flooding over her. "Yes, thank you. Would you take the children over to your camp? And see if you can find Mrs. Davis some water?"

A smile brightened Harriet's face. She took the girls' hands, Norman trailing behind. "I think my auntie packed some cake in our hamper. Should we check and see, Katie?"

Lillian arched her back and moaned. "Not here. All these people watching. I don't want my baby to be born in a park. It isn't supposed to be this way." She gripped onto Abby's fingers.

Abby freed one hand and fished around in a nearby basket filled with laundry. Drawing out a petticoat, she dried the mother's tears. "It'll be fine." She leaned close and forced a smile. "Just think of the stories you can tell him of the day he was born."

Lillian hiccupped, her tears morphing into a soft laugh. "My sweet baby, born in a park after an earthquake."

"That's right," Abby rubbed circles on the woman's back, like she had so many times for Cecelia.

Harriet reappeared with a tin cup full of water. "The little kids are with my auntie. And she has a big jug of water the doc can use, if he needs it."

Abby waved her to the mother's other side. "Lillian, let me help you sit up a little." She reached her hands under the woman's back.

Harriet held the cup as Lillian gulped down several mouthfuls.

Robert reappeared. "Not too fast, now," he warned. "It may come back up." He turned to Abby. "Why don't you tuck some of those laundry bundles under her back, so she can stay a little upright?" He crouched by Lillian. "Your husband said the baby wasn't due yet. How early is it?"

"About five or six weeks, I think."

Robert's eyes narrowed, his lips pressing into a line.

Abby's throat closed. He'd looked so confident earlier. She leaned close to speak into his ear, but a squeeze from Lillian's hand drew her back.

A look of horror crossed the mother's face, her jaw clenching. "It's coming—the baby is coming."

Robert jumped into action. An air of calm determination replaced the lines across his forehead. He reached his hand up and squeezed the woman's shoulder. "You can do this, Lillian. We're here to help. All right?"

She nodded, eyes wild. "Not much choice now."

Robert's gaze flickered between Abby and Harriet as he moved down to the woman's feet. With Abby on one side and Harriet on the other, a tight circle formed around the laboring mother, crowding out the rest of the camp. He spoke with conviction. "Are you ready, ladies?"

"Of course." Harriet beamed, obviously pleased to be included.

Abby swallowed, imagining all the places she'd rather be. At Robert's direction, she sat behind the mother, supporting her back and shoulders and clutching one hand.

The rest of the world faded away while Lillian strained. Abby watched over her shoulder, mesmerized by Robert's intense eyes as he coached the woman along.

Harriet's voice kept up a chanting litany. "You are doing fine. Just fine. All over soon."

The crowd faded into the background and Abby barely noticed as women hurried over from neighboring camps, bringing towels, blankets, and water. Harriet wet a handkerchief and mopped the mother's brow.

Sticky perspiration trickled under Abby's dress, her corset digging into her ribs.

Beads of nervous sweat shone on Robert's face as well. He swung an elbow upward, swiping his forehead, and knocking his derby askew.

Lillian bore down with a grunt, leaning hard against Abby.

The tiny baby slid headfirst into Robert's hands and a wild grin lit up his face. "And there we go—it's a boy!"

Lillian's chest heaved as she relaxed.

Abby wrapped arms around the woman's shoulders, squeezing. "You did it!" Her heart thudded. Abby wiped her forehead with sleeve cuff and looked into Robert's face.

His smile had vanished. His brows lowered and he turned, the child cradled in his hands.

Abby's breath caught in her chest, the air growing strangely still, as if all sound had been ripped away. She craned her neck for a glimpse. The baby, fitting perfectly in the palms of Robert's hands, looked like blue porcelain. The tiny form lay motionless with a thick coating of blood and fluid.

Robert turned the baby over in his palm and rubbed hard on the infant's back.

Lillian tensed, struggling to lean forward. "What's wrong? What's wrong with my baby? Why isn't he crying?"

Abby's throat tightened. *Please, no.*

"Doctor?" The mother's voice spiraled up pitch. "Doctor?"

Harriet grasped Lillian's hands as all eyes focused on Robert.

His concentration didn't stir from the infant. He pushed to his feet and turned away, supporting the infant with one hand and wrist. He reached for a towel.

Harriet rose up to her knees, pulling the young mother's hands toward her. "Listen here, everyone. Don't panic. Pray. It's time to pray."

Abby kept her gaze fixed on Robert's back, barely hearing Harriet's words between Lillian's gulping sobs.

Harriet bowed her head and entreated God for the child's life, her voice trembling.

Lillian wept. "God please . . . please . . . save my baby."

Abby squeezed her eyes shut, wishing she could stop the women's prayers reverberating in her empty heart. How many times had she begged Him for mercy? She pushed up onto her knees and wrapped protective arms around the shaking mother. She laid her cheek against Lillian's damp hair. *Not again.*

The prayers continued, words pouring from their mouths like water from a spring. Nearby people joined in until Abby could no longer hear distinct voices, just murmured pleas rising into the sky.

A sudden squalling cry cut through the din. Lillian gasped, head jerking upward and colliding with Abby's cheekbone.

Robert grinned as he held up the howling baby, tiny fists flailing in time with his cries.

"Praise God, praise God . . . " The words of the crowd began as whispers, but rose to cries of acclamation and erupted into cheers.

Abby sat back, her rear smacking hard against the ground.

ℒ

2:15 p.m.

Abby gazed down at the little red-faced bundle cuddled in her arm, every muscle in her body melting like butter. The infant gazed at her with steely-blue eyes and blinked. He scrunched his face into a yawn so massive it seemed as if it might detach his tiny jaw. She pulled the blanket back from his little arm, touching the miniscule fingers, marveling at the intricate details of baby fingernails on baby fingers. A tremble raced through her.

Had it been a miracle? The baby's mother insisted it had been, as did Harriet. As Abby stroked the feather-soft skin, her heart ached to believe.

And if her sister had lived—she would.

She gave Baby Albert a last pat and settled him back into his mother's arms, the little fellow's siblings looking over Lillian's shoulders.

Robert tapped her arm and gestured with his head away from the group. Abby pushed to her feet and followed, casting one last glance back at the group.

"We need to go. It's getting late and we still haven't found your family. There are more folks streaming into the park." His face grew grim. "Seems the fires are still spreading and this place is already bursting at the seams."

Abby brushed loose blades of grass off of her skirt. "Of course. I can't wait to find Mama and Davy. And to see Gerald and Aunt Mae." She wrinkled her nose. "And a bath wouldn't hurt either."

He rolled his sleeves back down and fastened his cuffs. "I found a bucket to wash up, but I wouldn't mind a bath either." He glanced around. "Of course, it's more than most of these folks will get tonight."

The air hung heavy with the scent of smoke. Abby looked out at the skyline and sighed. The past few hours had nearly washed away all thoughts of the ongoing disaster. Now it all rushed back—earthquake, fires, dynamite, missing family. She shuddered. Would life ever be normal again?

Of course not. It hasn't been normal for a long time.

She checked her pocket for Aunt Mae's journal. Her fingers wrapped about the comforting bulge, the stories contained within flooding her thoughts. *Maybe there's no such thing as normal.* She followed in Robert's wake as he snaked through the campsites and finally reached the edge of the park.

Robert paused, gazing down the long cobblestone street and looking oddly refreshed after their harrowing ordeal.

Abby, on the other hand, was still a sweaty mess. She twisted her hair into a loose knot, tucked it under her hat, and reset the hatpins. As soon as she released her grip, several locks slipped free and tumbled about her ears. With a sigh, she tucked the hair behind her ears. "What happened back there? With the baby? What did you do?"

A smile crossed his face. "One of the professors at med school lectured about early-term births. Most don't survive, but he said if you rubbed the baby's chest hard with a towel, clear the throat, and blow air into its mouth . . . well, it got him breathing. It was amazing, wasn't it?" He shuddered and looked up at the sky. "He never mentioned how terrifying it would be."

Abby glanced downward, breathing a sigh of relief. *Of course. Robert did it—not God.* Robert was the hero. The fact Harriet and Lillian were praying was coincidental. If God cared about what people wanted—what they prayed for—her sister would still be here.

Or else God just doesn't listen to me. Didn't Aunt Mae write the same thing in her journal? A dark cloud pressed around her.

Robert smiled, his brown eyes sparkling in the afternoon sunshine. "You surprised me back there. For a moment, I thought you were going to walk away. Thank you for your help."

"I wanted to walk away. Run, in fact." Warmth rushed to Abby's cheeks.

Robert offered his arm, his eyes crinkling. "You did a wonderful job. You kept her calm and focused."

She slipped her hand through the crook of his arm. "You were amazing. I love watching you work." As soon as the words dropped from her lips, she felt like crawling under the cobblestones. *Stupid girl. You should have stopped while you were ahead.*

Robert laughed, squeezing her wrist. "When I first spoke with Lillian, I nearly panicked. I kept thinking of all the things that could go wrong. I'm accustomed to having Gerald or one of the hospital doctors to fall back on—for a moment I was afraid I'd forgotten everything I'd learned."

Abby cocked her head, considering his confession. "But you looked so calm, as if you'd delivered countless babies."

"Actually, it was my first."

She gasped and choked back a laugh. "Really?" She glanced down at her hand, resting against Robert's sleeve, her eyes drawn to the tiny scar on her finger. Remembering Robert's gentle touch while he worked, a ripple of nerves started at her hairline and prickled down her back.

Robert pushed his hat to the back on his head. "So, you've been on your own since yesterday afternoon? Did you spend the night at the park?"

"No. I spent the night at a church with a group of Chinese women."

His eyebrows shot upwards, nearly disappearing under his hat. "You what?" He stopped in his tracks, looking her full in the face. "Chinese?"

She paused, taken aback at the dramatic change in his countenance. "Yes. Do you remember the Chinese woman we met at the hospital? And the missionary with the little girl? I encountered them on the street and they invited me to join them. They had evacuated, also. We stayed at a church on Van Ness."

"Abby." Robert furrowed his brow. "You should be more careful."

"What? Why?" Her back tensed.

He cast his eyes downward, a line pinching between his eyes. A long moment passed before he replied. "You're new to the city, so you wouldn't understand." Robert eyes darkened. "I've spent time in Chinatown with Gerald. Those people live by their own laws. Chinatown is full of gambling, opium dens, prostitution, and all kinds of horrors."

"*Those* people?" Abby choked on the distasteful words. Was this the same person who just blew breath into a stillborn baby?

Robert glanced around, lowering his voice before continuing. "People around here don't like them. And they certainly don't trust them. People will look down on you if you spend time around the Chinese."

Abby released his arm and took a step back. Kum Yong's vow of friendship still rang in her heart. "Why should I care what people think?"

"Have you been to Chinatown?" He stepped closer, eyes piercing. "The conditions are atrocious." He rubbed a hand across his forehead. "I knew I should have stayed with you. What will your parents think?"

A lump grew in her throat. "I think they would say not to judge a book by its cover. You can't muddle all people together." She balled her hands into fists.

Robert frowned. "These are desperate times. You must be careful. People will be quick to take advantage." His bushy eyebrows lowered, casting a dark shadow over his eyes. "I know you are a country girl, Abby, but you can't trust everyone."

Every muscle in her body bunched together, any ideas of rekindling a romance with this man going up in smoke. She tried to bite her tongue, but by the time the words reached her mouth, all control was lost. She surged forward, meeting Robert toe to toe.

"I am not some naïve child. You don't have to protect me. I can take care of myself."

He took a protective step backward, eyes widening.

Abby refused his escape, matching him step for step. "Those women seem to know more about God than you ever will. And they were kind enough to take me in—a country girl, as you say. Do they sound like desperate people who can't be trusted?" She reached out and grabbed his shirt to keep him from moving back. "You will never say those words to me again, you hear? Never."

Robert glanced down at the hand clutching his blood-stained shirt. "Abby—" he stopped short, lips parted. The color drained from his face. "I didn't mean—I—I was just concerned."

She shoved hard against his chest as he stepped back. "Don't bother."

Pressing a hand against her hat to settle it on her hair, Abby stomped off, a sudden ache settling in her stomach. Robert had lit a fuse with his words and she needed to escape before he encountered the flying shrapnel of her temper.

"Abby, wait!" His footfalls pounded the cobblestones, echoing off the wall of houses. "Wait!"

She quickened her pace, sending her skirt flapping against her ankles and the air searing in her lungs.

"Don't go off by yourself. Please." His fingers caught her sleeve.

She whirled, her hand colliding with Robert's wrist and knocking it away. "Don't touch me." *Didn't he understand his one touch would break her into a thousand pieces?* A gulping sob rent her chest, the street closing in around her—the tall houses looming like hungry vultures.

He stepped back. "I'm sorry. I won't." Robert raised his arms, holding them palms forward.

She gulped in air, each breath wheezing in her chest.

"It's okay." His voice lowered. "Everything will be fine."

The kindness in his eyes sent shivers racing through Abby. She covered her face, striving to maintain command over the crushing flood of emotions.

"No!" The sob stung her throat. "It's not! It's not okay. It will *never* be okay, don't you understand?" Abby wrenched the hat from her head, hatpins dragging through her hair. The tresses fell about her face, shielding her from Robert's eyes.

Robert stood frozen, his head cocked to one side, as if the odd angle could provide insight into her strange behavior.

What am I doing? What is wrong with me?

"I know. You're right. It's not okay. It's horrible. All of this . . . " Robert gestured to the street, "is terrifying. But, I don't understand—"

"I'm not talking about the earthquake." Abby trembled, the tremors dancing deep into her soul. "She's gone. She's never coming back. I'm alone."

His mouth opened and closed. "I know." Robert took a step closer, slowly stretching his hand toward Abby, like one would to a frightened horse.

She stumbled backward. "Don't." *If he touches me . . .*

Robert nodded, standing an arm's length away, hand outstretched.

Abby dropped the hat to the ground and drew her arms up over her face, stepping in a slow circle as if struggling in a whirlpool. She gulped in air to fill her lungs, but it refused to satisfy, the ache in her chest expanding until it consumed her. The edges of her vision blurred and a loud buzzing filled her ears.

Robert leapt forward, grabbing Abby's arms as she toppled. He pulled her back against his chest. Her body trembled against him as her muscles slackened, but she didn't seem to lose consciousness, her sobs cutting through the warm afternoon air. He lowered them both to the ground.

"Shh." He guided her head back against his shoulder, the lilac scent of her hair mingling with the smoky air. "I'm sorry. I'm so sorry." He squeezed her shoulder. "I wasn't thinking about my words. It was foolish."

She shuddered, her fingers digging into the flesh on his arm.

He pressed his forehead against the back of her head. Her pain tore at his heart.

"I want her back . . . " Abby buried her face against his arm and wept. "God took her, I want her back."

"I know." He rubbed her back, ignoring the strange looks cast in their direction from passersby. He closed his eyes and pulled her closer. "You've already been through so much—"

"I—I think I'm going to be sick," she interrupted, panting.

He chuckled, his speech forgotten. "Go ahead, if it will make you feel better."

Abby sobbed, hiccuped, and laughed, all in one breath. "I don't think so somehow."

Robert shifted his weight and pulled her closer, leaning her weight against his chest. "Put your head down low and take some deep breaths."

She obliged, folding herself forward and pressing her face down toward her knees, as her breathing slowed. She lifted a wrist and pressed it against her dripping nose.

Robert pulled a handkerchief from his pocket and pressed it into her hand. Winding his fingers through her lush chestnut hair, he lifted it off the back of her neck, hoping the cool air would ease her nausea. He shivered as the soft strands spilled through his fingertips.

She turned and stared up at him, her long lashes damp with tears, gold flecks glistening in her brown eyes.

His medical training dropped away, the beautiful woman in his arms consuming every thought, the wonder of the moment making the hairs on the back of his neck stand at attention. "Feeling better?"

She stared over his shoulder and Robert followed her gaze. Rolling clouds of smoke billowed into the gray sky above the tops of the nearby houses.

Abby shivered and drew in a deep breath. She closed her eyes and lowered her head back to his shoulder. "No. Not just yet."

36

3:00 p.m.

*E*ven with her eyes closed, life pressed back in, dragging Abby back to reality. Voices, rattles, hooves—the sounds of the city pointed an accusing finger at the odd picture of two people sitting huddled on the ground in the midst of chaos. A rumble rippled through the ground, the earth trembling.

Abby turned her head so she could gaze up at Robert's unshaven face, shadows haunting his brown eyes. She had no desire to push out of his secure arms, but he wouldn't want to sit here forever. Untangling her arms from his, she scooted away and reached for her hat.

A woman walked by, glancing down at them with a raised eyebrow.

Robert stood, brushed off his pants, and held out his hand.

She allowed him to hoist her to her feet, his hand grasping hers a moment longer than necessary. Abby straightened her skirt, discreetly tugging at her corset. Even though she hadn't tightened it since the earthquake, its edges dug into her ribs, stiff and confining.

"Ready?" Robert's voice was gentle, as if speaking to a frightened child.

Abby nodded, keeping her eyes low. When would she learn some self-control? If he thought she was a naïve country girl before, what must he think now?

Shuffling along beside Robert, Abby lost count of the blocks as they continued toward Gerald's neighborhood.

Every few minutes, Robert glanced her way. "Do you need to rest?"

She shook her head, trying to imagine Robert's thoughts. *One minute I'm friendly and the next minute I'm shouting at him. To top it off, I practically swoon in his arms.* She'd behaved like a character in her sister's dime novel romances. Except for the shouting part.

As they crested the hill on Haight, Robert halted, jarring Abby out of her self-critical trance. In the distance, charred buildings stood gaunt against the gray sky, like the bones of a creature left to rot in the desert. "I never dreamed the fires would make it this distance." He pointed to the east. "Look, so far up Market Street. Unbelievable."

Abby lifted a hand to shade her eyes. "What about Gerald's house? Is it gone, too?"

He grabbed her hand, picking up the pace. "I hope not."

Abby trotted to keep up as they hurried through the cracked streets. Wind picked up ashes and swirled them down the road, skipping across the cobbles like autumn leaves.

"I can't believe this." The gloom of the surroundings colored Robert's voice. "I knew of the fires, but . . . we were so busy—I didn't realize how bad it had gotten."

After about a mile of walking, Robert paused, giving Abby a chance to catch her breath.

She plunked down on a pile of fallen blocks, reaching down to run a finger around her sore ankle. A keening cry caught her attention, like the sound of a kitten mewling for its mother. She turned, the faint sound teasing her ears.

Robert sat beside her, pulling off his hat and running a hand through his hair.

Abby tipped her head to the side, trying to locate the sound. "Do you hear that?"

He turned, a question in his eyes, but she raised a finger to silence him. A distant explosion echoed. A man shouted encouragement to a sway-backed nag as it hauled an overloaded wagon down the road.

Amidst it all, a faint whimpering cry rang out. Robert turned back, examining the wreckage of a nearby building.

Abby jumped up and hurried toward the mound of bricks and wood. She grasped the closest board and flung it away. She clawed into the heap, pulling out stones and twisted pieces of metal.

Robert's long shadow fell across the pile. He strained against a large block. It shifted and slid to the ground, revealing a small dark opening.

The cries stilled. Robert leaned back on his heels. "Abby . . ."

"Hush!" she hissed.

A long moment passed in silence. The other noises from the street faded as Abby crouched over the opening, placing her ear to the hole. "I hear something. It sounds . . ." She frowned. It sounded like the baby she'd held in her arms just a few hours ago. Pulling on a stone block, it sprang free into Abby's hands and she stumbled, landing hard on her backside.

Robert stared, transfixed down at the place where the block had rested.

Abby clambered to her feet and hurried to his side. Dark stains marked the stones. Her stomach lurched.

Robert crouched down and cleared away the neighboring chunks of brick revealing a hand and arm so coated in dust it looked statuesque. His gaze met Abby's, his lips drawing back slightly from his teeth. Blowing out a long breath, he touched the wrist before withdrawing, shaking his head.

A wave of sickness clutched at Abby's midsection.

Robert mopped a handkerchief across his forehead. "Are you going to be all right?"

Abby swallowed hard and nodded, unable to remove her gaze from the unmoving hand. A simple gold band, coated in grime, adorned one of the fingers.

The bleating cry rose again, louder now, tugging at Abby's conscience. She reached for another chunk of stone. After moving a few more stones, the sounds increased in intensity and volume.

Robert hefted a wooden beam, casting it off to the side, uncovering a tiny form cuddled next to the dead body.

Abby gasped and reached out to touch the tender toes, the infant's skin cool against her fingers. A yellow blanket covered the baby's face and chest. Abby held her breath as she lifted the edge of the soft fabric.

Bruised and speckled with dried blood, the tiny face scrunched up against the sudden light, mewling cries coming from a rounded mouth.

Abby's hand trembled as she stared down at the crying infant. *How could something so small survive under this mess?* Her arms ached to pick up the child and cradle it—warm it with her body. But, it looked so weak—what if it died in her arms? She glanced up at Robert. "Should I . . ."

Robert reached down, his hands scraped and bleeding, and lifted the tiny form from its rocky bed. The baby flung its arms to the sides, sucking in shuddering breaths to fuel its cries. He ran his fingers over the torso and limbs, scrutinizing it with the eyes of a doctor before passing it to Abby.

Her heart pounded as she grasped the child, pulling it close to her chest. The cries softened.

Robert picked up the dirty blanket and shook it out before stepping close to Abby and helping her wrap it around the tiny form. "Now we're even. We've both delivered a baby today." His hand rested on the baby's head, his eyes warm.

After a few moments, the baby shoved its tiny fist into its mouth and began chewing on its fingers. Abby lowered her cheek to the soft head. "It's so cold." The little one's chest rose and fell under a filthy gown of eyelet lace, fringed with pink ribbon.

Davy's face jumped into her mind. *I am so glad I left him safe with Mama.* She sighed, remembering how Aunt Mae claimed God was watching over them. *Too bad He didn't watch after this little one's mother.*

Robert crouched over the dead body, running his hand down the lifeless wrist, his fingers closing around the gold ring.

Abby's stomach turned. "What are you doing? You can't just—"

"For the baby. She might want it someday. And maybe it will help us identify her." He twisted it off, examining it before passing it to Abby.

Abby closed her fingers over the cold metal, her heart lurching. She gazed down at the mother's hand, now bare. *I'm sorry. We'll see she's cared for.* Abby squeezed the ring in her palm. She didn't want to put it in her pocket, it might fall out on their journey, but she couldn't wear a dead woman's wedding band.

Robert watched her fumble with it. "Would you like me to hang onto it?"

"Yes, please." She placed it in his outstretched hand with a shudder.

Robert tucked the ring into his vest pocket. "We should probably move on."

Abby ran a hand along the baby's dirt-smudged cheek. "Will she be okay? Is she injured?"

He rubbed the back of his neck with a sigh. "There is a lot of bruising, but I don't think she has any broken bones. I don't see any signs of internal injuries, but . . ." He shook his head. "I just don't know." Robert wiped his face with his sleeve and cleared his throat.

Abby rocked the baby in her arms, her throat tight.

Robert's shoulders lowered as if exhaustion pushed them down. "We'll take her to Gerald and see what he thinks. There's nothing else we can do—the hospitals are overwhelmed. She'll probably have a better chance with us."

His words echoed in Abby's ears and heart. *"There's nothing else we can do." Do they teach them that phrase in medical school?*

"We can pray for her." Robert's face loomed over her, his eyes grave.

The words pierced Abby's heart. Would it hurt to utter one little prayer? She swatted the temptation away. The baby's life was in her hands, not God's. Abby stepped backward. "You can," she whispered. "Not me."

37

4:10 p.m.

The sun burned, a fiery red ball blasting through the veil of smoke that clung to the city, but too high in the sky to be an actual sunset. Robert pressed his knuckles against his nose, certain he'd never be able to erase the scent of the incinerating city from his memory. The cinders floating on the breeze reminded him of the story of God's manna. But these ashes were no blessing from God—more akin to the destruction of Sodom and Gomorrah.

Abby stumbled along by his side, her eyes fixed on the tiny shape clutched in her arms.

A shiver ran down his spine. As tired and bedraggled as they were, they must resemble a young family on the run from the flames. His mind wandered for a moment imagining Abby as his wife. He longed to take her into his arms and promise her Mrs. Fischer and Davy would be safe, but the longer they spent walking, the more concerned he grew. The fires were moving too fast.

As they turned the corner, Gerald's street stretched out before him, the row of fine homes standing defiant against the smoke-filled horizon. A rock lay in Robert's gut. The flames could reach the neighborhood before dark. There was no question of staying.

Abby looked up. "We made it." A shaky smile graced her lips bringing new light to her dirt and tear-smudged cheeks.

"Just another of our long walks, eh, Miss Fischer?" He rallied a smile despite the emotions swirling in his chest.

"I don't know about you, but I'd love to get off my feet for a few minutes."

Robert nodded, pushing open the gate and holding it for her to step through, the gangly roses spilling over the fence a reminder of lighthearted times long past.

Abby halted on the bottom stair.

"What is it?" He hurried up the walk to her side as she stared up at the door.

Instead of being greeted by Mrs. Larkspur's open arms, a crisp piece of white stationery fluttered in the breeze.

"Not again." Abby hung her head.

Robert groaned. He took the steps two at a time and tore the sheet from its tack. Mrs. Larkspur's genteel script matched the woman's grace, her gentle words reading as clearly as her own voice.

Dearest Clara,

Gerald is insisting on my leaving the city until the crisis passes. He is escorting me down to the ferry and I will be crossing the bay to Oakland and staying with my brother's family. If you and the children are able, come join us there. I will be watching for you. Gerald will return to the hospital, I fear.

I am informed the fires are heading this way. I am praying you and the children are safe. I told Gerald I wouldn't leave the city like this, but he has threatened to carry me off against my will. I know our Heavenly Father is watching over you and I will be on my knees interceding with Him until I hear word. I am thankful Abby is with you. You are fortunate to have capable hands to help during this time.

Remember Clara, "God is our refuge and strength. A very present help in trouble." Psalm 46:1.

With my love and prayers,
Your loving Aunt,
Mae Larkspur

Robert skimmed the note three times, his stomach sinking lower each time.

Abby tucked the baby higher up against her chest, like a child clutching a doll. "Tell me they're safe. Please."

He plodded down several steps. "Gerald's sent his mother across the bay. The letter is addressed to your mother—apparently, she hasn't been here."

Abby turned and sank onto the steps, her head falling forward. Her straw hat wobbled on its perch.

Crouching on his heels, Robert took a deep breath. "We will find them. I won't leave you, don't worry."

Her shoulders trembled, face hidden. "Why do you feel so responsible for my family? Where does it end?"

Robert touched her arm. "I care about you. You know I do."

She tipped her head back, meeting his eyes. "I blamed you for Cecelia's death."

His chest ached. "I know." He sat beside her, careful his shoulder did not brush hers. "I was eager to prove myself. The thrill of the research, anticipating an earth-shaking medical discovery . . . it was my only focus."

He searched for words. "I wanted to be the hero. I convinced your family to subject Cecelia to the treatment, even though I knew it would likely fail in the end."

She looked down at the baby, running a finger down the tiny arm. "And now?"

Robert set his hat on the step beside him and ran fingers through his hair, passing lightly over the lump on the back of his skull. "I didn't expect to fall in love with you."

Her head jerked up, brown eyes round with surprise.

He stood, climbed the stairs, and paced back down before turn-ing to look at her, heat growing under his collar. The tremble in her lower lip made his skin crawl, yet the emotions pounding in his chest refused to be ignored. "I mentioned before I was fond of you."

She straightened. "Yes, but . . ."

"It was inappropriate at the time, because I was your sister's doc-tor." He hesitated. Was it any more acceptable now? Hadn't her sister perished under his care? "I tried to keep silent. I knew you blamed me. But I can't deny my feelings."

Abby's face flushed under her freckles and she turned her eyes away.

Her silence cut like a scalpel. Robert took a step back, struggling to regain his control. "But I'll understand if you don't return my affections. Frankly, I'd be surprised if you did." He retrieved his hat from the step and turned away. Robert exhaled, his hopes dissipating into the air along with the smoke.

"I can't, Robert." Abby's voice shook.

Rather than facing her, Robert closed his eyes. He tapped his hat against his thigh. "We should gather some supplies. We can't stay here long, I'm afraid."

The wooden steps creaked under Abby's shoes as she rose. "I'm sorry, Robert. I wish things could be different."

Me, too.

Abby turned the doorknob and stepped inside the quiet house, cold and lifeless without Aunt Mae's vitality. Even the air tasted stale.

Robert followed her inside, pushing the door shut behind him. "We'll need food and water. And some milk for the baby, if there is any. Then we'll head for the hospital and see if Gerald has returned."

Abby shivered. *Does he think Mama and Davy are at the hospital? Or worse?*

"Or I could take you down to the ferry." Robert's eyes narrowed. "You could join Mrs. Larkspur in Oakland while I continue the search."

"I am not leaving without Mama and Davy."

Robert opened his mouth as if to reply, but he refrained. He nodded and strode off to the kitchen.

Abby took a deep breath, the weight of his confession crushing against her shoulders. Did he really say he loved her? Her emotions jumbled like the tangle of debris in the streets. When she fled from the ruins of her grief, she'd cast Robert aside. Had she loved him, or had she used him as a replacement for God?

Stepping into the parlor, she sank down into the same fine chair as yesterday morning. It seemed like another lifetime. Leaning her head against the high back, she remembered her Aunt's words: "*God is our refuge and strength, a very present help in trouble.*"

"I wish I had a faith like hers," Abby whispered to the baby. "A refuge sounds pretty good right now. 'A very present help in trouble'—we could definitely use some, couldn't we?"

She pictured Robert's face, his chocolate-brown eyes earnest and pleading. Her heart had leaped in response, but she knew it was all for naught. How could she love a man who had failed her so deeply? She lowered one hand to her lap, her fingers resting on the bulge in her pocket. Aunt's journal.

She pulled it from her pocket and set it on the end table. Aunt Mae had obviously expected her story to teach Abby something about God's faithfulness. But like Robert, God had failed her as well.

Abby closed her eyes, letting the exhaustion wash over her. How she would love to sit here and let sleep provide a temporary escape. Her arm ached from holding the slumbering child. She shifted against the soft chair. If she weren't careful, it's exactly what would happen.

Forcing her eyes open, her gaze settled on the journal. A few of the delicate pages hung askew. Freeing one hand, Abby opened the book to straighten them. The familiar handwriting beckoned.

September 1, 1856

I started school today with my cousins. It's strange to have family again. And such a big one! They are all so noisy sometimes I can't hear myself think. But when Uncle Harold says, "Let's pray" in his deep voice, everyone goes silent as a church mouse. I sit quiet with the others, but I don't pray. I gave it up months ago.

September 21, 1856

My new "sister," Lydia, is only one year older than me and it already feels like we've known each other forever. We talk about everything. The other night we were sharing secrets. Hers was about a trick she pulled on a boy at school. When she asked me for a secret, I told her about how I don't pray since He doesn't listen anyway. Her eyes went all big and round. The next thing I knew, she rushed off to tell her mother. Lydia's not much good at secrets.

Abby shook her head, remembering how she and Cecelia used to trade secrets. Abby staggered to her feet. There wasn't time for those kinds of thoughts. Clutching the tiny baby in one arm, she climbed the stairs and dug through the linen closet. Locating a few clean towels, she tiptoed through the hall to Aunt Mae's bedroom, feeling like an intruder in the deserted house.

Spreading one of the towels over the quilt, she laid the sleeping baby down, placing pillows to each side. *Too young to roll off, anyway, I suppose.*

She picked up the pitcher from the washstand and walked down the hall to the bathroom. Abby stared in surprise at the upstairs tub, already filled with water. Aunt Mae must have heard about the water problems and stocked up. Abby dipped the pitcher into the tub, enjoying the silky feeling of the water against her dusty skin.

Returning to the bedroom, Abby bathed the child with a wet cloth. The infant fussed, her tiny voice shaking, fists clenching. She sucked in a deep breath and kicked both feet, bringing knees up to her round stomach.

Abby smiled in response, the knot of worry in her chest lessening. *She has some strength after all.* Abby removed the stained shirt and soiled diaper, the dark purple bruises making Abby queasy. After a quick wash, she wrapped the baby in clean towels. The child stared up at her with round blue eyes. *So tiny and helpless.*

"My mama is gone, too," Abby murmured to the infant. "Well, not gone. Just missing—I think. I hope." Lifting her into her arms, Abby rocked her gently. "I'm sorry about your mama. But there must be someone else out there looking for you. If not . . ." She paused. "Well, we'll figure it out later."

The baby's eyes closed. After a few moments of watching her sleep, Abby laid her in the center of the big bed while she carried the washbasin back to the bathroom. She stopped and stared at the full tub. For a brief moment, she considered shedding her clothes and stepping into the lovely water. She leaned over and touched the still surface, skimming her fingertips like a water strider on a quiet pond. The cool water beckoned, her skin growing itchy and hot.

A sound of cabinets closing downstairs in the kitchen brought her to her senses. With a groan, she filled a basin, dunked the washcloth into the water, and held it up to her face. Running it across her skin, she wove it under her hairline, letting the water dribble down the back of her neck. The coolness reminded her of wading in the creek back home. She rolled up her sleeves and plunged her arms in to the elbows, washing the ugly combination of soot, sweat, and dirt from her skin.

With a deep breath, Abby withdrew her dripping hands from the basin and ran them through her hair. Grimacing at her reflection in the tiny mirror, she braided her hair, pulling the strands snug. She wound it into a knot and secured it to the back of her head with some pins from a basket on the counter. She hung the towel on a hook and cast one last wistful glance at the big bathtub.

After checking if the baby still slept, Abby climbed the rickety steps to the attic and searched through an old cedar-lined trunk until she located some baby clothes and some knitted blankets.

Abby dressed the baby, wrapping her in a soft blanket. Cradling the infant in her arms, Abby took a deep breath before trailing down to the kitchen to face the handsome doctor.

Robert was laying out some food on the table. He smiled at Abby, his eyes lingering. "You look refreshed."

She lowered the infant into his waiting hands and suppressed a smile as he gazed at the child with warm eyes. Spotting a small picnic basket, she stepped into the pantry and eyed the shelves. Not wanting to spend another day wandering with no provisions, she picked through Aunt Mae's stores, packing enough food for a day or two. She glanced over her shoulder to where Robert stood, his back to her, resting the babe against his shoulder. Where would they stay tonight? She moistened her lips. If they couldn't locate her mother or Gerald . . .

She couldn't imagine the alternative.

Turning back to the pantry shelves, Abby pulled Aunt Mae's spare apron from its peg and tied it behind her back. The pocket bulged. She reached in and withdrew the enormous ivory bow from Cecelia's gown. *It's still here.* She lifted it to her cheek, rubbing her face against its glossy softness. Closing her eyes, she pictured Robert's face, his brows knit together in concentration as he stitched the wound on her finger. *How embarrassed I was of my silly dress; now look at me.* She glanced down at her stained shirtwaist and torn skirt. Tears stung her eyes as she shoved the bow into her skirt pocket next to Aunt Mae's journal. Some memories were too precious to discard.

Abby wandered into the kitchen, gathering necessary supplies. Her hand settled on Aunt Mae's knife block. She slid the sharp blade from its place, her fingers closing around the familiar handle. Wrapping it in a dishtowel, she added it to the basket.

Robert sat down, the baby curled against his shoulder. "Aren't you hungry?"

Abby glanced at the food on the table. *Was she hungry?* She hadn't eaten since breakfast, and then it had been only a few bites. "Yes. I'm starving."

"Then come join us."

She set the basket on the floor, circled the table, claiming the seat across from Robert.

He reached a hand across the smooth surface. "Shall we bless the food?" His raised brows made his dark eyes look even larger than normal.

She grasped his hand and lowered her chin, fixing her gaze on his fingers. A tiny white scar ran along one knuckle. The warmth of his touch sent a tingle up her arm. Before he reached the end of the prayer, she closed her eyes so as not to be caught staring.

Abby handed Robert a plate, growing hungrier with every passing moment. She spooned up a helping of applesauce, adding it to her dish along with a slice of ham, a biscuit, and a slice of cheese. It took effort to keep from bolting the food down, but Abby smiled as she watched Robert lift large spoonfuls of the applesauce to his mouth.

He swiped a napkin across his lips. "I hope Mrs. Larkspur won't mind us helping ourselves."

"She won't. Nothing brings her more joy than feeding people."

Robert chuckled. "And there are few things that bring me more joy than eating her cooking."

"I know what you mean. It tastes even better today." Abby gathered the baby in her arms and tried spooning some milk into her mouth, but the infant gagged and turned away, squalling.

Robert reached for a clean napkin and dipped it in the glass. "Try this."

Taking the dripping cloth from his hand, Abby touched it to the baby's lips. The child closed her mouth on the fabric, but pushed it back out with a pink tongue.

Robert cleared his throat. "We should probably get over to the hospital. We can leave the baby there and Gerald can help us find your family.

"Leave her?" Abby bristled at the words.

"She might have injuries we don't know about."

She set her jaw. "I'll take her to the hospital, but I won't leave her there."

Robert narrowed his eyes. "She's not your kin, Abby. You can't just keep her. They will need to find her family."

"I'm not your kin, and yet you are helping me." Her words snapped in the quiet house.

He took another biscuit and shrugged. "It's completely different. We are friends. And you are my best friend's cousin."

A cold chill crossed her skin. Abby dug fingers into her leg. She pushed away from the table as the food settled into her stomach like a stone. "Yes, I suppose I am." She reached for the basket. "Perhaps we'd better be going. Let's not keep your best friend waiting." *And then you can be rid of me as well.*

38

*R*obert jostled two jugs of water in one arm, a canvas bag of supplies in the other, and a yellow quilt across his shoulders. The smoke hung heavy in the air, ripping away the peace of the past hour. He tightened his grip on the containers, lifting them a little higher and bracing them against his chest. All he needed was a trunk to drag and he'd look like every other refugee on the street.

Abby cradled the baby in one arm, a basket over her elbow and a second quilt on her shoulder. The glow of the sun through the gray clouds cast a warm light on her face, accenting her cheekbones and the spray of freckles on her nose.

He turned his eyes back to the street. It wouldn't do to be caught staring. Again. She'd made it clear she wasn't interested. Now he needed to learn to keep his eyes forward.

Robert lifted one shoulder, trying to shift the rolled-up quilt as a drop of sweat trickled down between his shoulder blades. If they didn't find Abby's family by sunset, they might join the rest of the displaced people camping in the open. He glanced at her, walking with her gaze centered on the baby. A man and woman alone—yet, chaperoned by thousands?

His neck burned under the soft quilt. *We have to find them. This evening.*

The smoke plumes loomed over the houses and the streets were crowded with people fleeing on foot. Discarded belongings littered the streets—cases, boxes, books, and piles of clothes were strewn everywhere. A massive painting leaned against a piano. A woman in a faded blue dress pulled a trunk over to the instrument and began to play "The Maple Leaf Rag." It brought smiles to a few faces, the bouncy song standing in stark contrast to the somber scene.

As Robert stepped over a twisted section of streetcar rail, a hand gripped his arm, wrenching his attention from the music. A soldier glared at him, a long rifle braced against one shoulder. "We need men to clear streets. My orders are to conscript every available able-bodied man."

Robert yanked his arm free. "I'd like to help, but I'm certainly not available." He scanned the ragged group of men shuffling about near a wagon. As if people didn't have enough to worry about today, now they had to avoid being put on work detail?

The soldier grunted. "It's what everyone says. I don't got a choice and neither do you."

Abby seized Robert's other arm, her eyes wild. "You can't just take men off the streets."

The man glowered at Abby, his soot-stained face lined with exhaustion. "Sorry, ma'am, but I got my orders. Your husband's got to put in six hours labor and after that you can have him back."

Robert set down the water jugs. He held his hands out in front of him. "She's not . . . um . . . I mean . . . we're . . ." His words hung in the air like the wisps of smoke.

Abby shifted the baby in her arms.

Leaning on his rifle, the soldier raised an eyebrow. "Listen, buddy, I don't care who she is. I care about you helping me get this street cleared so we can get supplies running. Now, get in line!" He gestured toward the group of men with his thumb.

Robert stepped clear. "I'm a doctor—you can't conscript me."

The soldier growled under his breath and spit onto the road. "You got papers?"

"I . . . uh . . ." Robert's mind raced. His identification was in Gerald's automobile.

"Just what I thought." The soldier's beefy hand shot out and latched onto Robert's arm, hauling him across the street.

Abby dropped the basket. "I can vouch for him. My cousin is Dr. Gerald Larkspur. Robert is his assistant."

Robert staggered as the man shoved him into the procession. The expression on Abby's face hurt more than his bruised arm. "Abby, head for the hospital and tell them what's happened. Have them send someone for me."

The soldier stomped to the front of the column. "You!" he pointed at an exhausted looking Chinese man with a long braid dangling down his back. "You're done. Hand your tools to the doc boy."

The Chinese man pushed his shovel into Robert's hands. As soon as Robert closed his grip, the man melted into the crowd.

"No, you can't do this." Abby's voice rose. "You can't just take him."

Robert slipped the bag off his shoulder and handed it to her. He grasped her shoulders, staring into her damp eyes. "Find your cousin. I'll come as soon as I can." He pulled the ring from his vest pocket and pressed it into her hand. "This should stay with the baby."

Abby shoulders slumped, the supplies scattered in a heap at her feet. "You said you wouldn't leave me."

Heart sinking, Robert pulled her against his chest and pressed his lips to her forehead. Stepping back, he hefted the shovel over his shoulder. "If I had a choice, I'd take your hand and never let go. But I don't. Gerald can get this waived—I have paperwork in his car and on file at the hospital."

The men began to move off, but Abby's concern kept him rooted to the spot. For a brief moment, he considered darting into the crowd. Would the soldier really come after him? He reached out and squeezed her elbow. "Everything will work out. I'll see you soon."

With a deep breath, Robert fell in line, casting a glance over his shoulder every few feet.

Abby remained fixed, her gaze following him.

Robert dug his fingernails against the worn wooden handle. Every step took him further from Abby's side. No matter how he longed to be close to her, something—fate? God?—kept getting in the way. He swiveled his head to the front, focusing on the grimy sweat stains on the man's shirt in front of him.

He'd haul rocks for the rest of his life if it meant he could keep Abby at his side.

The sun's rays burned orange through the hazy sky, casting a somber light on the line of men plodding away. Abby dug her fingers into her skirt, squeezing the material into a wrinkled wad and kicking once at the ground. The sudden motion woke the baby and she raised a keening cry. Abby hung her head, tears of her own dripping onto the blanket.

Abby lifted her face to the blood-red sky and the heavens beyond. "Stop it!" She hissed at God through gritted teeth. "Stop this. I know you can."

People walked by, unmoved by Abby's outburst. Abby closed her eyes and lowered her head. Apparently, on a bizarre day like today, a hysterical woman talking to the sky wasn't worth a second glance.

She unhooked her necklace and slid the ring onto the chain next to the golden locket. *I vowed never to pray again.*

39

*A*bby stood in front of the hospital ruins, despair settling on her like a chilling frost onto the orchard. Memories swept over her as she stared at the damaged building. At one time it had represented all of her hopes, for Cecelia' healing and Robert's attention. Now the building stood empty and broken, shards of glass littering the ground under every window opening.

Searching for signs of life, she walked to the rear of the quiet building. *Robert was inside during the quake?* She shivered at the thought. A flurry of motion caught her attention. A slender woman dressed in a stained nurse's uniform clambered out onto a low windowsill, and glanced about before dropping to the ground with a grunt. She clutched the corners of a long apron caught up against her bosom.

Abby hoisted the heavy bag higher on her shoulder, trying to avoid unsettling the rest of her load. "Wait!" She lumbered under the weight, arms aching. The wedding ring clinked beside her locket, bouncing against her chest in rhythm to her steps.

The woman turned, nurse's cap perched at an awkward angle atop her red curls. Her eyes widened. "I'm not looting—I work here!" She wrapped both arms around the bundle of items, pulling it close to her tiny waist.

Abby stopped a few steps away, catching her breath. "Where is everyone? The doctors?"

"We've set up a temporary medical camp down the street." Dark circles surrounded the woman's eyes, face tense and drawn.

Abby shifted the load in her arms, careful not to jostle the sleeping infant. "I'm looking for Dr. Gerald Larkspur. He's my cousin."

The nurse's frown lifted. "Dr. Larkspur? I haven't seen him since this morning. We could sure use him, though. We're shorthanded, and the soldiers are threatening to relocate us to the Presidio." She wiped a hand across her brow, dislodging a stray curl tucked under her cap. "I don't know how they expect us to move the patients again."

"Oh." Abby's heart sank. "Thank you. His partner, Dr. King, thought he might be here."

"Wait—you're Cecelia Fischer's sister, aren't you? I remember you." Her eyes traveled across Abby's face, her green eyes narrowing. "I'm sorry for your loss."

A breeze scattered some dried leaves, sending them bouncing down the glass covered walkway. Abby swallowed, her throat suddenly dry. "Thank you." She glanced down at the tiny face framed by the yellow blanket. "My name is Abby."

"I'm Nurse Maguire." She cocked her head to one side. "Where is Dr. King? We could certainly use his help."

Abby twisted, dropping the bag from her aching shoulder. "I'm afraid he was conscripted to help clear the road. He was hoping Gerald could intervene."

The nurse glanced skyward. "People with medical training cleaning up bricks in the street while patients die from their injuries? Has this city gone mad?" She huffed, the gust of air lifting the hair from her forehead. "Where are they? Maybe I can send someone over there; get him released early."

Abby gave the woman the necessary information as the nurse laid her supplies on the ground and reached for the baby, her features softening. "What a sweet little mite."

Abby dropped the rest of her load on the steps. The food basket had left a dent on her inner arm. She peeled off the two quilts she had wrapped around her shoulders like heavy shawls, the cool breeze a welcome diversion. Two sparrows picked through the dried leaves under a nearby bush, apparently in search of food. The familiar sound made Abby smile—even in the midst of chaos, life continued.

The nurse followed her gaze. "God watches over the tiniest sparrow, you know. He must have known you'd take good care of this little one." A dimple formed on Nurse Maguire's cheek as she returned the baby to Abby's arms.

Pulling the baby close to her chest, Abby swayed, hoping to rock the infant back to sleep.

Nurse Maguire reached out and touched Abby's locket. "This is lovely. Your sister's, wasn't it?" The wedding band jangled against the chain as the woman bumped it with a long fingernail before withdrawing her hand.

"Yes, it was." Abby tucked it back under her collar. "Thank you."

The nurse sighed, the corners of her lips drawing down. "I'll see if I can find someone to go after Dr. King. With the way people are acting today, I'm not certain they will release him, even with medical papers. Do you want to come with me?"

Abby shook her head. "I need to find my mother. I think she might be at Golden Gate Park. If you see Dr. Larkspur or Dr. King, would you tell them where I went?"

"I'll do that." The nurse gathered her supplies. "You take care, now—you and the little sparrow." She smiled, waved her free hand, and hurried down the street.

Abby rested on the stairs in front of the hospital, laying the baby across her knees. "Shall I call you Sparrow, then? It's as good a name as any, until we discover who you really are." Contemplating the walk back to the park made Abby's feet ache. Bouncing her knees lightly, Abby drew the journal from her pocket.

September 22, 1856

After Lydia spilled my secret, Aunt Joyce was real quiet. This morning, when all the other kids were outside playing, she came up and told me a story.

She said three years ago, when they heard my Mama was sick, they all started praying for us. One night God started whispering my name into her heart. Aunt Joyce started writing letters trying to find me. God wouldn't let her give up. She figured He was letting her know how much I needed them.

Isn't that strange? Here I wasn't even talking to God, and yet He was still looking out for me. I still don't know why He took my Mama. And I'll never understand why Papa had to go away. Aunt Joyce says I may never know, but whatever happens, I need to remember God is always with me.

So, I suppose I might try praying again. Maybe.

Abby closed the book with a sigh. God was looking out for Great Aunt Mae, and the nurse said He was looking after this baby. *If only He were looking out for me.*

Robert added three more bricks to his load, lifting them with a grunt. He pushed upright, hefting the bricks against his chest as black spots appeared before his eyes. A quick shake of the head only made them tap dance across his field of vision. Robert closed his eyelids for a brief moment, willing the ache in his temples to cease. So many others were in worse condition than he.

The man across the pile from him had removed a sling from his arm in order to work, certainly Robert could manage with a mild concussion.

He tossed the bricks into the wagon, wiping his palms on his pant legs before turning for another handful. He glanced down the street, hoping to see Abby or Gerald coming to retrieve him. How long had it been? An hour? More? Sweat trickled between his shoulder blades. A few weeks ago, he'd complained about working on the X-ray equipment's electrical wiring, but today the chilly basement laboratory sounded like a blissful retreat.

He grabbed some loose boards and tossed them into the wagon on top of the bricks. Unfortunately, his laboratory lay crushed under several thousand pounds of brick and concrete. And right now, he had about as much of that as he could stand.

Abby trudged down the street, the long walk back to Golden Gate Park passing in a blur, her eyes seldom straying from the path. After two long days of walking, the broken buildings had lost their fascination.

The sun ebbed over the horizon as she stumbled into Golden Gate Park. Locating a small scrap of unoccupied ground, Abby sank down in exhaustion. Digging through the remaining supplies, she pulled out a yellow quilt. Flinging the patchwork wide, she let it settle over the dirt before lowering Sparrow onto it.

Shouldn't she be crying? Davy was always crying when he was this size. The tiny infant laid perfectly still, her eyes following Abby's every move.

The evening light shifted from red to purple as the sky made its way to bed. Pulling out some bread and sausage, Abby grasped the sharp knife to cut off a thick slice. The food tasted like ashes, but her jaw worked mechanically.

Digging through the basket, the familiar smell of Great Aunt Mae's molasses cookies brought tears to her eyes. She pushed the paper-wrapped package aside in favor of a small jar of milk. Abby soaked a piece of bread and tried to feed it to Sparrow, but the baby's tongue pushed the strange stuff back out. She even turned her head away from the milk-soaked washcloth.

Leaving the food and the knife next to the basket, Abby laid down beside Sparrow, wrapping her body into a half-circle around the tiny form. Sparrow turned her head, keeping Abby's face in her field of vision. Abby ran a finger over the baby's cheek as Sparrow yawned, the tiny mouth forming a perfect "O". Abby drew her close and rubbed circles on her back like she remembered Mama doing for Davy years ago.

With a sigh, she slid Aunt Mae's journal from her pocket and opened it to where she had left off earlier, the violet sky coloring the pages with a lavender hue.

October 15, 1856

I'm praying again, for real this time. Now I know God loves me and cares about what happens, I feel different about Him, too. I used to think He was like a wishing star. Now when I pray, I can feel His love wrapping around me like Mama's arms. It doesn't matter so much if He says no, to what I'm asking, because I understand He knows best. It still hurts when I think about Mama. But if she's up there with Him, then maybe she's whispering in His ear for me, too.

"God is my refuge and my rock. An ever-present source of help in troubled times." I am learning this full well.

Abby glanced over the top of the journal to see the crimson-colored sun slipping below the skyline, the smoke towers drifting over the city like a thick woolen blanket.

Abby closed her eyes, her hand patting a steady rhythm on Sparrow's back. After about ten minutes, she reached under her collar and withdrew her chain, sliding the locket away from the ring. Abby rubbed the smooth, warm metal across her cheek, the noise of the milling crowd fading into the background like cricket song on a summer evening.

One more night. Tomorrow I will find them.

Friday, April 20, 1906
12:30 a.m.

Jerking awake, Abby blinked in the darkness. The flames from her dreams receded into the distant sky where the glow of the smoke suggested the true location of the fires. She shuddered, the real scene only slightly less surreal than the nightmare. Closing her eyes, she fought to steady her breathing. *Only a dream.*

The thought brought a jab of pain along with the peace. *Which means Cecelia isn't out there somewhere.*

The missionary's words floated back through her memory. "*She is not wandering frightened through a burning city. She is at peace in a way we cannot fully comprehend.*"

If she's at peace, why do I keep dreaming about her?

A nearby rustling caught Abby's attention and she rolled to her back. A shadowy figure crouched nearby. A long dark coat hung down over the bent knees, making the man look like a squatting gargoyle—a monster from a nightmare.

Only this one was real.

40

12:30 a.m.

*R*obert leaned over the groaning figure. In the flickering lantern light, the shadow of the curved hand resembled a raptor's talons preparing for the kill. "Steady now. Hold it tight."

The foreman nodded, closing his grip around the worker's injured hand.

Robert lifted a bottle of wine, the contents sloshing about. "Leave it to San Franciscans to salvage bottles of wine while the city's burning." Gripping the already-loosened cork with his teeth, he eased it out and spat it aside, fixing his gaze on the injured man's eyes. "This is going to hurt, so be prepared."

The man groaned. "Can't hurt much worse'n it already does."

As Robert poured the liquid, the man shrieked, his clawed fingers contracting in a sudden spasm. "Couldn't you just pour it down my throat? It'd do the same, wouldn't it? Such a waste."

Setting the bottle on the ground, Robert chuckled. "I'm not using it to deaden the pain, I'm trying to clean the wound." He gestured to the soldier hovering nearby. "Could you bring the lantern closer? I can't see what I'm doing here."

Robert hands were raw and bleeding after hours of lugging bricks, but examining his patient's crushed fingers, he offered a prayer of thanksgiving he had not been nearby when the rock wall had given way. He cast a glance at the soldier standing across from him. Likely as not, Robert wouldn't need paperwork to prove his medical status now.

He straightened the injured fingers as best he could in the primitive conditions. Peering closely, he gauged the man's reactions as he manipulated the bones. The second and third fingers seemed to be the only ones broken, possibly an oblique fracture of the proximal phalanx on one and the middle phalanx on the other, with the rest of the hand scoured with abrasions.

Using strips of cloth, Robert fastened each of the broken fingers to its neighbor, using the good fingers as splints. It was a ragged job at best, but he hoped the bones would heal straight. At least it would hold the man through the night.

The patient grasped the half-empty wine bottle with his good hand and cradled it to his chest. Obviously, he was not beyond self-medicating for pain.

Abby sucked in a quick breath, her voice croaking in the back of her throat.

The man dragged her basket a few feet away and dumped it onto the ground, pawing through the contents. Aunt Mae's book fluttered down, landing on top of the kitchen knife. He grabbed the meat and bread, shoving it into pockets on his loose, flapping coat. Turning his back he pawed through Abby's other belongings. The cookies spilled onto the ground at his feet. He scooped them up and added them to his stash.

A blast of heat climbed up Abby's throat, burning away any sense of caution. How dare this man steal her things? She jerked upright, hissing like an angry cat. "Hey, get away from there. You can't take those—they're mine." Jumping to her feet, Abby lunged for his arm.

The man spun and fastened meaty fingers on her wrists before she could reach into his pockets. Twisting her around, he locked a crushing arm around her middle and wrenched her back against him.

Abby shrieked and kicked backward, her heel smashing against a shinbone.

The man tightened his grip, uttering a few choice words, crushing a hand against her mouth before she could manage another cry. His arm squeezed her like a bellows, shoving the remaining air out of Abby's lungs. "Be quiet!"

She kicked again, catching his leg a second time.

Cursing, he hoisted Abby off the ground and flung her like a dirty dishrag. She slammed down on her stomach, just a few feet away from Sparrow, their supplies crushing under her body. A jolt of pain surged through her arm where it folded beneath her, her wrist catching the worst of the fall.

Before Abby could gather her wits, the attacker grasped her shoulders and flipped her over. Pinning an arm with his knee, he grabbed for her mouth with both hands.

Heart pounding, Abby arched her back and swung at his face with her free hand. She dug her fingernails into his cheek before he secured her wrist and pinned it down. He succeeded in latching a hand across her mouth.

He sneered, filling her face with sour whiskey breath, "I will take what I want to take, girl."

Abby twisted, trying to wriggle out of the man's grip.

He threw himself across her, jamming her into the ground. Releasing her mouth, the man shoved his forearm across her neck. He bent down, a sickly grin crossing his whiskered face.

Abby's throat closed under the weight, spots forming before her eyes. Clutching at his arm, she kicked her legs, struggling to draw a breath. A knobby protrusion dug into her back as his weight pressed down.

The man leaned in. "You can't get away. No one can help you." His hot breath flooded her face.

A sob struggled for release in Abby's throat. *He's right. I'm in a crowd of people, but no one even knows I am in trouble.* She dug her fingers into the dirty arm pushing down against her throat, but couldn't dislodge it. Starving for air, Abby's desire to fight ebbed away.

The man snorted a soft laugh into her ear as her movements weakened. "That's better. You be a good girl, now. Such a pretty little thing like you should be a good girl."

Abby's stomach twisted. Smoke rolled into her head, sounds fading as if she listened from deep underwater.

The man leaned back, reducing the pressure on her throat, his voice distant. "You gonna be good? Because if you scream—it won't be pretty."

Abby managed to drag in a partial breath and her eyes refocused.

Greasy hair fell into the man's eyes and a thick moustache rode the upward sneer of his lip. "Answer me, girl," he hissed. His weight increased.

"Yes," Abby used the precious puff of air to squeak out the word.

Slowly he lifted his arm from her throat, his body still pinning her to the ground. "I take what I want, you hear?"

Abby tried to nod. A twinge of pain shot through her shoulder, her hand pinned behind her back.

The man sat up, releasing Abby's throat. She squirmed, grasping for the lump under her back. Her fingers closed around it—a smooth, wooden handle.

"And you don't go telling nobody. Or I'll be back." He bent his grimy face down to her cheek and breathed the words into her ear. "Do you understand what I'm saying?" His breath reeked of whiskey and cigars.

Abby swallowed the bile rising in her throat. "I won't tell. Take the supplies, just leave me alone." Sparrow cried, softly mewling in the darkness nearby. Her fingers tightened.

Reaching out a grimy finger, he brushed the side of her face. His eyes traveled downward and he grasped at the chain, drawing the necklace from under her collar. He lifted the ring, hand shaking, his red-rimmed eyes growing large. "And what's this?"

In one swift motion Abby twisted, pulling her arm free from behind her back and jamming Aunt Mae's knife into the man's leg.

His shriek tore the night air and he jerked away, ripping his leg free of the blade.

Abby scrambled to her feet, the bloody knife clutched in her hand. As he writhed on the ground, she scooped a handful of belongings back into the basket and grabbed Sparrow.

A flurry of movement nearby suggested they wouldn't be alone for long. Abby glanced down at the dripping knife, heart pounding. She clutched Sparrow to her chest and ran like a frightened animal, stumbling over her feet and people's scattered possessions. Hiding the knife flat against her side, Abby's thoughts scattered, Sparrow bleating protests as Abby jostled her through the night. *Oh, God— what have I done? Where do I go?*

She darted into the street and staggered to a halt. Buildings loomed up against the sky, towering above her. Eerie glowing clouds billowed above their dark shapes. A soldier with a bayonet-topped rifle rested against his shoulder stared off into the fiery horizon. Abby wiped the bloody knife on her skirt and stashed it inside the basket.

There was nowhere to run. No place of safety. She shuddered. The man had said, "No one can help you."

But Aunt Mae's words also echoed in her heart: *"God is our refuge and our hiding place." Would God help me, even if I've turned away?*

She stole into the shadows and crept along the quiet street. A man rode by on a horse, the hooves loud on the cobbles. Abby pressed her back against a dark building until the rider disappeared into the night. After a few moments of silence, she rushed down the street in the opposite direction, racing blocks away from the park.

She paused in front of a drugstore, the front window broken and merchandise strewn across the floor. Abby glanced to the left and the right before stepping through the broken window and tiptoeing through the shop. She crunched over scattered pills and leaking bottles of sticky syrups and tonics, making her way to the back corner. She sank down behind a long counter and pressed her back against the wall, her trembling legs stretched before her.

Abby opened the basket. Not much remained—a towel, the journal, one water jug, and the knife. Pulling out the towel, she made a cozy nest on the floor for Sparrow, her arms too shaky to trust. Clutching the knife, Abby drew her knees up to her chest. No one would sneak up on her again.

She stared into the dark shadows, daring them to move. The faint glow from the front window reflected off the gleaming blade.

41

1:35 a.m.

*R*obert coiled a strip of cloth around his blistered hand as he hurried through the smoke-laced street, head throbbing. He'd finally stumbled back to the hospital, only to find it in disarray, the few remaining staff members loading patients onto army wagons en route to the Presidio. They needed help, but he was far too exhausted, too spent to help anyone. Besides, he had a promise to keep.

No one had seen Gerald since the morning. Perhaps he had escorted his mother across the bay and been unable to come back. There was no other choice but to return to the park. Abby had been so certain her mother would be camped there, it made sense she would retrace their steps after leaving the hospital.

But as he approached the grounds, his heart sank. The shadowed park contained countless huddled shapes, nestled under cloaks and blankets. How could he recognize Abby in these conditions? It had been difficult enough in the daylight—but now? Impossible.

He picked his way through the milieu, his throat aching with weariness. All he wanted was to slump down on the ground and fall asleep. Every muscle, every joint ached. And yet Abby consumed his thoughts. Was she frightened and alone? What about the baby?

Somewhere in the distance, he heard a shriek. He swung around, eyes searching the darkness, heart pounding.

Lord, let her be safe.

In the distance, a cluster of lanterns glowed in a tight circle. Maybe he could ask someone about Abby. Perhaps someone had spotted a young woman with a baby. A moaning wail caught his attention and he picked up his pace toward the lights. Obviously, there had been some sort of trouble. He pushed his way into the circle.

A dark figure writhed on the ground, spouting a string of oaths as another man pressed bandages to a wound on his leg. Robert drew in a deep breath, his legs shaking with exhaustion. Was he the only doctor in the city tonight? After a moment, he pressed forward. "What's happened?"

"Well, look what the cat dragged in." Gerald glanced up from his position over the wounded man, a wry grin lighting his face. "I figured you'd collapsed in exhaustion somewhere."

Robert fell to his knees, clasping an arm around his friend's shoulder. A wash of emotions swept over him, stealing the breath from his lungs. "And I thought you'd left town!"

"And leave you with all the fun? No, sir." He pressed a hand on the injured man's chest. "Look here, sir. I need you to stop struggling and lie still." He glanced up at Robert. "Do you think you could hold him down for me? I need to get a better look at this wound, but he's too drunk to listen to sense."

Robert stepped to the far side and kneeled. Bracing himself, he pressed the man's arms to the ground. The fragrance of sour whiskey and vomit mingled on the patient's clothes and his biceps corded under Robert's grip. "You'd better hurry. He feels pretty strong."

Gerald waved a few nearby men in to help. He pulled back the bandages and grimaced. "What's it look like to you, Robert?"

Robert lifted his head, gazing down to where the lantern light illuminated the oozing wound. "Stab wound?"

"Yes. I agree. And look at this." He gripped the man's chin and turned it toward the light. Three parallel gouges stretched from his eye to his chin. "We'd better inform the police." Gerald reached for his medical bag. "We may be seeing a lot of this over the next few days. Desperation and tight quarters."

A cold sweat broke out over Robert's skin. *And Abby's out there alone.* "Let's hurry up and get the wound closed. I want to find your cousin and get out of here."

Gerald's brow lifted, but he reached for his suture kit and set to work, not bothering with anesthetic. By the smell of the man, he already had enough to deaden the pain.

Robert kept a firm grip on the patient's arms, though the man seemed only half-conscious. For a few moments, he watched Gerald's careful stitches, but after a bit he let his gaze wander. The blanket under his knees looked familiar.

Robert's throat went dry. "Gerald . . ."

His friend glanced up.

"Don't you have a quilt like this?"

Gerald followed Robert's gaze. His brows drew down as he dropped the forceps. "Yes." He reached for the yellow patchwork. "My grandmother sewed it when I was a child."

Robert's gaze raked over the patient. A glimmer of gold shone from between his fingers. Releasing the beefy arm, Robert wrenched open the man's hand. A necklace slid from his grasp, gold locket and ring tumbling out onto the dirt.

Gerald shot to his feet. "Are those—"

"Where did you get this?" Robert lunged forward, shaking the man awake. He waved the necklace in front of the man's face.

"She done it," the man coughed, his stinking breath causing Robert to reel backward. "She shtuck me. A girl." The scratches wrinkled as the man curled his tobacco-stained lips into a sneer.

Robert's stomach twisted. He grabbed the man's shirt and jerked him to a sitting position. "Where is she now? What did you do to her?"

"She didn't have nothin' I wanted."

With a shove, Robert returned him to the ground. "Where is she?"

The man's eyes rolled back before closing.

Springing to his feet, Robert spun in place. He cupped his hands to his mouth. "Abby! Abby, are you out there?"

His voice echoed through the park.

Gerald stepped to his side. "Are you sure it's hers?"

Robert lifted the chain, the gold glimmering in the lantern light. "I gave her the ring myself."

Gerald's jaw fell open. "What?"

Closing his fist around it, Robert shoved the chain into his vest pocket. "We've got to find her. She could be hurt."

"We'll get the police. But we have to finish closing the wound."

"Why?" Colors flashed in front of Robert's eyes.

"He was the last one to see Abby." Gerald's lips thinned.

Crossing his arms, Robert stood guard while Gerald drew the last bit of thread through the man's wounded leg. He glanced around at the darkness, his heart too troubled to pray. Now he knew for certain Abby was out there.

And she was in trouble.

42

2:45 a.m.

*A*bby slept curled in a tight ball behind the counter, taunted by anxious dreams.

She found herself in a Chinatown alley, rows of silk-clad Chinese girls staring down from high fire escapes. Their anguished eyes cried out. Abby reached a hand up toward them and they vanished into the smoke.

Papa's voice called through the mist. "Abigail! Abigail, my little wanderer, where are you, child?" His thick accent colored the words as they echoed down the dark alley, the buildings closing in from both sides.

"I'm here, Papa!" Abby turned in a circle, unsure of her path.

Cecelia's song floated on the wisps of smoke. "Prone to wander, Lord I feel it. Prone to wander, prone to wander . . . "

She pushed toward the sound, jumping effortlessly across broken cobbles and giant cracks in the street. "I'm coming, wait for me!"

The song's gentle refrain beckoned. Abby ran toward it with every ounce of energy she had left, her breath wrenching from her lungs in wheezing gasps.

A burning building crumbled, sparks spewing across her path. She skidded to a stop as flaming beams of wood fell and splintered on the street. "No!" The wind, pulled by the heat of the flames, sucked through the street with a roar, stealing her breath and plastering her skirt to her legs. Her hair hung loose, locks tangling about her face.

"Come to me, Abigail." A voice spoke, whispering straight into her heart.

Abby held her breath, still and silent as a stone.

The wind died away, no longer pulling at her clothes and hair, the rushing noise fading into silence. The fire still raged, but the sound, heat, and wind scattered until nonexistent. Abby placed her hands over her cheeks, the sudden lack of sound causing her ears to buzz. The surreal scene unfolded like a silent film at the penny arcade.

Between two burning buildings, an alley stretched into darkness, a trail through the flames. The peaceful shadows beckoned. Following the path, Abby slid her hands along the cool brick walls until she stood at the base of the steps of an old church. Climbing, she pushed aside the heavy oak doors.

The shadowy church enveloped her. Light shone through massive stained glass windows, the colors streaming down into the front of the church. A young woman sat in the front row, golden hair hanging down her back in a single, long glistening braid. She turned, her smile—as always—lighting the room. "Abby . . ."

"Cecelia?" Abby's voice caught in her throat.

Her sister's skin and hair shone and her blue eyes sparkled with obvious delight.

"I heard you calling . . ." Abby raced to her side, reaching for her hands.

Cecelia stepped back, out of her sister's grasp. "I wasn't the one calling you, Abby." Her face glowed like the morning sun. "Open your heart and hear Him."

Abby pulled back, heart thudding. *God. She's talking about God.* Abby pressed her fingers to her lips. "I don't want Him. I want you."

Cecelia's eyes glistened. "Don't you see? Why can't you see? Open your eyes!"

"Come back with me." Abby reached for her sister.

Cecelia took a step further back. "God is not taking me away, Abby. You are the one wandering. Don't you see? I will always be with you. God will always be with you. But every time we get close, you wander off again." Tears shone on her cheeks. "You have to stop running."

Abby pushed hands up into her hair. "How has He helped me? He didn't heal you. And then the earthquake and the fires—all those people dying. He hasn't helped anyone."

Cecelia placed a cooling hand on Abby's hot, sweaty face. "He loves you more than you can imagine."

Abby held still, the frantic beating of her heart slowing under Cecelia's touch.

"God took every step with you today and every day. He knew when you were at the end of your strength and He led you to Kum Yong and Miss Cameron. He sent Robert, Harriet, Lillian, and tiny Sparrow. You have never walked alone. You have never been far from His thoughts. He is calling you now. Don't you hear Him?"

"But what about you?" Abby placed her hands atop her sister's. "I don't want any of those other people. I want you. Why did He take you away from me?"

Some kind of secret delight hid in her smile. "I can't tell you why. There are some things you will have to wait to learn. But trust me." Her smile widened as she leaned close, breathing the words into Abby's ear. "It'll be worth the wait."

Abby opened her eyes in the darkness as the knife clattered to the floor.

"You have to stop running."

Her chest ached. She sat up and gulped a breath of air, fighting tears. Abby lowered her head, staring at her knees. She had kept her vow for so long, it was difficult to know where to begin. "I am angry at you." The words tumbled out, her voice quavering. "You shouldn't have taken her away. It would have been easier on Mama and Papa and Davy if you'd taken me."

The tension grew and her throat squeezed. Abby pushed against her chest, trying to force her heart to stop racing. "I don't want to be the one left behind. Do you understand? I don't want to be alone."

A wave of warmth tickled her face and her breathing slowed. Abby leaned her head back against the wall, tears sliding down her cheeks. "If you are here . . . " She pressed her fists against her eyes until colored spots floated in the blackness. "If you care enough to be here with me . . . "

Abby took a deep breath, the pressure in her chest easing. "I guess Cecelia might be right. Maybe I'm not really alone."

Abby lowered her hands to her knees, palms open. She gazed up toward the ceiling. "I don't know if I can trust You, completely, God." A sense of calm tiptoed into her heart. "But, I'm glad You're here."

A tiny sprig of joy took root. Abby's tears flowed freely, like a summer shower washing the clouds after a long drought.

"Thank you for not leaving me." Abby reached down and touched the journal, sitting beside the basket. *It's what Aunt Mae was trying to show me.*

Sparrow slept peacefully, one tiny arm cupped around the side of her head.

Abby stretched her arms and leaned side to side, loosening stiff back muscles. She pulled herself to her knees before clambering to her feet.

At the front of the store, a glowing light drew her attention.

Abby swallowed, hard.

Flames.

43

3:15 a.m.

 $\mathcal{W}$ hat a waste of time." Robert ran his fingers across his bristly chin. "The policeman barely took any notes. How does he expect to find her?"

"I don't believe he does." Gerald sighed, folding the medical kit under his arm. "Half of the city's population is probably missing right now."

Robert squeezed the broken necklace in his fist, the warm metal a tangible memento of Abby's presence. If only it could lead him to her.

She never took it off—she'd told him so. Why then was it in the bottom-feeder's grasp? A chill washed over him like the glow from the X-ray tubes. The memory of the man's jagged wound put his teeth on edge. What must he have done to make her lash out like that?

Robert's stomach tightened. He couldn't let his mind go there. Where was she now?

Her parting words echoed in his ears. *You said you wouldn't leave me.* Robert balled the chain in his palm. If something horrible had happened to her, he'd never forgive himself.

Gerald scanned the shadows of the park. "We can search the grounds again, but in this darkness, we could walk right past and never see her, if she's even here at all."

"We have to do something." Robert ground his jaw, returning the necklace to his pocket. "She may be in God's hands, but I won't feel comfortable until we know for certain she's safe."

L♥

3:25 a.m.

Abby froze in place. Flames licked at the front of the store and thick gray smoke crept along the floor. A gentle tremor rattled the building, sending light fixtures swinging. Abby scooped up Sparrow, pushing toward the back of the building.

A side door led down into a basement room. Abby clambered over fallen shelves, clambering through debris to put distance between them and the smoke. "Sparrow, we have to get out of here."

Fresh air poured in from a narrow, horizontal window high on the wall. Abby wrapped Sparrow in the towel and tucked her into the basket for safekeeping. Placing it on the floor, she gathered loose boxes and fallen shelves into a pile and scrambled up to the window. She pushed on the sill, but the window refused to budge more than an inch. Abby plucked a loose board from the wreckage, the tottering pile shifting beneath her feet. She smashed the window, splinters of glass flying out into the darkness. Stretching her hands through the gap, her fingers brushed a cold metal pipe. She wrapped her hand around it, trying to pull herself higher.

She'd never fit through the tiny opening. A snake-like wisp of smoke wove its way under the door. *There isn't much time.* Sparrow's mewling cry drew her attention. Abby glanced up at the window. Even if she couldn't squeeze through, she could get the baby out.

She jumped down from the heap, kneeling beside the basket. Abby reached for the mother's ring, but her fingers stalled on the empty spot at her throat where the chain normally rested. *It's gone.* Her stomach tightened. "I'm sorry, Sparrow."

She wrapped the blanket tightly around the baby and clambered back up to the window choosing footholds with care. Abby took a last look into the tiny, angry face. "Sparrow, God is watching over you."

The baby howled in response.

Blinking away stinging tears, Abby eased the squirming bundle through the broken window and into the fresh air outside. The window sat at street level and Abby set her on the ground, pushing her as far away from the building as she could reach, hoping the blanket protected Sparrow from the broken glass.

"Help!" She pressed her face to the opening, rising on her tiptoes. "Help us! I've got a baby here!"

Sparrow's weak cries wafted in through the open window, wrenching at Abby's heart. Abby pressed herself against the wall, the cool night air filling her lungs. She stretched her fingers, caressing the soft blanket. She banged a fist against the wall. "Please, someone help!"

Abby pressed her forehead to the window frame, her breaths ragged in her chest. "Lord, keep her safe. I don't care what happens to me, but take care of Sparrow."

What do I do now? Just sit here and wait for the flames? She glanced back at the door, smoke seeping in through the cracks.

He walks with me.

Abby took a deep breath, filling her lungs with the fresh outside air. With one last glance at the squirming bundle, she clambered to the floor. She gripped a handful of skirt, fingers trembling, and reached out for the door. Abby crawled up the stairs, keeping her head below the smoke.

Abby struggled to breathe in the murky air. She pushed through fallen shelving, coughing and choking. Burning debris crumbled from the ceiling, sparking as it crashed to the floor. An unexpected cool breeze brushed against her skin and Abby swiveled her head, searching for its source. Beyond the fearsome wall of flame, a dark opening gaped to one side.

Springing forward, Abby scrabbled past the flames, pushing past broken boxes. The cool air grew stronger, like a river cutting through the smoke-laden air. Choking and sputtering, Abby followed its path to an open doorway. Lunging through, she burst out onto the dark street.

The cool night breeze caressed her stinging face. An unfamiliar peace filled her soul and she turned to gaze at the burning building, so close to being her death.

A sharp voice snapped her from the trance. "Hey, girl, get away!" A man grabbed her wrist, yanking her back. "Are you crazy? Why were you just standing there?"

Abby spun around, not fully comprehending. She opened her mouth, but her numb mind refused to form words.

Sparrow. Abby twisted and broke free of his grip. Hurtling around the building and into the dark alley, she spotted the bundle, sitting near the back of the store.

Abby fell to her knees, lifting the baby with trembling hands. Sparrow squirmed in Abby's arms, her face twisted into a mad howl, fists clenched. Abby touched her chin with a soot-smeared finger. "You are one lucky baby, you know?" She clutched Sparrow to her chest and swayed, turning in a tight circle. "I guess God does look after the sparrows. You and me, both."

The morning sun peeked over the edge of the horizon, painting colors on the curtains of smoke draping the San Francisco sky. What was the verse Aunt Mae had quoted? *Beauty for ashes.* Abby cradled Sparrow in one arm, sending up whispers of thanks. God had gifted them with a brand-new day.

44

5:30 a.m.

*R*obert rolled over onto his stomach, his hand sliding across the yellow quilt. After two long hours of searching the park, Gerald had finally convinced him to wait until morning.

"Though, I must confess, you're making me look like a lousy cousin." He shook his head. "But you can't make her appear out of the night by the sheer power of your will. She's in God's hands."

As much as Robert hated admitting it, Gerald was right. Stumbling through the dark had brought them no closer to finding Abby or Clara.

And yet, lying here on the ground wasn't much use either. Sleep was impossible. Robert dug his fingers into the corner of the quilt, wadding it into a knot. If God was trying to teach him something, somehow the lesson was lost on him.

Gerald shifted beside him, his shoulder bumping Robert's. "Sorry."

Robert exhaled, trying to release some of the tension growing in his chest. "I'm not sleeping anyway."

His friend sat up, rubbing a hand across his eyes. "Once dawn breaks, we'll get started."

Robert rested his head against his elbow, imagining Abby walking into his arms, a smile lighting up her coffee-colored eyes, but the scene blurred away into an image of her injured and alone, wandering flaming streets in terror. He pushed his brow against his forearm as steam built in his chest. If he waited much longer, he was bound to explode.

Robert knew Gerald would accuse him of trying to be the hero, but it had grown into much more. At this moment, he didn't desire Abby's adoration or gratitude. He needed her love, alone. His chest ached for it.

Gerald propped himself up on one elbow. "Would you like to pray with me?"

Robert rolled to his back. "Now? Here?" His stomach churned. He hadn't prayed aloud since his father's funeral.

His friend chuckled. "Can you think of a better place? I'm betting about half of the people here are praying."

Pushing up to a sitting position, Robert glanced around with a yawn. "Looks to me like they're sleeping."

"Like you?"

A glow appeared in the eastern sky, the sun announcing its impending arrival. Robert shrugged. "We might as well."

Gerald nodded before dipping his head and closing his eyes. He spoke in soft tones, entreating God for the safe deliverance of his cousins, wisdom for him and Robert as they searched, and comfort for the people of San Francisco.

Robert ran his damp palms over his trouser knees as Gerald finished speaking. His thoughts jumbled as emotions spilled from his heart, muddying his thinking. "God . . ." he paused and cleared his throat. He swept away his insecurity and tried to focus. "God, I don't have the words for what I want to say. You know my heart. I want to rush to the rescue, but You have made it clear it isn't my purpose. Every time I try to help, things seem to fall apart. So now, I'm turning Abby and her family over to Your keeping."

A warm presence wrapped around Robert's heart as the words flowed. "Protect them. Be their guard and protector . . ." his voice faltered. He cleared his throat a second time, taking a breath. "Lord, if I can be of help, please—show me the way."

Gerald clapped a hand on his arm. "Amen."

Robert opened his eyes, a new calm surrounding his soul. As he lifted his gaze, the sun burst over the horizon, light spilling out over the city.

6:30 a.m.

Abby retreated to the relative safety of Golden Gate Park. With all of the soldiers milling about the crowd, she doubted she'd see the thug from last night. A shudder tripped up her spine at the memory.

She found an open spot and sat down, legs folded to the side, her skirt tucked underneath. All around, families chattered, making preparations for the day.

Abby laid the sleeping baby on her legs and closed her eyes. Sparrow squirmed, giving a quiet whimper. Lifting the baby, Abby cradled her, rocking back and forth. Sparrow gave two soft mewling cries before falling silent. Abby remembered back to Davy's plump baby cheeks and reached down to stroke Sparrow's pale face. Babies were supposed to have round, rosy cheeks. Dark circles surrounded Sparrow's sunken eyes.

Caressing her face with the tip of a finger, Abby gazed into the baby's eyes. *I cannot feed her. If I don't find help, soon, she'll die.*

A woman sitting nearby stared at Abby with dark eyes. Abby continued gently rocking Sparrow.

The woman rose to her feet, walked the few steps to Abby's side, and crouched silently on her heels. Her stained dress hung loose on round shoulders, the fine fabric speaking of a high position in society. Her stare wandered from Abby to the baby and she lifted a trembling hand and pressed it against her lips.

"Yes?" Abby managed to speak, the pressure of the woman's silence weighing on her shoulders. She wrapped a protective arm around the child.

"Marta." A well-dressed man called to her, speaking in a soft tone. "Come have something to eat."

The woman remained crouched like a cat, staring at Abby and Sparrow.

Abby dug her heels into the ground and pushed back a few inches.

The man, clad in a rumpled suit, walked over and reached out a hand. "Come, Marta. Come away." Dust gathered in the fine lines around his eyes and mouth.

Marta stood, brushed off her mauve skirt, and strode back to her own camp with only one backward glance. Her full lips turned downward and her chin trembled.

Abby pushed up to her feet, Sparrow nestled in her arms. She glanced around, pondering a move to a safer location without so many prying eyes. A morning chill hung low over the park. Balancing the baby against her shoulder, Abby rubbed her palms together. Her skin tingled as the hairs lifted along her arms. She glanced about, heart skipping a beat. *Something feels . . .*

Abby's gaze returned to the odd woman, now sitting with her back turned. The black shirtwaist she wore emphasized the somber downturn of her shoulders, curved forward as if she cradled something in her arms. The man rested a hand on her knee, speaking so softly Abby couldn't make out the words.

The couple made such a lovely image, Abby's feet took two quick steps before she jerked to a sudden stop.

The man glanced up at the sunrise, the light washing over his face, deepening the shadowed grooves in his forehead. He closed his eyes, falling to his knees in front of the woman and laying his head on her lap.

Abby couldn't make out his words, but she sensed he was murmuring a prayer. The woman wept, her shoulders shaking with quiet sobs. Eyes still closed, he lifted his head, reached both hands behind her back and pulled her into his arms and onto her knees, facing him.

They remained on their knees, crying and holding each other, the private moment exposed for the entire city to see. Other refugees stepped around their camp, politely averting their eyes, but Abby could not turn away. Sparrow squirmed, offering a faint, mewling cry.

Abby's heart hammered as she felt a magnetic tug dragging her toward the couple. *Go.* She swallowed, her throat squeezing.

Straightening her shoulders, Abby managed the few steps over to the couple's campsite.

The man glanced up, wiping the tears from his eyes. He pushed himself to his feet, keeping one protective hand on the woman's shoulder.

"My name is Abby." She bit her lip, a flush working up her neck. *Why had she interrupted?*

The man reached out a hand. "I am Micah Webster. This is my—"

"Is this your baby?" The woman's dark eyes flickered between Abby and Sparrow.

Abby swayed, rocking Sparrow. "Well, no, but—"

"Your sibling?"

Sparrow's eyes closed, blue veins visible through the paper-thin skin on her eyelids. Abby's heart fluttered. *What am I doing?*

Mr. Webster placed a hand on his wife's arm. "You'll have to excuse our forward manner, Miss. We lost our infant daughter in the quake." He wrapped an arm around Mrs. Webster. "She was killed when the chimney fell into the nursery."

Mrs. Webster's dark eyes filled with tears. "I should've kept her in our room."

"I'm sorry." Abby's throat tightened. "My sister died, too." She didn't bother to mention it happened months before. It didn't seem to matter.

Mrs. Webster reached a trembling hand to touch Sparrow's blanket. "Helen was about the same age, I think. She looks so much like . . ." her voice faltered as she raised a finger to brush the tear from her cheek.

"Helen," Abby murmured the name. "How beautiful." She glanced down at the sleeping infant. "I call this one 'Sparrow.'"

The Websters exchanged confused looks.

A shiver coursed through Abby as the sliver of an idea grew in her mind. She told them the story of how she and Robert had rescued the child. "A nurse at the hospital said God watches over the sparrows."

Mr. Webster placed a hand on her shoulder. "Aye, He does indeed."

His wife covered her mouth with a trembling hand. "If only He had watched over my little sparrow."

A surge of energy rippled through Abby. "He never left her side."

The woman nodded, wiping her face with a worn handkerchief. "You're right. Of course. But it's so difficult to be the one left behind."

A settled feeling swept over Abby, leaving her no doubt as to her next step. Looking down at Sparrow, she cuddled the child close, rubbing the tip of her nose against the rose-petal soft cheek.

Abby tucked the towel around Sparrow and held her out to Mrs. Webster.

The woman reached out, hands trembling. "I may hold her?"

"Will you keep her?" The words rasped in Abby's throat. "At least for the time being?

Their eyes widened. "Abby . . ." Mr. Webster exchanged an uncertain glance with his wife.

"I believe God wants it this way," Abby laid the child in the woman's arms. "I can feel it in my heart."

"Are you sure, child?" Mr. Webster's voice crackled with emotion.

Abby nodded, eyes stinging. "I love her, but I cannot care for her. She is weakening every hour. She needs a mother. She needs someone who can feed her and someone to love her like she deserves."

Mrs. Webster pulled Sparrow close to her heart. "I can do that."

Placing a hand on her shoulder, Mr. Webster nodded. "We will need to search for her family, Marta."

"Of course." Her eyes glittered.

A hesitant smile grew on Mr. Webster's face. He reached his arms out and embraced Abby, gentle at first, but then nearly pulling her off balance. "God bless you, daughter." Tears coursed down his cheeks. "Perhaps we *can* help this child and perhaps she will help us as well."

Abby blinked hard, a lump growing in her throat.

He stepped back and gazed down at his wife, still staring in awe at the tiny face. "If we can't find her family, we will love her as our own. I promise you."

"Oh," Mrs. Webster glanced up. "I can't call this sweet thing 'Sparrow.' Do you mind if we come up with something else?"

Mr. Webster's lips parted. "Marta, you're not thinking of . . ."

Her eyebrows sprang upward, "Oh, Micah, of course not. There will never be another—oh, goodness, it's not what I was thinking at all." Mrs. Webster turned to Abby. A hint of delight grew in her dark eyes. "Abigail, what was your sister's name?"

Abby's breath caught in her throat, tears springing to my eyes. "Cecelia. Her name was Cecelia."

The Websters gazed at each other, conversing with their eyes.

"Cecelia," Mrs. Webster cooed at the baby. "Cecelia Sparrow Webster, you will be. At least until we discover who you *really* are."

45

*R*obert frowned as he stared out at the sea of people, the scent of smoke clinging to his clothes. Clambering up onto a stone bench, he drew a hand over his brow to shade his eyes against the rising sun. He'd already made a circuit of the park, but now that every square foot seemed to be occupied, finding anything or anyone seemed unlikely.

More refugees had arrived during the night, piling their belongings on every scrap of open ground, sleeping wherever they could. Barking dogs growled and snatched at any foodstuffs left unprotected.

Robert shouldered his pack, loaded with the few supplies he'd scavenged from Abby's ruined campsite. He shuddered, pushing away the image of Abby fleeing in terror with the baby. Where had she gone? Where was she now?

He turned, bracing his knee against the back of the bench, peering across the crowd, looking for a familiar straw hat with green ribbons—was she still wearing it? To the east, the lines of army tents multiplied, a sign of order being restored in the midst of chaos.

Robert scraped a hand across his bristly two-days-growth of whiskers. He probably looked more like a tramp than a respectable physician. He glanced back at the row of tents. If Abby were concerned for her safety, she might gravitate there.

Replacing his hat, Robert stepped off the bench and wove through the campsites. The scent of fried ham wafted through the morning air, mingling with the stench of campfires and open latrines. The crowd thickened along with the smells, everyone streaming toward a large tent marked with the symbol of the Red Cross.

Large notice boards stood on either side of the tent, covered in innumerable scraps of paper. Robert pushed through the gathering crowd until he could read the closest of the messages as they fluttered in the breeze. Robert scanned the notes.

> Margie, your cousin and I are going to Sacramento, meet us there.

> Seeking John Spencer, age 14, taken by the work crews. Please direct him to meet his family on the east side of the park.

> Uncle Tomas — Luis and I and the children are camped just south of the statue. We haven't found Auntie.

> Mary, house is gone. Meet us at Uncle Joe's in San Anselmo.

> Lost: Girl child, age six, named Berta. Please help.

Robert paced around the board, carefully reading and rereading each message, lifting corners to read other notices hidden behind.

A scrap of yellow stationery fluttered near the edge of the board, half-hidden by a scrap of brown paper. The large letters printed at the top caught his eye: "SEEKING ABIGAIL FISCHER."

A thin-faced woman jostled against Robert as she reached for a note, her arm blocking his view. She pulled a wrinkled scrap of paper from the board and rushed away. Robert stepped into the space she'd vacated, scanning the board for the note he'd spotted and then lost among the sea of slips. He ran his hand along the board, his heart beating out a rapid rhythm. Had he imagined her name?

He lifted a sheet of white paper and spotted the yellow scrap. Yanking it from the board, he stepped back as others rushed forward. Turning toward the sunlight, he lifted it close to his face, eyes hungry for the words.

"SEEKING ABIGAIL FISCHER: Abby, I'm at the northwest end of the park, by the corner. I'm so worried, please hurry. All my love, Mama."

A surge, like an electric current, rushed up Robert's arm as he clutched the precious slip of paper. He couldn't wait to show it to Abby.

Now he just had to find her.

9:35 a.m.

"I haven't seen anyone by that name, Miss." The olive-drab garbed soldier shook his head. He tipped his hat to Abby, the blue cord around the brim bouncing with the motion.

Abby thanked him and moved off, shrinking against the pressure of the milling crowd. She pushed up on her toes, but couldn't see very far through the gathering. The stench of unwashed bodies and desperation made her head swim. She pulled off her hat, grateful for the slight breeze finding its way under her hair, drying the sweat gathered on her scalp.

Perhaps she should head back to the Webster's camp. The couple had coerced a promise from her to return if she could not find her family within a few hours. Now as she milled through the throng of refugees, she wondered if she'd be able to find her way back. *And Mama is waiting out there . . . somewhere.*

The hours blurred into each other. Abby plopped down on a curb to rest, once again pulling Aunt Mae's journal from her pocket, to stave off any attempts at conversation from nearby campsites. Sliding her fingers along the worn leather binding, Abby tried to picture her aunt as a girl, her mischievous gray eyes hidden in a much younger face.

The journal's script matured as Abby flipped to the later pages, morphing from the carefully crafted penmanship of a schoolgirl to the more relaxed script of a confident young woman.

August 6, 1854

Yesterday was so frightening and overwhelming, I never got the chance to write. It was awful hot, so Lydia and I took the younger children swimming in the river. Baby Mildred waded too close to the current and was swept away in the waters. She stayed afloat, her little head bobbing above the surface as she spun off downstream. Our neighbor, Hiram Larkspur, jumped in and pulled her to safety. I was so relieved, but I trembled for the rest of the day, even after I went to bed. I gave up trying to sleep and pulled out Mama's Bible. A verse in Isaiah fit so perfectly with the day's events I cried tears of joy. I am going to inscribe it below. God was surely with little Mildred today. She should have drowned, but He held her up.

"When you pass through the waters, I will be with you; and when you pass through the rivers, they will not sweep over you. When you walk through the fire, you will not be burned; the flames will not set you ablaze." Isaiah 43:2

Abby reread the verse several times, her aunt's fine hand curling about the words. The crackle of the flames roared in Abby's memory, the choking clouds of smoke burning in her chest. She whispered the words aloud: "You will walk through the fire, you will not be burned; the flames will not set you ablaze."

She lifted her head, gazing at the dirty campsites and the children playing, forcing the image of flames out of her mind before skimming further through the pages.

> Went driving with Hiram Larkspur again this evening. I haven't told Lydia, since she's so miserable at keeping secrets, but I think he has the most handsome eyes. When he smiles, I can feel it all the way to my toes. And he speaks frequently of his faith, as if the Almighty were a personal friend. Hiram would make a fine minister, but he says he's going west to California to set up a store like his father's. He says San Francisco is growing quickly because of all of the men looking for gold.
>
> I cannot tell Lydia, but I think I may have already found gold . . .

Abby closed the journal and touched the empty spot at her throat where her locket should rest. She could still remember Great-Uncle Hiram's eyes—as blue as the California sky, just like Mama's and Cecelia's. *Who knew Aunt Mae was such a romantic?*

Glancing up from the page, she fixed her gaze on a nearby campsite. An older couple sat huddled together, her silvery head resting on his stooped shoulder. A brown-haired young woman handed the gentleman a cup and he held it steady as his wife raised her head and took a sip, a smile working its way across her lips. He held the cup to his own mouth, bracing his arm around her shoulders. After chatting for several moments, the young woman took a second cup to a broad-shouldered man stacking supplies nearby. He grinned, accepted the cup, and snagged her hand as well. Her easy laugh rang out through the morning air as he pulled her into a one-armed embrace.

An empty hole gnawed in Abby's stomach. The memory of Robert's kiss swirled around her heart like peach blossoms caught up in wind. She closed her eyes, imagining his strong arms circling around her waist, pulling her close, his chocolate-brown gaze melting her resolve. Why had she pushed him away? If he were here now, she'd grab on and never let go.

Abby thrust the journal back into her pocket and pressed up to her feet. Daydreaming would get her nowhere. She had to keep looking. She cast one last wishful glance at the young couple before turning her eyes forward.

A black derby atop a dark head bobbed above the milling crowd. Abby bit her lip. Most men wore the round hats these days and yet every time she spotted one, her heart jumped. As he walked away from her, Abby's breath caught in her chest. *Maybe.*

She surged forward, elbowing her way past three women and skirting around a pair of children playing jacks. She lost sight of the hat for a moment and she pushed up on her toes, heart pounding. She stepped over a pile of clothes, accidentally knocking over a stack of books. When she glanced upward, the man had reappeared, turning his profile to her.

"Robert!"

Abby remembered the day she'd seen him in front of the hospital. *Ladies do not call out in public.* She thrust away the memory and sucked in a big breath. "Robert!" Her voice rang through the din.

Abby pushed through the last few people, no longer caring what she stepped on, just eager to feel those arms encircle her. She jumped toward him, the momentum so powerful he rocked back on his heels, his eyes lighting up like a room filled with electric lamps.

Gripping Abby about the waist, Robert lifted her in the air. "There you are!" He crushed her against his chest. "You had me worried."

The pressure of his grip was both painful and glorious. She wrapped her wrists around the back of his neck and laid her head on his shoulder, leaning into his embrace. "I have never been so glad to see anyone in my entire life." The smell of sweat, dirt, and ashes tickled her nose, but she buried her face in his neck, breathing deep. She didn't want to miss anything.

After a long moment, she stepped back, gazing at him. "Look at you—stained clothes, dirty hands . . ." Abby took one of the hands, winding her own grubby fingers around his. She glanced up at his bristly chin, longing to rub a hand across it. "You hardly look like the same man. I'm fortunate to have recognized you."

Robert grinned, his teeth a brief flash of white in the grime covering his skin. "You're not the freshest of daisies yourself, Miss Fischer."

Abby glanced down and saw the state of her dress—covered in dirt, soot, and blood.

"Where is the baby?" he asked.

"I found someone better suited to care for her." She glanced down at their entwined hands. She really should let go, but the touch felt so right. "I lost her ring. I guess we won't be able to identify her."

Robert dug into his pocket, drawing out a familiar gold chain. "Do you mean this?" He pressed the locket and wedding band into her palm.

She gasped. "How—where . . .?"

He frowned. "It's a long story—one I want to hear as badly as you. But first, you might want to see this." Robert reached into his pocket a second time and withdrew a scrap of yellow stationery.

Abby's fingers tingled as she took the paper from his hand and unfolded it. The familiar handwriting brought tears to her eyes. "My mother!"

He claimed her hand again, squeezing it in his strong fingers. "I was just heading there. Come on, we're not far."

She clutched the paper to her chest like it was a message from God Himself. Her throat convulsed, a sob escaping from her gut. *Mama and Davy. Finally.*

Abby kept a firm grip on his hand as they pushed past campsites, refugees, children, dogs, and tents. He paused at the northwestern end of the park, eyes scanning the crowd.

Abby turned, pressure rising in her throat. *God, where are they?*

"Abby?" A woman's voice called from a distance. "Abby?"

Abby gasped, swiveling on her toes, trying to locate the sound.

"There!" Robert pointed, his face splitting into a wide grin. "Over there."

Her mother burst through the crowd, catching Abby in a massive embrace. Her fine dress soiled and tattered, Mama looked nothing like the fastidious woman who had stepped out on the porch right after the quake. "Abigail, you're here!"

Abby flung her arms around her mother's midsection. "Mama, I can't believe I finally found you!" She blinked back more tears, intent on not blubbering like a lost child.

"I've been praying in earnest, child, ever since the two of you left." She drew back and gazed deep into Abby's eyes. "I knew God was protecting you, but it feels so good to have you back in my arms!"

Abby cocked her head to one side "What do you mean, the two of you? I just ran into Robert a few minutes ago."

The color drained from Mama's face. "Abigail, where is Davy? Is he with Aunt Mae?"

The air whooshed from Abby's lungs. She pressed a hand against her stomach. "What?" Her voice sounded tinny in her ears. "What? Isn't Davy with you?"

Mama's face whitened, her lips parting and closing like a fish. "You took him to Aunt Mae's after the quake. I haven't seen either of you since."

"No, Mama," Abby's knees wobbled, her stomach tightening. "No, Mama, I didn't. He wouldn't come. He stayed at home."

Robert placed a hand under her mother's elbow. "Maybe you should sit down."

Her mother stumbled back a step. "Abby. Davy . . ." She covered her mouth with a trembling hand, her knees buckling.

Abby struggled for air. How long had it been? Two days? Three?

Robert crouched on one knee as he lowered Mrs. Fischer to the dirt, her shoulders heaving with sobs. Bracing her back with one arm, he glanced up at Abby, heart thudding. She didn't look much better—her complexion resembling the green glass bottle of quinine sulfate in the front of the office medicine cabinet.

Abby splayed her fingers over both cheeks. "But the neighborhood was evacuated. He couldn't still be there, could he?"

Robert leaned back on his heels. "He could have escaped with another family. Or the firefighters." A child, alone for two days—the weight crushed down on Robert, like all the times he had carried Davy on his shoulders. What chance did the little boy have with his world shattered and ablaze?

The glow on Mrs. Fischer's face had faded into the color of ashes. "My baby. I left my baby behind." Her hushed voice barely passed her lips, but the words cut into Robert's heart.

Hasn't this family endured enough grief, God? His throat closed.

"I'll find him, Mama. I will—I promise." Abby's voice rose. "I will find him."

"I'll go." Robert straightened. "You ladies stay here. I'll go back to the house." Likely as not, the house was already gone. The idea of Abby or her mother stumbling onto it twisted around in his stomach like a snake.

Abby's eyes narrowed. "I'm coming with you. It's my fault he's there."

Mrs. Fischer trembled in his arms. "How could I not know he was still home? How could I just leave him?" She clutched handfuls of her hair, burying her fingers in the long locks. "He's all alone."

Robert reached a hand out to Abby, who was edging backward as if she was prepared to leave immediately. "Abby, you should stay with your mother. We can't leave her in this condition."

The crazed look in Abby's eyes softened as she stared down at her mother. She dropped to her knees. "Mama, I'll find him. God walked every step with me over the past two days—I know He's watching over Davy, too."

Mrs. Fischer's breathing eased as she clutched her daughter's hands. "Yes, but—"

"I'll find him."

Robert watched Abby's head bob as she repeated the words with growing conviction. *Something has changed in her.*

Karen Barnett

Abby clutched her mother's arm. "We were all in the backyard when I was getting ready to leave. Do you remember? What happened then?"

Mrs. Fischer shook her head, dabbing at her eyes with a handkerchief. "It's such a blur. I was upset." Her brows pinched low. "I went inside to start cleaning up." She covered her mouth, eyes widening. "Maybe he followed you. Or he was still in the yard and I didn't even notice."

Her lashes flickered as her gaze darted between Abby and Robert. "Abby, I thought he was with you. I never would have left him there." Her voice rose, piercing the air.

Robert touched Mrs. Fischer's shoulder, the woman's grief palpable.

"I know, Mama. I know." Abby's chin lowered. "I should have taken him. And I should have come straight home. This is my fault."

"How could I not know he was there? What kind of mother am I?"

Robert rubbed a hand across his brow. "What time did you leave the house?"

"The soldiers came just before noon. I told them I needed to wait for Abby, but they wouldn't listen. I gathered a few things and left." She clutched at Abby's arm. "I hoped you and Davy had stayed with Aunt Mae. I tried to join you, but the streets were blocked. They kept telling me to go to Union Square. I never dreamed Davy was still in the yard." She dug her hands into her stained skirt. "He hasn't eaten since the morning of the earthquake. He must be—have been—so frightened." She lifted her hands to her throat. "He couldn't be . . ." Her eyes rolled. "It's been two days!"

"Shh, Mama. Maybe he's still at the house." Abby rubbed her mother's arms.

"But the fires—" Mrs. Fischer gulped back a sob. "And the dynamite—Robert, the soldiers said they were going to dynamite the area." She rocked back and forth on her knees, her hands pulling at the neck of her dress like it had closed about her throat.

Robert leaned forward, catching her shoulders. "Mrs. Fischer, you need to breathe slowly. Look at me."

308

Her head wobbled on her neck, her eyes darting around before finally meeting his gaze.

Robert took her face in his hands. "Keep your eyes on me and breathe."

She sobbed, gulping air between cries, eyes fluttering open and closed.

Abby jumped to her feet. "I'm going back to the house."

Robert jerked, his gaze lurching between the woman in his arms and the woman of his heart. "No. I'll go."

Abby pinned him with a glare, her hands settling on her hips. "There isn't time to argue. And there is no way I'm staying here while my brother is in danger."

Mrs. Fischer pushed Robert's arm away, pushing up to her knees and then her feet, swaying unsteadily. "I'm coming with you. We have to find him, Abby. We must. I will never forgive myself if something has happened to him."

Robert placed a hand under Mrs. Fischer's elbow to steady her. Maple Manor stood several miles from the park and up a steep hill—in the fire zone. His stomach tightened. The chances of finding the little boy alive were minimal. Could this family stand another tragedy? He glanced at Abby, the firm set of her jaw reminded him of their first meeting. *If there's one thing this family understands, it's slim odds.*

46

10:45 a.m.

*R*obert pushed through the crowd, clearing a path and leading the way to the edge of the camp. His stomach soured at the thought of what they might find when they approached the Maple Manor neighborhood. He'd walked the charred streets, seen the remains of the deadly combination of earthquake and flames. The firestorm offered no compassion. It wouldn't care whether a house contained a lone little boy. *Please, Lord. This family needs mercy.*

As they reached the edge of the park, he glanced at Abby, her shoulders back and head high. Even with tangles of hair draping around her face, the gleam in her eye and tilt of her chin suggested an inner strength and determination. He remembered the thug he and Gerald had worked on last night and a flare of heat burned through his chest. With all she'd survived, where did she find the fortitude to continue?

Robert picked up the pace once they cleared the park. The crews of workmen had removed much of the debris from the road, so other than dodging horses, wagons, and the occasional automobile, the journey went faster than before.

Mrs. Fischer grasped her daughter's fingers as they hurried along, her eyes rimmed with dark shadows. "We must find him. Losing two children . . ." Her voice faltered.

"Mama, let's not think that way." Abby's voice quavered.

Robert placed his hand on the small of Abby's back, the sudden urge to connect with her overwhelming his sense of propriety. He had no claim on her, or her family's struggles, and yet he couldn't— even for a moment—imagine walking away.

Abby's gaze met his, the glistening eyelashes surrounding her brown eyes providing him a glimpse into her heart. She reached for his hand, sending a wave of warmth through his arm.

Robert squeezed her fingers. Seeing the smoke roiling in the distance, his pulse accelerated. Even if the flames had not yet reached the house, it was a race against time.

Robert guided Abby and Mrs. Fischer up the hill. Reports of dynamite echoed through the air, a vortex of smoke billowing from nearby streets. Spotting that the neighborhood was still intact, a portion of the crushing weight lifted from his chest. Praying with each step, Robert was determined to follow Gerald's advice and turn this problem over to God. It was time to let Him be the hero.

Abby's pulse raced as she hurried along, gripping Robert's hand for strength. She'd walked every step in terror, expecting to find smoldering ruins. At the sight of standing homes, new hope sprouted in her heart.

But what about Maple Manor? Shivers broke out across her skin as she thought of the choking smoke she had experienced in the abandoned store. And now Davy could be in the same situation, all because she had been too lazy to take him along to Aunt Mae's. It seemed like years since the morning of the quake. *And Davy's been alone ever since.* She blinked away the tears, not wanting to let go of Robert's or her mother's hands.

Her parents wouldn't survive another loss. Abby gulped back the emotions rising in her throat and straightened her shoulders. *God, You said You wouldn't leave me. I am trying to trust, but it's so hard.* She glanced down at her dusty shoes, hurrying across the fractured road.

Pressure on her hand made her glance over at Robert. He lifted his brows, a question in his eyes.

She gathered a breath, trying to force a confident smile to her lips.

Robert nodded, his dark eyes shining with an inner light, and squeezed her hand a second time.

Abby pulled from his strength, even as he turned his gaze back to their path. *My fix-it man. The healer.* She sighed. *But you can't fix this one, can you?* She focused on the loose cobbles in the road, careful to keep her feet from stumbling. *It's too big for any of us. Davy's in God's hands—where he's always been.*

A pair of soldiers blocked the final approach onto O'Farrell Street from Van Ness. The men's olive drab uniforms were coated in filth, their soot-stained faces more fitting for chimney sweeps. Each toted a bayonet-topped rifle. One of the pair balanced his gun over a shoulder, while the younger man leaned against his.

The duo jerked to attention as Abby approached, Robert and Mama at her heels. One of the soldiers waved his weapon. "No one is allowed past here!"

Mama released Abby's hand and approached the men. "My baby is down there." She pointed a shaking finger into the smoke-filled street.

The senior soldier gestured with his rifle. "I can't let you folks go that way. We have orders. No one goes down this street without permission." The barrel of the gun bobbed with the cadence of his speech.

His partner stood silent, face pale and taut. His fingers wrapped around the grip on his rifle as he pulled it to his chest.

"I must get my baby." Abby's mother's voice grew slow, almost detached. She took several steps toward the men, hand outstretched, eyes imploring. "You wouldn't shoot a mother trying to rescue her child, would you?"

Abby's throat tightened at the sight of her mother's shaking hand. "Mama . . ."

The soldier lifted his rifle and steadied it against his shoulder in response, his blue-corded campaign hat casting a shadow across his narrow-set eyes.

Robert reached for her mother's arm, his face grim. "We'll find their superior officer. We'll get permission."

"There isn't time." Mama's voice crackled, like branches creaking in the wind. She shrugged off Robert's hand and took two more steps.

Abby edged to the side of the road, holding hers hands outward. "Don't shoot my mother. She's just trying to save my baby brother."

"Corporal," the younger soldier frowned. "Can't we—"

"You have your orders, Private."

The quiver in the younger soldier's hands made his rifle barrel vibrate. Abby's stomach churned as she watched the man track her mother's movements. Abby took another step to the side. *They won't be able to stop her. Mama's going to make a run for it.*

Mrs. Fischer's eyes flashed. "You will not keep me from my son."

Robert took two quick steps to the far side, drawing the soldiers' attention.

Abby's mother surged forward.

The older soldier cursed, throwing his body into her path. They collided, falling to the ground in a heap. The bayonet flashed in the morning light.

Abby screamed, leaping toward her mother.

As the younger soldier lifted his gun, Robert smashed into him, grabbing the rifle and shoving him against a wall. "Abby, go!"

Energy surged through her veins. She darted forward, sprinting through the gap and racing down the street toward Maple Manor. Abby lifted her skirts, her feet hammering down the cobblestones, running faster than she had ever done before. A shot tore through the air, echoing off the nearby buildings. Abby's steps faltered. She pictured her mother or Robert lying injured, but pushed the image away choosing to continue on her path. They wouldn't want her to turn back. She must reach Davy.

Flames licked through nearby houses and Abby closed her mind to both the scene behind and the one ahead. Sweat dripped down her face as she hurdled debris and threaded through abandoned belongings strewn in the road. Paper fluttered by on the breeze, lost and forgotten. *Lord, please. Lord, please.* Abby chanted the words in her mind in rhythm with her pounding feet.

Maple Manor faced the empty street, the structure still untouched by the flames. Abby stopped in front of the house, her breath ragged in her chest.

The front door stood wide open.

The breath blasted from Robert's body as he crashed onto the cobblestones.

The soldier rolled, gaining his feet—and his gun—in the time it took for Robert to suck in a breath of precious oxygen. Robert froze, the gleaming bayonet inches away from his chest. He laid his head back on the ground, hands held to each side.

The soldier pressed the tip against the front of Robert's vest. "Don't move!" Beads of perspiration stood out on the man's forehead, his campaign hat nowhere to be seen.

Robert wheezed in the scent of spent gunpowder as his lungs remembered how to function. *Move? Not likely.*

The silver blade tapped against Robert's top vest button in rhythm with the shaking of the young man's white knuckled hands. When the soldier risked a sideways glance, Robert followed his gaze, gravel scraping against the back of his head.

The older soldier gripped Mrs. Fischer across her midsection, the small woman lifted off her kicking feet. His sidearm lay on the ground by his feet. He glared at the man standing over Robert. "You're an idiot, Thompson. We're not supposed to fire at civilians unless they're looting!"

The younger man took one hand off the weapon to wipe an arm across his nose, red patches rising on his pale skin. "I didn't mean to, it was an accident. I didn't see the guy coming."

"If you'd shot someone—" the man wrenched the struggling Mrs. Fischer to Thompson's side, "Sergeant Haskins would have had you peeling onions for months."

Robert eyed the point bouncing against his sternum, splashes of crimson decorating the silver blade. *Blood?* A stinging in his hand drew his gaze to the laceration crossing his right palm. His stomach twisted at the sight of blood oozing down his wrist and staining his cuffs.

"What about the girl?" The private relaxed his stance, the bayonet retreating by a few inches.

"Well, it's her funeral, I suppose."

Mrs. Fischer twisted in his grip. "You're talking about my daughter."

"Corporal, sir, what do we do with these people?"

The corporal grunted as Mrs. Fischer landed an elbow in his gut. He took a step back, giving himself at least an arm's-length distance from the flailing woman. "I suppose we might as well let them pass at this point. The young lady is already past and I don't want to go retrieve her. It's probably better if she's not alone." He released his grip on Mrs. Fischer's wrist.

Private Thompson glanced down at Robert, still spread-eagled across the ground. "He attacked me."

Robert squeezed his fingers into a fist, applying pressure to the wound.

The corporal guffawed. "What're you going to do? Spear him? You're hands are shaking so bad you couldn't roast a sausage on that thing."

The private's cheeks darkened to a deeper shade of red.

"Actually," Robert waved his dripping fist. "He already has."

The private's face blanched and he scuttled backward, pulling the rifle up to his chest. "I didn't."

Robert sat up, bracing himself with his good hand. "It must have nicked me when I grabbed at the gun."

Mrs. Fischer hurried over. "How bad is it?"

He pulled a handkerchief from his pocket and pressed it to the wound. "I'll live. But we should go after Abby."

The corporal pulled out a second handkerchief and pressed it into Robert's hand. "Get out of there as quick as you can. And don't tell anyone about this. Got it?"

Robert pushed up to his feet, watching the smoke roll over the rooftops. "Trust me, we won't be there one minute longer than necessary."

❧

Abby stared at the door, running through scenarios in her mind. Had she left it open yesterday? Had Davy opened the door and wandered away? Had some stranger been inside their house?

She clambered up the stairs and crossed the threshold, slamming the door closed. The windows rattled with the sudden force. An echoing blast of dynamite answered, only a few blocks away.

Not much time.

Abby pressed her back against the door, the knob still clutched in her sweaty palm. *What if I find him dead?* She imagined her baby brother lying cold and silent, like Cecelia in her coffin. Abby drew in a slow breath, pushing away the horrific thoughts. God wouldn't let it happen. Not again.

Late afternoon shadows loomed as her knees and hands trembled. The smell of plaster dust and wood smoke tainted the air. She closed her eyes for a moment, gathering strength for whatever she might find. *Please, God, don't leave me now. Help me find him.*

"Davy?" Her voice quavered, echoing through the still house. Her throat ached, raw from days of smoke and dust. She cleared her throat. "Davy? Are you here?"

She tiptoed into the hall as if she were sneaking into a stranger's home. "Davy? It's Abby. It's safe to come out now." Abby's voice sounded unfamiliar to her own ears as it broke the silence of the cluttered house. She wandered into the parlor. Two shattered vases littered the rug. A second blast of dynamite set the light fixture swaying above her head. Abby crunched over the mess on the floor and pushed open the pocket door to the dining room.

The polished top of the cherry dining table hid under a thick layer of plaster dust, strewn with chunks fallen from the ceiling. Abby peeked under the table, one of Davy's favorite hiding spots. Empty.

She hurried to the kitchen. Food and dishes covered the floor, cornmeal crunching beneath her shoes. Earthquake damage or a little boy searching for food? Abby stepped gingerly through the mess, her toe bumping into something solid. A glass jar rolled across the floor. She grabbed it up, the sticky preserves adhering to her skin.

Calling Davy's name, she swung open the basement door and crept down the steep, creaky stairs, like descending into a dark throat. The dank air barely stirred as she revolved, peering into the shadows beneath shelves lined with canned fruits and vegetables. Wooden crates filled most of the floor space. A scraping noise sounded behind her and Abby whirled about watching for movement in the gloom. "Davy?" She held her breath.

A bristly rat peered out from behind one of the boxes, its dark eyes glittering in the dim light. Abby shrieked and dove for the stairway, climbing the steps two at a time using both her hands and her feet.

The methodical search over, she dashed through each room, calling Davy's name, her voice echoing throughout the house. Her bedroom stood empty, littered by the broken bed frame, shelves and bricks, the other bedrooms in similar states of disarray. She checked every corner, praying she'd missed something.

Her hopes dwindled. The last time she had seen her little brother he'd been playing outside. *Did he wander away, looking for us?* The idea of Davy wandering the city sent chills across her skin.

She hurried down the back stairs and into the yard, making a careful search of every shrub. His toy wagon stood ready by the garden gate, half-filled with stones and topped by a toy train. The yard seemed eerily empty, without even birds singing in the big maple tree.

Maybe he's hiding. She ran back into the house and searched it again. She dug through rumpled bedcovers, rummaged through closets and crawled under tables. The clock that had stood on a shelf above her bed lay smashed on the floor, its hands frozen at 5:12.

Abby paused in the upstairs hallways, spirits sinking through the floorboards. She leaned against the wall, a lump rising in her throat. *We can't search the entire city.* Abby kicked the wall, the wood giving slightly under the pressure. The sudden action brought a moment of relief. "What are You doing, God?" Her voice split the silence of the empty house. "I have to find him. Why won't You help me?" She kicked the wall a second time.

Clenching her fists, Abby dug them into her skirt. "God! Where are You?" Her voice echoed down the hallway. "I can't live like this! I can't live *with* this!" She pressed her fingers against her eyes, fighting back tears. Before Cecelia had become sick, she'd hardly ever cried. Now it felt like an everyday occurrence. Fresh tears spilled down her burning cheeks. "I let You back into my life and this is what happens?"

Abby ripped the journal from her pocket and threw the book onto the rug. It bounced, fluttering across the floor. "You are supposed to be good. How could You let this happen?"

Sinking to her knees on the hallway floor, Abby placed her hands on the Persian runner, tracing the geometric pattern before collapsing down upon it. She wept, her tears soaking the rug. "I can't do this."

Aunt Mae's words echoed in her mind. *"God is our refuge and strength, an ever present help in trouble."*

Abby held her breath, chest aching. A thought took hold, like a seed opening in her heart, its tiny roots sinking into her soul. *It's not about my strength. It's about His.*

Long minutes passed. A tremor shook the house gently, rattling the windows and sending the hall curtains swinging. A flood of emotions poured from the rift in her heart—sadness over Cecelia, anger at Robert, bitterness toward God, fear for herself. Abby pressed her hands against her chest. "I can't do it. But You can." Abby breathed slowly, holding each breath captive before releasing it. "But, will You?" The damp rug scratched at her cheek. "You can have this mess—my life. I don't want it anymore." She rolled to her stomach and flattened her palms to the floor. With closed eyes, she dug her fingers into the coarse rug. "Take it. Take my heart. Take my life. Take it all."

Her body shuddered, its own little quake.

Abby opened her eyes. Sunlight poured in the window, illuminating the particles of dust floating in the air. Weary and broken, Abby gazed up at them.

Up.

Abby lifted her tear-stained face, noticing the small door to the attic. The dark room had been her place of grieving—of refuge—for so many weeks, the place where she had wrapped herself in the memories of Cecelia.

The door was ajar.

Abby inhaled sharply. Pushing up from the floor, she hurried to the staircase. Ducking her head, she stepped into the dark, open area, the thick air warm and stuffy. The tiny dormer windows allowed only a few shafts of light to penetrate the gloom, the open area cluttered with vague shapes.

A soft sound cut through the stillness. Faint snores? Dropping to her hands and knees, Abby crawled across the rough floor, shoving boxes out of her way. "Davy?"

Scooting toward the window, Abby found the corner of Cecelia's quilt and followed it with searching fingers until she landed on her brother's warm, sleeping body. Warm tears sprang to her eyes. "Davy, you're here!" A bubble of laughter mixed with a painful sob.

She lifted him into the light, pulling him against her chest, sobbing and hiccupping as she knelt on the floor. "Thank you, God, thank you!" Her heart trembled, as if it were a building laced with dynamite. Any moment it would explode into a million pieces like a beautiful firework, arcing across the sky.

Davy's warm body stretched. "Abby? Is it you, Abby?" His hand reached up and touched Abby's face. "You're wet."

Abby laughed and sobbed. "Yes, I am." She rubbed her damp face on his shirt. "And I'm going to get you all wet, too." She buried her nose in his warm stomach.

Davy whimpered. "Abby you were gone, Mama was gone. I thought you weren't coming back."

Abby wiped her dripping nose on the quilt. "I'm here now." She gripped him under the arms and lifted him to her chest. "And I'll never let you go again."

A nearby blast of dynamite rattled the window sending Abby's thoughts scuttling back to Mama and Robert.

"I don't like those sounds." Davy tucked his head under her chin.

Abby stood, lifting him. "I think it's time to leave. Let's go find Mama." She bent down and retrieved Cecelia's quilt, wrapping it around her brother. She clambered down the narrow stairs and out into the hallway, settling Davy on her hip.

In a short time, this house will be gone. She pulled Davy tight against her side as he laid his head on her shoulder. *But, God has given me all I need.*

47

12:15 p.m.

*A*bby hauled Davy through the front door, the latch clicking shut behind them. Her brother squirmed until she loosened her grip, allowing him to slide down her legs. She grabbed his hand, relishing the touch of his skin against hers. They clattered down the porch steps together.

"I want to bring my rocks." Davy yanked at her fingers.

Abby glanced up at the rolling smoke. "Davy, we have a long walk. You don't want to carry them."

"Yes, I do." He pulled her to the pile near the gate and reached down for a handful, shoving the pebbles into the pockets of his short trousers.

A chunk of broken brick on the side of the heap reminded Abby of Kum Yong's Ebenezer stone. Abby knelt down and picked through Davy's collection until she found a smooth, flat rock. Picking it up, she noticed a thumb-sized indentation in its center. *God's thumbprint. His mark—His seal—on my heart.* Cecelia's hymn tickled the back of her mind. *Here I raise my Ebenezer, hither by Thy help I've come.* "Can I have this one, Davy?"

He frowned and grabbed for her hand.

Abby wrapped her fingers about it and lifted it out of his reach. "Hey, who just saved your life, little man?"

His bottom lip protruded. "But they're mine."

Abby stood, the stone warm in her palm. "I'll make a deal with you. Let me keep this one and you can fill *my* pockets with rocks, too."

Davy's face lit up and he scooped two giant fistfuls of pebbles, holding them up to Abby.

"I'm going to regret this, aren't I?" After a few minutes, Abby's skirt pockets sagged. She clasped Davy's hand and walked him to the gate. Abby gripped the small stone in her other palm, resting her thumb in the hollow. *My Ebenezer. Thank You, Lord, for helping me this far.*

Mama and Robert hurried toward them, Mama's skirt flapping as she ran, arms outstretched. Abby sucked in a quick breath, a smile rushing to her face as her heart rose. She released Davy's hand, giving him a gentle nudge.

The boy catapulted forward, jumping into his mother's embrace.

Mama swept him up, pressing Davy to her chest. "I thought—I thought—"

Robert came up behind, a massive smile extending across his dirty, sweat-streaked face.

Abby rushed to him, grabbing his arm. "I heard the shot—I was so afraid something horrible had happened."

He lifted his hand, clutching the blood-stained handkerchiefs. "Only a scratch. Nothing to worry about. I'm relieved to see you and Davy are all right."

Mama handed Davy to Robert and wrapped her arms around Abby. "Thank you, Abby. Thank you."

Abby, still holding Robert's hand, pulled him into their embrace—all four together.

As they walked toward safe ground, Mama wove her arm around Abby's back. "Abigail, your Papa will be so proud." She smiled, squeezing Abby's waist. "I think our little wanderer has come home at last."

Abby flushed. "God had a few things to show me, first."

"I can't wait to hear about it."

"I'm really hungry!" Davy tugged at her skirt.

Robert pulled a chunk of bread from his pocket. As Davy grabbed it, Robert hoisted the boy up onto his high shoulders. "Whoa, Davy—you're so heavy. What have you got in those pockets of yours? Rocks?"

Davy drummed on the top of Robert's hat. "How'd you know?"

✐❧

Saturday, April 21, 1906
9:15 a.m.

Robert stepped behind Abby as she gripped the ferry rail, circling his arms about her waist and resting his fingers on top of hers. His wounded hand was wrapped in a strip of linen Abby had given to him—torn from some part of her clothing. Robert tried in vain not to think about it. He pressed one foot behind him, leaning down so he could rest his chin on her shoulder. His heart beat slow and steady, weariness descending now she was safely nestled between his arms. The ferry's engines powered them through the bay, the water in their wake churned into frothy white waves. San Francisco retreated into the distance, a haze of orange smoke clinging to the broken skyline like a smothering blanket.

The salty breeze washed away the scent of smoke and he took a deep breath, filling his lungs with the first fresh air he'd tasted in days.

"I can't believe we're leaving." Abby leaned back against him.

"Only for a while. And think how excited Mrs. Larkspur will be to have all of you under one roof."

"And Papa will be meeting us at the dock." She leaned back against his arm. "I can't believe he got a message through to Gerald in all this chaos."

"I wish Gerald had come with us." Robert gripped the rail. "Now I'm going to have to deal with his mother's questions."

Abby twisted until she faced him, her back pressed against the railing. "You'll stay in Oakland, won't you?"

Robert inched his arms closer to her waist. "I'll head back to the city tomorrow. The hospital is in ruins and our office is gone, but they're going to need medical help in those tent camps."

The hint of a frown pulled at her lips. "Always the physician. Always the hero."

He lifted his chin. "Yes, ma'am. A doctor's work is never done." Robert chuckled, the truth of his words warming his chest. God had given him plenty of work. He thought back to the X-ray laboratory, buried under the remains of the hospital. The machinery could be replaced. *You are the hero, God. Thank you for watching over the ones I love.*

The ferry rolled over a swell, and Robert splayed his feet to keep his balance. "Good thing, too. I would make a horrible sailor. No sea legs at all."

She reached for his arm, pulling it back to her side. "Here, let me help you." She lifted an eyebrow, a pink flush spreading across the spaces between her freckles.

He stepped closer, encircling her with his arms and resting his hands back on the rail. "Your mother might have something to say about it."

"She took Davy to the front of the ship. He wanted to see where the captain stands."

Robert's pulse stepped up as he moved nearer. He lowered his face until it brushed against her hair, tiny wisps of brown floating on the breeze and tickling at his nose. He could still remember the touch of her lips, the feeling of her breath against his cheek. A sudden urge to repeat the experience gripped him. Robert let the swell of the ship push him closer. The lilac fragrance still clung to her hair, not fully obscured by the reek of smoke. He breathed it in, the tender scent assuring him of her nearness. Whatever happened, he would not let her get away again.

He lifted a hand to her chin, gently guiding her face upward until he could see the rays of the sun lighting up the gold flecks buried in her brown eyes. Holding his breath, he lowered his face until their lips met.

As the kiss ended, Abby pulled back with a sigh, her arms tightening around Robert's waist. She laid her head on his shoulder, thankful for the strong wind—an excuse to cuddle close. Her hat was long gone—probably left in the park.

Abby reached into her pocket, nearly empty since Davy had gleefully tossed most of the pebbles into the waves. She closed her fingers around the Ebenezer stone. *Hitherto hath the Lord helped us.* Cecelia would be pleased to know she had stopped running from God's love. She closed her eyes, picturing her sister's smile. Cecelia was alive, Abby was certain. God had borne her sister over the waters to heaven, just as the ferry now carried them across the bay. Cecelia's voice echoed in Abby's mind, strains of her song lifting on the breeze. *"Come Thou fount of every blessing, tune my heart to sing Thy grace. Streams of mercy never ceasing, call for songs of loudest praise."*

She ran her thumb over the stone's smooth surface. Kum Yong had said Miss Cameron planned to take the Mission girls across the bay. Had Kum stood on this same deck, watching the city—the place where she had once been enslaved—go up in flames? Abby closed her eyes. *Please, Lord, let me see her again. I want to tell her what her stories meant to me. How they nudged me to You.*

Robert rested his chin on the top of her head. "I am so thankful I found you again." His warm breath stirred her hair.

"Hey, I found you—remember?" Abby slid one hand behind his back, the other still tucked in her pocket. "Now I don't want to let go."

His arms tightened on her waist. "Don't. Not ever."

She glanced up, a shiver running across her skin.

Robert's brows pinched together, his hat pulled low over his forehead. "Don't let go. Stay. Forever."

Her heart jumped in her chest. "What do you mean?"

"Be my wife, Abby. Marry me." The intensity in Robert's eyes made her knees wobble.

She gazed into his face, the stone warming between her fingers. She released it into her pocket and placed her hand on his shirt-front. "Are you certain?"

He laughed. "Abby, I love you. I've been able to think about little else since the moment you *almost* fell out of that tree."

Her heart rose, like bubbles floating to the surface of the water. She'd been in the orchard then begging for Cecelia's life. And not to be alone. Somehow God had taken care of both, though not in a way she'd envisioned.

Her plans for a future of tending her trees—those dreams had crumbled like the city. But she had learned to trust, to love. Abby's heart swelled. "I—I love you, too, Robert."

"Then say you'll marry me." Robert squeezed her waist with his hands, grinning. "And I can go back to the city tomorrow trusting you won't have wandered off again before my return."

Her face warmed. "Wandered off? Who is wandering off here?"

Robert leaned in, resting his forehead against hers so she could barely make out the glint in his dark eyes. He cupped her jaw in his warm hands, the linen bandage soft against her cheek. He kissed her temple, his lips brushing her skin. "Will you marry me?"

A rush of energy raced through her, starting somewhere deep inside until it surged out to her fingertips. She grasped the lapel of his jacket and pressed her lips against his cheek. "Yes. Of course, I will."

He pulled her up to her toes, capturing her lips for another kiss. Releasing her, Robert pulled his hat from his head, his grin so wide it nearly connected his ears. He glanced back across the water. "With the city in rubble and flames, I feel a little guilty being so happy."

Abby stared out across the bay. The smoke curling up to the heavens from the ruins of San Francisco was testimony to the tragedy. A verse from Isaiah drifted through her mind like the smoke drifting on the breeze. *To give unto them beauty for ashes, the oil of joy for mourning, the garment of praise for the spirit of heaviness.* Abby closed her eyes and buried her face in Robert' shoulder. "Perhaps pulling joy from the ruins is exactly what God is all about."

Discussion Questions

1. Which character was your favorite? How do you relate to his or her struggles?

2. In the first chapter, Abby finds refuge in the limbs of a tree. Where do you hide when life gets overwhelming?

3. When Abby encounters Robert in the orchard, she almost falls out of the tree. If you're in a relationship, how did you first meet? Did you feel an instant connection?

4. Abby attempts to strike a deal with God. Have you ever been tempted to do the same? Did it work?

5. Abby finds herself shaken many times in this story. Her life is rocked by her sister's illness, Cecelia's death, the loss of her home, and finally by the earthquake itself. What sort of earthquake moments have you experienced? How did you cope?

6. Think about the spiritual life of each of the characters. Who are you most like?

   a. Cecelia—faithful, trusting

   b. Abby—doubting, leery of God's love

   c. Robert—trusting only in science and his own ability

   d. Gerald—respecting God's divine plan

7. Cecelia and Abby are both drawn to the hymn "Come Thou Fount of Every Blessing." Do you have a favorite song or hymn? What is it about the song that speaks to your soul?

8. Great Aunt Mae serves as a voice of wisdom in Abby's life, both in person and through her childhood journal. Who has influenced you in your faith walk?

9. What truths does Abby learn about God during the course of the story?

10. God reached out to Abby in many ways throughout the novel, and finally in a very vivid manner near the end. Can

you think of a time in your life when God has revealed himself to you?

11. Robert shelved his faith during medical school, choosing to rely on science instead. Gerald chose to view the human body as evidence of God's artistry. Have you ever felt pressured to set your faith aside? How do you view the conflict between faith and science?

12. Robert likes to rush to the rescue, but he learns to rely on God. Can you think of a time when you've been forced to rely completely on the Lord?

13. Abby made a difficult decision, handing baby Sparrow over to strangers. Here's your chance to finish her story—what do you imagine happened to Sparrow after Abby left? Was she reunited with her family? Does Abby ever see her again?

14. As Abby and Robert leave the burning ruins behind them, she looks back and thinks of Isaiah 61:3:

"To appoint unto them that mourn in Zion, to give unto them beauty for ashes, the oil of joy for mourning, the garment of praise for the spirit of heaviness; that they might be called trees of righteousness, the planting of the Lord, that he might be glorified."

Are there ruins in your life that could use a touch of God's beauty?